How could anyone lie so convincingly?

Jesse almost had Elissa believing he had come straight from some grueling mission that he wasn't yet ready to discuss. "I'm sure you had a hell of a time, Captain Garrett." The last two words sounded like a curse.

"Call me Jesse." It was an order, not a request. At her startled glance, he uttered, "I've waited a long time to hear you say it, Elissa."

The subdued passion behind the words rattled her. Inexplicably, she felt like crying. She drew in a breath, fortifying herself against the drugging effect of his nearness and the unmistakable message in his bold, heated stare. He wanted her. Here and now. And though he hadn't made a move to touch her, she felt his touch and thrilled to it.

When she finally found her voice, it shook. "Did you bring the waiver of parental status that I sent you?"

"No, ma'am, I did not. What makes you think I'd ever give up my son?" Although his expression hadn't changed, he suddenly looked dangerous. Intimidating. Every inch the battle-hardened commando. "Take me to him."

"He's not here," she lied. "He's with my parents. Now do me a favor, Captain Garrett, and get the hell out of my house."

Jesse glowered at her for one insolent moment. Then in a voice as soft as gunpowder, he promised, "I'll go, but I'll be back, Elissa. Never doubt it."

Dear Reader,

Did you ever notice that a truly strong man somehow makes those around him believe he's indestructible, that no power on earth can stop him from getting what he wants?

An illusion, of course, and one that makes the woman who's falling in love with him wonder what lies behind that tough facade. She'll look for his vulnerabilities— surely he has some! She'll arm herself with each one, *use* them if she must. And all the while, she'll hope to find a particular weakness, one that makes him vulnerable only to her.

Because sometimes in a moment of need, a man's greatest weakness can turn out to be his greatest strength.

I hope you'll enjoy Elissa's quest as she probes beneath the tough exterior of Captain Jesse Garrett...to find the surprise awaiting her there....

Happy Reading!

Donna Sterling

Books by Donna Sterling

HARLEQUIN TEMPTATION
586—SOMETHING OLD, SOMETHING NEW

Don't miss any of our special offers. Write to us at the following address for information on our newest releases.

Harlequin Reader Service
U.S.: 3010 Walden Ave., P.O. Box 1325, Buffalo, NY 14269
Canadian: P.O. Box 609, Fort Erie, Ont. L2A 5X3

POSSESSING ELISSA
Donna Sterling

Harlequin Books

TORONTO • NEW YORK • LONDON
AMSTERDAM • PARIS • SYDNEY • HAMBURG
STOCKHOLM • ATHENS • TOKYO • MILAN
MADRID • WARSAW • BUDAPEST • AUCKLAND

ACKNOWLEDGMENT
My heartfelt thanks...
To Kosmar, whose music inspired the creation of Jesse,
To my critique group—Melissa Beck, Marge Gargosh,
Susan Goggins and Carina Rock—for their advice and support,
To my family, for the love that sustains me, and to
Susan Sheppard, whose open mind and warm enthusiasm set my
soul free. This book wouldn't have happened without you.

ISBN 0-373-25728-7

POSSESSING ELISSA

1

THE DAMNED CONDOM had busted. That bothersome little detail flashed with neon clarity through Jesse's memory as he reread the letter for the umpteenth time in two days.

> Dear Captain Garrett,
>
> Hope this letter finds you safe and well. You might not like the news I have to share. I'm pregnant, and the baby is unquestionably yours. Don't worry—I won't complicate your life. I'm perfectly able to raise this child on my own. He's due in July. Let me know your thoughts.
>
> Sincerely,
> Elissa Sinclair

Belted into the seat of the homeward-bound army transport as it lifted off from the small airstrip, Jesse Garrett stared at the linen stationery until the handwriting blurred before his eyes. In the two days since he'd collected his back mail, the shock of this letter's news had somewhat worn off. He was able now to concentrate on the woman who had written the brief, impersonal note.

She hadn't been brief or impersonal the night they'd met. And she hadn't called him "Captain Garrett."

Of all the details he'd forgotten about her, Jesse remembered the heat that had gunned through his veins when she'd whispered his name. And he remembered her mouth. Smooth, sweet and incredibly arousing. And the provocative feel of her in his arms, writhing beneath him in bed... These were his memories of Elissa Sinclair; dreamlike impressions that had stayed with him, warming him, stirring him, night after night throughout the entire hellish year.

Get real, Garrett. She couldn't possibly have been as good as all that. It had been his last night of leave, and if his gut instinct about this covert mission had proved correct, it would have been his last night on this earth with a woman. Imminent death, mused Jesse, has a surefire way of intensifying one's appreciation of pleasure.

Striving to remember more about her, Jesse retrieved a second letter from his coat pocket—the last letter she had sent him, dated months after the first.

Dear Captain Garrett,

Enclosed is a birth certificate for Cody Sinclair, born on July 8. Please note your name appears as "father." If you care to claim paternal responsibility, advise me immediately. If not, complete and notarize the enclosed legal document.

Once your waiver has been received, you will never again be connected with this matter. Contact me at the above address.

Elissa Sinclair

Jesse shoved both letters into the inner pocket of his military overcoat. He supposed if he had answered the first letter, the second might have been friendlier. But he hadn't read either until two days ago. And it was already October.

Which made his son three months old.

His son. Jesse had little doubt that the baby was his. Why would Elissa lie? She was asking absolutely nothing from him; in fact, she seemed anxious to cut him out of the picture altogether. The timing was precisely right, the condom had broken, and his cousin Dean had raised hell all the way to the airport the next morning for "playing fast and loose with a woman like Elissa," one of Dean's closest friends since his freshman year in college. "Damn you, Jesse, she's not the kind of woman you're used to."

He'd been right about that. Jesse had known she was different within moments of meeting her. Classier. Softer. Infinitely beyond his reach. And he had wanted her more than anything he'd ever wanted in his life.

Guilt rumbled through him. Had he deliberately seduced her? He didn't remember it that way, but now he wasn't sure. How had the pregnancy affected her life? She was some kind of schoolteacher, wasn't she? In a small southern town. Jesse winced. Single and pregnant couldn't have been easy. Was she resentful? Would she take it out on the child?

At the thought, an unfamiliar pang clutched at Jesse. *Would the boy be loved?*

Cody. His name was Cody.

Jesse tightened his fists as an odd protectiveness washed through him. Elissa obviously expected him to sign a few forms, then be on his way. Before he'd left the base today, he had signed a few forms, all right. But not the ones she'd sent him. He had wanted to start the legal ball rolling so there'd be no doubt about his intentions.

Staring through the thick, smudged window, Jesse watched as the hazy green expanse of forest below gave way to the gray shadows of mountains. The men around him talked, laughed and lied about what awaited them stateside.

A sudden vibration shuddered through the aircraft. Jesse, like the others, ignored it. The vibration worsened; the engine spluttered. Conversations died. Jesse cursed with impatience. Not another delay. With his luck, they'd have to land in the middle of godforsaken nowhere.

It wasn't until the pilot's panicked voice crackled over the intercom that Jesse's premonition of death returned, no longer just the vague intuition riding heavy in his gut, but a looming, rational possibility.

Not now. His silent pronouncement was a fierce resolution, uncompromising and absolute. *I won't die now.*

The engine cut off; the pilot cursed. The nose angled down into a dive. Panic broke out among the men. Jesse refused to give in to it. He had to get back to Georgia to meet his son. To make sure he had a better start in life than he himself had had. To change his name to Cody Garrett.

And to douse with cold reality the memories of Elissa that made him want so damned badly to get back to her. He wouldn't rest until he had done at least that much.

Nothing, but nothing, would stop him.

TIPTOEING IN HER fuzzy purple slipper-socks past the sleeping children, Elissa gently laid the newborn down into the crib and covered her with a silky baby blanket.

Barely daring to breathe, Elissa then glanced into the corner crib where her own son dozed, his diapered rump high in the air, his chubby legs tucked beneath him. She removed the pacifier from his bow-shaped little mouth, brushed a kiss against his milk-scented cheek and tiptoed out of the room.

Nap time. At last, an hour or two of peace.

If she worked quickly, she could have her kitchen cleaned before the kids woke up. Savoring the time she'd have to herself, she clicked on her radio, turned the volume down low and found a station playing soft jazz blues. She bent over a bouquet of roses from Dean, indulged in a whiff of their fragrance, then set about her cleaning chores.

It had been one hectic morning, she reflected, moving her hips to the beat as she mopped up soup. Nine-month-old Jennifer, in a teething frenzy, had gnawed on everything...including Joshua's finger, which he'd obligingly stuck in her mouth. Cody had been whiny except while in his swing, which required cranking every five minutes. Heather, recently introduced to the potty concept, spent the morning racing to her potty-chair, whether she needed to or not.

Five children, mused Elissa as she tossed baby-food jars into her recycling bin, were harder to handle than she'd expected. Then again, she *was* managing to keep them all safe, dry, well fed and reasonably happy.

And she did so need the money.

She applied her soapy dishrag to the cookie mush and thought back to her days of lucrative paychecks, panty hose, lacquered nails and reasonable schedules. She couldn't help a certain wistfulness. Seven years of college, five years of professional experience, and where was she now? Chiseling a dried Noodle-O off a high-chair leg.

Every career had its challenges.

Resolutely she concentrated on the bright side. Her life plan had changed—drastically, yes, but not necessarily for the worse. She couldn't imagine living now without Cody. He was her joy, her sunshine, her happiness.

The ringing of the telephone startled her. She dropped her dishrag into the sink, dried her hands on the apron that covered her faded jeans and hurried to the phone.

"Elissa, is this a good time to talk?"

She sank down onto a kitchen chair and blew her dark, wayward bangs off her forehead, happy to hear another adult voice. "It's fine, Mom. They're all out for the count."

"So, have you made up your mind about Dean yet?"

Elissa squeezed her eyes shut. She'd known this was coming. "No, I told you I wanted to think about it. Marriage is a big step."

"But you've known him since your freshman year in college, Elissa, and he's been so good to you through this entire ordeal." *Better than you deserve.* Her mother hadn't actually said it, but Elissa heard the implication.

"Yes, Dean's a good friend, but we've never actually been more than that. I think he sees himself as my knight in shining armor. It's sweet of him, but I'm not sure if I—"

"Elissa, honey, your son's already three months old, and you're still single. How do you think he'll feel when he's old enough to understand his...you know... status?"

She stiffened, her hackles raised. "What exactly do you mean by status?" Politically incorrect words like *illegitimate*—and worse—hovered somewhere on the line between them, mercifully unspoken, but nonetheless hurtful.

"Oh, Elissa, you know as well as I do that a husband like Dean would mean security for you and Cody. Why, health care alone costs a fortune these days. Believe me, honey, you could use a knight in shining armor right now."

"I wouldn't marry anyone just for financial security." But she had to admit to herself that the small profit she made from her home day-care business was barely enough for rent, food and diapers. A hard-working, responsible partner *would* make their lives much easier.

"If you won't do it for financial reasons, then what about social? Once you're married, even *this* community will forgive and forget your...er..."

"Fall from grace?"

"I wasn't going to say that. But you know what I mean. Why, I'll even bet the school would rehire you."

"I wouldn't go back, Mom, even if they asked." The ludicrous relief on the faces of the administrators when she'd handed in her resignation had been almost laughable—if it hadn't cut so deeply. She hadn't been fired for her pregnancy; *that* was forbidden by law. But the disapproval of her co-workers—and the fact that the community would have questioned her influence over its impressionable teens—was enough for her to withdraw from her hard-earned position. Why submit herself or her child to public censure?

And then there was the real reason she'd quit her career as a high school counselor. She didn't deserve it. The position required impeccable judgment and clear-cut vision. She simply didn't qualify anymore.

"Elissa, you could hardly blame the school or the

community for disapproving of an unmarried high school counselor who gets herself knocked up."

"Mother!"

"And in this town, everyone knows you weren't even dating anyone seriously. How could they trust you to properly guide troubled teens if you yourself—"

"I know, Mom, I know. Let's just brand a scarlet *A* on my forehead and talk about something else, shall we?"

"Honey, you're a mother now, and it's time for you to wake up and smell the orange blossoms. Cody needs a father."

Ah, there was the argument she couldn't quite refute. She wanted her son to be raised with a father's love. And Dean would make a wonderful father—gentle, scholarly, loyal. And even though they had never been more than friends, Elissa knew that he wanted to be. She'd been the one keeping their relationship platonic.

"I know Dean cares about me, and I care about him. But..." Elissa paused, trying to find words to explain her hesitation. But the explanation was not one she could share with her mother. Or with anyone else, for that matter.

The fact was, she didn't feel especially *attracted* to Dean. Not in the way she had been attracted to...

She quickly squelched the thought. She refused to waste her time thinking about Jesse Garrett. Their one mad night together had resulted in too much hurt, too much shame. She couldn't understand what had come over her!

Captain Jesse Garrett of the U.S. Army Rangers—Dean's cousin—had unexpectedly dropped in for a visit on his way from Savannah to Atlanta. His last night of leave, he'd said, before shipping out for overseas duty. She hadn't met him before that night.

When his dark, restless eyes had sought hers—and held them entranced—her world had somehow stood still. She'd never forget the feeling; as if she'd plugged herself into some kind of spiritual light socket.

Spiritual? she thought derisively. *You mean sexual, don't you?* How could she have thrown away all her morals and common sense just for the sake of attraction? Powerful, mesmerizing, intensely sexual attraction though it was...

She shivered at the mere memory of it. No, she wouldn't think about Jesse Garrett with his hard, muscular body and his heart-stopping stare. Or the way his kisses had incited a frenzy within her.

She took a deep breath and purged her mind of the disturbing memories. Dean was the kind of man she needed. The kind of man her son needed.

"Don't worry, Mom," she said at last, cutting into a lengthy monologue on the virtues of any man willing to adopt a baby that wasn't his. Elissa leaned her head against the kitchen wall. "I haven't said I wouldn't marry Dean."

She had barely said goodbye and hung up the phone when a sound near the front door caught her attention. Not a knock, precisely. More like...footsteps.

In her living room. Her heart contracted. She switched off her radio to listen. *Someone was walking across her living room floor!* But she had locked the door. Hadn't she?

The footsteps drew closer.

A shadow darkened the kitchen doorway.

Her breath stopped in her throat. She reached for the heavy iron skillet on the stove beside her. Wrapping both hands around its cold iron handle, she held it in front of her, like a club, ready to clobber the intruder, if need be. Her babies were sleeping in the other room.

Only she stood between them and whoever had invaded their sanctuary.

A man filled the shadow. Tall and broad-shouldered, with wavy raven hair. Wearing a U.S. Army Ranger uniform.

Elissa froze in disbelief. His silver-eyed stare—oh, how she remembered that potent stare—swept over her, then connected solidly with hers. And once again, the world blurred before her eyes, and all she could see was him.

An incredulous whisper tore from her throat. "Jesse."

He leaned his powerful shoulder against the doorjamb, the corner of his wide, firm mouth lifting in a hint of a smile. "I like that better than 'Captain Garrett' any day." His deep, soft, southern voice sent warmth rushing through her like Georgia sunshine. His glance flickered downward to the iron skillet she held protectively in front of her. Wry humor glinted in his eyes when they again met hers. "That thing loaded?"

It was the warmth of humor in his eyes that released her from her shock-induced paralysis. That same understated humor, unexpected in a man as ruggedly *physical* as Jesse Garrett, had been her undoing the last time they'd met. It had charmed her, lulled her into a false sense of security, deepened the damnable attraction.

"How dare you scare me like that!" With trembling hands, she dropped the skillet onto the stove. "What do you think you're doing, barging into my house?"

"What do you think *you're* doing," he responded calmly, "leaving your door open? Don't you know what kind of trouble you're inviting? That old skillet wouldn't be enough to even slow me down if I had it in my mind to overpower you."

The reprimand brought a defensive flush to Elissa's cheeks. "My door was locked! I know it was. I always—"

"It didn't keep *me* out, did it?" Jesse sauntered across the kitchen, hands in his trouser pockets, and leaned his hip against the counter, gazing sternly down at her. "Don't ask me why, but I thought you'd be more responsible."

Between clenched teeth, Elissa seethed. "Don't you dare talk to me about responsibility. You didn't even bother to—" She cut herself off sharply. What good would it do to rail at him for ignoring her letters? She couldn't change what he was. All she could do was learn from her mistakes. And never, ever repeat them.

Jesse raised one inquiring brow. "I didn't even bother to...what? Answer your letters?" She said nothing, but knew her anger radiated outward in palpable waves. "I didn't get your letters until two days ago." His tone was not in the least defensive; merely factual. "My incoming mail was held at the base. I was out on a recon mission. It should have taken only a few months, but we ran into some—" he pressed his lips into a grim line and his eyes clouded as he visualized something she could only guess at "—complications." After a pause, he summarized, "I was gone longer than planned."

Elissa peered closely at him. How could anyone lie so convincingly? She could swear he'd come straight from some hellish ordeal that he wasn't yet ready to discuss.

He *had* to be lying, though. Dean had told her about each phone call he'd received from Jesse, usually from bars and brothels in Asia. Although Dean had tried his best to spare her feelings, he'd had no choice, under the circumstances, but to relate how Jesse hadn't wanted to talk to her, or about her, or about her "little problem."

And yet here he was, in her kitchen, acting perfectly at home. Fresh anger spurted through her. "Yes, I'm sure you had a hell of a time, Captain Garrett." The last two words sounded like a curse.

"Call me Jesse." It was an order, not a request. At her startled glance, he uttered, "I've waited a long time to hear you say it, Elissa."

The subdued passion behind the words rattled her as nothing else would have. Inexplicably, she felt like crying. The man was a compulsive heartbreaker, she reminded herself. Dean had warned her, even before she had left the party with Jesse that night. Why hadn't she listened?

She drew in a breath, fortifying herself against the drugging effect of his nearness—and the unmistakable message in his bold, heated stare. He wanted her. Here and now. And though he hadn't made a move to touch her, she felt his touch and thrilled to it.

"I've been gone a long time, Elissa," he said in a solemn, hoarse whisper. "Have you no welcome for me at all?"

With her heart in her throat, she forced herself to answer by resolutely turning her back to him and walking away. She stared through the lace-curtained window at the backyard, seeing instead the starkness she had glimpsed in his eyes...and an oddly urgent need. The need for what? Probably for a quick lay, now that he was back in the States.

When she found her voice, it shook, though she strove for nonchalance. "Did you bring the waiver of parental status that I sent you? Signed and notarized, I hope?"

"No, ma'am, I did not. What makes you think I'd ever give up my son?"

She turned and gaped at him. He didn't care about Cody! What game was he playing? Her maternal instincts rose in frightened protest. She didn't want him near her baby. "Don't call him yours. He's mine."

Although his expression hadn't changed, except for a tiny muscle flexing in his lean, square jaw, he suddenly looked dangerous. Intimidating. Every inch the battle-hardened commando. She sensed an awesome power barely leashed within his muscular frame. "Take me to him."

"He's not here," she lied, praying that none of the children would cry and draw his attention. "He's away with my parents. But Cody's no concern of yours. Whether you sign that waiver or not, he'll be raised by me. Now, do me a favor, Captain Garrett, and get the hell out of my house."

Jesse glowered at her for one insolent moment, pulled away from the counter and straightened to his full, intimidating height. In a voice as soft as gunpowder, he promised, "I'll be back, Elissa. To be a father to Cody. Never doubt it." He then strode out of her kitchen.

She backed up against the refrigerator door, needing it for support. Her heartbeats filled her ears. She didn't hear the front door open or close, but she knew the moment he'd left. The resultant coldness cut through to her heart.

The phone rang. She considered not answering. She had to calm herself before the children woke. But the ringing would wake them, she realized. Reluctantly, she answered.

It was Dean, his voice unusually somber. "Elissa, I have some bad news. It's about Jesse."

She gripped the receiver tighter at the mention of his

name. "About Jesse?" she repeated dumbly. "What about him?"

A short silence followed her question. "The plane that was bringing him back to the States," Dean said haltingly, "crashed this morning. He was killed."

"Killed? Jesse? Dean, what are you talking about? Jesse's not dead. Is this some kind of a joke?"

"Joke!" Dean's tone reminded Elissa that he never joked, let alone about death. "I know it's hard to believe. I can barely believe it myself. Jesse and I grew up more like brothers than cousins. We lived in the same house as kids. We went our separate ways as adults, but—"

"Jesse was here less than five minutes ago."

Dean took a moment to absorb what she had said. "That's impossible. The military called my aunt—Jesse's mother—an hour ago. The plane crashed this morning, around nine."

"He must have taken another plane. He was here."

"Elissa, it's only noon now. Even if he somehow got on another plane, he left from an Asian port around nine this morning. He couldn't possibly have flown to Atlanta, Georgia, in two hours. A flight straight through would take longer than that, not to mention the drive from Atlanta."

Elissa's brows knitted together as she paced across her kitchen, the receiver to her ear. The army had made some kind of error, of course. Jesse was certainly not dead.

"You must have been mistaken," said Dean. "The man you saw was just someone who looked like Jesse. Haven't you ever done that before, mistaken a stranger for someone you know?"

"It wasn't like that. I wasn't out in a crowd. I didn't

catch a glimpse of him in passing. He came to my house. We talked for at least ten minutes. It was Jesse."

The silence this time lasted a good deal longer. When he finally spoke, Dean sounded troubled and unsure. "I...I guess I'll call my aunt. When was he there, did you say?"

"He left just a few minutes ago."

"Okay. Let me do some calling around. And then I'll—I'll be over there. To make sure you're...okay."

She didn't argue, although it bothered her that he thought she might *not* be okay. It was a military mix-up, nothing more.

After hanging up the phone, she paced into her living room and peered out her front window, hoping that Jesse might still be out there, walking down her driveway. After all, she hadn't heard a car pull up or drive away. He might have hitchhiked. If she could find him, she'd have him phone Dean and set things straight.

But she saw no sign of Jesse from her front window. She decided to stroll down the drive and look down the country road. Donning her jacket, she hurried to the front door.

As she reached for the knob, she halted. And stared. The door was locked, just as she'd sworn it had been. And the steel bar of the dead bolt was jammed firmly in place, securing the heavy wooden door from the inside.

An odd chill crept over her skin and beneath her hair.

The only other door in the house was in the kitchen, where she had been. All the windows were locked and fortified with immovable outer storm glass. Clearly, she remembered the footsteps sounding across this living room.

How had Jesse come in? How had he gone out?

THE FOLLOWING WEEK was the longest of her life. Jesse didn't return to her house, which was not surprising after their last conversation. Nor had he visited his family. Still, Elissa knew without a doubt that he had visited her. The question of his entrance into her home remained a disturbing puzzle, but in the larger scheme of things it meant little. Jesse was alive and she intended to prove it.

Despite numerous phone calls placed by Dean, his mother and Jesse's mother, all at Elissa's urging, the military refused to consider the possibility of a mistake. Records indicated that Captain Jesse Garrett had been on that fateful flight. His death would be officially confirmed when his remains, or whatever could be found of them, had been identified. That investigation was under way.

Elissa couldn't let the matter rest there. They wouldn't find his remains, because he wasn't dead! How cruel that his family should wait indefinitely to know that he was alive. She anxiously hoped he would come back. If not for her, then for his family.

The entire week passed with no word from Jesse. Elissa pestered her way into a conversation with his commanding officer. "He's the father of my child, Colonel Atkinson. Doesn't that give me the right to confirm his death?"

The colonel's sigh came across the trans-Pacific phone line. "The only reason I'm speaking to you now, ma'am, is because Captain Garrett's mother initiated the call. What exactly is it you want to know?"

"Could he have taken another flight?"

"Ms. Sinclair, I personally watched him board the plane that went down." In a friendlier voice, he added, "Jesse was a damned fine soldier. I'll miss him."

"But I saw him. That very day, here in Georgia."

"Stranger things have happened, ma'am."

Nothing she said shook the colonel's stand. Elissa knew in her heart he was speaking the truth. "If he was on that flight," she said, finally acquiescing, "could he have survived somehow?"

"Highly unlikely. The plane had mechanical problems and went down in the mountains. We don't believe there were any survivors."

"As far as you know. But isn't it possible...?"

"Even if he had somehow survived, Ms. Sinclair, there is no way he could have found an international airport in the area where the plane went down, then flown to the United States in the time period you've described. I also know that Jesse Garrett wouldn't have done that. He'd have contacted headquarters at the first opportunity."

Again, she knew he spoke the truth. "One more question," she asked haltingly. "When Jesse visited me, he said he had been on a recon mission. Was that true?"

At first, she thought he was going to refuse to answer. "Jesse was involved with highly sensitive projects. I'm not at liberty to say what kind of mission he was on."

"Is there such a thing as a 'recon' mission?"

"Of course."

Of course. Elissa hadn't known that, though, military lingo was totally unfamiliar to her. She had never heard the term *recon* before. Not until Jesse had mentioned it.

She persisted. "He said he'd run into complications, and that the mission had lasted months longer than anticipated."

"I can't say that's incorrect," he admitted, guardedly.

"And his mail," she whispered, frankly shaken now.

"Was he able to receive mail while away on his mission?"

"No, ma'am, he was not. Any communication would have jeopardized his position. His incoming mail was held here at the base until he returned."

"And that was...?"

"Two days before the flight."

A sense of unreality flooded Elissa and her head swam. *Jesse had been telling the truth.* It had sounded so unlikely—the secrecy of his mission, the holding of his mail. Which meant that he hadn't deliberately ignored the news of her pregnancy and Cody's birth.

The implications boggled her mind. Her perception of Jesse had been based largely on his failure to respond...and on things that Dean had told her. She then remembered his phone calls to Dean, placed from bars and brothels across Asia. The only explanation was that Jesse's mission hadn't begun until a few months ago. Which would mean he *had* deliberately ignored her letters. "When did he leave on his mission, Colonel? What date?"

"I'm sorry, but—"

"How long did his mission last, exactly?"

"Ms. Sinclair, I really can't give you specifics. I'd advise you to keep an open mind about that visit from Jesse. I've seen a lot of death over the years and I could write volumes about unexplained phenomena."

"I don't doubt that at all," she whispered.

"As a matter of fact, something rather odd happened the day before Jesse's flight."

She clutched the phone tighter. "What was that?"

"He made out a will."

"A will? He made out a will?"

"Yes ma'am. As if he'd had a premonition."

In that moment, the first inkling of belief trickled through her that Jesse *might* really have died on that flight...and that his visit to her hadn't been on the physical plane. As the colonel had said, stranger things had happened.

Certainly not to her.

Three days later, Jesse's mother was contacted and told that remains had been found and identified through fingerprinting. Captain Jesse Garrett was declared legally, officially—unequivocally—dead.

Even after Elissa heard the pronouncement, she heard Jesse's last words to her. Spoken with quiet passion, they echoed through her heart. He'd said, "I'll be back, Elissa. To be a father to Cody. Never doubt it."

2

JESSE DREAMED of his own funeral. It was one of those dreams so rich in detail that he swore he was there. Yet he knew he was dreaming and fighting against a deeper, heavier sleep.

He was back in Savannah, beneath the sprawling live oaks with Spanish moss trailing over century-old graves. The earthy smell of the river filled his nostrils, sweetened by flowers and greenery. In the beautiful but somber twilight imposed by the oaks, magnolias and dogwoods, the October sun cast dappled rays upon the small gathering of mourners.

A preacher voiced a eulogy beside the family vault, extolling the virtues of courage and patriotism. He ended with a promise of life everlasting for the good.

From a vantage point possible only in dreams, Jesse noticed his mother's hand spasmodically clutching her elder sister's. The sisters shared a troubled gaze—one they had often shared over his head when he was boy. Even in his dreams they believed the worst of him. With good reason, he had to admit. Goodness had never been his forte.

He directed his attention away from his mother, who was now dabbing at her eyes with a handkerchief. His stiff-backed aunt was next to her, her silvering head held at its usual haughty angle. Behind them stood the small knot of mourners.

The turnout at this dream funeral wasn't very gratifying, thought Jesse wryly. His mother's family had dutifully put in an appearance, along with their army of servants. But he recognized no one as a friend. No one who would miss him.

With a surprising flash of insight, he admitted that he couldn't blame his friendless state on his career. He'd deliberately avoided personal ties, distanced himself from potential friends, even from lovers. Especially from lovers. Would all those one-night stands mourn his passing when his time came? A humorless laugh escaped him.

As he tried to remember faces, only one came to mind. Elissa. But he didn't consider her a one-night stand. In his dreams, he'd made love to her every night since he'd met her.

He didn't consider her a lover, either. She'd made her feelings clear on that point. No, Elissa was an adversary—one who had a knack for whipping up his fury. Worse yet, she had control of his son. Jesse tightened his fists. Why had he built their brief union up in his mind to be anything out of the ordinary? He must have been mission-bound desperate, or just plain crazy.

At a signal from the preacher, the restless crowd began their shuffle between the graves toward their cars. Watching the assembly disperse, Jesse felt very much alone.

He'd had enough of this dream. He wanted to wake up. *Now.* Wakefulness, however, didn't come. Beckoning him instead was a deeper, numbing sleep. A forgetful sleep...

A woman slowly passed him, swept along by the crowd. She was dressed in a tailored black suit and white silk blouse. Her hair, soft and dark as sable, was tied with a black scarf at the nape of her neck and cascaded down her back in smooth curls. Her head was bent; he couldn't see her eyes, except for the graceful contours of her profile.

Jesse's weariness instantly vanished. *Elissa.*

His cousin Dean walked beside her. Jesse saw his arm come up around her shoulders. In a possessive way, he realized. As if to announce ownership.

No, he had to be mistaken. Dean was nothing more than a friend to Elissa. A platonic friend.

And this, of course, was only a dream.

As ELISSA SAT in a parlor over Abercorn Street, she felt as if she was smothering. Jesse's aunt—Dean's mother—invited everyone after the memorial service to her home on a picturesque square in Savannah. Elissa had accompanied Dean, hoping for a sense of closure, because ever since Jesse's death had been confirmed, she'd felt oddly hollow. Stricken, as if she'd suffered a terrible loss. It was illogical—she hadn't known Jesse very well—but she found she couldn't shake it.

In fact, her melancholy mushroomed and grew until she could think of little else. Jesse was gone, with no chance of returning to her life. No chance to incite all those visceral emotions that would lay and had otherwise lain dormant. Gone, before she had fully expressed her fury at his neglect. Gone, before she could understand her absolute bewitchment.

Since his death, every passing day had increased her sense that she was somehow drifting from the right path, separated from her destiny, headed in the wrong direction.

The funeral hadn't brought her closure, and looking around, she realized she wouldn't attain a sense of closure from this gathering, either. Jesse's family didn't seem to share the feeling that there was a gaping hole where he should have been. Gossipers exchanged news, sports fans analyzed football plays and business types networked, but not a word was spoken about the man they'd come to mourn. She overheard Dean chatting with a cousin about teaching high school chorus, and then her attention was drawn to the guests behind her. Someone had uttered Jesse's name and Elissa's heart was pierced by a pain she hadn't expected.

"Of *course* there isn't a casket," one young woman was saying. "After all, there wasn't actually a *body*. His remains were cremated...at least, the remains they could find. You know how it is after a plane crash—especially when there's a lot of passengers involved. From what I heard, the military had to search the jungle for...*parts*...."

In sudden need of air, Elissa whirled away. As she shouldered her way toward the open side balcony, someone clamped a hand around her arm. "Elissa, darling." It was Dean, and an elegant matron with cropped silver hair, a pointed chin and thin lips that looked remarkably like Dean's. "I'd like you to meet my mother, Muriel Pholey."

Elissa struggled to murmur a greeting as sharp blue eyes assessed her. "So, Elissa, at last we meet. Did Jesse's commanding officer answer all your questions?"

"Yes, ma'am, he tried."

"Did you know Jesse very well?"

Her throat tightened. "No, not very."

"From our conversation, I assumed you'd been... close to Jesse. You seemed so positive he was alive. So...passionate about it." Her elegant silver brows arched.

For a stricken moment, Elissa said nothing. She *had* been passionate about it. But how could he have visited her? The only rational conclusion she could draw was that his "visit" had been a psychic connection...maybe even at the time of his death. She could accept this possibility; telepathy during a trauma had been documented in hundreds of cases. But the idea of Jesse reaching out to her in distress left her aching. She had refused his last chance at making peace between them. She had sent him to his ever-after without forgiving his neglect; without welcoming him home. "I was mistaken, obviously."

"How did you know Jesse?"

"She met him *once*, Mother," Dean snapped. "Just once."

Elissa's glance cut to him in reproach. What would his family think now when she told them Cody was his son? For she intended to tell them; intended for her son to know his paternal relations. It was the least she could do to make amends to Jesse. But then, she hadn't told Dean of her intention. She realized now that he wouldn't like it.

"You met Jesse only once?" said Muriel, her blue eyes gleaming.

"Her only contact with him was when I introduced them," said Dean, looking red around the ears. "She's been *my* friend for many years. In fact—" he slipped his arm around her "—I'm hoping she'll be more than a friend." He smiled at Elissa.

The air around them suddenly chilled, as if a door had come ajar in the dead of winter. But this was October in the South, a mild October at that. With a shiver, Elissa looked for air-conditioning vents, but found none near enough to cause the dramatic drop in temperature.

Crossing her arms to warm herself, she realized that no one else seemed affected.

Muriel actually appeared warmer than before, her face flushed in patches. "Then, why did Jesse's attorney ask for her address?"

"His attorney?" repeated Dean, baffled.

Everything seemed to slip out of focus. "The waiver I sent," she whispered. The waiver of paternal status. Jesse had told her he hadn't signed it, but obviously, he had. Why else would his attorney be contacting her?

Disappointment, illogical but strong, coursed through her. So he hadn't wanted Cody, after all. Even in his last-ditch psychic connection with her, Jesse had lied.

"What had you sent to Jesse?" prompted Muriel, annoyed that she hadn't heard.

"Oh, Mother, let's not discuss boring legalities. Elissa was in the process of transferring some property from Jesse," Dean lied.

"Which property?" demanded Muriel. "That place in the Victorian section? He was forever buying old houses."

"Uh, no," replied Elissa.

"The beach lot on Tybee?"

"Really, Mother, where's your famous hospitality?" Dean interjected. "Elissa hasn't tried your liver pâté yet."

"Not the house on Isle of Hope!" cried Muriel. "You didn't close the deal, did you? Did it bring a good price, at least? That house is a historic landmark. How he came by it I'll never know. Some underhanded way, you can be sure."

"Elissa hasn't bought the house on Isle of Hope," Dean assured her. With an agitated glance around, he whispered, "But if she had, Mother, it's none of your business."

"Delia's business *is* my business," she snapped. "I've handled her assets for years." Her glance darted like the tongue of a snake toward a gentle-faced lady with white hair who was chatting contentedly with the preacher. "If only Delia had listened to me," said Muriel, "she wouldn't have gone with that Garrett boy in the first place."

In an aside to Elissa, Dean muttered, "Jesse's father."

"He *forced* himself on my sister." Muriel waited expectantly for Elissa's reaction.

But she had heard the story before—from Dean, the morning after her glorious night with Jesse. And later, when she had told Dean of her pregnancy, he had asked with concern, "Did Jesse...*force* you?"

Visibly disappointed with her lack of response, Muriel reworded her revelation. "He violated Delia. Brought shame to the family. Oh, he married her in the end—Papa insisted. But the louse didn't stay. Left Delia holding the bag—or the cradle, I should say. That misbegotten son of hers was exactly like his father. Bad from the minute he was born. He could charm the skirts off the ladies...for his own satisfaction, no matter what the cost to them. I remember the time he broke into the girls' dormitory. We had the charges dropped." Darkly, she muttered, "He sprang from bad seed. The blood of a rapist ran through Jesse's veins."

Elissa didn't want to listen. Cody had sprung from the same seed. The same blood ran through his veins. Shaken, she leveled Muriel a look as cold as the air that had grown so frigid around them. "I have to go now, Mrs. Pholey. I want to meet with Jesse's attorney. If you could please tell me his name and address—"

"Peter Thornton, on River Street," she said, "but—"

"Elissa, darling, we can't leave now," protested Dean.

"No need for you to leave, Dean. I have personal business to attend to."

He frowned, looking affronted. "But we drove together in my car. How will you—"

"It's only a few blocks to River Street. I'll walk."

"Well, if you insist. But call me when you're finished. If we leave for home by five, we'll be there around eight."

"You can go back without me. I have a friend in Savannah I'd like to visit." It was a lie, but Elissa felt desperate to be alone. "I'll take the train home."

Dean followed her to the front door. "Elissa, I know mother upset you with her talk about Jesse, but every word she said is true. And everyone who's anyone in Savannah knows it." Discreetly, he whispered, "Do you understand why it's so important we keep Cody's...ah, paternity...a secret?"

Muriel broke in, "Dean, go see what's wrong with the thermostat. It's freezing in here."

Elissa made the most of her opportunity to escape. As she hurried down the front steps into the balmy afternoon, she saw that the windows of Muriel's town house had begun to frost over.

"YOU DO UNDERSTAND, don't you, Ms. Sinclair?"

As if from far away, the attorney's voice droned through the fog that had settled in her mind. Understand? No, actually, she didn't. She'd been expecting to hear about the waiver of paternal status. So why was this lawyer talking about a fortune Jesse made during the urban renewal boom?

When she continued to stare blankly at him across his desk, the attorney explained, "To put it simply, your son has inherited Jesse's estate. His properties and his funds."

"My son?" she finally said.

The attorney sat back and removed his glasses. "Yours and Jesse's, according to the documents he signed the day before he died."

Slowly, the news sank in. Jesse had left all his belongings to Cody. He had named him as his heir. He had acknowledged him as his son. He had cared.

"He also left a tidy sum to you. According to the will, he wanted you to have the choice of staying home with Cody."

And as the attorney went on to explain about her role as caretaker of the properties and trustee of Cody's funds, Elissa buried her face in her hands and cried.

JESSE WOKE FROM THE DREAM with his teeth painfully locked. Elissa had been there with his family, letting them poison her mind. Against him, against Cody. He knew how potent that poison could be. He couldn't stop it from affecting her view of him; he had known from the start that she'd eventually discover the truth about him.

But he couldn't let the gossip affect her love for their baby. *If* she had any love for their baby. He still had to find that out. His son would grow up feeling loved, he swore, even if he had to strap him into his backpack and take him on missions.

Jesse sat up in bed and threw the covers aside, wondering about Dean's relationship with Elissa. Could there be any basis in reality for *that* part of his dream?

Had he subconsciously picked up clues to a closeness between them?

It was then, as he rose from the bed, that Jesse noticed his surroundings. The spacious bedroom with its leaded-pane windows; its polished pecan floor and woodwork aglow in the afternoon sun; the oversized Georgia pine four-poster bed with its hand-sewn quilt; the framed photo on his dresser of his old platoon gathered around a Bradley. He was home in Savannah. In his house on Isle of Hope.

But how had he gotten here?

He couldn't remember. He couldn't remember the trip from Elissa's house to here. He shook his head, feeling disoriented. Why couldn't he remember?

A sound from outside disrupted his concentration. A car, pulling into the drive. A car door slamming. Jesse peered down through the quartered panes of the side window.

A woman stood on the walkway in the front garden as a taxi pulled away. Her sable brown hair was tied back by a black scarf, with haphazard curls cascading down the front of one slender shoulder. She wore a slim black suit and a white silk blouse. In the last golden glare of late afternoon, her expression looked dazed and somber.

His dreams had never come true before, but it seemed part of his last one had. Elissa was here, in Savannah, looking exactly as she had in his dream.

A crosscurrent of emotion held Jesse in its grip: anger that she had sent him away without letting him see his son; suspicion over why she was here; and a stubborn desire to catch her up in his arms, anyway.

He wouldn't, of course. He hadn't been allowed to even touch her the last time they'd met.

He saw her graceful fingers dip into her purse as she advanced toward the front door. A moment later, he heard a key grating in the lock. *A key.* How did she have a key to his house? The only person who had one was his housekeeper.

And why did Elissa feel justified in using the key, however she happened to come by it? By God, she had some explaining to do. Jesse dropped the sheer drapery back into place, curiosity roiling in his chest. Curiosity, and fierce anticipation. For whatever the reason, justified or not, Elissa was here. In his home. Tonight.

WITHDRAWING THE KEY from the lock, Elissa paused on the front porch of the brick cottage set high on the bluff above the Skidaway River. Her first reaction to the place had been shock. She had never expected such beauty.

Huge moss-draped live oaks canopied the driveway that sloped upward from the riverfront road. The house itself, built of Savannah brick with its soft red-gray hue, its shingled roof and leaded windows, reminded Elissa of a quaint British cottage nestled in a profusion of greenery. Ivy, grape and confederate jasmine vines festooned its aged brick walls, dappled by the shade of fig trees, oaks, pecans and palmetto palms. The scent of semitropical foliage, the taste of brackish river mist and the ambience of this historic southern coastline came to her on the twilight breeze, hauntingly appealing.

This wild, soulful beauty had once belonged to a man every bit as compelling. A man who had drawn her to him with the same magical enchantment his house now invoked. Loneliness squeezed her breathless.

The place belonged to her son now. She should be gladdened by his good fortune, and by hers. But she could think of nothing but the man who had bequeathed it. *Jesse*. Her heart ached to see him, touch him, just one more time. Of course, she never would.

She knew what she had to do now. She had to make her peace with him. To say her final goodbye. What better place than his home? What better time than now?

Bracing herself, she pushed open the glossy oak door. Inside, shadows engulfed her. The heavy door creaked shut, and she battled the impulse to fling it open. Instead, she stood perfectly still at the threshold, allowing her eyes to adjust to the dimness.

She sensed a different aura than she had outside. A cool, menacing presence. As if the house, having lured her inside with its quaintness, now scorned her presence. But no, it wasn't scorn, or disapproval. It was... anger. Yes. Anger. *Against her?*

A trill of fear shivered through her, and for no logical reason, she remembered Muriel's harsh whisper. *He sprang from bad seed. The blood of a rapist ran through Jesse's veins.* Was it a lingering evil that she sensed so strongly here? Whatever it was, the presence seemed to be growing stronger. Or maybe just...closer.

No. She squared her jaw and stood her ground. She could not believe that Jesse had been evil. A heartbreaker, yes. But not evil. He had provided a secure future for the son he'd never met; certainly not the action of an evil man. She would not allow doubts raised by his aunt's whispers—and by her own perplexing experience with Jesse—to interfere with that certainty.

What she felt now was merely her own longing for a connection with him...and the sinister aura of solitude in an unfamiliar house at dusk.

The high heels of her leather pumps clicked purposefully against a stone floor as Elissa ran her fingertips over textured plaster walls in search of a switch.

The shadows intensified around her. A chill snaked its way down her spine. She felt that if she were to reach out through the darkness, her hand would encounter a presence, a solid presence, of whatever or whomever it was....

"Is anyone here?" she called out. She was answered only by her own eerie echo. Her now convulsive groping at last produced the switch, and she exhaled in relief as illumination brightened the room.

Again, she stood motionless.

The vast living room was floored with pinkish flagstones, the walls textured with an earthy gray, evoking a southwestern flavor. The oversize furnishings were cushioned in shades of peach, green and cream. Area rugs and pillows abounded. Luxuriant ferns spilled from hanging baskets; large-leafed plants grew near the floor-to-ceiling windows. The mirrored blinds were drawn. Bookshelves flanked a massive fireplace whose mantel was lined with souvenirs of travel: carvings of animals, figurines, pottery, bottles, artifacts and models of ancient ships.

Again, a wistfulness seized Elissa. The room—open, warm and intriguing—abounded with character. But the source of that character was only a memory, reflected in earthly trappings like these that could never bring him back.

She turned away from the living room and wandered through an archway to a flight of stairs bordered by gleaming oak handrails. Jesse had certainly had a taste for elegance. Solid, masculine elegance. She hadn't known that about him. Hadn't been given the chance. Her sense of loss sharpened.

On the second floor, she walked from room to room, the decor and furnishings barely registering in her mind. Only weeks ago, the place had been readied for Jesse's return from overseas. He should have been here. He should have been guiding her tour.

In the largest bedroom, she stopped. The handsome pine four-poster bed had been left unmade. Elissa frowned. Why would the housekeeper, obviously efficient, leave a bed unmade? Jesse hadn't returned here. Who, then, had slept in his bed?

She slowly ventured into the room. Traces of a familiar scent lingered. Jesse's aftershave, she realized. The scent activated vivid memories of the night they'd shared, when the heat of their bodies had intensified the fragrance. That scent would be forever linked in her heart with raw, carnal passion.

Had it meant anything to him? Anything at all?

Drawn to the bed, she reverently ran her hand over the pillow, swearing she saw the indentation from where a head had rested. Could she feel a warmth there, too? *Could she?*

Nonsense. It had been more than a year since he'd been home.

"Jesse," she whispered into the utter stillness, the name catching in her throat. "Jesse, oh, Jesse, why did you have to leave before I even had a chance to know you?"

And through the twilight silence of that bedchamber rang out a laugh—brief, wry, utterly familiar—that spun her heart around and sent it plunging toward her toes.

"You have a pretty short memory, darlin'" came the deep, hoarse drawl. "The way I remember it, you told me to get the hell out."

3

HE STOOD IN THE BEDROOM doorway, his night black hair tousled from either wind or sleep, his skin a golden umber from the Asian sun. His arms were crossed; one sinewy shoulder wedged against the jamb. He wore only loose-fitting military khaki pants, leaving his lean waist bare and his muscular chest covered with only a mat of dark curls. Although one corner of his mouth curved upward, no smile disturbed the cool silver of his eyes.

Shock drove the air out of Elissa's lungs.

How could he be here? *He couldn't be.* But there he was, standing half a room away, wearing a powerful, piercing stare. The same stare that had set her back an intimidated step when they'd parted company.

"Where'd you get the key to my house?" he demanded quietly. "And why? Did you think I wouldn't let you in if you knocked?" His gaze held her—a granite-hard gaze, yet oddly warming. "I would have let you in, Elissa. We have business to settle, you and I."

She tried to draw a breath, but couldn't. It seemed her lungs had collapsed, or maybe just stopped functioning. She'd never fainted before, but dizziness threatened her now.

"Or was this your way of getting back at me for surprising you in your kitchen?" With a brief, mocking tilt of his head, his eyes grew even colder. "Touché. And I'm not even armed with a frying pan."

She opened her mouth and drew in a tortured semblance of a breath, but it seemed to carry no oxygen. She caught at the bedpost as the room spun around her.

"You owe me an explanation, Elissa. Among other things." Through a blue-tinged haze, she watched him approach, his eyes as fierce and dark as thunderclouds. "You wouldn't let me see my son, and now I've caught you breaking and entering into my home." The very air around her changed as he neared, vibrating with his animosity.

Instinctively, she cringed away from him and his tightly leashed anger. Still, that anger quavered through her like an electrical charge. Her gasp drew air into her lungs and, ironically enough, jump started them out of their paralysis. Clarity filtered back, and she managed to rasp, "Jesse!"

"You're surprised to see me. Just what the hell were you planning to do here in my absence?"

She didn't reply. How could she? She barely believed he stood there!

His anger visibly swelled. "Damn it, Elissa, tell me."

But incredulity seeped in to take the place of her shock. "Jesse...is it really you? Oh, God. Jesse!" She reached out to touch his face.

Out of sheer reflex, he evaded her, flinching, as if she had thrown a punch.

"It was all a mistake," she whispered in soft wonder. "The whole thing—a terrible mistake."

Jesse frowned at that, and at the emotion glimmering in her sherry brown eyes. Was it...joy? Was she *glad* to see him? Foreboding filled his gut. "Is Cody okay?"

"Cody?" She sounded surprised to hear the name, or

surprised that he remembered it. "Oh, yes, yes, Cody's fine. He's with my parents. But, *you...*" She held her hands open wide, and her gaze swept over him. The unexpected welcome in her eyes seared through the armor he'd built up against her. "We thought you were dead!"

"Dead?" He'd been prepared for just about anything but that. His brows drew together. "Who thought I was dead?"

"Everyone."

Thunderstruck, he stared at her. "I've been called a lot of things, but 'dead' has never been one of them."

Despite his sardonic tone, or maybe because of it, her expression grew more solemn. "I swear to you, Jesse, the military officially pronounced you dead."

Her earnestness sent a shard of doubt through his certainty that she was, for some reason, bluffing. "Impossible. Why would they think I died after I successfully accomplished the mission? I returned to the base, and the brass promised me a promotion. Until then, I'm on a month's leave."

She planted a hand on one hip—a slim but rounded hip, he noticed. "I talked to Colonel Atkinson," she said.

That shook the sureness right out of him. "Don't be ridiculous. The colonel knows I'm not dead. He saw me off when I left the base."

"Someone obviously made a mistake."

A mistake. How could he argue with that? "Damned army," he grumbled. Another screw-up to straighten out. Dead, of all things. It had just better not interfere with his pay, he swore, or he'd have someone's head.

As she sank down onto the bed, which caused her slim black skirt to ride slightly above her crossed knees,

Jesse strode to the bedside telephone. Elissa said with an open-palmed gesture, "I *tried* to tell them that I saw you after the plane crash, but…"

"Plane crash?" He paused with the receiver halfway to his ear.

"A transport crashed on its way to the States from the base where you were stationed. The colonel swore you were on that very plane. But you…you must have taken another."

His frown deepened as he struggled to remember his flight home. A strange fog obscured much of the memory. He recalled saying goodbye to the colonel and boarding the transport, headed for the States.

And then…yes, there had been some kind of trouble. The pilot's voice had come over the intercom. Something about an engine failing. The plane had rolled to the right, and nosed down into dive. But then what?

He couldn't remember.

"Was there more than one flight headed for the States that morning?" Elissa queried. "There must have been. The colonel was simply confused about which one you boarded."

Jesse didn't reply. There hadn't been any other flight. And he'd never known Colonel Atkinson to be confused.

"They supposedly used fingerprinting as the method to identify your…your—" Elissa paled "—to prove your death." A visible shudder went through her. "But there's always the possibility of human error."

Decisively, Jesse dialed the colonel's number. The foreboding in his chest worsened as he listened to the ringing at the other end. Why couldn't he remember the finish of his trip home? If the plane had crashed, how had he gotten here? The questions rumbled through ·

him as he waited for Colonel Atkinson's phone to be answered.

On the third ring, the feminine voice of the colonel's after-hours service answered. Jesse asked her to put through an emergency call to the colonel. She responded with, "Hello? May I help you?"

Impatient, he repeated, "This is Captain Jesse Garrett, and I need to make an emergency call—"

"Is anyone there?"

He gripped the phone tighter. "If you can't hear me, I'll try the call again. The connection must be bad."

"Hello-o-o?" There was a resounding *click* as she disconnected.

With a soft curse, Jesse dialed the long-distance operator, who answered promptly and clearly. But she couldn't hear him, either. Frustrated, he dropped the receiver. "It's probably this phone. I'll try downstairs."

Elissa accompanied him down the oak-railed stairway and into the living room. Even in his agitated state, he couldn't help but watch as she kicked off her pumps and folded her mile-long legs beneath her on the sofa. Her gypsy-dark hair curled around her face, tendrils dancing free from the scarf tie. She lifted worried eyes to him.

He looked away as he dialed the phone on the end table. Her beauty infused him with a tension he didn't need.

He waited, the receiver to his ear, and when the colonel's answering service picked up, he muttered a few words, then halted. *She still couldn't hear him.* Slowly, he hung up the phone. "The trouble must be in the lines."

Elissa bit the corner of her full bottom lip; a teasing thing for her to do, as far as Jesse was concerned. "Let's go use a phone somewhere else," she suggested. Her voice was slightly throaty; a detail he hadn't paid nearly enough attention to in his fantasies. "We have to talk to your family, too. They still think you're dead."

"My family." He tried to keep the scorn out of his voice. Shoving fists into the pockets of his khakis, he ambled toward her. A sudden thought occurred. "Did they, by any chance, hold a funeral service for me?"

She nodded, her brown eyes glinting auburn. "Today."

He dropped down onto the sofa beside her. "It seems I've developed a new talent." Although he spoke with self-mockery, he'd learned enough about the human mind not to doubt its capabilities. Wouldn't the military have a heyday if their training had endowed him with remote-viewing skills? He wouldn't doubt that it had. Their research and training was specifically aimed at stretching the limitations of his mind.

"I dreamed of a funeral," he admitted slowly. His contemplative gaze cut to Elissa. "You were there. And you were wearing exactly what you have on now." The spark of awe in her eyes told him she believed him. "And before that," he recalled, more to himself now, "I had a premonition of danger. It lasted days...before my plane crashed."

"But *your* plane didn't crash. You had to have taken a different flight." A tremor shook her otherwise reassuring voice. "Didn't you?"

He didn't answer. He had no answers, although he knew that rational ones existed. He was in no mood to search for them now.

Settling back against the sofa, he extended his bare arm along the seat behind her. A silky tendril brushed against his forearm, its color a few shades warmer than his own wiry black mop. He hadn't noticed that about her before—the secret fires burning in every dark strand whenever the lamplight caught it. And he wasn't sure if he had fully appreciated the creamy smoothness of her skin. Or the warmth and softness of her slender shoulders...

Jesse drew in a slow, steadying breath. His memory would return, he had no doubt. The telephone lines would clear. And this fiasco about his so-called death would resolve itself. But not tonight. Nothing could be settled tonight.

And he might never have Elissa to himself again.

Her scent, elegant and sensual, wafted to him from her hair, her skin. Gazing at her mouth, he remembered the taste of it—sweet and sultry and endlessly inviting. It had been so damned long since he'd kissed her.

He wanted to kiss her now.

The strength of the wanting stunned him. He'd felt the same the first time he'd laid eyes on her. All demure and proper, she was, socializing with Dean and his teacher friends. Too chaste and shy for a beast like Jesse. He had stalked her, anyway, with his eyes, with his wits, until he'd cornered her. But she was no one's prey. She had turned on him with concealed weapons—well concealed, brought out privately for him—her warmth and sensuality. Lord, he had wanted her.

One short night with her had barely whetted his appetite. She had haunted him throughout the long brutal months that followed, even after his mission had ended. There'd been women at the base—slim young nurses, more than willing to give him a taste of the softness he'd been missing. But he'd had no appetite for them.

He'd wanted Elissa.

He allowed his gaze to play over her elegant features,

reacquainting himself with every curve, every hollow. Hoarsely, he asked, "So...did you believe I'd died?"

Elissa tilted her face up to his, only partially surprised to find herself tucked in the warm curve of his bare arm and shoulder. He hadn't lost his boldness, or the smooth, casual way he somehow always placed her in close physical proximity to him.

Thrilling with that proximity, she tried her best to reply in an unaffected voice, but a husky one answered, anyway. "When they first told me you were dead, I didn't believe it. How could I? You'd been to my house that morning." She glanced away from him with that memory, embarrassed by her treatment of him. "But when the military declared you legally dead—" She paused, unable to explain her feelings. *Unwilling* to explain them.

"What, then?" he probed. "What did you make of my visit?"

With his warm, fragrant breath stirring her hair and his strong body vibrantly close to hers, Elissa felt foolish for ever having given in to theories of deathbed telepathy. "I didn't know what to make of it."

He studied her for a long, unnerving moment. "Is that why you nearly choked when you saw me tonight? You thought I was...a ghost?"

The last softly spoken word sent a shiver up Elissa's arms, beneath the sleeves of her suit jacket and thin silk blouse. "Of course not. I was just surprised to see you."

Silence descended around them, thick and intimate.

"Why did you come here, Elissa? To my house." The quiet question reverberated in the vast, stone-floored room.

"You bequeathed it to my son."

"Our son."

Elissa's breath caught, and the old argument between them came rushing back, startling her. She had denied him access to Cody. Refuted his right to see his own son. She'd been wrong; she knew that now. Jesse had a God-given right to see the baby they'd made together. "Yes. Our son."

"If you thought I was dead," Jesse persisted, lifting a curl from beside her ear and slowly twisting it around one long, hard finger, "who were you talking to, upstairs in my bedroom...with your hand on my pillow?"

She felt her cheeks warm. "I was saying goodbye."

He raised his brows, his eyes meeting hers. "To...?"

"To you."

A mesmerizing fire lit in his eyes, and he asked in a low, gruff whisper, "Did you grieve for me, Elissa?"

She felt it then—the slow burning away of her emotional defenses. She had no business feeling so deeply tied to this man. *She barely knew him.* But she couldn't lie, not when he'd caught her in such a telling gesture. "Yes," she finally whispered. "I grieved for you."

Some emotion flared deep within the quicksilver of his eyes, and she felt his hunger, strong and ever so seductive. "Then, you owe me, Elissa," he softly growled. "You owe me a welcome home."

His gaze forcibly held her as he lowered his mouth. Longing welled up within her. She wanted to kiss him. Wanted to indulge in the keen, sensual pleasure of his mouth, his hands, his hard, powerful body.

Alarmed, she realized she was doing it again, letting this mesmerizing stranger slip beyond her prudence and common sense—the few virtues she had left after their last explosive union.

"Jesse," she said in a panicked whispered, "I don't think we should—"

"Then, don't think," he breathed.

And with slow deliberation, he brushed his mouth against hers—lightly, reverently—from one corner to the next, the contact a mere whisper of heat across her lips.

Elissa closed her eyes and thought she'd die from the pleasure. Erotic sensations washed through her in a heated torrent, leaving her trembling as it ebbed. Trembling, hot, and wanting more. If she had doubted at all the proof of her eyes, there was no denying this. Jesse was back, and igniting a potent heat—with only the lightest of touches.

She opened her eyes, seeking him. He angled his head for another kiss, his gaze burning an unmistakable message. This would be no mere whisper.

Elissa parted her lips, ready for it. Ready to throw caution and hard lessons to the wind.

But a sudden sound jarred her. A chime. *The doorbell.*

"Jesse," she whispered, half dazed, "someone's here."

"They'll go away," he muttered against her mouth.

The next sound disproved that theory. A key turned in the front door lock. "Ms. Sinclair, are you here?" rang out a woman's cheery voice from the foyer.

Jesse's eyes darkened with thwarted desire. Beneath his breath, he cursed. "Suzanne. My housekeeper."

Still trembling from Jesse's feather-light assault, Elissa managed to call out weakly, "Yeah, I'm here."

A lanky blonde in a T-shirt and faded jeans approached them with a snap of chewing gum and a look of mild surprise. Elissa recognized her from Jesse's funeral. "Oh, there you are," she said. "I figured you were upstairs, since the light's on up there. I'm Suzanne Hancock."

Elissa's cheeks blazed with embarrassment as she rose from the sofa. She felt as if the woman could easily divine the scope and nature of the tension so tangible between Jesse and her—the sexual need that had been whetted and then left brutally unfulfilled.

Mercifully unfulfilled, she corrected herself, her good sense slowly returning.

Jesse, meanwhile, shirtless and impossibly sexy, stood up and raked a frustrated hand through his unruly black locks as he ambled toward the shadows. When he turned back to face them, his mouth, eyes and wide-legged stance expressed unbridled annoyance.

Elissa stepped forward to break the awkwardness. "I'm Elissa Sinclair. It's good to meet you."

"Looks like I caught you napping," Suzanne said with a grin. "Sorry if I woke you."

Elissa's eyebrow quirked. She thought they'd been *napping*?

With a hint of self-consciousness, Suzanne said, "I thought I'd make sure you got in okay, and give you a key to the garage." She held out a key. Absently, Elissa took it.

Jesse emitted a deep, husky sound between a laugh and a snort. "You've got a hell of a sense of timing, Suzanne."

Elissa admonished him with a frown.

But Suzanne didn't so much as glance his way. Her attention dwelled solely on Elissa, in a friendly open manner without a hint of embarrassment.

Jesse tightened his lips, crossed his muscle-corded arms and leaned against the mantel. "Hello to you, too, Suzanne. It's only been a year since I've been home."

Suzanne ignored his mocking retort and launched

into an account of problems she'd had with the kitchen appliances.

Elissa gaped at her. She hadn't acknowledged Jesse's presence by the merest glance, let alone a greeting. It then occurred to her that Suzanne should be more than mindful of his presence—*she should be stunned by it*. She had attended his funeral that very day!

An eerie tension stiffened her spine, and she looked back at Jesse for some clue to the woman's behavior. He appeared to be as bewildered as she, watching Suzanne as she cataloged the contents of the pantry.

"Suzanne," she interrupted, "I no longer need to know any of this. Nor will I need a key."

Suzanne tilted her curly blond head as Elissa pressed the key into her palm. "Aren't you the new owner of the house? The lawyer told me that your son is Jesse's heir."

"True enough," said Jesse, a hint of amusement softening his irate, almost belligerent voice. "Let's just say that the change of ownership's been postponed for a while."

Elissa awaited her reaction.

But none came. *None*. Suzanne's questioning gaze remained steadfast on Elissa, as if she hadn't heard a word Jesse had said.

"Suzanne!" exclaimed Elissa. "How can anyone inherit this house when Jesse's *not dead?*"

Surprise, at last, disrupted her calm. "Not dead?"

Elissa regarded her in disbelief. Couldn't she see that for herself? She cast an incredulous glance at Jesse, who stood with a fist on his lean hip, a frown on his mouth and an expression of fascinated puzzlement in his gaze.

"Oh!" exclaimed Suzanne, holding up a finger, her

cheeks ruddy. "You mean he's alive in some sort of spiritual way."

Elissa's jaw dropped.

"Now, that's questionable," Jesse quipped.

Bothered, irritated and just a touch frightened, Elissa snapped, "Don't make light of the situation, Jesse. There's obviously some...some *problem* here."

When she swung her gaze back to Suzanne, uneasiness had crept over the young housekeeper's face. "I'll just leave the key on the end table," she said, sidling toward the door.

"Wait, Suzanne, don't go...."

Suzanne had turned her back and now made a beeline toward the door. Baffled, Elissa followed her out onto the porch. "Please, Suzanne, I need to talk to you!"

The housekeeper beat a steady path down the drive toward her car. Tense and confused, Elissa watched the headlights flare and fade in the cool Georgia night.

A vague resentment embraced her. Why had Suzanne ignored Jesse? She obviously wasn't blind, and he'd been standing in clear view. Didn't she comprehend the monumental significance of his presence? Didn't she realize that a man—her employer—had been falsely declared dead? Didn't that warrant a comment or two?

Elissa didn't know what to make of it. Maybe it was a psychological thing. Maybe Suzanne's refusal to acknowledge his presence had been caused by denial—to protect her from a surprise too jarring. She found that hard to believe, though. If she herself had survived the shock of finding him alive, anyone could.

Wrapping her arms around herself, she shivered against the October chill as she walked back into the house.

"Jesse," she called on her way into the living room, grateful for the golden lamplight illuminating the vast room. "She left, without ever saying—" She halted. He wasn't in the living room. "Jesse?" She peered into the dining room, then paced to the kitchen. He wasn't there, either.

"Jesse!" she yelled from the bottom of the stairs. No reply from the second floor. Only her own eerie echo. "Don't tease me like this. It's not funny."

He didn't answer.

Forcing a calm she didn't feel, she methodically searched the house, room by room, shadow by lonely shadow. Her efforts proved to be in vain.

Jesse had simply vanished.

DRIZZLE-GRAY LIGHT seeped through the hotel room's blinds and permeated Elissa's fitful sleep the next morning, a Saturday. Before she had fully awakened, the events of the previous night crowded in on her, resurrecting the questions that had stormed through her then.

Where had Jesse gone? Why had he made such a sudden exit, without an explanation, without a goodbye? Those were the questions she *allowed* herself to ponder. But just beyond those lurked the ones she refused to examine—the ones that had suggested unthinkable possibilities throughout the hellish night.

As she lay alone in the hotel suite staring at the ceiling, those unasked questions imposed themselves on her. Why hadn't Suzanne acknowledged Jesse's presence? Why, when she'd later searched his room, had she found no signs of occupancy, other than the unmade bed? No clothes or shoes out of place; no coins or sundries on his dresser. His toothbrush, toothpaste,

comb, razor—even bar soap and shampoo—were all
stored away in cabinets. In the kitchen, the refrigerator
had been void of food. The trash containers stood
empty and unlined.

Perhaps he was simply neat. She'd heard that the military often instilled obsessive neatness. In her heart,
though, she believed that Jesse hadn't spent a single
night in his house since his return from overseas.

Which brought her to the next set of questions. How
had he returned from overseas? And why hadn't he
known about the plane crash, which had been on television, radio and in newspapers? Where had he been
since he'd left her kitchen that morning a few weeks
ago? And why, when she had telephoned for a taxi
from his house last night, had her phone call gone
through unimpeded?

Jesse's hadn't. The colonel's answering service and
the long-distance operator hadn't been able to hear him.

Huddling beneath the covers, she drew her knees up
and tucked her chin to her chest, trying to stop her
trembling.

Everyone thought Jesse was dead. Should she notify
his family that she had been with him last night? She
imagined what Suzanne's version of events might be:
Ms. Sinclair thought Jesse was with us, but I didn't see him.

Her trembling worsened. *What are you thinking?* she
asked herself wildly. *Just come out and admit it.* But she
couldn't even fathom the possibility that this last encounter had anything to do with paranormal phenomena. He'd been there last night—solid, warm and alive.

Which meant that he had been there, *physically* been
there, in her kitchen three weeks ago. Again, a question
reared its ugly head. How had he popped in and out
through solidly locked doors and windows?

She had come to believe that that encounter had been a telepathic link with him as he died. Telepathy wasn't too hard to understand; she herself had experienced vague bouts of it from time to time. But that's *all* she had believed it to be—a reaching out from one human mind to another, with brain waves much like television or radio waves. She had never for a moment allowed herself to believe that the visit had been of a spiritual nature.

And, of course, it hadn't been. He'd been in her kitchen then, just as he'd been in his house last night, fully alive. How could she believe anything else? *He had touched her.*

Hadn't he?

A serpent-cold doubt slithered through her. He had brushed his lips against hers. Thinking back, she remembered a profusion of sensations that had coursed through her. But had she felt the actual contact of his mouth?

No. She hadn't.

Stop it, just stop it, she told herself. Ghosts couldn't kiss like that. Ghosts, if they existed at all, which she strongly doubted, were spiritual beings, with no mass or substance. No sexy smiles, or muscled biceps, or lightly furred chests. Ghosts were like illusions; holograms; vaporous masses; tricks of light, temperature or air pressure. *Weren't they?*

Of course they were. Her trembling lessened.

There was always another possibility, she realized with growing dismay, another one that she wouldn't entertain for even a moment. Maybe she was losing her mind.

She had to pull herself together. Had to ground herself in reality. Shoving her hair back from her eyes, she sat up by the bedside phone and called her mother. After asking about Cody and his teething problems, she had her mother hold the receiver to his little ear.

She felt a foolish warmth rush to her eyes. "Hi, baby. It's Mama. I love you." And though she knew that at three months of age, he wasn't actually responding to her greeting, he nevertheless made a contented gurgling sound, the kind he made after a comfy nap. Her throat tightened up. "You're my sunshine, my angel, my heart." Her eyes blurred; she knew she was being ridiculous. She'd only been away from him for one night, the first he'd ever spent apart from her. "Did you miss me last night? I missed you," she whispered.

Her mother reclaimed the phone. Elissa assured her she was all right and said she'd be home later that day, after breakfast and the four-hour train ride.

As her mother issued her usual warnings about traveling alone, an appetizing aroma wafted over from the adjoining sitting room. *Coffee.*

She remembered noticing a coffee maker on the countertop when she'd arrived last night. Had it been set to brew this morning? A lovely idea. Odd, considering the hotel had no way to know when the occupants would rise.

As she promised her mother that she'd follow her instructions to the letter, a voice rang out from the sitting room. A gruff, familiar, masculine voice.

"You take yours black?"

4

As THE AROMATIC COFFEE drizzled into the pot, Jesse wondered if Elissa had heard his question. Probably not. Her attention was obviously monopolized by her phone call. And that was precisely why he had brewed the coffee—for an excuse to interrupt her.

Who the hell was she talking to, anyway? Her words weren't clear, but her tone and pitch were. Soft, intimate murmurs. A hint of tears held in check. The sound of a kiss being sent across telephone wires.

If she didn't hang up the damned phone soon, he just might have to hang it up for her. The ferocity of the impulse rooted Jesse to the spot. Her phone calls were none of his business, and he knew it.

Was it Dean on the other end of that line? Jesse shook his head in self-disgust. What did it matter who was at the receiving end of those soft endearments? Just because she'd never spoken to *him* in that tender voice wasn't any reason to feel like he'd been punched in the gut.

Dammit, she'd practically been *cooing* in there.

It was everything he could do not to go to her now and make her forget all about the guy at the other end of that intimate conversation. He could, he swore he could. He'd make her see that he, Jesse, should be the only one she would ever...

His thoughts screeched to a halt. What was he thinking? He'd be gone in a month—one short month—off to his next assignment. He certainly had no intention of tying himself to anyone, or tying anyone to him. If she wanted to whisper love talk to some S.O.B., that was fine with him. Just fine.

But it wouldn't stop him from claiming some of her time. And her mouth. And her body. *Soon.* The shortness of his leave time added a kind of desperation to his resolve.

As the coffee finished brewing, Jesse morosely reached for the cups beside the coffee maker, then experienced a profound realization. *He didn't know where he was.*

Stunned, he stared around at the room—green plaid furniture, a coffee table, a miniature refrigerator with a price list posted on its door, floor-to-ceiling draperies that most likely covered sliding glass doors. A hotel suite.

With Elissa?

Why couldn't he remember? He looked down at his favorite pair of faded jeans, ones he hadn't seen in ages, and a T-shirt he'd practically lived in during his last leave. He couldn't remember dressing in any of it. His memory was blank.

This much he vividly recalled—Elissa and he had been interrupted by Suzanne at the start of a kiss. Even now, his body responded to the memory. Though he had barely brushed his lips across hers, the tantalizing taste of her had been even sweeter, more intoxicating, than he'd remembered.

A question hit him squarely in the libido. What if he'd made love to her and couldn't remember it? *That* possibility was more than he could bear. Something had to be done. He'd have to see a doctor about these memory lapses.

He suspected that the problem had something to do with the trauma of his last mission. The lack of food, the intense cold, the filth of the prison, the less-than-hospitable treatment he'd received at the hands of his terrorist hosts. All this may have somehow left an effect on him. Delayed shock syndrome, he guessed, thinking of what some of his men had suffered after various missions.

As he began to unwrap a coffee cup, movement from the open doorway caught his eye.

Elissa stood there, staring at him. Her long pink robe was loosely tied at her slender waist and her white lace gown was open at the throat. Her dark hair glinted and fell in a glorious, uncombed billow; her lips glistened a smooth, natural pink. She had very obviously just risen from bed, and Jesse wanted nothing more than to take her back there.

He then realized that the glow in her amber brown eyes was *not* desire. It was anger. Incredulous anger, as if he had sprouted horns before her very eyes and incinerated her favorite sofa.

"You do want coffee, don't you?" he asked.

She didn't reply, but stood glowering at him, her fists clenching and unclenching at her sides.

With a half shrug, he offered, "Orange juice?"

Slowly she advanced, her bare feet peeping out from beneath her robe, her eyes seething. He set down the coffee cup. He'd seen her angry before, but never to this extent. Her full bottom lip was tight and a vein pulsed at her temple. "You!" she finally spat out in a tone of loathing.

Baffled, Jesse frowned. "Care to elaborate on that?"

Immediately she complied. "You are despicable.

Vile! The worst, the very worst person I've ever known."

"That's plenty 'nough elaboration for me." He eyed her in total bewilderment.

"What's your game, Jesse?" she cried. "Are you trying to drive me crazy? You left me last night, just vanished, letting me search all over the house for you."

"I left *you?*" *Impossible.*

"And that thing with Suzanne. Why did she act like she didn't see you?"

"I have no idea. Maybe I ticked her off. Seems like I'm pretty good at riling up women without even knowing it."

Elissa paced back and forth like a caged lioness, glaring at him. "And those phone calls you supposedly tried. When *I* called for a cab, *my* call went through just fine."

"Good for you. But how should I know why mine didn't? The lines were obviously messed up. Maybe the army's covertly taken over the running of the telephone company."

"Were the lines *really* messed up?" she scoffed, ignoring his feeble attempt at humor. "Or was that whole scene part of some scheme?" Her eyes widened at another possibility. "Is Suzanne in it with you? Are you pretending to be dead to hide from the military?"

"Don't be ridiculous."

"If this *is* a scheme, it's cruel. *And* illegal. How does it involve me?" Another thought lowered her voice by a decibel. "And how did you know where to find me this morning?" Her tone took on the hush of disbelief. "You must have followed me last night!"

Jesse could only stare at her in dismay. He hadn't the first clue as to what the hell he'd done last night.

Vaguely he remembered a weariness overtaking him; an insidious drain on his energy. But what happened after that?

Elissa interpreted his silent reflection as guilt. "You *did* follow me! How did you get into this private suite?"

Again, he had no answer. Not even a reasonable guess. And in her current state of mind, she probably wouldn't buy the truth—that he simply didn't remember. One lesson he'd learned in the military: when in doubt, keep your mouth shut.

Never had he been more in doubt.

She was circling him now, her eyes blazing with contempt. "Did you use some maneuver you learned in your juvenile delinquent days to pick the lock of my hotel door? Or did you lie to the front desk clerk, tell her we were together, ask for my room key? If anyone else tried that, it wouldn't have worked. You're a con man, Jesse. You had *me* believing things that are too crazy to even admit. I should have listened to your aunt. She said you've always had ways of charming the ladies, no matter who got hurt...."

"Ah, so that part of my dream was true, too." Anger had, at last, stirred him. "Did you enjoy my aunt's little spiel about how I sprang from bad seed?"

A fission of eeriness penetrated Elissa's anger. His aunt had said exactly that. "You dreamed that?" she asked skeptically. "You dreamed she said those words to me?"

"And what about the fact...notice, I say fact, that the blood of a rapist runs through my veins?" His voice had grown soft and harsh; his glare burned her cheeks. "She also mentioned the incident in my teenaged years when they 'apprehended' me in the girls' dorm. What did you make of that, Elissa?"

His glowering nearness forced her back a step. She moistened her suddenly dry lips with the tip of her tongue. "You...you hadn't been accused of...*rape*...had you?"

"Close." He smiled, entirely without humor. "Breaking and entering."

"You do seem to be rather good at that."

"Think, Elissa. With parentage like mine, what else would I have been doing, lurking in the hallway of a girls' dorm in the middle of the night?"

"V-visiting a girlfriend?"

Jesse halted his forward advance and stared at her. She was the only person, *the only one*, who had given him the benefit of the doubt and hit on the truth.

"A girlfriend who was afraid to say that she'd invited you up to her room?" guessed Elissa hopefully.

He shook his head, dumbfounded. "I don't understand you, Elissa. Why would you give me the benefit of *that* doubt when you just accused me of hatching schemes, conning you for some unspecified purpose and breaking into your hotel room?"

"I didn't accuse you," she protested, now thoroughly confused. Because she *had* accused him...and at the same time, hoped it wasn't so. "But Jesse, you're standing right here, in my hotel room, and I didn't invite you. I didn't let you in. Why and how are you here?"

Again he stared at her in silence.

She wanted very much to slap him. Why wouldn't he defend himself? Why wouldn't he answer her questions and give her some hope of believing he wasn't as bad as everyone warned? "Where did you go last night? Why did you leave?"

"Do you really think that I would have voluntarily left you last night?" His gaze suddenly held her transfixed. "In case you've forgotten what we were doing when Suzanne interrupted, let me assure you, I haven't." His voice roughened in a way that set her pulse to pounding. "We were about to kiss. I was about to pin you down on that sofa and remind you just what we've been missing. I fully intended to finish what we started, Elissa." His gaze settled on her lips, then rose to her eyes with bold, sensual longing. "Make no mistake...I still do."

An answering warmth rose within her, making her all too conscious of the bed just one room away. Regardless of where he'd been last night, he was with her now, and they were alone. Temptation beckoned with alarming appeal.

Damn him! Damn him for bewitching her so...with nothing more than softly uttered words and a heated gaze! "Are you saying someone *forced* you to leave, and you didn't even have a chance to let me know?"

His maddening, unreadable stare slid back into place. He obviously couldn't think of an excuse for leaving without a goodbye.

Her suspicions flared once again. "*Are* you involved in some kind of fraud? Do you have accomplices? Is Suzanne one of them?" Raising her hands to her head, she spun away from him, frightened by her own inability to think of rational answers. "I'm starting to sound paranoid. You're doing this to me, Jesse. Dean was right about you. You *are* dangerous."

"Dean said I was dangerous?"

"A heartbreaker, he told me. A reckless, womanizing—"

"Yeah, but...*dangerous?*"

Elissa glared. In soft deadly accents, she swore, "I've never met anyone more dangerous. You have me doubting myself, and that's where I draw the line." Coming to a decision—a surprisingly painful one—she announced, "I never want to see you again. Never. Now, get out."

"I'm not going anywhere." He crossed his arms with arrogant stubbornness.

She squared her jaw. "Then, I will." With self-righteous fury she stormed into the adjoining bedroom.

Jesse followed her. "Damn it, Elissa, let's talk."

"I tried to talk to you." She snatched up her overnight bag from the luggage rack. "It didn't work."

"You didn't try to talk to me. You demanded answers, and I admit, I don't have many of them."

She whirled around to face him, holding up one hand like a traffic cop. "Don't say another word. You're not going to embroil me in whatever scheme you've hatched. Thank God I learned your true nature before I got any more involved." With her overnight bag in hand, she headed for the bathroom.

Jesse stepped in her path, his anger visibly building. "You're forgetting one very important thing."

"I hope to forget everything about you."

"I'm talking about Cody."

She blanched. "I'd rather die than let you near him." As she marched toward the bathroom door, she felt his rage growing behind her.

Before she reached the bathroom, an odd heat swept over her—a dry, invisible inferno that swirled around her, blasting her skin, clothes and hair like dragon's breath. And in the sudden fury of that hot cyclone, the bathroom door slammed shut with an ear-splitting *bang*.

Intense silence followed.

The wind ceased, but the unnatural heat grew even

hotter. Elissa stood stock-still, gaping at the closed door. *He had slammed it.* He had slammed the bathroom door from clear across the room!

Into the silence, Jesse growled, "One thing I will not do is stay out of your lives."

The quaking began in Elissa's knees and quickly spread to the rest of her body. *He had slammed the door without touching it.* Slowly, she turned to face him.

The heat, she realized through her shock, was radiating *from him.* For a moment, the briefest moment, he seemed to shimmer and waver, like a desert mirage. Then the heat lessened and the shimmering aura abated.

Fear, like none she'd ever known, possessed her.

His voice, low and quiet, shook through her like a muted roar. "I'm Cody's father, and nobody can change that."

She heard not the words, but the threat in his tone. "Jesse," she managed to whisper, wanting to calm him, needing to exert some kind of control. "Please..."

But the anger still blazed in his eyes, and he seemed fixated on one thing—whatever point he was trying to make. "You will not use my son as a weapon to get back at me for any wrongs you imagine I've done you."

"The d-door," stammered Elissa, "h-h-how..."

"A child isn't a pawn. Cody won't be used like that."

Jesse's eyes continued to smolder, and Elissa suspected he was unaware of his anger's effect—the heat, the slammed door, her mind-numbing fear. His attention seemed concentrated entirely on whatever it was he was saying.

"Do you understand me, Elissa?"

"Yes!" she cried, nodding, although her mind hadn't grasped anything beyond the fact that he'd slammed the door from across the room and nearly roasted her with his fury.

"Good." The anger in his eyes slowly dissipated until they had cooled into an unreadable ash gray. He frowned. "Why are you staring at me like that?"

"I'm not," she swore, clutching her overnight bag to her chest like a shield.

He studied her for a silent moment, as if he hadn't been glaring at her steadily for a seeming eternity. "Yes," he corrected her softly, "you *are* staring at me. Like...like I'm the devil himself."

She felt her eyes widen and her heart slow to a beat that shook her.

She fought off the onset of hysteria. She had to get a grip on herself.

"Elissa, what the hell's wrong with you?" The concern in his gruff voice softened the rebuke as he stepped closer.

She dropped her bag and jumped away from him, her back hitting into the closed bathroom door. "I'm fine. Fine."

Puzzled, he halted a short distance away. "I'm sorry if I yelled, but he was born three months ago. And I haven't seen him yet."

The stark, simple longing in his eyes broke through her terror. Was he talking about Cody? Of course he was. Who else would he be talking about? Born three months ago, hadn't seen him yet. Yes, he meant Cody. *Her* Cody.

"Do you have...a picture?"

She nodded. Yes, she had a picture.

"Do you have the picture with you?" he gently prodded.

Again, she cautiously nodded. Unable to move away

from the door supporting her, she pointed with a trembling finger toward the dresser where her slim leather purse lay.

"May I see it?"

"Yes. Yes, of course." Realizing he expected her to physically procure the picture, she forced her rubbery legs to move, to carry her, past Jesse and across the bedroom.

As her body resumed normal motions, her mind kicked into overdrive. What kind of man slammed doors without touching them... elevated the temperature...popped in through locked doors...vanished into thin air...couldn't be heard by phone operators... couldn't be seen by Suzanne...traveled thousands of miles in record time without a verifiable aircraft...*had been declared legally dead*....

Elissa swallowed a sob as she reached for her purse. Was she losing her mind? Was she?

From her side view, she saw Jesse sit down onto the unmade bed, his knees spread in typical male fashion, his muscled forearms resting across them as he watched her. "Do you need help finding the picture?" he offered, a frown in his dark, intelligent eyes and on his blatantly sensual lips as she stood absently holding her purse.

"Oh, no, no, I'll find it." She opened her purse and fumbled through it. Her wallet—the picture was in her wallet. By rote, her fingers sought it out and flipped through the photos until she came to the most recent one.

Jesse rose and extended his hand. "May I?" She suddenly didn't want to give it to him. This was Cody he was wanting to see. Her maternal instincts rose up in protection.

He reached with his hand—a large, long-fingered hand, bronzed by the sun; an appealing, masculine, seemingly *human* hand—and plucked the wallet from her. She watched in dry-mouthed desperation as he looked down into her baby's face—the chubby dimpled cheeks, the dark hair that stood straight up, the cola-colored eyes that sparkled in merriment.

Jesse didn't offer the usual compliments as he pored over the photo. But after a moment, the harsh planes and angles of his dark, commando face softened. A vertical groove deepened beside his mouth. "He looks like you." His soft, hoarse comment held a note of reverence.

"His chin's like yours," she admitted in a whisper. "See that cleft?"

He studied the photo closely, his concentration intense. A husky little laugh soon escaped him. "I see it."

And when he raised his gaze to hers, she recognized the glow of paternal pride...and something stronger; something that glazed his eyes with a sheen she hadn't expected to see.

Warmth blossomed within her and very tangibly around her. A strong, peaceful warmth that nourished her spirit like a sun-washed day, blooming flowers and simple happiness.

She knew then. Beyond a doubt. He wouldn't hurt Cody.

Jesse cleared his throat. "You, uh, have another one of these? I mean, can I...keep this?"

She nodded, fighting not fear this time, but affection—and attraction—for the father of her baby. She watched as his big, blunt-tipped fingers cautiously removed the photograph from its sheath. What was she to think of this man who handled his baby's photo with such tender care? Who was he? *What* was he?

"I want to spend time with him, Elissa," he said. "I want him to know me as his father."

It seemed a reasonable request. Except the fear she'd felt only moments before hadn't entirely receded. *She wasn't even sure what kind of being he was.* "When?" she hedged.

"I want to stay with him for the rest of my leave. To act as his father. It may be my only chance in a long time to...now, what's the term?...*bond* with him."

"Bond with him? For the rest of your leave? At my house?" she asked in growing alarm. She imagined doors slamming on their own, the temperature sharply rising, the neighbors talking about her invisible house-guest....

"Do you have a problem with that?" inquired Jesse.

The truth trembled on her tongue—that his unnatural powers and sudden disappearances scared her, *worried* her, made her doubt her own sanity. But before she could phrase it in an inoffensive way, a coolness hardened his gaze.

"So you *do* have a problem with that." A muscle tensed in his jaw. "Then, I'll just have to take Cody to my house."

Elissa gasped, her fear reactivating with full force. "You can't take Cody! I won't let you. I'm his custodial parent. I'll have a warrant sworn out to keep you away."

He ventured nearer, his face close to hers. "And do you think it will?"

She felt it growing again—the unnatural warmth emanating from him in waves, building along with the anger in his eyes. She realized with terrifying certainty that no power on earth would keep him away.

"A baby that young can't be separated from his mother for very long," she explained in a frantic whisper. "I'm still breast-feeding him. He needs me."

"Then, you'll have to stay with us." Although he didn't smile, she sensed he was pleased with the solution.

"But I have a job. A business. I can't just drop everything and leave. I'm not independently wealthy."

"I intend to pay you enough child support to give you the choice of staying home with him. Or staying at *my* home with him, as you will this month." His stare grew harsh. "I'll give you three days. If you're not at my house with Cody by Wednesday—" his eyes darkened "—I'll come for him."

They stared at each other—he adamant, she appalled.

"Thanks for the picture," he finally murmured. And he extended her wallet to her.

Elissa knew then what she had to do. If she were to even consider bringing her baby near this man, she had to touch him—firmly, solidly, so there could be no doubt that he was, at least, a flesh-and-blood being.

Holding her breath, she reached to take back the wallet. As her fingers curled around the leather warmed from his grasp, she pressed the back of her knuckles into his palm.

The callused hardness was exactly as she remembered from the night they'd spent together. Vividly she recalled the exquisite roughness—and the surprising gentleness—of these hands on her skin. Blessed relief coursed through her.

But before she could pull her hand away from his, that reassuringly human contact began to change. Or rather, her perception of it did. An odd warmth generated from the point of contact and traveled up her arm. She lost sight of where she was, what she was doing; forgot her intent and her questions. A sweet blindness stole over her and plunged her into a dimension of feeling—sensation at its purest.

Memories surged of moments they had shared, with every sensation magnified. Taste, touch, smell, sound...an intimate caress, a kiss, a smile, a groan. Snatches of conversation that had meant little at the time. Colors shone brighter, deeper; emotions ran stronger than their tentative relationship would justify. Coursing beneath the vivid sensations was a current of forceful determination, stronger than any Elissa had known. All this in a blinding flash.

But at the edges of perception hovered a curious pain; an imminent danger. A darkness pressing in, trying to blot out the brilliance, trying to foil the determination.

With a cry, she snatched her hand back from Jesse's. The disconnection jolted her, like an electrical shock. Dull red blotches floated before her eyes, as if a camera had flashed too close to her face. Gradually, her vision cleared, and she found herself holding her wallet in both hands and staring at Jesse. His palm remained outstretched, and his face reflected the same shock she had felt.

Slowly he withdrew his hand. But the pain, the darkness, was now in his shadow gray eyes. Hoarsely he whispered, "Wednesday, Elissa. My house. You and Cody." He turned, and with an odd, lagging stride, pushed open the bathroom door, then closed it behind him—manually this time.

Elissa wasn't sure how long she stood there, gazing at

that closed door. Questions, fears and possibilities tumbled through her mind as she waited for him to rejoin her. She paced through the hotel suite, the fragrance of coffee drawing her to the sitting room. She poured herself a cup and, after a few sips, decided she'd waited long enough.

Approaching the bathroom door, she called, "Jesse?"

No answer. She called again and briskly knocked. No reply. She tried the knob. The door pushed easily open.

There was no one inside.

And on the cold, white tile of the bathroom floor lay the photograph of Cody. Wherever Jesse had gone, he obviously hadn't taken it with him.

5

ELISSA LEFT THAT HOTEL room a woman obsessed. During her train ride back home, her teary-eyed reunion with Cody and her long, sleepless night, thoughts and questions about Jesse haunted her incessantly.

She spent Sunday researching paranormal phenomena via her Internet connection and the public library. Theories and studies answered none of her questions, or even began to alleviate the ache in her heart when she thought of Jesse.

He'd seemed so strong and vital. She didn't want to think of him as some disembodied spirit. She wanted him to be a flesh-and-blood man, in the same live body that had held her, laughed with her, made love to her. *She didn't want him to be dead.*

Was that the crux of the problem—a psychological one? Were these encounters the result of her deep-seated desire to keep him with her? No, she couldn't believe that. None of the encounters had gone the way she would have dreamed, if they'd been products of her own wishful thinking.

Monday afternoon, after her young day-care charges had all gone home, she visited the private college where Dean and she had graduated. With Cody snoozing in her arms, she entered the stately brick building that housed the humanities department and hurried down echoing corridors to the cramped office of her favorite professor.

Dr. Lehmberg lounged in her worn leather chair with her feet propped up on her neat desk. She wore a tweed jacket with elbow patches, dark jeans and hiking boots. Her ginger hair hung down her shoulder in a thick braid. Rimless glasses dominated her unadorned face as she looked up from her cup of plain yogurt and waved for Elissa to be seated.

As Elissa removed Cody's blue knitted cap and loosened his sweater, careful not to wake him, she wondered how the petite woman regarding her from behind the desk had ever managed to intimidate students without so much as raising her voice. But during Elissa's time here, few students cut Lehmberg's classes, failed to turn in assignments or disobeyed any mandate issued in the course of her teaching.

The professor's sedate gaze settled on Cody. "Yours?"

"Mine."

She nodded with wordless approval. "I heard you left Central High to have a baby. Planning to go back?"

"No." When Lehmberg's thin brows rose above her glasses, Elissa explained, "I want to stay home with Cody."

"Nothing wrong with that." She took a spoonful of yogurt. "Unless, of course, you let some narrow-minded fools run you off like a dog with its tail between its legs."

Her throat tightened. "No one ran me off."

"Think you're not good enough to counsel students, now that you're an unwed mother?"

As usual, she'd hit upon the truth. "I suppose some people might question my judgment. My...morality."

"I didn't ask about some people. I asked about you."

"I'd be happy to discuss it with you, Dr. Lehmberg, *if* you're ready to discuss *your* personal life with me."

That closed the professor's mouth. And turned it up in a begrudging grin. "Come on, now. We both know that I don't have a personal life...as far as my colleagues can tell."

The mutual glance lengthened—both women acknowledging the point and establishing a subtle new equality. Lehmberg lowered her booted feet from the desk. "If I can't bully you into spilling your guts, what *have* you come to discuss?"

"The articles you wrote about paranormal phenomena."

Interest brightened her eyes. "I've documented quite a few cases. Remote viewing, where the subject sees a scene taking place miles away. Psychokinesis, where objects are moved by sheer mental force. Telepathy, which is thought transference. Astral projection, also called out-of-body experience. Precognition, or awareness of future events..."

"But all of those involve a living subject, right? Not someone who's...dead?"

Surprise rendered the professor silent.

Shifting her sleeping baby in her arms, Elissa hesitated to pursue the topic, then cleared her throat and forged onward. "I want to know about...ghosts."

Lehmberg studied her closely, as if trying to gauge her sincerity. At long last, she queried, "What about 'em?"

"I've researched materialization. You know...apparitions."

Lehmberg nodded.

"Some researchers believe they take form from a substance called ectoplasm," said Elissa. "I'm wondering what ectoplasm *feels* like. I mean, can an apparition feel solid? Warm?" In a near whisper, she added, "Muscular?"

"Descriptions recorded of apparitions and their feel vary. But I, personally, don't believe apparitions are formed from ectoplasm. I think they're projected by the psychic energy of the departed. If the life force that drives a human being—his spirit, some might call it— does *not* cease to exist when his body dies, then I believe it's possible for that energy to project itself to the living. And to stimulate our senses: vision, hearing, smell, taste." With a slight smile, she added, "Touch."

"You mean, a spirit might be capable of making me *feel* something that's not really there?"

Lehmberg steepled her fingers beneath her chin. "If a spirit is present, then he *is* really there. How can he move things or be felt to the human touch? By the power of his mind, I say. A good hypnotist, for instance, can make his subject believe he's experiencing anything he describes. Why shouldn't those who inhabit the spiritual realm use similar methods to communicate?"

"Ghosts with hypnotic powers?"

"In a manner of speaking." Lehmberg leaned on her elbows and continued with quiet passion, "I think the capabilities of a person's spirit depend entirely on the strength of that person's mind. The strongest minds, especially when trained, can attain miracles. Like barefoot men walking over red-hot coals without blistering their skin. Masters of meditation levitating above the ground. Psychokinesis experts bending metal utensils with their thoughts. Faith healers curing diseases. Who knows what boundaries a well trained mind can exceed—*especially* after crossing over into the spiritual realm?"

Elissa sat spellbound by the possibilities. "What do you mean by a 'well trained' mind?"

"Psychic abilities are like other skills. The more one practices, the better one gets." Lehmberg lounged back in her chair, her hazel eyes brimming with curiosity. "May I ask what brought on your sudden interest in parapsychology?"

Elissa hesitated, not quite ready to share the details with anyone. "An experience in Savannah."

"Ah. Savannah. This experience didn't take place at the old Pirate's House Restaurant near Bay Street, did it?"

"No."

"One of the renovated mansions on the squares? Or the antebellum plantation house off the expressway?"

She shook her head and volunteered no specifics.

Lehmberg opened her bottom desk drawer. "Here's a list of psychical research centers you can contact—in North Carolina, Pennsylvania, California, England, Germany." She handed a page to Elissa. "Call one of them."

Grateful, she took the paper and rose. "One more question, Doctor. Do you know *why* a spirit might appear?"

Lehmberg shrugged. "Case studies suggest that reasons might be revenge, vindication, protection of a loved one, the desire to right some wrong or assuage some guilt. Whatever the goal, it's one the spirit feels passionate about. And until it's met, chances are he'll remain."

Jesse's demand rang in her memory: *I want to see my son.* Was that the goal that kept his spirit chained to this

level of existence? Or was it guilt that kept him here—
guilt because he'd avoided her and Cody while barhop-
ping in Asia before his last mission? Either way, his
"passionate goal" was obviously to see Cody.

Elissa paused in the doorway. "Is it painful for the
spirit," she somberly asked, "to be kept here after
death?"

"That's hard to say. Some spirits seem playful
enough. Others, angry and obsessed. But channelers often describe a sense of anguish emanating from them. I
can only surmise that as time wears on, it *does* become
painful for the human spirit to be blocked from its final
destiny, whatever that might be. Painful, and maybe
even destructive."

Elissa knew then in her heart what she must do. She
had to help Jesse achieve his goal. She had to take Cody
to him.

AFTER ARRANGING FOR a licensed substitute to handle
her day-care business—no small feat—Elissa faced an
even more difficult task: telling her parents, and then
Dean, of her decision to leave town with Cody for possibly as long as a month, with no greater reason than to
"get away for a while."

As she had expected, her parents bombarded her
with questions, pointed out difficulties and plied her
with long, searching looks, but eventually agreed to respect her right to privacy as long as she kept in contact
with them.

Dean, on the other hand, fervently objected. She
wished she could tell him the truth about Jesse, but
when she had casually asked if he believed in the para-

normal, he dismissed it as "the silly ravings of sensa-
tionalists."

Even on Wednesday morning as he helped pack luggage into her car, he complained. "It's absurd, leaving
town on a whim. Who knows how this could hurt your
day-care business!"

"You should accept my credentials as a professional
counselor when I say that for the sake of my emotional
well being—and therefore, Cody's—I need some downtime."

"Downtime? Okay, so I'll take a few days off and we
can drive into Atlanta, see some plays, tour some mu-
seums."

"Not that kind of downtime." She removed a box of
diapers from an awkward corner and fit it into the
travel bassinet. "I want time away, so I can think. Just
me and Cody." Resolutely she slammed the trunk.

Dean grabbed her hands and held them, capturing
her full attention. "Is it something I said or did? Whatever it was, I'm sorry. If I sounded put out yesterday, it
was only because I'd been looking forward to your pot
roast."

That she believed. He hated any change in their routine, but especially when it came to food. He was used
to a home-cooked supper at her house every Tuesday,
but she'd been too busy to cook.

"You haven't done anything wrong, Dean." She
squeezed his hands and gazed into his beseeching blue
eyes, hating to upset him. "I'll make you a pot roast
when I come home."

"But...but...who will watch our TV shows with me?
How can I play 'Jeopardy' by myself?"

Aware that he was somewhat joking now with that

lost-little-boy expression that went so well with his
sandy brown curls, Elissa patted his cheek. "Know that
I'll be beating you just as badly from a living room in
Savannah."

Softly, he said, "I hope all this thinking you'll be doing has to do with us, and that you'll decide on 'yes.'"

She didn't disillusion him, but she'd almost forgotten
about the marriage proposal he'd made last month. He
slipped his arms around her and kissed her. It was a
pleasant kiss, as most of his were. But she backed away
before he could deepen it. She simply wasn't ready for
further intimacy. "Now, get going," she said, "or you'll
be late for school."

Obediently he trudged toward his station wagon—a
tall, sturdy figure in his blue oxford shirt, navy tie and
tweed trousers already rumpled although his workday
hadn't yet begun. He called from the car window, "If
you wait until Saturday, I can drive you. It's dangerous
for a woman and baby to travel alone."

"Don't worry. I've traveled alone before."

A few hours later, on a deserted highway miles from
anywhere but dense Georgia forest, with a flat tire and
lug nuts that had rusted too tight to budge, Elissa's assurance rang mockingly in her ears.

The two huge black motorcycles that rolled to a halt
on the grassy shoulder beyond her car did little to allay
her anxiety. Two men climbed off and ambled toward
her. The noonday sun glinted on the beer cans in their
hands...and the disturbing gleam in their eyes.

IN THE COMFORTABLE clutter of his own garage, the satisfying smell of gasoline and engine oil filled Jesse's
nostrils; the feel of the screwdriver in his hand made

him whistle a merry ditty. He'd been thinking about fixing the carburetor on this old bass boat engine since his last leave. Odd, what months of forced idleness could put in a man's head. Someone who'd never been a prisoner might guess his thoughts to have been strictly of the life-and-death variety. But his had often wandered to details he'd left unfinished at home. Like this boat engine.

And Elissa.

She'd be coming today. She'd stay the night. Anticipation sluiced through him. He'd have a whole month of days and nights with her. And he'd hold his son for the very first time. Cody.

Jesse contentedly tightened a screw on the boat engine. Life couldn't get much better.

As he discarded his screwdriver and reached for the oilcan, his attention was caught by a sound. A cry. An urgent cry. He angled his ear to the open garage door and the woods beyond, listening intently.

The cry came again. *Elissa.* It was her cry; he knew it. But it wasn't an actual cry. It wasn't a sound at all. It was a sense. A sudden, urgent awareness.

Danger.

SHE ROSE TO HER FEET from where she'd been kneeling in the grass beside the flattened tire. Her hand tightened around the wrench as the two men drew near.

The husky, bearded one wore shabby jeans and a dirty sleeveless T-shirt, and had snake tattoos on his sunburned biceps. The other wore shabby jeans and an open leather vest—shirtless, to show off his thin, snake-tattooed chest. Both men reeked of beer and old sweat.

"Looks like you could use some help, ma'am,"

greeted the bearded one in the T-shirt. His appraising gaze settled not on the flat tire, but on the swell of her breasts beneath her sweater, then slithered downward to the curve of her hips beneath her jeans.

"No, thanks," she replied in a voice that shook only slightly. "I've already called for help on my cellular phone. They'll be here any minute." She'd have given anything for that to have been the truth.

"Hear that, Bones?" He elbowed the lanky one in leather. "She's got one of them fancy car phones."

"I'd sure like to see that phone. Wouldn't you, Fuzz?"

A sick fear skittered through her. She hadn't locked the car doors. Cody lay inside. The can of pepper spray she'd brought as protection remained in her purse on the floorboard. Would she have the courage to use the tire wrench against the men? And would it stop them or only enrage them?

"M-my husband took the phone with him," she improvised, edging toward her car door, holding the wrench behind her, "into the woods. He had to...you know...take a short walk. But he'll be back very soon."

"Your husband?" said the husky one called Fuzz. "Where was he when you stopped at the gas station? He didn't pump the gas. Or pay for it, either."

Her heart dropped. They'd been following her...for miles, it seemed. The last gas station had been at least fifteen minutes back. Maybe they'd even punctured her tire!

"Yup, sure is funny," ruminated Bones as he pressed in closer, "I didn't see no man in the car with you at all."

Her mouth went dry, and frantically she tried to fabricate an answer.

Before she could think of one, a reply resounded from an unexpected direction—from behind her, past the rear bumper of her car, near the edge of the deep, pine-scented woods. "Maybe you just weren't looking hard enough." The quip, softly spoken, was rife with masculine challenge.

Jesse stood there, just inside the forest's shadows, his eyes gunmetal dark and deadly.

6

"JESSE! THANK GOD."

The stark relief on her face told Jesse all he needed to know. They'd scared the hell out of her. Anger, cold and intense, gusted from him. A sudden wind whipped the dry, rustling leaves at his feet into a miniature cyclone.

He wanted to kill the bastards.

Their progress toward Elissa stopped as they followed her gaze. Jesse stood ready for them; ready to tear off their thick skulls with his bare hands. His stare alone should have conveyed this mind-set. It was a look that had stopped fully armed enemies dead in their tracks, when he himself had been weaponless.

But these scum bag fools didn't even focus their eyes on his face. They seemed to look clear through him, the same way Suzanne had. Their eyes swept the forest's edge, lingering only on the leaves swirling at his feet.

The skinny one mumbled, "Who she lookin' at?"

The hefty creep turned his attention back to Elissa. "You're seeing things, sugar...or tryin' to pull a fast one."

Stunned by their reaction to him—or rather, lack thereof—Jesse stood motionless. Couldn't they see him? He couldn't buy that. They were ignoring him. *Had* to be...

"Somethin's whooping them leaves around, Fuzz."

An apprehensive frown formed on the skinny one's face as he watched the commotion of the leaves. "And it's gettin' cold."

Fuzz had other things on his mind. "What did you plan on doing, sugar?" he murmured to Elissa. "Running off while we was lookin' the other way?" He took a step closer and his voice lowered to a purr. "What happened—you decide to stick around for some fun with Bones and me?"

She cast another panicked glance at Jesse. "They can't see you!" Her fear jolted him into action, and he strode toward her, his anger building with every step.

Fuzz then made a tactical error of critical proportions. He reached out to touch her.

Jesse's fury erupted. He rounded the back bumper of the car and lunged, his right fist whistling as it caught Fuzz under the chin. His left fist then drove into his solar plexus, and Fuzz responded with an audible "oof."

Fuzz's head jerked sideways with the first punch. The second doubled him over. The next smashed into his nose and propelled him backward toward the asphalt highway, where he skidded on his rump.

"What was that?" cried Bones, his bloodshot eyes wide and fearful. "What the *hell* was that?"

"She punched me," murmured Fuzz in dazed amazement, shaking his head as if to clear it. Droplets of sweat and blood flung from his face like water from a wet dog.

"B-but she didn't move." Bones stared at his bloody-nosed cohort in confusion. "No one punched you."

"The hell I didn't," muttered Jesse. With another long stride, he caught Bones by the throat and wrapped his fingers around the column of his windpipe. His mouth gaped open like a beached fish as he gasped for air. Jesse drew back his fist for another satisfying slug.

"Jesse, stop!" cried Elissa. "You'll kill him!"

Her words penetrated his red haze of anger, and he realized she was right. The thug was choking in his punishing grip. With a distasteful shove, Jesse released his stranglehold and sent him sprawling on the ground in a gasping heap of leather, hair and snake tattoos.

The heap rolled to its bony knees and scampered while the other thug stumbled toward the black motorcycles. Curses and mutters about a voodoo woman floated back on the autumn breeze. Engines roared to life. Grass flew from beneath spinning tires. Rubber burned against asphalt.

Voodoo woman? Had they been talking about Elissa?

There was no time to ponder. A tiny sob and a choked "Thank you, Jesse" swung his attention to where she stood beside the hood of her car. Her face was pale, her lips trembling. "I needed you," she whispered, "and you came."

Something in Jesse's chest rolled over. She'd needed him. He moved toward her, wanting to touch her.

She came willingly into his arms, pressing her cheek against the curve of his neck, her arms around his shoulders. Her body molded to his with utter, aching perfection.

The effect was immediate. An electric current crackled through his veins, stunning him. A tumult of emotions surged from her to him: the aftereffect of an adrenaline high; a dizzying relief; intense curiosity; profound awe. And thick, smothering apprehension. Other emotions rushed by too quickly to understand, but packed their wallop all the same.

These were *her* emotions storming through him,

without a word spoken. A connection beyond his comprehension. But the power blasting through him steadily grew into an unbearable force, as if to drive her from his arms.

Elissa seemed to sense his turmoil and tried to withdraw from his embrace. Jesse's resentment flared against the intrusive force. He wanted to hold her, and hold her he would. He'd worked wonders with his mental powers before. He'd bent metal with his mind, for God's sake. Surely he could tame whatever force now plagued them.

The chaos surged with an even greater strength, prying them apart. Fiercely he concentrated, fighting it with all of his might, utilizing skills he'd perfected over his lifetime. Locked in their embrace, the two of them swayed as the turbulence swirled and coursed.

It took a while, but gradually the turbulence lessened. Like sunshine after a storm, pleasure—bright and clear—replaced it. With his eyes closed and his jaw buried in her jasmine-scented hair, Jesse treasured the exquisite feel of her, the womanly warmth—sensations he had waited so long to savor again. How many times had he held her like this while alone in that godforsaken prison, or holed up in the rain-deluged jungle?

"Are you all right?" he whispered against her temple.

She raised her eyes to his, her sherry brown gaze aglow with a warmth that made him feel more intensely alive than he had in a long, long time. "I am now."

He wanted to kiss her. His gut burned with need for it. He lowered his mouth to hers.

"Jesse, wait," she cried in an anxious whisper. She stopped him with her fingertips against his lips. He kissed them, one by one...and drew the last into his mouth.

Her eyes darkened in sensual response. But with a soft little cry, she pulled her fingers away. "We can't!"

A car whizzed by them, its wind blasting their hair and clothes. He saw what she meant. They needed privacy. He meant to kiss her thoroughly, explicitly, and for as long as he damned well pleased.

Without breaking their hard-won contact, he swept her to the passenger side of her car, away from the highway, in the cozy shade of the forest. "There." His arms, strong and determined, pulled her solidly against him. How perfect, the fit of their bodies...

"No, you don't understand. I don't think we're from the same *world*, you and I."

"You knew that when we met. But it didn't matter then, and it doesn't matter now." He ran his roughened hands along her velvety cheeks until he'd captured the fine oval of her face. Gruffly, he reminded her, "You still owe me my welcome home."

An odd vulnerability lit her gaze. The claim had, for some reason, affected her deeply. And she affected him deeply. Too deeply.

With stubborn resolve, he lowered his head.

"Please, Jesse!" she cried, her whisper anguished. But she failed to specify the exact nature of her request.

So he kissed her. A slow, sensual sampling of her lips and mouth. A thousand delicious sensations swirled through him. He'd been craving her for far too long. His kiss plunged deeper then, his concentration intense.

And somewhere along the way, she lost her reservations. Wrapping her arms around his neck, she joined in and welcomed him home. Thoroughly.

The impact of that welcome ambushed Jesse. It

packed a much greater punch than the warmth, the sweetness, the excitement he had expected. Without ending the kiss, he backed her up against her car door, his hips bracketing hers. She moaned deep in her throat—a wildly seductive sound. He thrust his fingers into her hair and slanted his mouth for deeper exploration.

She broke away from his kiss with a breathy gasp. "Stop! We can't do this!"

Closing his eyes, he leaned his forehead against hers, the need to make love to her a physical ache. "I'm sorry. I know this isn't the place. Let's go up to my house."

"Jesse, it's more than that." Her breathing sounded as labored as his. "I tried to tell you, *we have to talk.*" The quiver of her voice and body soothed him somewhat. It hadn't been easy for her to stop, either. "I think you're a ghost."

It took a moment to absorb her words.

"You think I'm *what?*" He could have easily countered philosophical arguments—nonsense about respect, commitment and the like. Or even indictments against his character. But this was a new one on him. She thought he was a *ghost?* In his astonishment, he allowed her to pull away.

As their bodies parted, an odd dizziness overtook him. A deep, drugging weariness seeped into his mind and sapped his strength. He'd felt the peculiar draining before—in the hotel suite, shortly after Elissa had touched him. As if contact with her somehow used up too much physical energy.

"Think about it," she said with passionate earnestness. "The military declared you dead. Your family held a funeral service for you—a funeral that you saw!

You disappear without a moment's warning. You appear in a locked suite without an apparent way in...."

Interesting points she had raised. But ridiculous. He shook his head to dispel the fuzziness clouding his mind.

Her eyes glimmered with concern. "Are you okay?"

"I'm fine." He wasn't, though. Intense weariness tugged at him and his vision had dimmed at the edges. Did these symptoms precipitate the blackouts? That's all she'd need—an unconscious man to worry about, along with the possible return of her assailants. Anger flowed within him—anger at the inexplicable ailment. What the hell was going on?

"Was it...our touch?" she whispered.

Jesse gaped at her in surprise. So she'd felt it, too. Which meant it wasn't just some psychological thing— a symptom of post-traumatic shock like some of his army buddies had suffered. Uncomfortable with questions he had no answers for, he hid his concern behind nonchalance. "At least you can't say there's no chemistry between us."

She didn't find his quip amusing. Crossing her arms, she leaned a shapely hip against her car. "Did you notice that those two buffoons couldn't see you?"

Apprehension curled through him. He'd noticed, all right. "They didn't want to see me," he muttered. "Selective perception, I'd call it." He blinked against the weariness that weighted his eyelids.

"And what about Suzanne?"

Regardless of his flip answers, the whole issue did baffle him. No one had ignored him before—ever. Even when he was a kid. They might have hated him, mistrusted him, even feared him. But no one had ignored Jesse Garrett.

"Face it, Jesse—people can't see you."

"You can."

"Well, yes." She didn't offer an explanation for that neat little fact.

"Are you in the habit of seeing ghosts?" he asked.

"No, of course not!"

"Good. I'm glad to hear that." He forced a hard little smile. "I'd better change that flat tire before I, uh, disappear." Although he'd meant it sarcastically, the statement sent an odd prickling down the back of his neck.

Elissa caught her bottom lip between her teeth.

Jesse turned away and strode toward the rear of the vehicle where the flat tire needed tending. With every step, he felt as if he were straining against a strong wind on the tilted deck of a ship.

There was something wrong with him, he had to admit. Vitally wrong. The gaps in his memory, the way people looked right through him these days. The damned shock that nearly fried him when Elissa and he touched. He'd have to take care of *that* problem soon. Real soon.

In the meantime, he wasn't about to buy into that ridiculous notion of hers! He'd have to see a doctor, plain and simple. A shrink, maybe. And he'd make an appointment for her, too.

Determined to finish his task despite the cloudiness in his mind, he wrenched the rusted lug nuts loose as Elissa busied herself with something inside the car. The tire change took longer than he expected; the weariness taxed every move he made. With acute relief, he finally bolted the spare tire in place, packed the flat one in the rear of the vehicle and turned to find Elissa watching him.

At least he could still see her. And that was no small

thing. With tiny pearls glinting at her ears and throat, in her white cashmere sweater and tight jeans, her dusky hair flowing around her shoulders, she was simply the most beautiful woman he'd ever seen.

In a solemn undertone, she queried, "What do *you* think your problem is, Jesse?"

"A woman I want so damn bad I can't see straight." He pressed in closer to peer down into her face, his breath stirring the tendrils of hair near her temples. "The same woman who pulls away from my kiss for no good reason."

A delicate flush crept into her cheeks. "Be serious."

"You don't think I am?"

"About the...the ghost issue. You have to at least give it some thought." She was flustered and he was glad.

Tightening his lips, he moved past her to the car door, feeling as if he were wading through neck-deep quicksand. "Better get going. No sense in standing here on the highway."

"That's another thing. How did you get here, to this isolated spot on a country road?"

Fighting the dimness that framed his field of vision, he opened the door for her, then leaned his forearm across the top of it. "I walked through the woods."

"But how did you get to the woods?" she persisted. "And why did you appear right when I needed you?"

The insidious heaviness was worsening, and his vision had narrowed into a thin tunnel. "The woods are adjacent to my property." He heard the slur in his words and hoped she would miss it. "I was in my garage when I heard you." Remembering his work on the boat, he looked down at his hands. They were covered with black motor grease. With a grimace, he glanced up at her. Smudges of grease marred the sleeves, shoulders and sides of her white sweater.

Following his glance, she noticed the smears herself. Her brows, like angel wings, lifted in surprise.

"Sorry," he said. "I'll buy you a new sweater. When we get to the house, you can take this one off." The thought of helping her out of the sweater blurred his vision even more.

"I don't care about the sweater. Jesse, your garage is nowhere near here. Your house is an hour's drive away."

The weariness bore down on him with an awesome weight, and he struggled to make sense of her words. "Don't be ridiculous. My house is just through those woods."

"No, it's not. Look around." Her gesture encompassed the highway and surrounding forest. "Do you recognize this stretch of road as one that borders your property?"

He pretended to inspect the landscape, but could barely focus his eyes. "Of course." Fiercely he concentrated on staving off the encroaching dimness.

It was then that he heard the cry—a plaintive wail of an infant. It came from inside the car. A smile lightened Elissa's expression, probably because of the surprise that must have crossed his features. She leaned into the car and reached into the back seat.

Realization hit Jesse like a bucket of cold water. *It was Cody. Cody was here, in the car.* He had asked her to bring him, but in the commotion of the fight—and then the heat of their kiss—he hadn't given the baby a thought.

He bent to peer around Elissa, trying to see his son. His vision had blurred so much, he could make out only vague outlines.

Elissa soon emerged from the car, her face very near his as she gazed up at him in the narrow door opening. "He lost his pacifier," she explained, her voice hushed.

"He's already back asleep. He fussed the first couple hours of the trip, so he should sleep awhile longer."

A ground swell of emotion lifted Jesse's heart. His son was here; the child born from the love Elissa and he had shared. He wanted to pull the front seat forward to see him better, but the weariness had grown too heavy to hold off.

He had to leave her, had to be alone. He didn't stop to analyze the need; it was too urgent, too basic. Clenching his teeth, he said with an effort, "I'm going up to the house. Meet me there." He turned and headed for the woods.

"But your house is an hour's drive away from here!"

"It's just around the bend." He didn't break his stride, but a disturbing question occurred to him. If he had actually passed out during those lapses in his memory, why hadn't Elissa found him lying somewhere? He'd been in his own house the first time, in her hotel suite the second. Even if he'd wandered away before succumbing to unconsciousness, surely someone would have found him.

"Jesse!" wailed Elissa. "Come back!"

From the cool shadows of the forest, he called, "I'm going home to clean this grease off my hands." He forced a smile into his next words. "I plan on holding my son."

And you. Through a whole month of nights. No force on earth would stop him.

ELISSA COULDN'T QUITE bring herself to drive away from the roadside spot. How could she leave him without a ride home?

Silly, she knew. He had appeared out of nowhere, and would apparently go back the way he'd come. The problem was making herself believe it.

How could a ghost kiss like that? How could their bodies fit together with such perfection? In the space of a few thunderous heartbeats, he'd swept her away to a dimension of pure sensual longing. No man in her entire life had ignited her passion so quickly, so fiercely—except Jesse. She remembered the last time he'd kissed her, the night she had thrown a lifetime of scruples to the wind and made love with a perfect stranger. His kiss hadn't changed, not one iota.

So how could he be a ghost?

When she finally forced herself to pull back onto the highway and resume her journey, she almost expected his house to be "right around the bend," as he had predicted. But it wasn't. Her map plainly indicated that the nearest town was a good sixty miles away from his home on Isle of Hope.

So how could he *not* be a ghost?

The questions went on and on. When she stopped in Savannah to grab a sandwich, feed Cody and change his diaper, she looked down at her sweater and suffered another surprise. It was clean, without the slightest smudge of grease. But she had seen the black smears with her own eyes....

Elissa thought about Dr. Lehmberg's theory. If strong-minded spirits could stimulate the human senses, make one see, taste, smell, hear and feel things that might not actually be taking place, was this the case with Jesse? Virtual reality?

She leaned her head back against the headrest and closed her eyes. The heat of his embrace, the thrill of his kiss, the passion he incited, had surely felt like reality. He had made *her* feel truly alive.

She pulled into the oak-canopied driveway of Jesse's home on the river bluff and looked at her watch. One-thirty—one hour since their roadside tryst.

His house, with its red-gray Savannah brick festooned with vines, its quaint shingled roof and leaded
windows, stood quiet and dark beneath the profusion
of exotic, semitropical trees. Holding Cody tightly in
her arms, Elissa ventured up the front steps to the
glossy oak door and pressed the doorbell.

Chimes echoed within. A mournful, lonely sound.

No one answered.

Her heart sank. Where was he? With the key his attorney had given her, she unlocked the massive door
and found the place exactly as she had left it—cool and
vacant. No food in the refrigerator, no trash in the trash
container, no clothes in the hamper, no toiletries out of
place. The house had obviously not been lived in for a
very long time.

Of course not, she chided herself. *Its owner is dead.* Anguish struck her anew. What had she expected—a fire
in the hearth, a meal on the stove? It occurred to her that
she had no guarantee even of his company. He might
not return.

Had he disappeared because their kiss had robbed
him of vital energy? Although he had tried to hide the
weariness, she had seen it overtake him, just as it had in
the hotel room. Had he disappeared in the solitude of
the forest? Again, their contact had been her fault; she
had lunged into his arms without thinking. Would he
come back this time?

Squaring her jaw, Elissa resolved to buck up and
adopt an optimistic outlook—Jesse would return. Allowing herself no idle time to entertain doubts, she busied herself settling in. She unpacked her luggage and
set up Cody's travel crib in the bedroom across from
Jesse's. She stacked firewood on the stone hearth for an
evening fire. She drove to the nearest grocery store and
stocked the kitchen with food. All the while, she lis-

tened for Jesse's footsteps, bracing herself for his sudden appearance.

Jesse did not appear that day, or the next.

With his house dark and brooding around her on that second night, she readied herself for bed, struggling to maintain her optimism. Not an easy task. Jesse hadn't had the chance to hold Cody, or to even get a very good look at him. Had he gone to his ever-after without accomplishing his final mission? What sad irony for a proud soldier.

She wanted to pray, but wasn't sure what to pray for.

She truly did want the best for Jesse, whatever that might be. Yet she had to admit that she also wanted to see him again. At least one more time.

Sleep eluded her. As midnight struck, she lay peering into the bedroom shadows, searching the darkness for movement, wondering whether shadows walked the halls this night. She shivered beneath the bedcovers, very much afraid—not that the house was haunted, but that it was not.

Her fear took an entirely different turn in the morning. It grabbed her heart with icy hands and squeezed tight. When she had reached into the small crib near her bedside, she had found that it was empty.

7

SHE TORE MADLY through the house, from room to room, her heart thundering, her fears ranging from common everyday kidnapping to vengeful spirits. She clung to the hope of something in between. She prayed that Jesse had returned and would be waiting downstairs with Cody safe in his arms.

No one awaited her downstairs, or in any other room of the house. Fear pounded through her as she stopped her wild pacing in the center of the vast living room, trying to marshall her thoughts and form a plan.

That's when she heard it—the low murmur of a voice coming from the back yard. Behind the mirrored vertical blinds, the sliding glass door to the walled garden had been left slightly open. With her heart in her mouth, she edged toward that garden door and drew the blinds aside.

There he was, the kidnapper. The vengeful spirit.

With his bare back against a muscular, T-shirted chest, his diapered rump supported by one large sun-bronzed hand, a huge thumb supporting his drool-shiny chin, and gigantic fingers splayed down the length of his pinkish, chubby body, Cody blew spit bubbles, kicked his dimpled legs and gazed around the garden with bright-eyed contentment.

Unaware of his adult audience, Jesse turned the baby toward a particularly lovely tree between the terra-cotta stucco wall and a small wrought-iron gate. "And *this*," he instructed, "is a tea olive. You smell that?" He inhaled through his nose with dramatic vigor—obviously so that Cody would catch on and do the same. "Mmmm. Nothing in the world smells better than that, son. Except a woman's hair and skin. But you've got quite some time before you'll know about that." He stepped toward the tile-bordered pool, where tiny jets of water stirred the lily pads. "And over here..."

Jesse stopped in the center of the courtyard, his gaze lighting on Elissa, who watched him from the doorway. A corner of his mouth quirked up into a grin, and his eyes greeted her with all the warmth of the Georgia morning sun.

A smile tugged at her lips, fright replaced by giddy relief—and another tender emotion that she dared not name.

"And over here," he said, "we have this lady we call your mama." His leisurely gaze took in all of her—her uncombed hair, her unmade-up face, her long pink nightgown that was neither attractive nor revealing. She tossed her tangled curls behind her shoulder, crossed her arms and pretended not to care that she looked her absolute worst.

Jesse continued with his tour-guide approach to parenting. "This lady, who's finally graced us with her presence, is not only your mama, but one heck of a kisser. You ever hear of a woman kissing a man senseless? Probably not. But this woman can. Not that it's any of your business, son. It's my business." Jesse ambled closer, his voice taking on a husky quality, his gaze descending to her lips. "And I plan to tend to it, soon as possible."

Elissa felt her cheeks warm and glanced away from

his hypnotic silver gray eyes. "Time for a diaper change."

"His diaper's already been changed." Jesse planted a kiss on top of the baby's head, where dark, wispy hair stood up in all directions above bright, cola-colored eyes. Cody looked so tiny and fair in Jesse's virile, sun-tanned arms—but in many ways, the resemblance between the two was uncanny. The arc of their eyebrows, the cleft of their chins, the shape of their mouths and noses.

"You changed his diaper?" Elissa asked in surprise.

"Yes, ma'am. And it was a nasty one, too."

She gaped disbelievingly. "Where and how?"

He raised one arrogant brow. "Oh, ye of little faith. You think I don't know how to take care of my own son?" When her unrelenting gaze pressed for an answer, he said, "I took him out back and hosed him off."

Elissa gasped. "You washed his bare little bottom with cold hose water?"

A frown protested her slant on the incident. "The weather's nice. In fact, by eight-thirty, it was warm as all he—" he paused, glancing down at his son "—as all *heck* out here. At least eighty-five degrees." Elissa had to admit, the weather was unseasonably warm. "He might have been a little surprised at first," Jesse allowed, "but he's a staunch little soldier." His gaze dropped to Cody with paternal pride. "He's got that Garrett blood in him."

Elissa rolled her eyes, stepped barefoot into the stone-floored courtyard and took the happily gurgling baby from Jesse's arms. Critically, she inspected his job of diapering. He had certainly made an elaborate production out of it. Intricate tucks and folds fitted the diaper with tailored perfection to Cody's bottom—not a gap or uncomfortable wrinkle anywhere in sight. Of course, he *had* used every one of the dozen pins from the diaper bag to accomplish this feat. Nevertheless, it was a truly impressive finished product.

"You kept him still enough to do…all this?"

"He had his rubber duck to gnaw on."

Her lips curved with suppressed laughter. "You found Mr. Duckie?"

He bent her a quelling glance. "A man's got to do what a man's got to do."

She nodded, her eyes bright with merriment. "You did a fine job, Captain Garrett." With her free hand, she saluted him. He looked inordinately pleased at the compliment. "What did you do with the dirty diaper?"

"What else? I trashed it."

"But that was a cloth diaper."

He shrugged. "I'll buy him more. As many as he needs."

Elissa stared at him. Could this possibly be the same man who had called Dean from a brothel in Asia and said he didn't want to hear about her "little problem"?

The old doubts came fluttering back. Was this lavish show of fatherly concern merely for her benefit—to make her fall into his bed during his month's leave? Elissa pulled herself up short. What was she thinking? This wasn't a man standing beside her; it was a *ghost*. She mustn't forget that. He hadn't hung around this mortal plane just to get her into the sack. It was Cody he had stayed for.

It then became quite clear just what Jesse's final objective was—to make up for his earlier, callous neglect. He apparently hadn't developed his parental conscience until it was too late. Postmortem.

His timing ticked her off.

She tried to soothe herself with the fact that he had named Cody in his will. On the other hand, if he'd really experienced a premonition of death, as both Colonel Atkinson and Jesse himself had told her, that little legality might have been a last-ditch effort to ease himself through judgment day.

Peeved, she hugged Cody tighter and turned to seek the privacy of the bedroom. "Time for your breakfast, angel," she murmured against his soft, rounded cheek.

"Great," said Jesse. "I'm starved."

"Not you."

"Oh." He shot her an irrepressible grin. "Then, I'll just watch."

"Cody prefers to breakfast in private, thank you." As she made a move toward the doorway, she stopped with a sudden thought. "Jesse, when you and I touched, we both felt something. It was as if we...shouldn't be touching."

He leaned a broad shoulder against the doorjamb and frowned down at her. "I felt the shock, but I wouldn't jump to *that* conclusion about it."

"Did you feel it when you touched Cody?"

"No, of course not. It wasn't that kind of touch."

Her brows rose. "You think it happens to us because of something...sexual?"

His voice lowered an octave, and his eyes turned a smoky gray. "Don't you?"

"No, I don't." She hoped her sudden flux of body heat wasn't visibly apparent. "When I touched you in the hotel suite, I hadn't been thinking about sex."

A roguish smile lit his eyes. "Maybe *you* weren't."

"Jesse, this isn't a joking matter!"

"And I wasn't joking." His gaze drove home that point. A tension-filled silence ensued. After a moment, he quietly asked, "How long did it take you to get here?"

Although his tone hadn't actually changed, Elissa sensed a sudden sobriety in it. She knew he meant from the location of their roadside meeting. "A little over an hour."

He said nothing, but she could see the news stunned him.

"Where were you since then?" she asked.

"I don't know." He stared at her in perplexity. "I found you in bed sleeping, so I assume our roadside visit occurred...yesterday?"

She shook her head.

"Couldn't have been today. It happened around noon, I'd say, judging from the sun...."

"Noon, yes. Two days ago. That was Wednesday," she reminded him. "Today's Friday."

Every trace of Jesse's former joviality vanished. "I'll go find us something for breakfast," he finally murmured, "while you feed Cody. We need to talk."

"SO WHAT DO YOU MAKE of all this, Jesse?"

They were sitting in the dappled shade of the quaint walled garden, a basket of buttermilk biscuits, a bowl of fresh strawberries and mugs of coffee all but forgotten on the glass-topped table between them.

Cody had fallen asleep in his windup swing as Jesse told Elissa about his memory lapses. They had discussed the fact that no one seemed able to see him or hear him except her; they pondered his ability to answer her silent call for help from many miles away; they commented on the strange circumstances surrounding his flight home from overseas. She also reminded him that the government had declared him dead—the fact that carried the least weight with Jesse.

"If only I could remember what happened after the plane went down. It rolled to the right, then angled into a nosedive...." He squinted in an effort to concentrate. After a few moments, he shook his head. "Then nothing," he reported glumly. "I can't remember a damn thing after that."

"So you're sure you were on the plane that crashed?" She heard the disappointment in her own voice. In her heart of hearts, she'd still been hoping for some bizarre mistake.

His lips tightened into a grim, white line. "No doubt in my mind." A plethora of unasked questions hovered between them. "You really do think I'm a...ghost... don't you?"

It had been difficult for him to say the *g* word, she knew. It was difficult for her to say it, too. "Can you think of any other explanation?"

"Of course."

Hopefully, she waited.

"Some crazy Asian medical syndrome, obviously."

Her hope again died. "A medical syndrome that makes you invisible to everyone but me?" She sat back in her chair and raked a clump of wayward curls from her forehead. "If you think that's it, why haven't you called a doctor?"

"I did. The receptionist couldn't hear me."

"Funny, the phone's been working fine for me." She couldn't help the sarcasm. "Dean called me just last night."

Jesse frowned. "Dean?"

"Your cousin, remember?"

"Of course I remember. Why was he calling you here?"

"Just to check up on me. Make sure I'm okay."

"Why the hell wouldn't you be? You're in my home, with me."

"Jesse, don't you understand? He thinks you're dead. Everyone thinks you're dead." She flattened her palms on the table and leaned forward, her dark eyes bright and earnest. "*I* think you're dead."

"That's a hell of a thing to say. I serve you biscuits, brew your coffee, and what thanks do I get? 'Jesse, I think you're dead.'"

"Stop joking about it," she reprimanded him sharply. "It's true. *You are dead.*"

Silence followed her outburst.

Jesse leaned back in his chair, folded his arms and studied her. She wasn't crazy; he knew that. And she truly believed what she was saying. If he were to be honest with himself, he'd admit she had some good reasons to believe as she did. But his years of covert military experience had taught him to look beyond any explanation that didn't sit well in his gut. Her explanation weighed far too heavy there. "You're a peculiar woman, Elissa."

She threw her hands up and fell back against her seat. "And you're a stubborn man, Jesse Garrett."

He stroked his beard-stubbled chin. Things could be a lot worse, he reflected. Elissa was here, with his son, to stay for at least a month. He cocked her a tentative smile. And after a few moments of stubborn resistance, she grudgingly gave in and answered his smile with a slight one of her own.

Squeaks from the windup swing and an exuberant

squeal diverted their attention from each other to Cody—wide-eyed, kicking and ready for fun.

Elissa reached for him, her smile now so radiant that Jesse's throat constricted. No matter what pain and sacrifice the baby's existence had caused her, she loved the little tyke with the kind of love that could bring only happiness. That kind of love Jesse himself had never known. He'd been an embarrassment to his own mother, proof of a wrong done to her, a social blight. Elissa could have so easily felt the same about Cody. But she did not.

A deep tenderness welled up in him, not only for the baby boy who shared his blood, but for the woman who so obviously treasured him. With playful zest, she plucked Cody out of the swing and nuzzled his neck, making him laugh and squeal with delight. She laid him in her nightgown-clad lap, cooed at him, growled against his tummy, played "patty-cake, patty-cake, baker's man."

Her thick, dark hair was tangled, her pink gown was an oversize T-shirt, her face betrayed distinct laugh lines in the morning sun. He'd never seen a woman he wanted more in all his life.

"And do you know who that is, over there?" She stood Cody up in her lap, facing Jesse, and spoke against his pudgy little cheek. "That's your Dada."

"Dada?" repeated Jesse in surprise.

Her cheek dimpled. "Yes, Dada. Can you say that, Cody? Da-da-da?"

And though Jesse managed a creditable smirk—as if he objected to the infantile form of address—his heart swelled beyond capacity. She was including him in their family circle. More than that—she was acknowledging his place at its very heart. She could have paid him no finer tribute; given no finer gift. He could have wept with the joy of it.

But weeping wasn't his style. He swallowed—admittedly hard—and reached out a finger for Cody to wrap his little hand around. "Give me a shake, there, boy. A handshake for your old pa." He saw Elissa's brows rise in response to his preferred title. "Can you say that? Pa-pa-pa?"

He had watched Cody reach for Elissa's fingers during their play. He had watched his face light up in response to her smile. But as Jesse leaned across that table, waving his finger in the baby's plain view, Cody did not reach out. His eyes didn't even focus on the finger...*or on Jesse's face.*

A bone-deep chill seeped through him. With slow deliberation, he waved his hand in front of the baby's eyes. Cody didn't so much as blink.

"He can't see me." Jesse turned his gaze to Elissa.

The bleakness there tore at her heart. She wished she could tell him he was wrong. She wished she could make it not so. But she knew from Cody's lack of response that Jesse wasn't mistaken.

The stricken look remained for only a very short time before a familiar determination hardened Jesse's eyes to a granite gray. "Get your car keys, Elissa. And Cody's stroller."

"Why? Where are we going?"

"Into town. I think it's time I do a little investigating about this condition of mine."

THE EXCURSION STARTED out predictably enough. They drove into the historic section of Savannah, where Elissa pushed Cody in his stroller down the bricked pathways of lush green squares and on sidewalks past restored historical homes, inns and shops.

Jesse, for the most part, walked with them. But it had been immediately apparent, from the moment he'd climbed from Elissa's car and greeted a young couple jogging by, that no one else could hear or see him.

Things only got worse from there.

He waved his hand in people's faces and marveled when they failed to react. He tapped a fashionably attired businessman on the shoulder and asked for the time. The man turned and lifted his brows at an elderly woman, who marched by with a righteous tilt of her head and girlish blush on her weathered cheeks. Jesse scolded a purple-haired teen for having too many gold studs in her nostrils—"I like my women with one. Two, at the very most." The girl slinked on without so much as a scowl.

Even that wasn't enough for Jesse. He lifted a cap from a kid's head and set it on his little sister, which instigated a loud altercation. He caught a ball that another boy had been tossing up into the air. The boy gaped at the ball Jesse held, then tugged at the woman in front of him. "Look, Mom, look! My ball's stuck in the air!" She absently patted the boy on the head and continued her conversation with the woman beside her.

Elissa couldn't help but intervene at that point. "Jesse!" she admonished from a few yards away. With a sheepish grin, he tossed the ball back to the boy, who examined it with wide-eyed reverence.

Jesse returned to Elissa's side and escorted her across a shady street toward a sidewalk café. "It's the damnedest thing I've ever seen," he muttered. "They can't see me, they can't hear me, but they can feel my touch."

Elissa had to bite her tongue to keep from asking what he felt when he touched them. People sat at outdoor umbrella tables, casting her casual glances and brief smiles for the baby. What would they do if she started talking to an invisible man? Cart her off to a padded cell, that's what.

"What do you think would happen," mused Jesse, "if I blocked their way? Would they bump into me?"

Foreboding shivered through Elissa. "Don't try it!"

The plea drew the attention of ladies seated at a nearby umbrella table. She looked down at Cody and, in a rush of embarrassment, stuck the pacifier into his mouth. "Don't...don't throw your pacifier again, sweetie, or we might not find it this time."

Cody accepted the pacifier in sleepy contentment as Elissa wheeled him beyond earshot of the sidewalk café.

Beside her, Jesse muttered, "I have to know what I'm dealing with here." And with his thumbs hooked in the pockets of his tight, faded jeans, he stepped into the path of an oncoming crowd.

Elissa flinched as a long-haired, husky youth with headphones walked into him. But there was no collision. The youth, and the crowd behind him, walked on without interruption. Elissa heard a woman remark, "Oh, do you feel that chill? I'll bet we're in for some rain." Her companion mumbled in agreement.

Elissa stood with her fingers wrapped tightly around the stroller bar, staring in dry-mouthed horror. Jesse was gone. Gone! Vanished in the midst of that crowd.

"Jesse?" she whispered when the crowd had passed. No one answered.

With shaking knees, she forced herself to stroll to the end of the block, casting hopeful glances around the city streets, praying to see Jesse among the pedestrians. Where had he gone? What had happened to him? Had he broken some cardinal rule of the spiritual realm, damning him to some netherworld for all eternity?

Oh, Jesse. Please come back.

But he didn't.

She returned to his house alone, her stomach knotted, her nerves frazzled, her hopes set on something she knew to be foolish. Why *should* he return? If his unresolved goal had been to see and hold Cody, he had accomplished it. And by bequeathing his house and money to Cody, he had provided for his future, as well. What more could the most conscientious ghost hope to accomplish in regards to his son?

This earthly plane was no place for Jesse anymore. It was right for him to move on to whatever his destiny held in store, Elissa told herself. He belonged elsewhere.

It was only her heart that begged to differ.

HE WAKENED TO the chirping of crickets, the humming of insects and the croaking of frogs, with the scent of autumn grasses and river mist heavy on the cool October night air. His first inclination was to listen for movement: voices, footsteps, faraway gunfire.

But by the dim light of a hazy crescent moon, he quickly recognized his surroundings—the driveway of his home, not a riverbank in some foreign thicket. And though he had just wakened, he found himself not lying down, or even recumbent against some tree, but walking with cautious, determined strides, as if on patrol.

Jesse frowned. Where the hell had he been since this afternoon? He remembered his trip to town with Elissa and his experimentation there. He remembered standing in the path of an oncoming crowd. Then what?

Nothing. A total absence of memory.

What had they done to him? What the *hell* had the military done to him now? He'd gone along with their psychic experiments, submitted to their testing, honed his mental powers into a viable force that had won them success in situations that would have otherwise proved impossible. He had bent metal with his mind for them—freeing hostages from terrorists' prisons, jamming weapons that would have otherwise destroyed cities, disabling enemy aircraft at the most crucial of times. Yes, he had allowed the military to strengthen his mental powers with methods their researchers had perfected.

But he had always drawn the line at drug experimentation or anything that could physically affect him. Had they tried some new drug or technology on him without his knowledge? Was *he* their guinea pig—their newest weapon?

He clenched his fists in fury. What else could explain his condition? He strode up the driveway, his footsteps crunching like so many necks breaking. He'd find out who was behind this, he swore, and he'd make them sorry.

Questions flashed through his mind at rapid-fire pace. Why had they allowed him to leave? Had they really intended to set him loose in a civilian setting? Did they know where he was, or were they searching for him now?

Doubts whispered through him.

Elissa had said she called the colonel and told him of his first visit. If the military was conducting some bizarre experiment with him, why hadn't the colonel believed that she saw him? Why hadn't he asked for the details and sent someone to follow up? Common sense answered that question: because the colonel thought he was dead.

The puzzle pieces didn't fit. Jesse didn't like it.

Forcing his anger to subside, he climbed the steps to the front porch. He couldn't afford the luxury of anger. He had to keep a clear mind if he hoped to find the truth.

He tried the door and found it locked.

Elissa's car was still in the driveway, he noted. Which meant she was here. He wanted badly to see her; *needed* to be with her. She was his sanity in a world that had ceased to make sense.

Checking the pockets of his pants and shirt for his keys, Jesse realized he was wearing his army fatigues. He also realized he had no key. With a muttered curse, he lifted his hand to knock, then stopped. Hadn't Elissa accused him of appearing in locked rooms without an apparent way in? He stared at the door for a doubtful moment. What would happen if he...?

Taking a step back, he braced his shoulders, covered his head with his arms and forged slowly, steadily, onward. He fully expected the heavy oak barrier to stop him.

He encountered no barrier.

Lifting his head, Jesse found himself inside.

The magnitude of this discovery—and all the others he'd made today—washed over him in icy waves. Whatever the cause, he was no longer a normal, flesh-and-blood man. He was something quite, quite different. Would this difference be...permanent?

Determination tightened the muscles of his jaw. He could not allow that. He would diagnose the exact nature of the problem and take whatever measures were necessary to correct it. Strengthened by his resolve, he glanced around the darkened living room. Elissa was obviously upstairs.

He took the steps two at a time.

When he reached the upper corridor, he paused in the open doorway to her bedroom. The only light spilled from the door left slightly ajar to the adjoining bath. The bed was neatly made, with no one sleeping in it.

He'd been hoping to find her there.

The rhythmic breathing of the baby in the crib drew Jesse to the far corner, where he gazed down at his slumbering son. "I promise you, Cody, you'll grow up with a father," he vowed. "A real father."

The gentle swoosh of water and the slurp of a drain lifted Jesse's head toward the bathroom door. Elissa, it seemed, had been bathing. His anticipation sharpened into hunger. He wanted to see her. Touch her. Renew his soul, his life force, by making long, hard love to her.

The bathroom door slowly opened and blossom-scented steam wafted out. The bathroom light flicked off, pitching the bedroom into an even deeper darkness, relieved only by a night-light near the bed.

Quietly she tiptoed, her hair wet, her skin dewy, her slender body wrapped in only a thin white towel, fastened by a tuck between her breasts. She didn't immediately notice him, but headed for the baby's crib, where she peered down at the sleeping infant.

"Our stroll must have worn you out," she whispered, adjusting the blanket around him with a tender smile. "It's past your feeding time." She then turned and reached for her pink nightgown, which lay draped across an armchair.

Jesse caught hold of the nightgown first, and whisked it sufficiently beyond her reach.

8

THE NIGHTGOWN FLEW OUT of her hand, startling her.

A figure loomed in the shadows, then materialized in the dim light—he was taut and powerful, his wide shoulders squared in a vaguely threatening stance. He wore army fatigues, stained and torn, the shirt open at his throat and chest. His wind-tossed hair gleamed black as the October night and curled down onto his neck, much longer than she'd ever seen it. His smoke gray eyes glittered with a dangerous allure in the harsh, unshaven planes of his face.

He looked wild. Driven. As if he'd spent months on a desperate mission. Relief welled up in Elissa with such ferocity, it choked her. He hadn't gone. She hadn't lost him yet. Her breath caught on a sob. "I was afraid I'd never see you again."

"I'm not going anywhere." His gaze said much more.

She was in his arms, then, and something like lightning bolted through them. There was a blinding rush of sensation too intense to endure; a hellish force bent on parting them. His muscles strained to keep her against him, his arms were protective bars around her as he waged battle.

Elissa, too, fought the preternatural force with all her strength. She wanted so to hold him, to hold *on* to him, for as long as possible. She wanted to feel his breath against her cheek, his muscles beneath her fingers, his heartbeat against her own. That desire doubled as it forged with his.

"Elissa, I want you so much," he breathed against her ear.

She shut her eyes and inhaled his lusty male scent. He brushed his mouth along her jaw, then trailed hot, moist kisses down the side of her throat.

She dug her fingers into the hard muscles of his shoulders, relishing the sheer, primal joy his body gave her. He exhaled in a heated rush and from the base of her throat he dragged his tongue to the underside of her chin.

A response like thunder shook her to the core.

She met him in an openmouthed kiss that tasted of danger and freedom and a dark sweetness that was all his own. She matched him, thrust for thrust, swirl for swirl, drawing him in ever deeper. His large, rough hands slipped beneath her towel—caressing, rubbing, teasing her in ways that left both of them trembling with need.

He tugged her towel away and slung it down.

And then he stared. The pebbled tips of her breasts and the palms of his hands were wet and glistening. Mother's milk. Her cheeks flamed as she realized what it was. She moved to shield herself. He caught her arms and held them at her sides, his surprise turning to awe.

Bending her backward slightly, he lowered his mouth to her breast. With consummate reverence, he savored first one breast, then the other until she ached for him in a way she'd never ached before.

Her fingers found the rock-hard column behind his zipper and he growled under his breath. With tightly leashed passion, he reclaimed her mouth.

One kiss led to another. Deeper, hotter, wilder. His

hand skimmed down the curve of her hip to the velvet of her inner thighs. Then, ever so slowly, it traveled upward, to her most intimate valley.

Elissa inhaled sharply at his unexpected touch.

His fingers lightly played there. His tongue danced in her mouth. Pleasure flashed through her in waves, bringing her blood to a full simmer.

Whimpering deep in her throat, awash in relentless sensation, she clung to him. She pushed against him writhing, her hip brushing against his hardness. He groaned, clutched her tighter and broke out in a sweat.

His ministrations slowed. Then intensified.

She dragged her mouth away from his to cry out, but suddenly his fingers ceased their taunting and came to rest, feather-light, against the threshold she so wished him to enter.

Poignant anticipation held her virtually paralyzed. Her mouth opened wide in a silent gasp. Her eyes sought his.

Slowly, obligingly, he deepened the touch.

Pleasure blossomed within her to an unbearable force.

His gaze, hooded with passion, burned into her like molten silver. In a hoarse, almost pained plea, he asked, "Will you let me love you, Elissa?"

Unable to summon her voice—or even to nod, for fear she'd shatter to pieces, Elissa merely gazed at him with all her heart. He had asked her permission the first time they'd made love, too. He had forced her to say it out loud. His need to do so suffused her with a profound emotion. Hadn't he known she was his for the taking?

If he hadn't, he did now.

He read it in her eyes.

Jesse lifted her off the floor, onto the bed. Elation blazed through him, along with the fiercest desire. If she had refused him, he surely would have died. For the heat had consumed him entirely, with much more devastation than it had even in his fantasies.

He needed her now, in the worst way. Needed to taste her again. To trace with his mouth the seductive path his hands had forged. To bring her to the brink of delirium, then pull her back, until she begged him with her eyes and her whispers and her body. To plunge himself into her again and again until her very soul merged with his.

AT HER SON'S HUNGRY WAIL, Elissa opened her eyes and stretched with languid contentment against the hard male body behind her. She'd been possessed last night—every intimate part of her—with a thoroughness she had never imagined, by the only man who had ever incited her to passion.

Her muscles ached with a delicious soreness, and as the memory of their lovemaking returned in full, her blood fairly sang with feminine power. For she had possessed *him* last night, too, as fully as a woman could possess a man.

If she were a violin, she thought with a smug smile, her strings would still be humming.

As she thought of the bow that had played her with such exquisite artistry, her hand appreciatively caressed the furry, muscular arm wrapped around her midsection. If only the baby wouldn't holler so; she'd love to spend a few more hours snuggled in these powerful arms.

But Cody demanded his breakfast, and she couldn't allow him to remain hungry for even a second longer than necessary. Reluctantly, she lifted the arm that lay heavily across her waist. But as she sat up to slip out from under it, a shock of cold horror pulsated through her.

She couldn't see the arm. She could feel it in detail: smooth, muscle-corded, hairy. But she couldn't see it!

Her heart stood still for a petrified moment. Chill bumps rose on every inch of her still-naked body. Winding her fists in the bedsheet that was tangled around her waist, she peered over her shoulder toward the masculine being who breathed rhythmically beside her.

No one lay there.

Her scalp prickled, as if her hair stood on end. Blood rushed to her head in a dizzying *whoosh*. And with a panicked cry, she scrambled from the bed, lunging and falling across the room, yanking the tangled bedsheet with her.

Behind her she heard a surprised mutter, a vivid curse, and the violent *thump* of a large body hitting the floor on the other side of the bed.

"Jesse!" she cried, quivering where she stood, clinging to the bedsheet as if to shield herself from further horror. "What's happened to you?"

Another descriptive curse, and then he said, "What the hell do you *think* happened? You pulled the sheet out from under me. Rolled me out of the damned bed!"

"But you...you...I can't...I can't..."

"*You* can't?" The utterance sounded weak, almost dazed, and still came from the floor, as if he hadn't fully risen. "Hell, I feel like a goddamn tank's run over me." After a pause, he noted in an almost pained whisper, "Baby's crying."

"Jesse!" Concern washed away a good deal of her

horror. She sprang out of her stupor and shrugged into her bathrobe. "Are you okay?"

"Can't say I am." It was little more than a hoarse rasping. With a weak attempt at wryness, he croaked, "Not enough lovin'."

Worry now gnawed at her, and she dashed around the bed, hoping to see him lying there in full living color. But when she reached the far side where he had fallen, she halted in dismay.

She saw not a sign of him anywhere. "I can't see you," she burst out in an agonized whisper. "You're inv-visible." She thought she heard a dry expletive, but with Cody's howling, she couldn't be sure. "Is this because...because we...made love?" she cried, wishing she could see him.

In reply came a strangled "Hell, no."

She edged toward the head of the bed, feeling carefully along the floor with her bare feet. Surely she'd feel him sitting or lying here, maybe nursing a morning headache....

"Jesse, where are you?" She knelt near the head of the bed, groping the air in all directions as if she might have missed him in the narrow space between the bed and the wall.

But she felt nothing. No warm male body. Not even a mysterious cold spot. Jesse, it seemed, had left her again.

At least, she supposed he had.

"Dr. Lehmberg? Elissa Sinclair." She was sitting with her knees against her chest on the Persian carpet in Jesse's living room, her back against the sofa and the telephone receiver to her ear. As she spoke, she absently watched Cody play with Mr. Duckie on the blanket she'd laid out for him. "I have another question."

"Sure," encouraged the professor. "What is it?"

"What would happen to a ghost if he—" she hesitated a moment, then forced the words out "—if he made love? With a live human being, I mean."

Silence echoed loudly over the telephone line. She could visualize her former teacher's surprise as the seconds ticked by. "What do you mean, made love?"

"Oh, you know. The usual." Elissa cleared her throat and rubbed the back of her neck, which had grown uncomfortably warm. "Would it...*hurt*...the spirit? Weaken his life force somehow?"

"Are you saying that you know of a spirit that made love with someone?" Lehmberg's voice had undergone a subtle change—to one Elissa might have used as a counselor.

"Well, no, of course not." She already regretted her question. "Not personally, I mean."

"Then what did you mean?"

She couldn't think of a single lie.

"Elissa, have you seen the apparition again that we discussed in my office?"

"Yes," she admitted, clutching the receiver tighter.

"Does it take the shape of a...man?"

"Uh-huh."

"You're not crying, are you?"

"Not quite," she warbled, holding back tears.

"Oh, Elissa, calm down. I've already told you how strong-minded spirits can create multisensory illusions that could be quite convincing to the average person."

"This wasn't an illusion. It couldn't have been. I felt it, he was here, k-kissing me, and..." She stopped and dashed a tear from her cheek. "It was real, I swear."

"This man—did you know him when he was alive?"

Sensing a trap, she replied cautiously, "Somewhat."

"Somewhat? So he wasn't a loved one?"

The simple question hit her with surprising force. Was Jesse a "loved one"? In that moment, a profound realization swept through her.

"Yes," she whispered. "He is." And it was true. She loved Jesse—in a way she'd loved no other man. She had from the moment she'd met him. "He's the father of my child."

A sigh, or something suspiciously like it, sounded in the receiver. "You should have told me that to begin with."

"Does it make a difference?"

"Not technically speaking. But—" Lehmberg paused, as if trying to pick her next words carefully. "I'm not saying that you haven't experienced a spiritual visitation. But often when a person sees the ghost of a loved one for any longer than a brief appearance, it has more to do with grief than with anything paranormal."

Elissa stiffened, her disappointment strong. "You think I'm imagining all this?"

"I didn't say that, exactly. But sometimes a person's psyche can conjure up whatever he or she most desires."

"You, a scientist in the field of parapsychology, think I'm just hallucinating? You think I dreamed up Jesse for company, or maybe a hot date on a lonely night?"

"I wouldn't put it in those words, but—"

"I know what grief is, Dr. Lehmberg, and I know the difference between wishful thinking and fact. Sure, I wish he hadn't died. Sure, I wish we could have had a future together." Her voice broke, but she kept on, her indignation painful. "That doesn't mean I've flipped my lid and now go around making love to illusions."

"Pity. That might have its advantages. Less worry about sexually transmitted diseases."

It took a stunned moment for Elissa to realize that Lehmberg was joking. The muted humor helped her regain perspective in a way nothing else would have. The professor wouldn't joke with a person she suspected might be crazy, would she? With a mollified sniff, Elissa mumbled, "Saves money on contraceptives, too."

That provoked a brief laugh. Elissa felt relieved, as if their relationship had been somewhat restored. "The Elissa Sinclair I know," said Lehmberg, the sobriety back in her voice, "would be the first to doubt any phenomena that couldn't be fully explained."

"That's right."

"Which is why you have to consider all possibilities. If this apparition truly is from the spiritual realm, the first thing you have to do is convince him that he's dead."

"I tried. He wouldn't believe me."

"That's not unusual. Ask any psychic who's worked with earthbound spirits, and they'll tell you. The spirit usually doesn't realize he's dead. It's up to you, Elissa, to convince him otherwise. Then you may have to guide him."

"Guide him? Where?"

"To the other side. Think of him as a traveler who has lost his way. He needs to be directed toward the light."

"What light?"

"Haven't you read accounts of near-death experiences? Documented cases date way back into history, and almost all of them share a common element: the departing soul is beckoned toward a brilliant light, usually at the end of a tunnel. If you really want to help this spirit, Elissa, you'll have to make him understand that he must leave this mortal plane and move on toward the light."

Dismay curled through her. She didn't want to imagine Jesse walking through that tunnel. "But maybe he's not ready. Maybe he hasn't achieved his final goal."

"If that's the case, he probably won't go," she replied with characteristic aplomb. "But he'll find no peace, no happiness, until he does. Who knows what damage he'll suffer, the longer he's kept from his destiny?" Somberly she added, "Perhaps he'll simply cease to exist."

Elissa swallowed a sudden lump in her throat; a painful heaviness pushed against her chest. "What if he doesn't reappear to me?"

"That would probably mean he found his way on his own."

Her vision slowly blurred, and she foolishly nodded above the receiver, not trusting her voice enough to reply.

"It's odd," murmured Lehmberg, "the degree of communication you seem to have established with the departed. Are you, by any chance, psychic?"

"Me? No. I mean, I never thought of myself as psychic." After a reflective moment, she mused, "But my mother did often accuse me of reading her mind. And a few times, I knew when a friend was about to pay an unexpected visit. I just felt it, somehow."

"So you've always had some psychic tendencies."

Elissa shrugged. "I suppose."

"That might account for the degree of communication you've established. You know, Elissa," she said as if pondering a new idea, "I've read theories that a truly psychic individual could actually summon the dead."

"Summon—? You mean, *I* might have held Jesse back from his final destiny?"

"It's just a theory. Other parapsychologists dismiss it as a bunch of nonsense. I tend to agree with the latter. I feel that only the individual himself could make the choice of whether or not to follow that beckoning light."

Elissa shut her eyes, more confused than ever. "But maybe my...my wanting him...is keeping him here longer than he would have otherwise stayed."

"Maybe. Anyway, try what I've told you. Guide him toward the light." Professor Lehmberg then wished her luck and murmured a pleasant goodbye.

But before she broke their connection, she imparted one last bit of advice. "It wouldn't hurt for you to talk to a grief counselor. The entire problem may be an emotional one. Sometimes when it comes to love, it's just too hard to let go. That unresolved business might actually be your own."

Elissa hung up the phone with an even greater ache splitting her heart. She had to send Jesse away, toward his final destiny. And she couldn't allow her own feelings to hold him back.

If only she didn't love him so.

SHE SPENT THE REST of that Saturday morning pacing around the house and yard with Cody in her arms, on constant guard for sound and movement. Inside, she jumped at shadows and settling noises of the old house; outside, at every whisper of wind or crackle of leaves.

Could Jesse still be with her, but unable to appear, or to speak? The horror she'd felt that morning at finding him invisible returned with almost as much force.

"Jesse," she found herself saying out loud, "are you here? Can you hear me, can you see me?"

If so, he wasn't saying.

It didn't stop her from talking to him, though, all that day and night. As she lit a cozy evening fire in the hearth, she asked if he was sharing it with her. As she climbed the staircase, she asked if he was following. And as she undressed for her bath and soaked in the jasmine-scented water, she gazed around and asked if he was watching.

She wished he were.

She dressed for bed with slow, deliberately seductive moves, in the soft, pearl-white gown she hadn't yet worn for him. She sat at the mirror of an antique vanity and brushed her hair, watching for movement behind her. She even sprayed her wrists and breasts lightly with perfume, all in an attempt to lure him out into the open.

But Jesse failed to put in an appearance.

Proof, she thought. He positively wasn't here.

The following morning, a cloudy Sunday, she dressed Cody in the little yellow sweater and cap she had knitted for him and pushed him in his stroller down the driveway, across the narrow road, to the sharply sloping bluff above the Skidaway River. Tall grasses rippled in the autumn breeze down the slope to the hazel green water. Long, wooden planked walkways above the marsh grass led to boathouses along the river bluff. Seabirds from the nearby Atlantic Ocean swooped and cried from the gray-and-white patchwork sky, their calls echoing her oppressive loneliness.

"I can't take much more of this, Jesse," she said, more from habit now than hope of eliciting a response. She stared out at a shrimp boat gliding past, its mast pole and cables glinting in the morning sun. "I can't stand not knowing where you are, or how you are, or if you'll come back."

"You think *I* like it?"

She jumped violently at the deep, quiet reply from beside her. He stood with his hands in the pockets of his gray trousers, a blue-green polo shirt emphasizing the incredible breadth of his chest. His jet hair rippled in the breeze like the marsh grass before them as he gazed solemnly across the river. "I don't like it worth a damn, not knowing when or where I'll black out, or come to."

It took Elissa a long moment to regain her breath from the shock of his appearance. "Don't do that!" she cried, a hand to her heart. "You scared me half to death!"

"We'd be there together, then, wouldn't we?"

She stared at him, surprised that he'd say such a thing. "Well, yes, I suppose 'half to death' would pretty much describe where you are." Her heart gradually stopped galloping and her voice returned to a civilized pitch. "So, you believe me now? That you're...dead?"

"Of course not. I was humoring you." He flashed her a mischievous grin, then bent down to gaze eye level at Cody in the stroller. The baby was totally occupied with stuffing all ten of his chubby little fingers into his mouth. "Come here to your pa," Jesse mumbled. And he reached to take the bright-eyed baby from the stroller.

"No, don't touch him."

He stopped with his hands inches from Cody and plied Elissa with a dark, questioning frown.

"People might see and wonder how he's hovering in midair. Besides, you shouldn't touch anyone. I'm afraid you'll disappear. Maybe this time for good."

Jesse settled his hands on his hips and stared at her. As much as he wanted to argue, he knew she was at least partially right. Something about physical contact with other people did put a drain on his energy. And he didn't want to fade off into unconsciousness again. Yet neither could he abide the idea of not touching Cody or her. No, that wouldn't do at all.

He made another move for Cody, and Elissa pulled the stroller back from him. "Aren't you worried about yourself? You saw the reaction of the people in town. They couldn't see you! And where did you go after that? It's not exactly normal to be bothered by pesky disappearing spells."

"Of course I'm concerned," he replied. But not as much as he knew he should be. In fact, nothing seemed too terribly important—his health, his mysterious ailment, even the military screwup about his alleged death. The only thing that mattered, he realized, was making Elissa want him with the same urgency he wanted her.

He stared out at the river, stunned by the depth of his need for her. He'd always been the one to hightail it out of a relationship at the first sign of intimacy. Now he found himself craving it, like some addictive drug. He was hooked, irrevocably hooked, and he meant for her to be just as needful of him.

His pondering was interrupted by the soft, throaty voice that had haunted his dreams, both sleeping and waking, for a full dozen months. "Does it hurt you, Jesse? Disappearing?"

"Yes." He turned his gaze fully on her. "It hurt like hell to leave your bed."

Her sherry brown eyes warmed beneath his stare, reflecting the intimacy of their lovemaking. She broke their gaze, a delicate flush rising on her cheeks. "That's not what I meant. You're deliberately avoiding the issue."

"I'd say you're avoiding it." His eyes spoke with a seriousness that raised her temperature. "Let's go inside and build a fire in the hearth. Then you can take a bath with that oil that glistens all over your skin." His glance took in all of her, as if he was envisioning it. "Then after we dry you off, I'll help you brush your hair."

She cast him a wondering glance. His plan sounded very much like her activities of last night.

"And maybe you can find some fancy gown." His voice had grown husky. "You know, like the ones with those thin little straps and see-through lace, clear down past here." He swept his finger from her shoulder to the tip of her breast, not actually touching her, but gliding above her thin sweater with an aura that sizzled right through it.

"Jesse, stop!" Ridiculously aroused, she crossed her arms and glanced around. "Someone might be watching."

"I thought you said they can't see me."

"Probably not, but—"

"So I can do anything I want...and no one would see."

She recognized the teasing light in his eyes—and the sensuality that sizzled beneath it. "Were you there," she whispered, "in my bedroom last night?"

"I dreamed I was there. I dreamed you wore a sexy white gown, with your hair all shiny and loose around your shoulders. And you sprayed perfume between your breasts. It smelled sweet—like oranges and powdered sugar. I wanted to taste it on you."

Her breath caught. "I wore a gown like you described. And sprayed perfume that smells very much like…"

"Did you whisper to me?" he interrupted hoarsely.

She nodded. And they slipped into a gaze, deep and warm with mutual longing. As his lips neared her, she abruptly came to her sense. "Jesse, *we can't touch.*"

"The hell we can't." And he reached for her.

She had anticipated the move and drew away. "I'm afraid you'll disappear!"

"That's just something I'll have to learn to control. I can use the practice."

"Practice!" Resolutely, she locked gazes with him, somber and earnest this time. "Listen to me, Jesse, and believe every word that I say. This might be a hard concept to grasp, but it's important that you do. *You are dead.*"

He nodded, slipped his hands into his pockets and tried not to curse. Her confounded "dead" theory was definitely cramping his style. "I understand why you think that. This invisibility thing…well, it *is* hard to explain."

"What other explanation is there?"

"Could be the result of a military experiment." But in his heart, he knew better. Whatever was happening to him went much deeper than his body, or even his mind. He knew that now with a clarity beyond reason. He also knew he couldn't give in to it, whatever it was. He had to overcome it.

"If some technology turned you invisible," reasoned Elissa, "then why can I see you?"

He shrugged, at a loss for an answer. "If I am, as you say, dead…why can you see me?"

"Because you're haunting me."

"Haunting you!" He frowned at her, incensed. "What, like some paranormal stalker?"

"When we talked, you said you couldn't remember anything from the times we're apart. Your spells of consciousness all take place while you're with me. Is that still true?"

"Well, yes, but—"

"That's because *you're haunting me.* If a ghost is haunting a house, he stays with it. He doesn't take a night off to paint the town. Face it, Jesse—you're haunting me."

"Now, why would I do a thing like that?"

"I'm not sure." She averted her eyes, looking somewhat secretive, as if she knew full well why he'd do it, but preferred not to say. "My research says," she began slowly, "that ghosts often remain earthbound because of their desire to fulfill some unachieved goal or obligation."

"What goal have I left unachieved?"

She pressed her lips together, obviously reluctant to answer. Just when he thought she wouldn't, she said, "At first, I thought you wanted to see Cody, and to hold him. But you've already done that and you're still here."

"Yes, I am. At least we agree on something."

"Maybe your unresolved business has something to do with guilt."

"Guilt?" he repeated in surprise. "About what?"

"Failing to contact me when I informed you of my pregnancy. And when Cody was born." Though her voice remained level, he could hear her resentment. "It wasn't until your deathbed, Jesse, that you regretted your neglect."

"Neglect! I didn't neglect Cody or you."

"Death endowed you with a conscience. Apparently you now feel the need to atone."

A muscle in his jaw throbbed. "Damn it, Elissa, I told you I was on a highly sensitive, covert mission. My mail was held until I returned to the base—"

"I know. The colonel backed up your story. Your mission clearly accounts for the last few months of my pregnancy. But what about the first half dozen? He refused to say when your mission started, or how long it lasted."

"Of course he refused to say. That's classified information. But I swear, I didn't receive your letters until I returned from my mission, two days before my flight home. The minute I knew of his existence, I legally acknowledged Cody as my son. Furthermore, I couldn't have 'regretted my neglect' on my deathbed because I haven't *been* on my deathbed yet!"

She would have believed him about the letters, about his immediate interest in Cody, except for what Dean had told her about the calls from brothels in Asia. Dean had begged him to at least talk to her about the pregnancy, but Jesse had refused. *Just because I play a game of pool,* he'd said, *doesn't mean I want to lug the pool table around with me.*

Thinking about those conversations that Dean had reluctantly relayed to her brought back all the hurt and humiliation she had suffered. She wanted to fling those heartless comments in Jesse's face, just to watch his new postmortem conscience kick him in the butt.

But wasn't his conscience kicking him hard enough already? Hard enough to keep him from his ever-after!

Besides, she had promised Dean that she'd never use the things he told her to drive a wedge between his cousin and him.

"Just forget I said anything about guilt," she grumbled, ashamed of herself for almost betraying Dean's confidence.

"You don't believe me, do you." Jesse's dark gaze bore into her with patent incredulity. "You really think I read those letters and chose to ignore them."

Goaded by his act of persecuted innocence, she retorted, "Mail isn't the only method of modern communication."

"What do you mean by that? Did you try to call me? If so, I never got the message, not even after I returned to the base. Tell me who you spoke with, and we'll confront them together."

My, but he was convincing! She rounded on him in barely leashed fury, "You can't confront anyone. You're dead!"

His jaw clenched, his stare simmered, but he answered with impressive restraint, "I am not dead. And whether you believe me or not, the only unresolved business I have is to be there for Cody, as his father, while he grows up."

A bright flash of pain sliced through Elissa's anger. She wished it could be so. She wished it with all her heart. But a future of any kind was impossible for Jesse.

Her thwarted longing made the memory of his past betrayal hurt all the more. "Yes, I suppose that does make sense," she reflected with quiet anguish. "That would be a way for you to atone for your initial neglect, whether you ever admit to your guilt or not." To her horror, she felt her eyes blur with tears. "Sorry to tell you, though—you're one lifetime too late!"

He muttered a curse and grabbed her, his hands hard and forceful on her upper arms. "I intended from the first moment I knew about him to be a father to Cody. Trust me on this, Elissa. Trust me."

The familiar electricity flashed through them at his touch, but he didn't fight it this time. He wanted to saturate her with his emotions.

She felt his righteous anger, his determination to be believed, and above all, his burning need. The force of it was too powerful to endure and pried them apart, propelling her from his grasp.

Shaken to the core, Elissa caught her balance against a tree, too dizzy to see straight, too confused to make sense of things. She'd felt no guilt from him. No deception. He truly seemed to believe what he was telling her.

But how could that be? Dean surely hadn't lied, especially not when he'd known how dire her situation was.

"Trust me, Elissa" came Jesse's ragged whisper.

She released her supporting hold on the tree trunk and looked around for him, but he was nowhere to be seen.

"Jesse!" she cried. "Don't you dare leave me now!"

She received no answer. Disappointment, frustration and self-blame violently assaulted her. Why had she goaded him into a quarrel? Why had she allowed him to touch her? She hadn't even tried to guide him toward the beckoning light. She hadn't had a chance to forgive him...regardless of what he had or had not done in the wretched past.

Heartsick for wasting what might have been her last encounter with him, Elissa weakly returned to where Cody sucked his fingers and watched her from his stroller.

A fog had begun to descend in wispy swirls above

the river. The black Spanish moss on the branches of the towering oaks swayed ghostlike. A seagull dove from a low-hanging cloud, his cry sharp and mocking.

Elissa blindly stared into the thickening mist, her throat aching with wasted chances. "I'm not finished talking to you yet, Jesse!" she admonished out loud, grasping the stroller bar until her fingers hurt.

Though he hadn't quite enough energy left to voice a reply, Jesse thought, *I'm not finished with you yet, either.*

A car motored past Elissa on the narrow road, then pulled into Jesse's driveway. A dusty tan station wagon. The look of surprise on her face told Jesse she hadn't been expecting visitors.

The car door opened and a familiar stodgy form with sandy brown curls and wire-rimmed glasses unfolded from the driver's seat.

Dean. With a small bouquet of roses in one hand and an overnight bag in the other.

9

"DEAN, WHAT ARE YOU doing here?"

Elissa's wide-eyed greeting gave Jesse no clue as to whether she considered the surprise a pleasant one. He himself would have phrased the question differently. He would have said what the *hell* are you doing here.

Unfortunately, his brief contact with Elissa had siphoned his energy to a dangerous low. He tried to speak, but found he had no voice. And he was obviously invisible even to Elissa.

This handicap was getting more annoying by the moment.

From the grin on Dean's face as he shuffled toward Elissa, Jesse knew his cousin felt confident about the welcome he'd receive. "I was worried about you and Cody being here alone. And I missed you too much." He planted a kiss on her cheek. "So I spent yesterday working on plans for my sub, and arranged personal leave for tomorrow and Tuesday."

He handed her the bouquet of red roses with a courtly bow. It had been just that kind of cornball move that had earned Dean jeers throughout school—and had drawn Jesse into fistfights to vindicate him.

As Elissa murmured her thanks, Dean squatted down beside the stroller. "And how's our little man?" He pulled from his sweater pocket a yellow, pretzel-shaped teething ring that squeaked as he squeezed it.

Cody reached for it with a smile, his chubby legs kicking beneath the stroller tray.

A vague ache twisted through Jesse. His son responded immediately to Dean, but hadn't even seen Jesse. Brusquely, he told himself he should be glad that Cody liked Dean. He was, after all, his cousin. Probably the closest Cody would ever have to an uncle. *And maybe the closest he'll have to a father.* Jesse scowled at the thought. *He* was Cody's father, and always would be.

Why, then, did Dean's presence fill him with resentment? Dean had been like a younger brother to him all through their boyhood—irritating at times with his holier-than-thou attitude, but always an ally at home where the adults stood united in chronic disapproval of Jesse.

Dean and he had fished together near the family's beach cottage on Tybee Island, and they'd water-skied. Or rather, Jesse had skied while Dean drove the boat and muttered dire predictions about the shark-infested waters. Jesse had shown him his first girlie magazine, back when that was high excitement. They'd been like brothers.

The night before Jesse was to ship out for his overseas mission, the premonition of death had been riding heavy in his gut. He had stopped to say goodbye to Dean; an impulsive visit, but one that had seemed important.

The visit *had* proven important, but for a different reason than he'd expected. That night he'd met and made love to Elissa.

It was only now, as he watched Dean play up to her, that his resentment kicked in. Dean ruffled the baby's dark, wispy hair, then rose from his squatting position. Reaching into the pocket of his cardigan, he brought out a rectangular box and handed it to Elissa. "And this is for you."

Hesitantly, she opened it and eyed the contents in surprise. "A telephone."

"Cellular. I couldn't sleep a wink after you told me about that flat tire you had on the way here. Thank heavens you were able to change it."

Her cheeks pinkened and she avoided Dean's gaze. So, she hadn't told Dean about his presence. Her words from Friday morning returned to Jesse with new importance: *Everyone thinks you're dead. I think you're dead.* Did she plan to carry on as if he weren't there?

"This is sweet of you, Dean, but I can't accept—"

"I've already paid for the first month of basic service. Keep it at least until you're back home, safe and sound."

Jesse's lips stretched taut. As always, Dean had done the right thing. She *did* need a cellular phone while she was on the road. He himself should have thought of it.

With a sudden flash of insight, he recognized the look in Dean's besotted blue eyes as Elissa thanked him. It had been there when Dean had nursed obsessive crushes on girls at school. He hadn't acted on any of those crushes, way back then. He'd slept with their photos beneath his pillow, phoned them to hear their voices before he hung up, scrawled their names in his notebooks a thousand times over.

Jesse had been very careful to keep his hands off any woman Dean wanted. Dismay lodged like a rock in his stomach. Elissa would have to be the exception.

He watched as she scooped up Cody. Dean folded the stroller, packed it into her car and retrieved from his trunk two bags of groceries, which, he said, included fresh apples from a fruit stand, since he knew she loved them.

Jesse realized that he himself hadn't a clue as to what Elissa loved. Food-wise, at least. Then again, he knew exactly how to please her in other ways. Important ways. Ways that whetted a very different appetite.

Did Dean?

With teeth on edge, Jesse followed the couple as they climbed the front steps and entered his house. The oak door swung closed behind them and he put out a hand to stop it. The door didn't even slow as it shut in his face.

Jesse drew back and stared at his hand. *The door had passed right through it.* He tried to turn the knob, but his hand wouldn't connect with the solid material.

For the first time since he'd become aware of his "condition," alarm buzzed through him. He had passed through this door before, but only because he had wanted to, not because he couldn't open it.

With a technique he had deployed during the worst of his military endeavors, he cleared his mind of the alarm. He couldn't waste energy on unnecessary emotion. When his inner calm had been restored, he passed through the heavy oak door with only the slightest depletion of precious energy.

Once inside, he tried to lift an ashtray.

He couldn't, and the attempt left him weaker still. He had to rest, to marshal his strength, to stay silently on the sidelines. Until he could do more, of course. In a way he didn't fully understand, he retreated to an altered state that required the least amount of effort.

Throughout that Sunday afternoon, he observed their actions and heard the murmur of their conversation, but from an oddly distanced perspective. As if he were dreaming it.

Elissa took Dean on a tour of the house, then walked him around the gardens. They strolled down to the river, arm in arm, with Cody snuggled against Dean's shoulder. It wasn't until that evening, after they'd put Cody to bed and shared a supper of pot roast and vegetables, that Jesse's faculties sharpened. Elissa washed the dishes and Dean dried. They handed each other plates and glasses with smooth regularity, as if they'd been doing this kind of teamwork for years.

Cozy. Too damn cozy.

It hit Jesse then like a radar-guided missile: if he never returned to normal, if this affliction remained or grew worse, Dean would be a good husband for Elissa. A good father to Cody. He wondered if Elissa was in love with him.

Bleakness, gray and suffocating, descended on Jesse. She was a vibrant young woman, alone with a child. Why shouldn't she have fallen in love with a man who was always there for her?

A sick heaviness crowded his chest. He couldn't stand to think of her in Dean's arms. In Dean's bed. In Dean's life, as his woman, as his wife.

No, he couldn't accept that. Elissa was his. He didn't question the truth of this any more than he questioned his own existence. How could she not be meant for him? She filled up the emptiness that had once comprised the greater part of his soul. She'd replaced that emptiness with substance, warmth, vigor and light. No other man would claim her. Not if he could help it. But that's where the problem came in.

If this peculiar ailment continued, he'd be little more

than a fly on the wall. Maybe he was being selfish to want her for himself.

Shaken, Jesse tuned in to their conversation, determined to hear every word. He realized they were speaking about him.

"I'll miss him," Dean was saying as he dried a bowl. "Oh, I know we didn't have much in common. But we...we looked out for each other, Jesse and I."

Guilt weighted Jesse down. Here he was, fully intending to take Elissa away from Dean, while Dean stood mourning him.

"Not that Jesse was ever an angel." Dean shook his head at some amusing memory. "I could tell you some kind of stories."

Elissa lifted a brow, her interest caught. "Oh?"

Mild displeasure shaded Dean's eyes, as if he hadn't expected, or wanted, too much response to his melancholy musing. "Nothing you'd want to hear, actually."

"No, but I would. He *was* Cody's father," she reminded him. "I'd like to know as much as I can about him, to someday share with Cody."

His thin bottom lip drew so tight it almost disappeared. "You might not want to share Jesse's antics with an impressionable child."

Jesse raised his brows. Which stories had Dean planned to tell? As he thought back, though, he couldn't think of many he'd want Cody to imitate.

"Jesse couldn't have been all that bad," countered Elissa, "or he would have ended up in jail."

"He barely missed it. If it hadn't been for the family's influence..."

"Are you talking about the girls' dormitory incident?"

"That, and others. He started on the wrong road

early. While I was at my Scout meetings, he was loitering with a gang at the corner store, shoplifting."

It was true, Jesse had to admit. The thrill of danger had appealed to him even then.

"He stole his first car when he was thirteen," Dean went on. "Hot-wired the principal's Cadillac in the school lot."

Yep, Jesse remembered. He'd parked it three miles down the road. His popularity with the wild crowd had soared. He'd wondered at the time if it was his "bad blood" that made him crave the notoriety these pranks earned him.

"His *first* car?" said Elissa, looking clearly dismayed.

For the first time since it had happened, Jesse felt a stab of regret for the crime.

"He stole others, too?"

One, thought Jesse. Just one. Another prank.

"Oh, yes. Jesse was quite good at hot-wiring cars."

Jesse frowned. Dean made it sound as if he'd made a career out of stealing cars, but then, Dean's worst infraction had been turning in a poetry project late. Jesse must have seemed pretty hard core.

"He needed more guidance," pronounced Elissa, handing Dean another sudsy salad bowl.

"Guidance? Hah! He needed a lot more than guidance."

At Dean's resentful tone, Jesse narrowed his eyes on his cousin's face. Something was wrong here. He'd never heard or even imagined Dean talking about him with such hostility.

Yet, if Dean had been in love with Elissa, which he plainly was now, he couldn't have liked the fact that Jesse had slept with her. And fathered her child.

How stupid not to have seen it earlier! He hadn't realized Dean's feelings for Elissa until now.

Why hadn't Dean staked his claim to her that very first night they'd met? Why hadn't he at least mentioned how he felt about her before Jesse left the party with her? But Jesse already knew the answer to that. Because he had wanted her so damned badly, even then, and he'd made no bones about that fact. A head-on confrontation—especially with Jesse—had never been Dean's style.

"He wasn't only a juvenile delinquent," said Dean, sneering, "he was a bully and a heartbreaker, even in high school. He terrorized the boys—the good, decent ones—and used the girls for sex...the most vulnerable girls."

Poking her tongue against her cheek, Elissa scrubbed a skillet with unnecessary force. She wished she hadn't encouraged Dean to reminisce. He'd hit her where it hurt the most...in an old but not quite healed wound. Had Jesse pursued her that last night of his leave simply because he'd sensed she was vulnerable?

A sudden chill crept into the kitchen—an odd, unnatural cold. She glanced around, searching the shadows. She saw no trace of Jesse. Unnerved by the idea of him listening to their conversation—and by the hurtful conversation itself—she murmured, "It's not uncommon for high school boys to date a lot of girls."

"Yes, but—"

"I think I've heard enough about Jesse."

Silenced by her curt interruption, Dean gaped at her.

From beside her, Jesse's deep voice rushed against her ear, "Thanks for the defense, counselor. Took you long enough to shut him up."

Elissa dropped her dishcloth and sloshed water over

the sink basin. Grasping the counter to steady herself, she turned to find no one beside her. Or rather, no one visible.

She glanced back to Dean and realized he hadn't heard Jesse. Dean stood watching her through his wire-rimmed glasses with concerned bewilderment. "I'm sorry if I offended you, Elissa. I never meant to." In a low murmur he added, "Perhaps it's best for you that Jesse's gone."

She wanted to shout that it wasn't. She wished desperately that Jesse were alive and permanently visible.

"Aren't you going to tell him I'm here?" asked the wry, disembodied voice of the man who was making her crazy.

"No!"

Dean broke off in the middle of a statement about his desire to see her with the roses back in her cheeks. "Pardon me?" he said, blinking.

"Nothing," she muttered. "I just...chipped a nail."

"Tell him to go," Jesse directed. "This is my house, and I don't want him here."

Elissa bit her tongue, afraid that she might be goaded into responding again. How would Dean react? He certainly wouldn't believe Jesse was here. He'd think she'd gone crazy. Unless, of course, Jesse started moving things around the room or slamming doors.

Anxiety hummed through her as she envisioned it. Knowing Dean, he'd call whatever authorities he felt should be notified. The so-called experts would then come to study Jesse. Some might try to exorcise him. The media would sensationalize him. Who knows what else would come of it?

One thing was certain—she would no longer have

the opportunity of staying alone with him. He'd belong to the curious. She would lose him.

"Excuse me, Dean, I'd better go check on Cody." She dried her hands, hurried from the kitchen and raced up the stairs.

She ducked into her bedroom, closed the door and turned to find Jesse standing there, solidly visible in a pair of close-fitting jeans and a dark sweater, his arms crossed and his smoke gray eyes impatient.

"You have to stop disappearing and appearing like that," she railed. "It's driving me crazy! How can I talk to Dean when you're standing a few feet away from him, invisible?"

"I agree, it poses a problem. Send him away."

"If I asked him to leave now, he'd know something was wrong and then he'd refuse to leave. What would it hurt, letting him stay one night? After all, he *is* your cousin."

"I don't care if he's my long-lost twin." His gaze arrested hers with all the urgency he felt building inside him. Gruffly, he whispered, "I want to have you alone."

Warm color touched her cheeks. Her hand fluttered to the base of her neck, where he swore he could see her heartbeat. "But I can't send Dean away tonight." Despite her words, her voice had deepened to a honeyed richness.

Jesse loved the fact that he could affect her so. But on the heels of that gratifying thought came a tormenting one: *could Dean?*

"His feelings would be hurt if I asked him to leave." Her eyes were the luminous color of candlelit burgundy. "Besides, he's worried about me. It would be better to show him that Cody and I are perfectly all right here by ourselves so he'll go home satisfied."

"Judging by those roses, I think it'll take a little more than peace of mind to 'satisfy' him."

She stared blankly at him for a moment, then slowly lowered her jaw. "Are you insinuating he brought me those roses just to—to—" She spluttered into speechlessness, then burst out, "How dare you cheapen his kindness that way! Just because *you* can't think past your zipper doesn't mean Dean can't."

Jesse wanted to grab her by the shoulders and shake some sense into her. Or maybe kiss the sense right out of her. But he couldn't touch her. He couldn't risk losing contact with her again. "Those roses mean one thing and one thing only. He can't wait to get his hands on you." *And then I'll have to kill him.*

Elissa stiffened and lifted her chin. "I've spent a lot of time with Dean in the past ten years, and he's always been kind, considerate, generous...."

"Are you telling me you haven't slept with him?"

She planted her fists on her hips and glowered. "I'm not telling you anything."

He stared at her hard and long, as if rifling through her thoughts to find an answer to his question. On a peculiarly jagged note, he finally queried, "Are you in love with him?"

She opened her mouth to tell him no, but stopped. How unfair to Dean to tell Jesse something so personal about their relationship before she explained it to Dean himself.

When she didn't answer, Jesse shut his eyes in a brief, hard wince. When he reopened them, they'd grown infinitely colder. His voice emerged as smooth and polished as a sea-washed stone. "Has he worked up enough courage yet to pop the big question?"

"He *has* asked me to marry him, if that's what you mean."

Though Jesse hadn't been moving much to begin with, he seemed to lapse into a concentrated state of immobility—as if breath itself had left his body. "And...?" he prompted.

"And what?"

"Do you plan to marry him?"

"That's none of your business."

Movement returned to him then in the form of a harsh scowl. "The hell it's not. The man you marry will live with my son, at least part of the time. You don't think I'd let you and Dean have full custody of Cody, do you?"

She retreated a step, her hand to her heart, her back to the solid oak door. "Jesse, you can't—"

"Don't be too sure about what I can or cannot do. If you marry Dean, I'll damn sure share custody of my son."

"And if I don't?" she asked faintly.

"Then, when I'm home on leave or stationed nearby, I'll keep Cody. You'd be welcome to stay with us, if you'd like. Or, to simplify matters—" his gaze intensified and his voice lowered to a rough whisper "—we can marry."

Elissa gaped at him, stunned. "You and I?"

"No, I thought we'd advertise for spouses in the personal ads. Of course, you and I."

"You'd do that, for...Cody?"

His lips tightened, his nostrils flared. "I don't see why not. I intended to change his name to Garrett, anyway."

Her bottom lip jutted out with sudden anger. "I'll marry whomever I damn well please, and I promise you this—it won't be you. I don't ask for much in a man, but I do prefer him alive!"

"Elissa?" Dean's voice intruded from the other side of the bedroom door, startling her. "Who are you talking to?"

"I'm...talking...on the phone," she improvised. "Why don't you go downstairs and make that popcorn you brought? It's almost time for your television shows."

"They've already started." He sounded petulant, just short of whiny. "I thought you'd be down there by now."

"I'll be down in a moment." She waited until his footsteps thudded down the stairs before she turned back to Jesse. "Dean doesn't deserve to be thrown out of your house like a sack of garbage. He's a good man. An honest man. A man who stood by me when *others* didn't."

Her emphasis on the word "others" furrowed Jesse's brow. "Do you mean me?"

"If the shoe fits..."

"That's the whole problem between us, isn't it, Elissa? You think I ignored your letters. I'm telling you one last time: I didn't even see them until I got back from my mission. For one thing, you used my old address. A *very* old address. I was lucky they even reached—" Jesse stopped. "Where did you get that address?"

She pursed her lips and stared, refusing to say.

"It was Dean, wasn't it." And the picture slid into clear focus. Disturbingly clear focus. Anger—and a dull sense of betrayal—flushed through him, washing away illusions built over a lifetime. As the initial surge of anger ebbed, Jesse realized another truth. He hadn't ever counted too heavily on Dean's support. He hadn't—

and didn't—believe too much in *anyone's* support of him.

He'd always known deep inside that he was alone.

"You're angry about Dean giving me your address," Elissa said. She crossed her arms and watched him with eyes that glittered accusingly. "He said you would be. Don't you dare hold it against him. I was pregnant with your child. To Dean, that was justification enough to break his promise."

"He told you I made him promise not to give you my address?" No wonder she'd been so peeved. Clever, Jesse had to admit. In one fell swoop, Dean had alienated Elissa from him *and* sabotaged their communication.

"Why didn't you want me to have your address, Jesse?" she probed, both anger and sadness in her voice. "What were you afraid I'd do with it?"

"I never told him to keep my address from you. In fact, I deliberately gave him my current one." He plied her with a searching gaze. "Why do you think he gave you an address that hasn't been good for more than eight years now?"

She blinked, taken aback, but after a moment, she shrugged. "He obviously thought that was your current address."

"He wrote the real one on the back of his hairstylist's business card and slipped it into his wallet."

That surprised her, though she refused to be swayed into doubting her knight in shining armor. "None of that matters now. If Dean has to leave this house to-night, so do I."

Anger tightened every muscle in Jesse's body. "Go ahead. But you won't take Cody. I'll make sure of that." A bluff, and he knew it. His energy level was too low now to do much of anything, or he would have already strangled Dean. In truth, he barely had enough energy to remain visible to Elissa. Fortunately, she wasn't aware of that. Another lesson he'd learned in the course of his military career—when low on weapons or men, *bluff*.

Elissa squared her jaw. "Don't threaten me, Jesse." With one last glare, she stalked out of the bedroom.

He knew then that he'd made a gross tactical error. Instead of making her see that Dean was the intruder, he had placed himself in that role. *He* was the enemy now, as far as she was concerned. She might even turn to Dean for help.

Jesse gritted his teeth. He'd been a damn fool, trying to keep her with him by force, virtually holding her baby hostage. What the hell kind of strategy was that? No better than a terrorist's.

He wanted his son, yes. And he wanted Elissa. But not under duress. He wanted her to know the truth about him and his reaction to her letters. He wanted her to stay with him of her own free will. He wanted her to want him.

How to make her believe his word against a man she'd known for ten years as a friend and maybe a lover? She'd known Jesse for days, not years, and in that brief time, he'd brought her only misery and shame.

He cursed the mission that had kept him out of touch with her, cursed his cousin for his sly deceit. Most of all, he cursed his own blind stupidity.

He clearly saw the enemy now.

Time for a forward advance. He had no weapons. He couldn't as much as lift an ashtray, let alone assert physical force. He couldn't be heard to issue challenges or ultimatums; he couldn't even be seen, except by Elissa.

Nevertheless, the battle line would have to be drawn. His cousin would have to defend his actions or pay the price for his sabotage. Elissa would have to choose *her* side of that battle line.

10

ELISSA RETURNED TO the living room, gritting her teeth. Jessie had gone too far this time, trying to pin the blame for his own neglect on Dean. If Dean had indeed given her the wrong address for Jesse, it must have been an innocent mistake.

Besides, even if her letter hadn't reached Jesse in time, Dean had spoken with him over the phone, not once, but many times before his mission began. According to Dean, Jesse hadn't wanted to speak *to* her or *about* her.

A sudden doubt permeated her anger. Was it fair to Jesse to withhold her knowledge of those calls? Should she have broken Dean's confidence and demanded that Jesse explain? He'd only deny making the calls. What else could he do?

But the niggling doubt persisted. Was Jesse a liar? *Was he?* She honestly didn't know. She wanted to believe he wasn't. But his own family had warned her repeatedly that he had ways of convincing women—especially vulnerable women—of anything. And with Jesse, she was indeed vulnerable.

He'd had the gall to ask her to marry him in order to "simplify" his visits with Cody. As if she had nothing better to do with her life than to make things convenient for him. The man's ego was nothing short of delusional.

And yet, for the briefest moment, she'd been tempted to accept his offer!

If that wasn't proof of onsetting insanity, what was?

Silently admonishing herself for allowing any man to demolish her better judgment, she settled back against the sofa cushions beside Dean. Absently, she toyed with the crossword puzzle in her lap—another of Dean's gifts, and part of a ritual they'd fallen into: television, popcorn and crossword puzzles. She stared in the direction of the television that had already mesmerized him into a stupor.

What, she wondered, would be Jesse's next step? The question made her nervous. She'd infuriated him, she knew. It was only a matter of time before he'd retaliate. Unless, of course, he faded out again.

Despite her irritation with him, worry spiraled through her. Surely he wouldn't fade away for good, just because she'd angered him?

No, she told herself, remembering the insults he'd just slung at her. He was too mean to vanish that easily. But he wouldn't hurt Cody or her, and she seriously doubted he'd hurt his own cousin. So whatever his next move might be, she'd simply ignore him.

She fiddled with her pencil above her crossword puzzle, and her thoughts returned to his flippant marriage proposal. Marriage obviously meant very little to him if he could offer it so casually. Why should that bother her so?

And why was she having such a hard time remembering that he wasn't a man, but a ghost? A ghost with no earthly future; a ghost whose marriage proposal meant nothing, regardless of his shallow motivation for making it. Sadness at that thought overwhelmed her.

Beside her, Dean, in his Mr. Rogers-style cardigan

and tassled loafers, took another huge, buttered hand-
ful from the popcorn bowl in his lap and munched in
dazed contentment. Every now and then he'd let out a
guffaw of laughter at the rerun of the "Donna Reed
Show." Next would be "Father Knows Best." His enjoy-
ment wasn't lessened at all by the fact that they'd seen
every episode many times over.

Elissa bent her attention to her crossword puzzle, determined to expunge Jesse from her mind.

"Hot date, huh?" The comment, lightly spoken, held
only a trace of wryness—but a heavy dose of resentment.

She stiffened. Jesse stood a few feet away, his booted
feet spread in a classically virile stance, his thumbs
hooked in the belt loops of his jeans, his gaze centered
on her.

After a quick glance at Dean, who was still occupied
with his television and popcorn, Elissa forced her attention back to her crossword puzzle, reminding herself
that no matter what Jesse did, she'd ignore him. She
read the first clue to the puzzle—one, across.

"I'm sorry I said that Dean had sex in mind when he
brought you those roses," said Jesse. "I apologize if
I...cheapened the gesture."

Elissa read the clue to her puzzle again, but couldn't
quite focus on its meaning. She moved on to the next.

"Guess I just didn't like the idea of another man
bringing you roses."

The print swam before her eyes. She wouldn't look at
him. She swore she wouldn't.

He ambled closer, until his legs and thighs encased in
worn denim intruded into her peripheral vision. He
leaned one hip lazily against an armchair. "But you

weren't quite right when you said I can't think past my zipper."

A dull heat crept into her cheeks, and a crushing witticism sprang to her tongue. She longed to barb him with her retort, but Dean sat fairly close beside her on the sofa.

As much as she tried to resist, Jesse's gaze drew hers—too compelling to ignore—and held her with a seriousness that took her breath away. "The truth is," he whispered gruffly, "I can't think past *you*."

Warmth pulsated through her.

"You believe that I made love to you that night, then went overseas without giving you another thought. That our lovemaking meant nothing to me." He sank down into the armchair, his knees apart, his forearms resting across them, his eyes now level with hers. "That just ain't so."

The heated sincerity in his stare blinded her to everything but him. She felt herself sinking deeper and deeper into another dimension. A dimension of emotion, of undiluted need. "What about you, Elissa?" he rasped. "How did you feel about our night together? Did it mean anything to you other than a good time?"

"Of course it did!" The low cry rushed from her lips before she could prevent it.

Dean cocked her an asking glance.

"I'm just...just trying to figure out this crossword puzzle," she uttered lamely. She needn't have worried. His attention immediately bounced back to the screen—and to the remote control he kept poised to fend off commercials.

"Tell me, Elissa," Jesse persisted, his gaze beseeching her with a dark magnetism, "what did it mean to you, that night we...found each other?"

Everything, she thought. Moisture coated her eyes. Here she was, fighting back tears and proclamations of love, after swearing to ignore him! She had to find more strength than this. She had to harden her heart. In desperation, she scribbled on the corner of her crossword puzzle, *Can't talk now*. With a sideways glance at an impervious Dean, she tipped the page to an angle for Jesse to see.

He read her message, and his gaze entwined with hers. "If our lovemaking meant anything to you, anything at all, you *will* talk now. And you'll tell Dean that I'm here."

Her lips parted in dismay. Again, she put her pencil to the page and wrote, *He might call too much attention to you*.

"I'm not afraid of Dean or anything he can do."

I am, she scribbled, underlining the words.

"Afraid that you'll lose him?"

She battled her inclination to tell him he was wrong. She wasn't afraid of losing Dean; she was afraid of losing Jesse.

"You don't love him, Elissa," he swore with a soft harshness. "If you did, you wouldn't have gone to bed with me. Not the first time, and not the second." In a scalding whisper, he added, "You might not know me, but I know you." Anguish glinted deep within his stare and touched her heart.

Why do you want Dean to know you're here? she wrote.

He read the question, and when he lifted his eyes again, the anguish had vanished, leaving only stark, gray ice. "We have things to settle, Dean and I."

His tone, his demeanor, the tense lines of his body, all communicated a threat that scared Elissa. What did he mean to do, and why? *Leave us alone, Jesse,* she wrote, hoping that by some miracle he'd listen.

When he'd read her reply, he drew in a long, quiet breath. Then he plied her with a look of utter disappointment—and an odd resignation that pierced her. "Is that what you want? *Is it?*"

Even before the question had fully registered, his presence changed. He began to fade. Before her very eyes, his image lost its vividness, and then its solidity, until it wavered like a hologram, transparent and surreal.

"Jesse!" she cried, reaching for him.

And then he was gone. Vanished.

She leaped to the armchair where he'd been sitting and groped the air, desperate to pull him back. "Oh, Jesse, Jesse, I didn't mean—"

"Elissa?" The word was a sharp admonishment as well as a question. She turned to find Dean staring at her with an astonished look. "What in heaven's name—? Had you fallen asleep? Were you dreaming?"

Perched on one knee at the edge of the armchair, she gazed at him in mute agony, a sob lodged in her throat. "No. No, I wasn't dreaming."

"You were calling Jesse."

She searched wildly around the room, hoping against hope that he might still be there. But the resignation in his gaze remained vivid in her memory. She'd made a choice, and he had honored it. The sob worked its way from her throat to her lips. All he'd asked of her was honesty—to let Dean know he was there. Could that request have had something to do with his final goal? If so, she had failed him miserably.

Coming to a decision, she returned to her place on the

sofa and faced Dean. "There's something you should know. Something I should have told you earlier."

He frowned and lifted a shoulder. "What?"

"Jesse..." Her throat closed at the mention of his name, and she struggled to clear it. After a moment, she managed to say, "Jesse has been here."

Dean's sandy-brown eyebrows scrunched together. "Of course he's been here. He lived here."

"No, I mean recently. This evening. He was...with us."

Dean barked an uncomfortable little laugh, as if she'd made a joke he didn't quite understand. With a decisive move—one that proclaimed the seriousness of the subject—he aimed the remote control and lowered the volume of the television. "Surely you don't mean that literally?"

"Yes, actually, I do. His ghost has been haunting me." As her words sank in, Dean's brows rose. Determinedly, she pressed on, "I told you about the first time I saw him—the morning of his death. He appeared again after his funeral, when I came to look at his house. And quite a few times since. That's why I'm here. To communicate with him."

He stared at her. "You mean you really believe Jesse is here," he summarized in droll amazement, "in this room with us, right now?"

"No." The word sounded bleak, even to her own ears, and she resented the relief that spread over Dean's face. "He left a few minutes ago."

"Good Lord, listen to yourself, Elissa! Babbling about ghosts and communicating with spirits!"

"I know it sounds crazy, but—"

"You're obviously going through denial." He reached out and drew her closer to him on the sofa with a gentle yet insistent arm around her. Concern shone in his pale blue eyes. "I'm sorry I didn't realize sooner how...attached...you'd grown to Jesse." His voice, though warm, resonated with a undeniable edge of bitterness. "I guess I should have seen it—your touchiness every time his name was mentioned, your certainty that he was alive."

She pulled away from the patronizing embrace. "I knew you wouldn't believe me." With forlorn hope, she called out to the room at large, "Jesse, if you're here, I could use some help."

"You could definitely use some help," muttered Dean, his stare laden with disapproval. "You have to stop this craziness, Elissa. Now, let's look at things rationally. The first time you saw his...ghost...was while your day-care charges were sleeping, wasn't it?"

"Yes." She wondered what that had to do with anything.

"So you were probably napping yourself and didn't even realize it. You just dreamed that Jesse was there."

"It wasn't like that. I walked around and talked to him. Argued with him, for heaven's sake. I've seen him a dozen times since then—spent whole days with him." Since she'd gone this far, she decided she might as well sound completely bonkers. "He has extraordinary powers now. He can appear and disappear. He can walk through walls. He even slammed a door without touching it."

The quality of Dean's stare changed—from unrelenting disbelief to what Elissa swore was uncertainty. As if her last statement held more validity than the rest.

His lips tightened to a thin white line, and his eyes narrowed. "Did Jesse, or maybe my mother, say anything to you about his...well, his talent?"

"Talent? No. What talent?"

He hesitated, as if debating the wisdom of telling. "It wasn't a normal skill. It never did anybody any good."

"What was it?" she demanded.

Looking sullen, Dean took a deep breath, rose from the sofa and paced across the living room. "When Jesse was a kid, sometimes he'd get angry and things would...well, happen. Doors would slam, things would fall off shelves."

She stared at him incredulously.

"If you've already heard about that," continued Dean, "your subconscious mind probably twisted it out of proportion and now you're having nightmares. Waking nightmares."

"You're telling me that Jesse moved things with his mind *before* he died?" The thought stirred a memory of Professor Lehmberg's theories. Something about well-trained psychic minds gaining even more power in the spiritual realm...

"Damn it, Elissa, I wish you'd never met him," swore Dean. "Jesse always meant trouble for me. I knew when he showed up at my door that I shouldn't let him near you. He always drew the attention to himself, no matter where we were. Everyone saw only Jesse." Realizing he'd gotten sidetracked, he ranted, "He was the devil's spawn, Elissa. All the girls went crazy over him. Even the boys followed him around like he was some hero. No one knew him like I did. He took real pleasure in hurting people...especially me."

Resentment stirred in Elissa. In the past when Dean had told her negative things about Jesse, she'd taken it as a friend's warning against a heartbreaker. Now his words seemed only malicious. "I don't believe that Jesse would intentionally hurt anyone."

Dean glared at her as if she'd gone mad. "And I don't believe your blind defense of him! I'd have thought that you, of all people, could see past his muscular physique and handsome mug to the real person. He's the by-product of a rape. And from things I've heard, he's a chip off the old block. He himself wasn't above forcing a girl now and then."

"You must have been misinformed about that." Her voice shook, but she managed to keep it level. "One thing I know for sure is that Jesse's no rapist. Both times I was with him, he made a point to stop and ask my per-mission, even when I was on the brink of...of..." she halted, appalled at what she'd been about to tell Dean.

"On the brink of what?" The curious prodding came not from Dean, but from the very air around her. And the voice, the deep, vibrant voice, was the one she'd been longing to hear.

Awash in relief that he'd returned—and embarrass-ment at what he'd heard her say—Elissa felt color heat its way up her neck to the very roots of her hair. "Never mind. That's not important now." And with unfocused eyes, she spoke to the vibrant air, "But I finally under-stand what is." She directed her gaze back to Dean, who obviously hadn't heard Jesse's remark. "Just rest as-sured that Jesse Garrett is far from being a rapist."

Dean's thin lips twisted. "Did you say, *both* times you were with him? When could you possibly have been with him a second time? Unless we're counting a post-mortem visit."

Her warm color refused to recede. "I'm sorry, Dean, but that's none of your business." The question proba-bly wouldn't have bothered her so much if Jesse hadn't been listening to every word. "Jesse, if you'll just make your presence known, this confrontation will go much smoother."

Can't. The reply was too quiet to be called a whisper. It was more of a thought that shimmered through her mind.

Dean stared at her in horror. "Do you really believe that you're conversing with Jesse now?"

"No, I wouldn't call it conversing. It seems he needs more rest to build up his energy to a sufficient level."

"Rest? He needs more rest? For God's sake, he's dead! How much more rest can he get?"

Tired of Dean's negativity, she spouted, "Dead is as dead does!"

Burying his head in his hands, Dean sank down onto the sofa. "You're cracking up, Elissa. Cracking up over Jesse." When he lifted his head, his eyes were shiny with tears. "He's not worth it, I'm telling you! Don't you remember what he did to you? He screwed you, then took off, without even answering your letters." The air around them suddenly chilled, deeply and dramatically. Elissa felt it and shivered, but Dean was too caught up in his distress to notice. "You should have heard him when he called me from those brothels in Asia."

Brothels? The word exploded in her mind like a tossed hand grenade.

She bit her lip in consternation. "Are you sure he was calling from brothels?"

"Hell, yes. He told me!" insisted Dean. "I heard the women giggling in the background. You didn't really think that a stud like Jesse would go for even a few days without having himself serviced, did you?"

Again, a silent reply ripped through her: *Self-service only, that whole damned year. While I was thinking about you.* Elissa could virtually hear the growl in Jesse's voice; see the anger in his eyes, invisible though he was. Her blood warmed to him.

"You must have misinterpreted the situation," she said to Dean. "He was probably calling from a restaurant or bar."

I made no calls to Dean.

Elissa froze. No calls? He'd made no calls? But how could that be? Surely Dean wouldn't have lied...would he? Jumped to false conclusions, yes, but not lied.

"I told you what Jesse said when I mentioned your pregnancy," reminded Dean, a brutal edge to voice. "He laughed. Then he said, 'Just because I play a game of pool doesn't mean I want to lug the pool table around with me.'"

The plunge in temperature this time was too severe to be ignored by even the angriest man. Dean shivered, looked around and rubbed his arms. "It's getting cold in here," he muttered. "Damned cold."

Elissa was more mindful of a tension in the air, an odd, watchful tension, as if Jesse were waiting. Wondering whose side she would believe...

She gazed keenly at Dean, who was now chafing his hands to warm them. Could he have told her such destructive lies at a time when she'd been in desperate emotional need?

"Dean," she said quietly, "that address you gave me for Jesse. Where did you get it?"

His gaze jerked back to hers. "Where did I get it? From my address book. Jesse's mother gave me that address."

Wrapping her arms around herself to fight off the bitter cold and the trembling that had taken hold of her, she asked, "Jesse didn't give you an address? A more recent one?"

Dean frowned. His neck and face slowly turned an unbecoming red. "No." The word sounded suspiciously tentative. "I guess he just didn't think of it. He knows I'm not one for writing letters."

"May I see your wallet?"

"My wallet?" He blinked. "Whatever for?"

"Humor me, Dean."

"But I don't understand why—" He grabbed for his back pocket, too late. His wallet had slipped through his hand and fluttered to the floor. With a start, he stared down at it in disbelief.

Elissa knelt and picked up the wallet that had fallen open on the Persian carpet. She gathered the folded money and business cards that had rained out.

Dean stuttered, "H-h-how did...how did that..."

"Jesse obviously wants me to see it." Her voice had grown cool and curt. She took no pity on Dean despite the little-boy look of bewilderment on his stunned face.

"You did that, didn't you?" he whispered. "You have the same psychic power as Jesse. I never knew you could do that. I don't think you should. I hated it when he made things move...hated it...."

Elissa ignored his flustered rambling. One by one, she flicked through his business cards until she found his hairstylist's—Pierre's House of Beauty. With a heaviness already weighing down her heart, she turned the card over. She knew full well what she'd find.

"An army base in Asia." She raised demanding eyes to him. "Whose address is this, Dean? It's not the one you gave me for Jesse."

"I...I forgot all about that address. It was so early in the morning when he wrote it."

"You lied to me." Her faint voice shook with sad, incredulous discovery.

"Lied to you? I didn't lie to you!"

"Things might have been so different for Jesse and me."

"Damn it, Elissa, he wasn't good enough for you."

"I should have been the one to judge that."

"I was protecting you! I love you. Jesse never did."

"At least he never lied to me."

"You only met him once."

"And you meant to keep it that way, didn't you."

With a curse, Dean grabbed her by the shoulders and dragged her to him. "I know what you're missing," he fumed, "and it's not Jesse." Twining his arms forcibly around her, he panted, "He's not the only one who can give it to you."

Startled, she wrenched away from his desperate attempts to kiss her and shoved at his chest. He staggered backward with much more force than her push had warranted. In fact, he crashed against the end table and flipped over it, as if a huge, angry man had slung him there.

As if.

Stunned, Dean pulled himself to his feet, too outraged to question the strength of her shove. "It's my turn, Elissa," he ranted, beating at his thin chest with one fist. His face and neck had turned a blotchy red and sweat trickled from his forehead. "It's way past time for my turn. I was good to you. I was willing to marry you even after your scandal. I was ready to take in Jesse's bastard!"

Elissa gasped as the razor-sharp hurt of betrayal sliced through her. He was talking about Cody, her baby, with a malice that shocked her.

"You like it this way, don't you?" he spat, advancing

with a resentful gleam in his eyes. "Rough and dirty must be your style—or you wouldn't have jumped into the sack with Jesse. I knew you for years, Elissa. Years! Jesse was a damn stranger. So why the hell did you go to bed with him, but not with me? How could Jesse's touch turn you into a—"

He never got the chance to finish. He was jerked up by the throat—as evidenced by choking noises and a gaping mouth—and slammed backward against the stairwell wall so hard that pictures jumped and crashed to the floor.

Dean hung there choking, pinned to the wall with his tassled loafers kicking uselessly above the floor. Doors all over the house slammed, lights flickered and a wintry wind blustered around the living room.

The vase of roses Dean had brought her leaped from the mantel and shattered, strewing the flowers across the hearth. The popcorn bowl flipped off the sofa and sprayed kernels into the wind, which howled like a pack of banshees.

"Stop it, Jesse!" cried Elissa, her hair whipping furiously around her as popcorn bounced off the walls and flower petals fluttered before her eyes. "Just stop it this instant!"

The commotion kept on. Books fell off shelves, vertical blinds clanged together, and Dean's head banged violently against the wall as he choked to a ghastly purple.

Elissa crossed her arms, lifted her chin and tapped her slippered foot. "Go ahead, Jesse. Kill him. But if you do, I won't speak to you."

It took a moment, but the chaos gradually lessened. First the wind died down, then the lights stopped flickering. Doors quit banging; books stopped leaping from their shelves. And finally Dean was lowered to the floor.

He collapsed there, gulping for breath and trembling. Wild-eyed, he gazed around the room. "It *is* you, isn't it, Jesse," he squeaked when he finally regained his voice. "Even death couldn't keep you in your place."

A gold letter opener rose up off the cluttered floor, launched across the living room and stuck in the wall beside his head, vibrating with an audible *twang*.

Dean whimpered and cowered away from the daggerlike weapon. "There's no reason for you to be mad, Jesse. You should be grateful. Grateful!" He took a moment to swallow as he inched his way along the wall toward the front door. "You told me to watch out for Elissa until you got back. That's all I'm doing—watching out for her. Who else is going to take care of her now that you're dead?"

The coat-closet door opened and slammed with eloquent fury. Elissa winced.

"Stop deluding yourself, Dean," she said. "I've been the one taking care of *you*." With cool arrogance, she then sauntered closer, the frigidity of the room matching the state of her heart. "I thought you were a friend," she said. "You hurt me. Deeply. But I thank God for that. Because now you'll never get the opportunity to hurt my son the way you and your pompous family hurt Jesse." Clasping her trembling hands behind her, she nodded toward the door. "Now, you'd better get the hell out of here...before I let Jesse decapitate you."

With a grateful sob, Dean scrambled to his feet and loped toward the foyer. As he neared it, he either performed a remarkable leap in a uniquely arched position, or an invisible foot connected with his backside and booted him out the door.

11

"SHHH, IT'S OKAY, CODY. Everything's okay." Elissa hugged the wailing baby fiercely to her. The noise of banging doors and shattering glass undoubtedly had woken him. Cuddling him against her shoulder, she rocked and hummed and pressed her cheek against his sleep-warmed head, savoring his baby scent.

She loved him so much. Why hadn't she seen the danger she'd almost subjected him to? If she'd married Dean, Cody would have grown up with the same steady diet of poison that Jesse had been fed as a child. For all his caring ways, Dean had resented Cody with a spite that shocked her. He'd called him "Jesse's bastard."

Pain shot through her—not for herself, but for her sweet, innocent son; that anyone would scorn him, devalue him as a person, before his personality had even formed, before he had a chance to develop a defense against the hatefulness.

How had Jesse prevailed against such malice, aimed at him from birth? She thought back to his funeral and his aunt's viciousness, his mother's lack of grief. The pain in her intensified—this time for Jesse. "Oh, God, Jesse, hadn't your own mother defended you against the family's spite?"

My mother's not to blame. The quick, silent reply came

to her as clearly as spoken words. Elissa glanced around the darkened bedroom, but saw no one.

"Not to blame?" she repeated in a pained whisper. "How could any mother *not* defend her child against hatred? How could she let them say you were born from bad seed, with bad blood...."

"She didn't understand any of that." This time, the words were spoken aloud, quietly, from the direction of the doorway. "As an adult, I came to realize that."

"What do you mean, she didn't understand?" Elissa continued to search the shadows, desperate for the sight of him.

"She had a severe case of scarlet fever as a child. She'd been exceptionally bright before that, from what I gathered. A writer, a poet. But the fever...well..." Sadness hung heavy in the darkness. "She believed whatever my aunt told her."

Elissa wanted to enfold him in the same kind of hug she now held Cody in. She sensed within his spirit a raw, gaping wound, and wanted so much to heal it. Through a tightened throat, she asked, "Then how did you turn out so good?"

Silence answered her—and Jesse materialized in the shadows near the foot of the crib, a stunned look in his cloud gray eyes. Wariness gradually crept into his stare, as if he was waiting for the inevitable put-down....

She realized then that she had wronged him far worse than Dean and his family. She'd fallen in love with him, given him a son, and still refused to see the honor in him.

He had asked Dean to watch out for her until he returned from his overseas duty. All he'd received in return had been her brief, cold letters notifying him of their baby—and demanding he relinquish his parental rights. Even so, he had provided for Cody and her in his will. Death itself hadn't stopped him from coming to see them, trying to resolve the conflict she had created. She'd sent him away even then, her mind set against him by gossip. Why had she allowed herself to be so swayed? Why hadn't she listened to her own heart?

She listened to it now. "You *are* good, Jesse," she swore fervently. "I'd want no other father for my child."

Silence hummed between them. And Jesse's image grew bright—intensely so, as if some electrical surge had increased his energy tenfold. But too soon, the brightness faded. His image wavered, and he disappeared into the bedroom shadows.

Elissa's throat constricted with torturous self-blame. Her blindfold had been ripped away too late.

She hugged her baby, who slept soundly in her arms. She needed the comfort of his warmth, his closeness. Jesse's blood ran through his veins, and though she'd always loved her son beyond limitation, his parentage now filled her with a bittersweet pride and tenderness.

Cody squirmed in her arms; she'd been holding him too tightly. She bent over the crib to lower him into it.

A low whisper tore from the shadows, "No, bring him."

She lifted her eyes and saw no one. "Bring him—?"

"In here."

A baby blanket rose from the crib, clutched by invisible hands. She followed it out into the corridor, down the hall and into the master bedroom. The blanket wafted down onto a pallet of large floor pillows that had been arranged in front of the bedroom hearth. As she stood watching from the doorway, a spark flared in the fireplace, and a flame burst from the kindling. Behind an antique fire screen, a small fire soon crackled and danced.

"Come here, Elissa." The quiet invitation drew her attention to the floor pillows where Jesse reclined, solidly visible in the golden firelight, leaning on one elbow beside the outspread baby blanket. "Lay him down here."

Slowly she approached, breathing in the redolence of polished hardwood flooring, firewood and Jesse's subtle aftershave. Folding her jeans-clad legs beneath her, she sat on the pillows and nestled her baby on the blanket beside his father. A potent contentment soon replaced the chill that had seeped into her bones.

Feeling unaccountably breathless as she watched Jesse gaze down at his slumbering son, she managed to whisper, "It's good to see you, Jesse." The cliché took on a whole new meaning. He smiled slightly in acknowledgment and she breathed easier. She'd been so afraid of never making him smile again.

"It would be good to touch you," he said.

Longing rushed through her as their gazes locked. She wanted his touch. She wanted to be in his arms, to assuage the ache in her soul with the awesome power of his lovemaking. "We can't," she whispered.

"We will." He made no move to touch her.

Unable to contain her guilt a moment longer, she said, "I'm sorry, Jesse. I wronged you so badly."

"I'd rather be wronged by you than loved by anyone else."

Though her heart swelled with fierce love for him, she wouldn't be distracted from her apology. "I doubted every word you said. I believed Dean without question. When I think of the mistake I might have made, allowing him to act as a father to Cody!" She shuddered. "There's no telling the psychological damage he would have inflicted. How could I have been so blind?" A possibility, a likelihood, then struck her. "Is that why you came back, Jesse? To show me Dean's true nature?"

"I'd like to say it was, but I'd be lying. Dean had me fooled, too. I thought we were family."

Although his expression hadn't changed, her sympathy went out to him. She'd forgotten that he, too, had suffered a betrayal, perhaps worse than hers.

"I came back for you." His voice softened with a sensual gruffness. "Dean was wrong when he said I never loved you. I did. From our very first conversation."

Her lips parted in surprise. "Our first conversation? But I...I didn't say much." She'd been awed by him that entire evening—by his masculine beauty, yes, but more by the raw, sensual power that had drawn her irresistibly to him.

"You might not have said much in words." His stare warmed her with its heat. "But we didn't need words then. I think we do now. I love you, Elissa. Marry me."

Emotion lifted her heart, then twisted it painfully. She was elated that he loved her; astonished that he could, after her hateful distrust. And she was agonized that their love could never be. She wanted to say yes, to spend the rest of her life with him, to disregard the fact that he was visible only to her, and then only at certain times. But she knew better than to hope that a future together was even a remote possibility. He belonged elsewhere.

"Don't answer me," he said curtly, "until there's not a doubt left in you."

Tears slowly filled her eyes. She had never loved him more. "Jesse, it's not a question of doubting love—mine or yours. We can't possibly marry. You have no future in this world. You died in that plane crash. You should be headed toward your...destiny."

Annoyance flickered across his rugged face. "Let's not start with that nonsense again."

"I wish it were nonsense, but it's not. You're dead." Seeing that she was getting nowhere with this tactic, she asked, "When you experienced those blackouts, did you see anything you didn't quite understand?"

"Like what?"

She didn't want to tell him. She didn't want him to leave her. But what choice did she have? "In the near-death experiences that have been recorded, most have one thing in common—a tunnel that the spirit seems to travel through. There's a light at the end of that tunnel. A parapsychologist told me that earthbound spirits should be directed toward that light. Have you...seen it?"

"No, I haven't seen any damn tunnel or any damn light." He paused, then slanted her a considering look, as if hesitating to confide in her. After a moment he murmured, "I do remember something about the downed flight, though. You know, the plane crash that...*killed* me."

She winced at the sarcasm and chose to ignore it. "What do you remember?"

"I remember the plane taking a dive and panic breaking out among the men. Then earsplitting noise and smoke and pain. It seemed to go on forever."

"Oh, Jesse!"

"And then there's snatches of other memories that I can't quite put together. Blurred faces, babbled voices. I thought I heard the word *dakrah*."

"*Dakrah?*" she repeated, mystified.

"It's a word I learned on an undercover mission two years ago, when I worked in an Asian village. We needed information about a terrorist, and I was the only one who spoke the language well enough to get by."

"What does the word mean?"

A muscle moved in his jaw. "It means dying." After a grim moment of reflection, he shrugged. "But then I also remember hearing Colonel Atkinson, shortly after that."

"Colonel Atkinson?"

"Yeah." With a half frown, half smile, Jesse shook his head. "The colonel said, 'I'll eat green grits for you, son.'"

"Green grits!"

"It's a private joke between us. Has to do with a Saint Patrick's Day we spent here in Savannah. He could take the green beer—plenty of it—but not the green grits."

"Oh, Jesse, it sounds like you were dreaming. Delirious, probably." *On your deathbed.*

His stare seemed to probe her thoughts. "You really think I'm dead, don't you. What the hell can I do to prove I'm not?" He reached for her, and she drew away.

"Don't risk touching me, Jesse! I'm afraid that if you do, you'll disappear again, before we even have a chance to—" She broke off midsentence.

He wasn't listening. He had drawn back his hand and now frowned down at it as he examined his little finger.

"Is something wrong with your hand?" She resisted the urge to take it in her own to better see it. She couldn't touch him. She dared not endanger whatever life force he had left. "Does it hurt?"

"No, it doesn't hurt, but—" He balled up his fist, then

slowly released it, watching his little finger. "My finger's been giving me trouble. It's numb."

"What do you mean, numb? Like, pins and needles?"

"Like, no feeling in it at all."

His explanation sent a shard of fear through her. Professor Lehmberg had theorized, *"Maybe he'll simply cease to exist."* Elissa's panic flared. No. She couldn't bear to believe it. "Maybe you hurt your finger when you were choking Dean."

"I did that with my mind, not my hand."

"Oh. Well, maybe you jammed your finger when you fell off my bed the other morning."

"No, I remember it bugging me before that...when I changed your flat tire."

"Could it be from punching those men in that roadside fight?"

"I hit 'em with my right hand, not my left."

A dark foreboding gripped her. Would he gradually lose *all* feeling? "Oh, Jesse, please listen to me! It's starting to happen, just like Dr. Lehmberg warned it might. This is serious, *real* serious."

"My finger?" He let out a brief laugh. "Over the last fifteen years, I've been shot more times than I care to remember, holed up in deserts and jungles for months on end, chained in foreign prisons with electrodes attached to my—" he stopped. His lips tightened. "Let's just say that I'm not going to die over a numb pinkie."

Stunned by his casual revelations, Elissa wanted to take him in her arms and blot out those painful memories with good, loving ones. But it was too late for that.

"Jesse, that numb pinkie might be just the start. The longer you stay trapped from your destiny, the more you'll suffer. Please open your mind to the possibility that I'm right."

The passionate concern in those brown eyes almost made Jesse forgive her for not saying that she loved him. Almost, but not quite. He wouldn't let her get away without saying it. "If someone told you that you were dead, would you believe 'em?"

"No," she admitted, "but that's an entirely different matter. I'm not invisible!" Expelling a harried breath, she raked loose, sable dark waves from her face and smoothed them behind one ear. "Humor me, then, Jesse," she implored in the low, smoky voice that always stirred him to thoughts of lovemaking. "There's obviously some goal you haven't attained, some need left unfulfilled that's very important to you. Think what it might be."

Only one came to mind. *He had to make her his.* He had to make Elissa Sinclair love him as he loved her—eternally, unconditionally, and at any cost.

But of course, he also had a whole lifetime of other, less compelling business that he fully intended to handle. He damned sure wasn't dead. If he were, he'd be the first to admit it.

"Can't you think of anything?" she prompted. "Any goal that you feel passionate about achieving?"

"Just one." Straining to resist the powerful urge to pull her into his arms, he whispered, "I would defy death itself for a lifetime of loving you."

Her stare—her passionate, caring stare—darkened with a curious emotion, the last one he expected to see there. Alarm. "Me?" she breathed. "I'm keeping you here?" With an almost inaudible sob, she wrenched her gaze away from his, gathered up the sleeping infant and stumbled toward the door.

"Elissa!" he called.

But she didn't stop. She didn't even glance back. The

door to her room across the hall shut. The lock clicked into place.

Astonished by her reaction, Jesse stared off in the direction she had fled. He had opened his heart to her, as he had with no one else in his life. And she had refused him. Locked her door against him.

Why? How could the need, the desire, the love that consumed him be completely one-sided? And what, Jesse wondered, made her think that a mere locked door would keep him out?

He rose to follow her, but the weariness set in. It felt deeper and more debilitating than ever.

SHE HAD INTENDED TO GO—to pack her bags, bundle Cody up in his blankets and drive far, far away from here. But common sense prevailed before she'd packed a single bag. She couldn't outrun Jesse. He had appeared at her house, at an isolated roadside spot, in a hotel room and near the river. He had accompanied her into town; he had spirited Cody away to his backyard garden. Where could she possibly go that Jesse couldn't follow?

Even now, she kept glancing around the bedroom, waiting for him to appear. Oddly enough, he did not.

With a sense of impending doom, she gave up her plan to leave, changed into her nightgown and slipped beneath the bedcovers, her misery roiling within her. *She* was the one keeping Jesse trapped in this mortal world. Her love for him, her need to be with him, had obviously spanned the miles—and the boundaries of life and death—to hold him back from that final trek to the other side.

Even if she hadn't actually summoned him away from the beckoning light, she had given him reason to stay with her. She'd laughed with him, cried over him, made love to him. She'd given him a son. Dangerous things to do with a man like Jesse. He was simply too strong-willed to let a good thing pass. And their love *was* a good thing, the very best thing that she'd ever found in her life. Or rather, it could have been…if only he were still alive.

But he was not. And it wasn't only Jesse denying that fact. She herself had not accepted it. Even now, as she lay agonizing in his guest room, knowing that her love was destroying him, she wanted to hold him again. She wanted to love him.

She had to fight that love. She had to deny its very existence, even to herself. Only then did she have a chance of saving Jesse, of motivating him to leave.

Hardening her resolve to send him away if he should appear, Elissa lay on her side, her hand tucked beneath her cheek on the pillow, her eyes resolutely closed. She had to sleep. She would need her wits about her tomorrow. First thing in the morning, she'd pack her bags and leave for home. If Jesse followed, she'd make him wish he hadn't.

A clock downstairs chimed twelve, a lone dog howled somewhere in the distance, and the big old house creaked around her. Slowly, Elissa drifted into slumber.

It was sometime later, hours, maybe, when movement in the bed disrupted her sleep, and her eyes fluttered open.

"Don't open your eyes." The whisper rushed across her ear from behind, and she became aware of a warm, male body against her back. She knew instantly who it was, and before her mind could censure her response, her heart rejoiced.

"Close your eyes, Elissa," he commanded softly. His hand brushed down over her eyelids and forced them closed. "You wouldn't be able to see me right now, and I'd rather not end up on the floor." His wry comment reminded her of the fright she'd suffered earlier in the week, finding him invisible in her bed. "It seems that if I don't waste energy on trying to appear," he explained, "I can...touch you."

She realized with a little shock that it was true—he was touching her. Yet she felt no hellish force prying them apart, no psychic current running through them.

His hand drifted away from her eyes, which remained obediently closed, and he pulled her closer, his arm around her waist. "I'd give up visibility forever if it's the only way I can hold you."

Longing coursed through her as his solid, muscular form cradled her, their bodies fitting spoonlike. Sensuality bloomed within her, its roots reaching deep and low.

"Jesse," she implored, struggling to resist its sweet lure, "I'm leaving tomorrow."

"Why?" Though no more than a drawn-out whisper, the word resounded with disappointment, frustration, opposition.

"To get help. Professional help. I...I don't know how to deal with a...a ghost." She felt his body tense—as if from a physical blow—and she had to force herself to continue. "I'm going to hire a channeler, or whatever kind of psychic might be able to guide you to the 'other side.'"

He cursed softly and thoroughly. The bed creaked, and with an abrupt movement, he rolled her onto her back. From the proximity of his voice and the way his breath fanned her cheek, she knew he had braced himself above her. She kept her eyes closed. She didn't want to replace the comforting image she held in her mind's eye with the frightening reality—an angry, invisible Jesse.

"Damn it, Elissa," he swore, "I'm not a ghost."

"Then why can't I open my eyes?"

"Go ahead and open them. But I don't have the energy to appear. Not if I want to touch you. And I do want to touch you," he added on a gruff whisper.

"If you're not a ghost, then there's only one thing you could be." She steeled herself against the inevitable pain. "You must be a figment of my imagination. A fantasy conjured up by grief. In which case—" she choked out the words, holding back tears "—I'd better see a grief counselor, or maybe a shrink."

A sharply indrawn breath told her the words had hit him hard. After a tense moment, heat tingled over her; the dry, unnatural heat powered by his anger. Ever so softly, he scoffed, "A figment of your imagination, am I?"

"You must be."

His muscles shifted with sudden purpose, and before she knew what he was doing, he'd leaped from the bed and scooped her up into his arms. She cried out, her eyes flew open, and sheer darkness spun alarmingly around her. She shut her eyes and clung to the warm, muscular neck, shoulders and chest that she wasn't able to see.

"I'm taking you to my bed," he uttered hoarsely, "where you belong."

"I don't belong there," she said with an anguished sob.

"I want to remember you there, anyway."

In a few long strides, he'd crossed the hall and

reached his bedroom. Above her riotous heartbeats she heard the crackle of the fire in the hearth, felt its gentle warmth. When Jesse halted, she peeked down to see the bedcovers of his huge pine bed peel magically back from the pillows.

She closed her eyes again as she tumbled down onto the mattress. Jesse swiftly joined her there, his bare, iron-strong legs, arms and torso sliding over hers, trapping her neatly beneath him.

"Get off me," she demanded between clenched teeth, struggling to free herself from his sleekly muscled body.

"Are you talking to me?" he asked in a ragged whisper, his breath warm against her mouth and chin. "Or to yourself?"

She understood then. He intended to force her into acknowledging that he was certainly more than a product of her mind. "Maybe I *am* talking to myself," she retorted. "I must be delusional—wrestling with a man who isn't even here." To prove her point, she defiantly opened her eyes.

But he *was* there, heart-stoppingly real—all human, all male, and furious as a thundercloud. His silver-hot gaze fused with hers, and traitorous joy sparked in her heart. She'd wanted so much to see him, to hold him....

"If I'm just your imagination, Elissa," he whispered as he lowered his dark, glowering face, "then let your imagination run wild."

His mouth accosted hers then with persuasive insistence—laving, tasting and probing until the kiss slanted and flowed. Caught up in the sensuous revelry, she kissed him back with a vengeance. If this was madness, then mad she wanted to be.

His muscles hardened in immediate response and

erotic heat flared between them. His fingers worked at the buttons of her nightgown, then tugged at the interfering fabric until he had stripped it completely off of her. He then drew her against him with another kiss, this one deeper and slower.

Elissa lost herself in the feel of his skin pressing against hers, the smooth brawn of his muscles bunching beneath her palms, the exquisite heat of his mouth as it glided in a swirling path to her throat, to her breasts.

He worked his way steadily downward. She wove her fingers through his silky hair as he kissed her in provocative, lingering ways that made her tremble.

With his hands hard and controlling, he captured her mobile hips and laid siege. Every advance heightened her sublime sensitivity, until involuntary shuddering set in.

And then he stopped. Withdrew his mouth, his hands.

"Jesse," she breathed, "what are you—?"

He started again—a strategic attack, using every weapon in his arsenal this time. She gasped as his hardness probed, entered and slowly inched into her. The pleasure steadily compounded and grew acute. Too soon, he retreated.

Through a swelter of need, she cried in a tortured whisper, "Don't you dare stop!" Then with a breathless sob, she moaned, "You're driving me crazy...."

His body lunged across hers and he caught her hands above her head, pinning them against the mattress. With his gaze dark and determined, he thundered, "Who's driving you crazy, Elissa? *Who?*"

She knew she could distract him with moves of her own—moves that would drive all rational thought right out of his head. She saw the barely leashed desire straining behind the purpose in his steel gray eyes.

But that purpose stopped her. He wanted her to admit that he was real, and here, and loving her. That was one admission she couldn't make. She had to send him away before her love destroyed him.

Surly and hoarse, he demanded, "Who?"

She squared her jaw. "No one."

"No one?"

"No one."

His bottom lip curled, his hands tightened on her wrists. And slowly, intently, he rocked forward. His male hardness pushed in, completely in, filling her to capacity.

Pleasure radiated to every fiber of her being; pleasure, and the love she struggled to hide. He gave another smooth, hard thrust, his gaze locked intently on hers. She couldn't stop her body from meeting his thrusts, couldn't stop her gaze from dancing with his.

He released her wrists, braced himself on his knees, and deepened the penetration. His rhythm quickened, his urgency grew, until each gliding thrust lifted her hips off the bed.

"I want more from you," he growled, "and you know it."

She loved him too much to give it.

With a groan of desperation, he lowered his fevered body to hers, his hardness still throbbing inside her. His fingers slipped into her hair, his thumbs rested beside her mouth. "Believe in me, Elissa," he begged. And he kissed her with a deep, aching need.

She melted into his all-consuming kiss, undone by his ragged plea. Their arms coiled tightly around each other, their legs intertwined, and their bodies writhed in slow, sensual opposition.

Later, when the tremors of aftershock had subsided, Jesse whispered into her ear, "You love me, Elissa. I feel it."

She did love him, so much it hurt. So much that she couldn't fathom losing him. And though she felt as if she were ripping her own heart out, she whispered, "No, Jesse." The acute pain of those two words almost defeated her, but she had to persevere, for the sake of his very existence. She choked out the blackest lie of her entire life. "Whatever it is you think you feel, well—" she even managed a shrug "—it's just your imagination."

Suffocating bleakness overtook her as she disengaged herself from his embrace and edged away until she no longer touched him. She fully expected him to reach for her, to pull her back.

He did not.

She felt as though she'd never sleep again. But soon enough, a drugging slumber blotted out her anguish.

A similar lassitude overtook Jesse—similar in its narcotic effect, yet very different. Different also from the numbing weariness that had so often attacked him these past few weeks. This sleep submerged him into a pulsating darkness, then plunged him headlong into some vacuumlike abyss. He tried to fight it, but found he hadn't the energy—or the reason—to resist.

She had wanted him to leave her. The pain of that realization sapped his strength way more than anything so far. To find her, then to lose her, even as he held her in his arms and loved her with all his heart...

The pain grew into a live, gnawing force. The darkness hummed as he sped through it, hummed with an inhuman wailing. Gradually the wailing turned into a dull babble of voices. Though incoherent, they seemed to be calling to him, not by name, but unmistakably beckoning in tone. He strained against a blinding wind to see. Vague forms hovered around in the murky distance.

Why had Elissa turned him away? Had they been right, all those monsters of his youth, lurking in every darkness, taunting him with the likelihood that no one could ever love him? He hadn't known then exactly what he'd been missing. He hadn't known until she'd shown him.

The pain intensified.

The darkness narrowed, tunnellike.

He looked for it. He looked for the light.

12

SHE SHOT UP IN BED with a violent start, her heart thundering. She had to hurry. *Hurry.*

In panic, she gazed around until she recognized her surroundings—Jesse's bedroom. The sun hadn't yet begun to filter through the morning darkness. The terrible urgency pumping through her veins had to have been caused by a nightmare.

Weakly, she leaned against the pillows. She couldn't remember the dream. And though she knew that there was no reason to leap from the bed and scramble into her clothes, the urgency continued to drum in her heart. *Hurry. Hurry.* But to where, to do what?

With a trembling hand, she turned on the bedside lamp. The fire in the hearth had dwindled to ashes and chill bumps had risen across her skin. Her nightgown lay on the floor, and only a linen sheet covered her. The soreness of her muscles, the swollen feel of her lips, and the musky male scent of Jesse that clung to her skin brought back vivid memories of last night. Jesse, though, was gone.

She stared at the indentation in the pillow where his head had rested. She was alone, she knew. He wouldn't reappear, or whisper to her from thin air, or even watch her from some mystical vantage point. He had finally left her.

She should be glad that he had gone, that she had

sent him in the right direction. Instead, she felt only an aching sense of loss...and this peculiar urgency.

It had to be a reaction to his departure. How *would* she face the prospect of living her entire life without love, without passion, without laughter? Without Jesse? She certainly couldn't face that prospect right now. The pain of it nearly doubled her over.

She gave in to tears—silent, anguished tears—for the man she had sent away. For the bleak, empty future she faced without him. After a while, when she'd cried herself out, she realized the urgent feeling that had awoken her remained. As if someone essential to her was in mortal danger.

Unnerved, she hurried from the bed to Jesse's closet and, looking for a robe, rifled through his shirts, pants and military uniforms. The sight of his clothes pierced her with fresh anguish, but she couldn't wallow in her grief. She had to figure out what was causing this odd rush of adrenaline.

At last she found a bathrobe, shrugged into it and padded across the hall to peer down into Cody's crib. The baby lay peacefully sleeping. So why did she still feel this sense of impending disaster? As she slipped her feet into her bedroom slippers, a shrill ringing split the silence. The doorbell this early?

The emergency had come to her doorstep! She took the steps two at a time, flicked on the light in the foyer and unlocked the door, bracing herself for whatever awaited her.

Her parents stood in the predawn darkness.

"Mom, Dad!" she exclaimed.

They peered at her with worried eyes, their mouths straight and grim as she ushered them inside. Her mother's auburn hair hadn't been curled, and her lips hadn't been polished their usual frosted pink. "Are you okay, honey?" she asked Elissa with perplexing concern.

"Me? Of course I'm okay. What's this all about?"

Her parents exchanged an anxious glance, and her lanky, silver-haired father said, "Dean stopped by."

She stared at them in dismay. He must have gone straight from here to their house. What had he told them? She turned away from their probing eyes and led them out of the foyer. "What did he tell you?"

Her mother watched her anxiously. "He said you think you're being...haunted."

Her lips tightened with anger at Dean. She hadn't expected such a low blow. "Dean and I had a disagreement, and I asked him to leave. But other than that, everything's perfectly—" Her assurance broke off as she flicked on a wall switch that illuminated the living room.

The place resembled a war zone. Shattered glass glinted in the debris that littered the Persian carpet and flagstone floor—books, vases, paintings, model ships, sculptures, rose petals, popcorn. Every lamp in the room had been smashed; every picture yanked off its moorings. Her parents gaped at the wreckage in stunned silence. She searched her mind for an explanation, but couldn't think of one.

At a little shriek from her mother, Elissa swung around to see her pointing at the gold letter opener buried a good inch in the wall where Jesse had barely missed Dean's head last night. "Dean told us about that," whispered her mother, aghast. "Oh, Elissa, you could have killed him!"

"I didn't throw that at Dean!"

"Then, who did?" countered her father.

She took refuge in righteous indignation. "I appreciate your concern, but I'm perfectly capable of dealing with my own problems. Dean and I are having difficulties—in fact, we parted ways—but he shouldn't have come to you."

"Your difficulties become my business when they involve your mental health," exploded her father, "and the safety of my grandson." The mention of Cody's safety filled Elissa with new foreboding. Her father continued, "When I get a visit in the middle of the night from a young man who looks like he's been mugged, and he tells me my daughter flew into a rage and attacked him because she thinks she's possessed by the ghost of that no-account drifter who—"

"Don't call Jesse that," she admonished him sharply. "He's the father of my child and deserves your respect."

Her father stared at her incredulously. "Was Dean right, then? You think you're possessed by his...his ghost?"

"Of course not." Her throat closed, and she worked furiously to open it. She wished she could simply tell them the truth, but that would be tantamount to locking herself away in a padded cell. "I do feel a connection with Jesse," she admitted, "emotional more than spiritual. I mentioned that to Dean, and he obviously took it too literally."

"Is that Jesse's robe you're wearing?" asked her father.

She glanced down at the oversized robe and felt her embarrassment rise. "I didn't have time to find my own."

"Staying in his house, wearing his clothes..." Her father looked white, drawn and older than when he'd walked in. "I had no idea," he murmured more to himself than to her.

Anxiety curled like sharp talons in her stomach. "I'm okay, Dad. I swear."

"Of course you are. You're a bright, fine girl." His eyes welled up with sudden shininess. "This Jesse just got under your skin, that's all. You weren't used to men like him. You were too sheltered. You should have dated more."

"I'm going to call the doctor," said her mother in a voice that warbled with unshed tears. "We'll take her to Peachtree Hospital, Walter." She addressed her husband as if Elissa weren't present. "It's one of the best private hospitals in Georgia. She'll get good help there...."

"I'm not going to a hospital, Mom." She couldn't possibly waste that much time when this bewildering sense of urgency beat through her with an even greater force than before. *Hurry. Hurry.* But what crisis called out to her?

"It's for your own good, Elissa," insisted her father. "And for Cody's. We'll take care of him until you're home."

"You'd rather believe I'm crazy than doubt Dean's word?" She tried to forget that she herself had believed him implicitly until Jesse had shown her better.

"Not crazy!" reproved her mother, visibly appalled. "Just...emotionally overwrought. Professional help might ease you through the worst of it, honey. And there's no need to blame Dean. He only confirmed our fears. You haven't been yourself since you met Jesse. Going to bed with him when you didn't even know him. Swearing he was with you after he'd died. Leaving your home and business on an impulse. And now, look!" Her mother lifted her hands in a gesture that encompassed the ravaged living room. Pain glazed her eyes as they met Elissa's. "Can't you see that we have to get some help for you? We can't take the chance of you hurting yourself, honey. Or hurting others."

Elissa's anger gradually seeped out of her, like air from a deflating balloon. They were doing what they truly felt was best for Cody and her. Realizing she'd get nowhere arguing, she swallowed her pride. "Okay. I'll see a doctor."

"At Peachtree Hospital," her father pressed. "Today."

AT LEAST HER PARENTS allowed her to take a shower before she left. Most of her luggage would be loaded into their car by now. Cody, whom she had woken and fed, would be freshly diapered and dressed.

"Emotionally overwrought," they'd called her. She couldn't argue with that. She wasn't even sure she could argue if they'd called her "crazy." If she hadn't gone at least a little nuts, why was every beat of her heart reverberating with warnings of disaster?

She leaned her forehead against the glass door of the shower stall and let the water beat against her. *Jesse, oh, Jesse, I need you.* But she couldn't allow herself to think that. What if her own panic somehow drew him back again from his ultimate destiny?

Have you found your way to the other side, Jesse? Are you happy and safe now? The only answer she received was an increase in the panic she barely held at bay.

Believe in me, Elissa, he had begged her last night. He had wanted her to believe he wasn't dead, that they could have a future together. But she'd have to discount the evidence of her own eyes, her own senses, to believe him.

Her heart whispered, *You were wrong before.*

She had to acknowledge the truth of that. She had come to believe Jesse before only because of cold, hard proof—the business card on which he'd written his address for Dean. Would she ever have believed him— that he hadn't received his mail in time and hadn't deliberately ignored her pregnancy—if she hadn't seen that black-and-white evidence?

She blanched at the mistake she'd almost made in trusting Dean...and remembered the lesson it had taught her: *Listen to your heart.*

But her heart wanted her to believe that Jesse wasn't dead. Which was, of course, preposterous. Wasn't it? An odd, shivery heat crept beneath her skin. At one time, she had considered the existence of ghosts to be preposterous.

As she lathered shampoo into her hair, she thought back to every occurrence, every conversation she'd had with Jesse. She'd reached the conclusion early on that he was a ghost, and assumed he had to be dead. But what if she'd been wrong?

Again the compelling sense of urgency pulsated through her, stronger now than ever. And she saw her own words and actions of the past few days in an entirely different light.

Oh, God, she thought with a plummeting heart, *what if I was wrong?*

FULLY DRESSED AND PACKED, she flipped through the cards in her wallet to be sure she had the ones she would need: credit cards, identification, passport. With an anxious glance at the locked bedroom door, she then dialed the number of a travel agency on her cellular phone. Little had Dean known that his gift would provide her with a separate line to the outside world when she needed it most.

"Let's go, Elissa," called her father from outside the bedroom door. "We have a long drive. Dr. Harrison will be waiting for us at the hospital."

"I'm almost ready, Dad."

His footsteps thudded down the stairs. A travel agent answered the phone. In a hushed voice, Elissa inquired about flights to the army base in Asia where Jesse had been stationed. It would take two connecting flights, she was told, and a bus trip to the base. By the time she had mapped out her route, another knock pounded at her door.

"Are you talking to someone?" called her mother. Elissa, however, was in the middle of reading her credit card number to secure a flight. Hushed panic entered her mother's voice. "Walter, I think she's talking to herself in there. Does she think she's with that ghost?"

Breaking her connection, Elissa hurried to open the door. "Calm down, Mom. I'm on the phone."

Her mother gazed at her with both sheepishness and relief. Slipping the cellular phone into her purse, Elissa kissed her mother's pale cheek, scooped up her overnight bag and descended the stairs. "Are you sure you don't mind taking care of Cody?"

Two steps behind her, her mother replied, "Of course we don't mind. We love keeping Cody."

"We'll bring him to visit you," promised her father. She kissed his cheek as she passed him in the foyer. "I'm sure you won't be away from home long," he said reassuringly.

She forced a weak smile, palmed the car keys she had

slipped into her pocket and strode directly out of the door. As she passed her parents' car, she saw Cody in his car seat. She longed to kiss him goodbye, but knew she couldn't risk it. Her parents were convinced she needed to be saved from herself, and they'd stop at nothing to protect her. Tough love, she'd heard it called—although this time, their toughness was somewhat misguided.

Hadn't she practiced "tough love" on Jesse, sending him away for his own good? Had she been similarly misguided?

"Wait a minute, honey, we're taking my car," her father called from the porch as she headed for her own vehicle.

"We'd only have to come back for mine," she said as she slipped in behind the wheel.

Her father hurried to the driver's window, which she obligingly rolled down. "I'd prefer that you ride with me, Elissa. It's not safe for you to drive right now."

She started up the engine. "I'm fine, Dad. And there's something I have to do before I go to the hospital."

"Elissa!" He gripped the window's edge and walked along as she slowly pulled forward.

Her parents' car blocked her from behind; she'd have to drive onto the grass to reach the road....

"Stop this car right now," her father shouted.

"I'm sorry, but I can't." She caught his gaze and held it. "Trust me, Dad. Please. You always have before. Don't stop when I need your faith the most." Swallowing a tightness in her throat, she cut the wheel and drove onto the grass. Her father let go of the window's edge and stared at her. "I'll call you," she promised.

"Elissa!" cried her mother from the porch, "if you

don't come with us right now, we'll...we'll start court proceedings. We'll take custody of Cody!"

She slowed her car as she turned onto the paved road. They'd take Cody from her? It was a mother's fear talking...fear for her daughter, for her grandson. Would she actually carry out the threat? If her parents were truly convinced that she posed a danger, she knew they would.

How could she risk losing her baby? She'd already lost her reputation, her career as a counselor, and Jesse, the love of her life. Now she stood to lose Cody, too.

But how could she not follow up on every lead that might take her to Jesse? She wasn't sure how, where or *if* she'd find him, but this compelling urgency pushed her to look for him—she now felt sure of that much.

If by some miracle she found him, her parents would have to acknowledge that she was acting on more than an insane impulse. Once they realized she wasn't crazy, they'd happily return Cody to her.

But what if she was wrong? What if this sudden need to investigate Jesse's death was nothing more than desperately wishful thinking? Her parents then would have even more grounds to believe she'd lost her mind. "She flew to Asia to look for a dead soldier," they'd tell the psychiatrists. By that time, they'd have found corroborating testimony from others. Like Suzanne, Jesse's housekeeper, who could say, "She thought she was talking to Jesse, but I didn't see anyone." And Dean, who would launch into his lie about how she'd attacked him with the letter opener....

She brought her car to a halt a few yards down the road. Should she go? Should she stay? Her soul cried out for guidance.

Believe in me, Elissa, Jesse had begged. *Believe in me.*

Uttering a silent prayer for forgiveness in the event that she was wrong, Elissa clenched her jaw, shifted into gear and pressed the gas pedal steadily to the floor.

13

HE WASN'T GOING TO HELP her. She'd come all this way—twenty hours in the air, a mad dash to make connections, exhausted sleep in cramped seats and an endless bus ride with chattering locals and their livestock—only to have Colonel Atkinson stare at her from beneath his woolly, copper-colored brows and mutter, "No sense wasting your time and ours, Ms. Sinclair. Captain Garrett is dead."

Elissa leaned forward in a chair beside the colonel's desk. "All I'm asking is to see where the plane went down."

He frowned, his gaze direct, impersonal and alive with an intelligence that had undoubtedly earned him his rank. He was a bear of a man—broad and commanding—and his gruff voice sounded like a growl. "It's a jungle out there. Dangerous. Just what do you hope to find?"

"I'm not sure. I—" She shut her eyes briefly, gathered her courage and countered with a question. "Exactly how much of Jesse's remains were actually found?"

The colonel's lips thinned with impatience. He clearly considered her question a waste of his time. "The plane crashed into a mountainside, Ms. Sinclair. I don't like to be crude, but everyone in that plane was blown to bits. The biggest body part we found was a hip connected to a thigh."

She suspected he was being deliberately shocking. Forcing her into comprehension. She repeated her question with forced composure, "How much of his body was found?"

"I'd have to check with forensics, and even then, I—"

"Please, Colonel. You have to admit that Jesse wasn't like most people. He moved objects with his thoughts and bent metal with his mind. You know he did that, don't you?"

"Well, yes, but—"

"Then, why is it so hard to believe that he contacted me telepathically?"

His frown took on a different quality—a reflective one. "You still think he appeared to you?"

"I *know* he did. He said he heard people talking after the plane crashed. Maybe someone found him and took him in." Something else Jesse had told her surfaced in her memory, but she hesitated to mention it. It may have meant nothing; a figment of delirium. Telling it now might weaken her credibility even more. Then again, Jesse had considered it important enough to relate to her. "There was something else he said, although it didn't make much sense to me."

"What was it?"

"After the plane crash, he heard *you* talking to him."

"Me? Impossible. I was here the entire time."

"He thought you said, 'I'll eat green grits for you.'"

All color drained from the colonel's face. He couldn't have looked more stunned if Jesse himself had appeared. Slowly he turned away and opened his bottom desk drawer.

Elissa's eyes widened as he drew out a gun.

"See this, Ms. Sinclair?" he mumbled, examining the weapon. "This gun won't fire. It's workings are jammed." He glanced up at her. "Jesse was a tough young private when I first heard about his so-called 'powers.' I called him over to me during target practice and told him he was full of bull. He saluted me and said, 'Yes, sir.' I told him to quit the magic shows—this wasn't a kid's party and he wasn't a clown." A brief smile bent the colonel's mouth. "The longer I kept at him, the warmer the gun grew in my hand, until it nearly branded me. I had to drop it." Incredulity glimmered in his eyes even now. "When it cooled enough for me to shoot it, the damned thing was jammed. Permanently."

"Excuse me, Colonel," said Elissa, distracted by the urgency she'd held at bay these last twenty-some hours, "but what does all this have to do with the color of grits?"

He let out a laugh. "Not a damn thing. But it does have to do with the power of Jesse's mind. When I heard about the plane crash, I took out this gun and thought about him. About the good times we'd had, and a bet I'd lost to him over a football game. The payoff was that I'd eat green grits, Savannah-style, every Saint Patrick's Day." His voice grew hoarse. "I said those words out loud after he'd died, Ms. Sinclair. I promised I'd eat green grits for him."

After a solemn moment, he returned the gun to his drawer, picked up the phone and uttered instructions involving forensic files. A while later, he set down the receiver. "There wasn't much of his body found—only one part. But we were able to make a positive identification."

Elissa's heartbeats slowed. "Which part was it?"

"His finger."

"Which finger?"

"Ms. Sinclair, this morbid preoccupation with—"

"Was it his small one? His...pinkie?"

"Why, yes," he replied in surprise. "It was."

She pressed her lips together to stifle a cry. His pinkie finger—the only part of his body in which he'd lost feeling. "Don't you see, Colonel? All that proves is that he lost his finger. The rest of him might still be alive."

"I'd say that's rather a long shot." But he picked up the phone, anyway...to arrange for a vehicle and a driver.

THE SITE OF THE PLANE crash was a whole day's drive from the base. Colonel Atkinson himself accompanied Elissa, along with a driver who spoke the language well enough to translate. They drove on rutted roads canopied by dense, tropical vegetation, questioning ragged farmers and their families who toiled beneath the hot Asian sun, most wearing large straw hats and working in fields, some clustered around thatched-roofed huts. The colonel showed a picture of Jesse he'd taken from his files, and each time, Elissa prayed for a spark of recognition. That spark never came.

Near evening, they checked into a hotel, which necessitated another long drive. The colonel promised they'd continue tomorrow.

Early the next day they set out in determined silence. Elissa's urgency had progressed to full-blown obsession. If not for the colonel's insistence, she would have foregone eating and sleeping. Again, their quest proved fruitless.

"I'm sorry, Ms. Sinclair," he said as they returned to the hotel that second night. "We've covered every village near the crash site. An injured man couldn't have wandered any farther." His voice cracked with disappointment. "I can't justify the time or expense of another day's search."

Exhausted, frustrated, yet driven by a relentless need, Elissa spent half the night pacing in her hotel room. "Jesse," she whispered aloud, "am I wrong to be searching for you? Have you moved on to your ever-after?" She waited in the darkness, yearning for a response that didn't come.

But as she fell wearily into bed, she remembered something else he had told her. The people he'd heard talking after the crash had used the word *dakrah*. He'd said it meant "dying." "*It's a word I learned on an undercover mission two years ago, when I worked in an Asian village.*"

Could the term be unique to that area—a localism? She hadn't mentioned it to the colonel because it hadn't seemed important. But what if it could pinpoint a region?

She approached the colonel the next morning. He hadn't heard the word *dakrah* before, and neither had his driver. "We have to find out where they use that word," she insisted.

"Ms. Sinclair," the colonel said with a deep weariness, "just because Jesse heard those people talking after the crash doesn't mean that they were physically with him. He heard me, and I was hundreds of miles away. It was probably another psychic thing...."

"He learned that word when he was on an undercover mission in an Asian village two years ago. You'd know where he worked then, wouldn't you?"

"Even if I did, I wouldn't be at liberty to tell you."

"Is it anywhere near the crash site?"

He raised his eyes to the ceiling as if praying for the patience to deal with her. "Do you understand the meaning of undercover, Ms. Sinclair? Covert? Top secret, maybe?"

"If you won't help me, Colonel, I'll contact the embassy, universities, language experts, investigative reporters—*anyone* who could help me pinpoint where the word *dakrah* is used. Then I'll hire a guide to take me there."

"You'll get yourself killed," he growled, his neck turning a dull red, "and compromise security in the process."

"I'll try my best not to."

He stared hard at her for a long while. "You never say die, do you."

"I did once," she whispered through a tightened throat. "I won't make that mistake again."

Later that day, Colonel Atkinson checked Jesse's files and located the village where he'd worked undercover two years ago. It lay just beyond where they had searched.

He then ordered a background check on one Elissa Sinclair. When it came back clean, he reached a decision that ran contrary to his usual prudence—mostly because he knew this particular woman would make his job a living hell if he didn't. He took her to that village.

"This place has been a hotbed of military unrest for the past decade," he warned as their jeep made its way down the muddy road of the village with its thatched huts and sloping farms surrounded by wooded mountain peaks. "Soldiers of any kind won't be welcomed here."

Not a comforting thought, reflected Elissa, considering they were riding in a military vehicle driven by a fully armed, uniformed soldier in the presence of his commanding officer.

"If Jesse isn't here—and I seriously doubt he is," he muttered, "these people won't know that he was a U.S. soldier. He worked here posing as a civilian volunteer. It would be damaging to our cause and dangerous for any current or future deployments to advertise the fact that we planted a spy here. We're not going to flash his picture around. The only one I have shows him in uniform. We're simply going to ask the villagers if they know anything about an injured American. We'll say your husband is missing, and that the embassy sent me to help you look for him. One thing is very important, Elissa. Let me do all the talking."

She nodded, her hope riding high in her throat. The driver stopped to begin his questioning, and she noticed the villagers' reluctance to approach. She heard him use the word *dakrah*, and they nodded in apparent understanding. Then they shook their heads and backed away.

"But he has to be here," she said, her hands balled into tight fists in her lap. "He has to be."

They stopped at each hut along the winding mud road. Villagers trailed them, watching with suspicious eyes. No one, it seemed, had seen or heard about a man found injured.

But as the afternoon grew late and the driver questioned the family at the last home in the village, Elissa gave in to desperation. Shouldering her way past the driver, she begged the ragged farmer, "Please, *please* try to remember if you've heard anything about an injured stranger. He's tall, with dark hair. His little finger is missing." She held up her hand and waggled her pinkie finger.

From the blank gazes of the farmer and his family, she knew her pleading was useless—they probably didn't understand a word—but she couldn't bring herself to stop. "He was hurt in an accident. He might be dying. *Dakrah...*"

"They can't help us," the colonel interrupted, coming up behind her and taking her arm. "Let's go, Elissa."

Stricken, she stared at him as if he'd condemned her to death. In a way, he had. He was taking away all hope....

"Ay-lees-a?" echoed an elderly woman from the family hovering behind the farmer. "You...Ay-lees-a?"

Startled, she replied, "Yes, I'm Elissa."

The woman's mouth opened wider, and her wrinkled hand came up to cover it. She then whispered something fast and fierce to a younger woman. The farmer muttered in angry disapproval, and a muted argument broke out among them.

Elissa exchanged a puzzled glance with the colonel and his driver. Why should her name cause bickering?

The elderly woman finally broke away from the huddle, and despite the farmer's tight-lipped glare, she ventured closer, her graying head held high. There was no mistaking her for anything other than the matriarch of the family. "You stay," she ordered. "GIs go."

The farmer uttered some oath and threw his hands up. The colonel barked, "What? We can't leave her here!"

The driver snorted a contemptuous, "No can do."

Elissa spoke only to the old woman, whose eyes were fixed on hers. "Do you know something about an injured man?"

"No." She shook her head and pointed toward the road that led down the mountain. "GIs go. You stay."

After a bewildered moment, Elissa turned to the colonel. "Please do as she asks."

"I can't leave you here! Who knows why she wants you to stay?" Quietly, he muttered, "Some folks have mighty odd customs. You might end up married to one of her grandsons."

"Or held hostage," warned the driver beneath his breath.

"I'll stay. Or—" she deliberated "—I could always return later, on my own...."

Tight-lipped with disapproval that matched the farmer's, the colonel handed her a radio. "If I don't hear from you within one hour, we'll be back to find you."

"Thank you." A sheen of gratitude blurred her vision.

He shook his head. "Never thought I'd say this to any woman, but you're a damned good match for Jesse." Brushing past the driver, he climbed into the jeep. The soldier reluctantly slid behind the wheel.

The small mob of villagers, who had been watching from a distance, gazed in stony silence at the military vehicle as it drove down the muddy road. The moment the jeep was out of sight, the old woman snatched the radio from Elissa. "Me keep." Tucking it into the folds of her long, loose dress, she hobbled across the grass onto the muddy road.

Swallowing her trepidation, Elissa followed.

The hike down the narrow path that wound through dense, tropical growth was not a long one, but altogether unnerving as she dodged a snake-laden limb, crashed through spiderwebs and listened to the hum, buzz and hiss of unseen wildlife.

When they reached their destination, she gaped in astonishment at a huge, two-story stone house. A spaceship wouldn't have surprised her more in this primitive village.

A convent, she deduced, or maybe a mission. Two slim nuns in white stood talking near the front door, and another worked in the garden. Elissa's elderly guide approached the nuns and spoke in low tones while gesturing toward Elissa.

A stern-faced nun addressed her in halting English. Elissa recognized her accent as French. The nun didn't smile; her look was more distrustful than even the villagers'. "Your name?"

"Elissa Sinclair."

"You come with soldiers, *oui*?"

Remembering the colonel's warning about this region's chronic military upheavals, she firmly asserted, "They're only helping me search for my...my husband."

"Your husband?" She glanced down at Elissa's left hand, which bore no ring. "This husband...he is not a soldier?"

Remembering the colonel's fear of blowing Jesse's cover, Elissa floundered. If Jesse was here, would they know he was a soldier? He would have been wearing a uniform—wouldn't he? Could it have been burnt or torn beyond recognition...?

The nun's thin brows rose. "It seems you do not know. Maybe you can tell me his name?"

Again Elissa stared, nonplussed. Would they know his real name—or the one he'd used when he worked undercover? The colonel hadn't told her the name Jesse'd used; he hadn't wanted her to know it, or to speak to these people at all. He hadn't felt comfortable "compromising security" any more than was strictly necessary.

"I...I call him Jesse," she finally answered.

"We have no 'Jesse' in our hospital," she stated. "No

strangers here at all. You and your soldiers can go away."

Disappointment, awful in its power, racked Elissa with piercing pain. "No, please, wait!" she cried. "You might know him by another name. I'm not sure what, but... He's tall and dark, and he's missing a finger." *She couldn't leave this place without him.* Digging wildly in her purse like the madwoman she'd become, she yanked out her wallet and fumbled through the pictures until she came to one of Cody. "Look, sister, look! Do you see this chin? Jesse has the same chin! Yes, and his eyes—they look very much like these—not the color, but the shape. And his nose...you might recognize that nose...." She looked up from the photo with a soul-deep desperation. Like a victim sinking in quicksand, she glanced at each woman around her, from face to unreadable face in a speechless plea. If he wasn't here...if she couldn't find him...if she never saw him again...

Something in the nun's gaze lost its granite edge. "Come inside, *madame*," she murmured, "out of this heat."

Amazed that her body could respond when her mind and heart whirled in the throes of agony, Elissa allowed herself to be guided into the side entrance of the stone house and through its cool, dim interior. Vaguely, she was aware of other nuns, other people, but she couldn't focus on them.

"One of our patients," said the nun in a conversational tone as she led the way down a corridor that smelled of illness and antiseptic, "is a man who worked in our village. A good man, who helped us save lives."

She stopped outside a door and rested her hand on its knob. "In monsoon rains he went out into jungle alone to find a lost child. He sucked poison from snakebite in an old man's leg. He gave his own blood to save a dying baby. We would never turn him over to soldiers, *madame*. Never." The passion in her voice left no doubt about her devotion. "Our boys found him wandering. I do not know how he managed to walk. He is badly hurt." As she pushed open the door, her gaze bore solemnly into Elissa's. "By the time they brought him to us, he was unconscious. He will not wake." Softly, she added, "But in his sleep, *madame*, he calls your name."

Trancelike, Elissa approached the bed, which was wired with life support tubing and monitors. There lay a man, obviously comatose, his face heavily bearded and scabbed, his body and head swathed in bandages.

Jesse.

"You think you have found him," whispered the nun, her voice choked with sorrow. "His body is here, yes. But his soul, I think, is not."

14

SHE COULDN'T SPEAK, not even a whisper, so tightly clenched was every muscle in her throat. Nor could she cry; her emotions ran too deep for tears.

But she could touch him—at long last she could touch him—and that realization almost undid her. She lay trembling fingers against the only smooth, uninjured skin on his face—along his protruding cheekbone, just above the gaunt hollow darkened by his overgrown beard. As her fingertips rested there, a fierce love washed through her...and a profound, unearthly awe.

She'd only touched this man once before. A year ago.

These large, dark hands that lay bandaged at his sides had not stirred her to feverish passion in these past couple of weeks. These wide, pale lips had not kissed her into sweet delirium. These eyes, now closed, had not glinted with seductive intent as he'd whispered to her beside his bedroom hearth. These arms had not crushed her against him.

No, all the while she'd been falling deeper in love with him at his brick cottage on Isle of Hope, this man had been lying here, still as death, thousands of miles away.

"Oh, God, Jesse," she whispered through an aching throat, "you reached out to me and I...I..." The ache grew too sharp to continue. She had done much worse than merely turn him away—she'd deliberately urged him on toward death.

Her tears began then—bitter, recriminating tears—and sobs that violently shook her. She lay her face against his chest and cried with every ounce of energy left in her—cried for the mistakes she had made, for the time she had wasted, for the love she had withheld.

She had told him she didn't love him.

"I'm so sorry, Jesse. If only I'd believed you."

"Don't cry," soothed the nun, stroking her hair. "You cannot blame yourself. There was nothing you could have done. We tried everything."

But in her heart, she believed she could have made a difference...or else why would he have reached out for her in such a powerful, compelling way? She had wanted to know his goal, his unresolved business. He had tried to tell her—it was life itself.

"Come, have some tea," urged the nun, "and maybe something to eat. You are much too pale."

Elissa wouldn't go; wouldn't move from his side, not for a minute. What was it the colonel had said to her? *You never say die, do you.* Lifting her head, she gazed at Jesse's deathly pale face and swore not to say it now. There had to be a way to bring him back. She would move heaven and earth, if need be. "I have to call the colonel," she said. "He'll bring doctors, medicine, equipment...."

"No, no, you must not tell the soldiers!" cried the nun.

Elissa frowned, uncomprehending.

"When our boys found him, he was wearing a soldier's uniform, or what was left of it. We do not know why. If he is American soldier, there are those here who would kill him. If he is not, the American army might kill him as spy!" The nun shook her head. "You must not tell the soldiers he is here. It could mean death for him—and much trouble for us."

Elissa covered the nun's hand with her own. "There will be no trouble from the soldiers, I promise. Colonel Atkinson is a good man. We can trust him."

"But it will do no good, asking for more doctors and medicine. The doctor who works here with us studied at your American universities. He said we cannot move him. His condition has worsened in these last few days. We called a priest to his side, *madame*. Your husband...he is dying."

"Find the woman who has the radio," instructed Elissa. "If I don't call the colonel or he doesn't find me, there will be much more trouble for this village... believe me."

With a sharp intake of breath, the nun paled, nodded and hurried off to find the radio.

HE WAS NO LONGER speeding through the long, dark tunnel. He now drifted weightlessly, barely moving at all. He'd lost all sense of time, or maybe time had simply lost its meaning. The drifting calmed him, lulled him. Lessened the pain...

The darkness began to flicker into colors, shapes, sounds. Like a three-dimensional movie, forms took shape. His mother, his aunt, his family. Scenes played out. His life, he realized, every moment, thought and emotion. Hurtful ones, mostly, in his early life. Loneliness, anger, shame.

As he grew, his defenses toughened, and even those emotions lost strength. He lived life on its surface. Never deep, except when he faced danger and adrenaline pumped him full of emotion. Only then did he truly feel. There was plenty of danger to keep him going, mission after mission.

And then suddenly, there she was—*Elissa*. Like a dam bursting, emotions gushed in fierce, unstoppable currents—warm, deep emotions—flooding every corner of his soul. Elissa. He'd had to leave her for another mission. His last mission. A hellish one made more so because he had tasted a richness he now craved.

The pace of his remembering slowed, and he saw himself boarding the plane for home. The premonition of death had been riding in his gut and now sharpened as he stepped on board. He read Elissa's letters, longed to see her and the son they'd made. Then the pilot's voice came over the intercom, talking about engine trouble. The plane rolled, angled into a dive. Panic broke out among the men.

But then the aircraft leveled out. The pilot announced that the problem had been fixed. "Relax, boys. You're on your way home." The men cheered and joked with giddy relief.

Jesse knew better. They had to leave the plane or they'd die. He strode down the aisle to the cockpit and informed the pilot of the danger. He couldn't pinpoint the problem, though; he couldn't explain. The pilot muttered bland assurances and strained to see through thickening fog.

Jesse went back to the men, his sense of impending disaster throbbing. "Prepare to jump."

They stared at him in disbelief.

"But we're going home, sir."

"The danger's over."

"No need to jump now, sir."

He reworded his terse command into a direct order. As the men exchanged stunned glances, he prepared his own gear and moved to the emergency exit.

"B-but that might be hostile territory below, sir," stammered a young soldier.

"We'll head north," he told him. "I have contacts...."

"But we're headed home, sir," said another.

They weren't responding to his order.

"You always said you wouldn't expect us to do anything you wouldn't do, sir."

"Yeah—you go first."

He felt the danger nearing. Angry, determined, he opened the hatch and shouted for them to obey. The plane took another roll, lurching him forward. He felt himself falling, falling. He yanked his cord, his chute burst open, and he was jerked upward by the billowing canvas. An explosion thundered above him. Pain struck like a poisonous spear. His hand...his hand had been hit by the debris.... And then a pain jolted through his head. Images jumbled. He tried hard to hold on to the survival skills that had kept him alive for the last fifteen years—he had to shrug free of his gear, trek to familiar ground—but darkness pressed in on him. Darkness that grew ever deeper...

"Jesse!"

Was that Elissa's voice? It spiraled through him with a glowing, visceral warmth. But it couldn't be her. She hadn't wanted him. Hadn't loved him enough. She'd sent him toward his death....

The colors and shapes faded into a dim, solitary point. Gradually, though, it brightened and grew...this time into a brilliant white beacon. Irresistibly, it drew him.

COLONEL ATKINSON SPENT the evening with Elissa by Jesse's bedside, uttering profuse apologies for not having believed her sooner, praising her courage for sticking by her convictions. "You did it, Elissa. You found him, and now I'll make damn sure he gets the best care that money and rank can buy. We've got the finest specialists in the world standing by. We'll airlift him out of here in the morning."

Elissa nearly cried with gratitude. The colonel believed there was hope...virtually *promised* that Jesse would pull through. For the first time since she'd found him, sweet hope buoyed her up. She fell asleep in a chair beside his bed, holding tightly on to that optimism.

A shrill ringing startled her awake—an alarm on some monitor—and a young nun shouted into the intercom in rapidfire French.

"What is it?" cried Elissa, stumbling half dazed from the chair. "What's happened?" It didn't take medical training to soon understand—the monitor at Jesse's bedside had ceased graphing its rhythmic peaks and valleys...and now hummed, showing a steady, flat line. His heart had ceased to beat.

Elissa stared in numb, horrified disbelief. How could this be? The colonel was going to airlift him out of here this morning...he'd get the very best of help....

The room burst into activity—nuns, nurses and doctors swarmed around, yelling instructions to one another, pushing her aside as they clustered around Jesse. In a haze of shock, she realized they were administering emergency treatment, trying to jolt his heart into action. She heard counting, buzzing, banging and occasional muffled sobs.

Then all of it stopped...and there was only weeping.

All but one doctor had backed away from the bed, Elissa realized. "It's no good," someone whispered, "he's gone."

Gone.

She somehow found her way to Jesse's side. Everyone, everything, faded from view but the man lying so still before her. "Don't do this, Jesse." The voice she heard was her own—quiet, but steady. "Come away from that light. Come away from it, do you hear? I was wrong to send you toward it. It's not time for you to die. Come back to me!"

Hands clutched at her, tried to pull her away. She shrugged them off, reached for Jesse's face, held it between her palms. "We could have a life together. A good life. You and Cody and I. You can raise him, be his father. He needs you. Cody needs you, Jesse!"

She gazed down hard at him, willing him to respond. Her desperation turned into anger. "You told me you'd defy death itself for a lifetime of loving me. If you meant it, Jesse, do it now," she ordered, her teeth clenching. "Do it!"

"*Madame*, he cannot," murmured a sad voice from behind her. "You must let him go."

"Did you lie to me, then, Jesse?" she cried, ignoring the nun's somber words. "Did you lie to me, damn you?" In her mind's eye, she saw him frowning. But not the slightest movement disturbed his face.

As suddenly as it came, her anger left her. She swept her hand into his hair, and her voice broke. "No, you didn't lie. You never have. You never would." Anguish welled up to choke her. "Please, Jesse, please," she said, sobbing. "Come back to me. I need you. I love you. I love you!"

Although the liquid heat in her eyes blinded her, she saw him quite clearly with her heart. As the distant hum of a monitor broke up into slow but distinct beeps, a harsh wheezing sound erupted from the bed. *An indrawn breath.*

And Jesse opened his eyes.

Epilogue

IT HAD BEEN A DAY of surprises. A month of them, actually, Jesse reflected, as he lathered soap across his chest and let the steamy, pulsating shower beat against his deeply scarred back and shoulders.

He still hadn't gotten over the shock of waking in that hospital to find Elissa at his side, swearing that she loved him. Some things are just too good to take in all at once; he planned to savor *that* surprise for a long while to come.

When he had realized the lengths she'd gone to and the danger she'd faced—grateful though he was that she found him—he damn near kicked the colonel's butt for letting her. The only thing that stopped him, other than his deep respect for the man and his rank, was the fact that he knew how hell-bent stubborn the woman could be. The colonel might make his Special Force commandos quake in their boots, but he hadn't really stood a chance against Elissa Sinclair.

Or rather, Elissa Sinclair Garrett. A fission of warmth, pride and something too profound to define spiraled through Jesse. She was his now.

He'd married her before they'd even left the hospital, though the marriage so far had been in name only. It had taken weeks of full-time therapy in the finest Georgia hospital to get back the full, fluent use of his body. His mental faculties, however, according to the astonished doctors, remained as sharp as if he hadn't lost consciousness at all during his month-long coma.

Jesse smiled. As far as comas went, his had been a relatively pleasant one. Damned pleasant.

And if the doctors wondered at his quick recuperation, it was only because they hadn't gazed into Elissa's eyes to see what awaited him there. They hadn't suffered the temptation of her kisses...the sweet, intoxicating ones that made him push himself harder than his therapists recommended. He ached for more than her gazes, for more than her soul-stirring kisses. He wanted to possess her, his wife, entirely.

He would do so tonight.

They'd be alone—without nurses, therapists, doctors or well-meaning friends—for the first time since he'd woken from the coma. He'd made sure of that by booking a suite in an out-of-the-way Savannah hotel where no one would find them.

Not an easy task when the colonel had invited soldiers from all corners of the globe to surprise him with a reception today. Men he hadn't seen in years showed up, embarrassing him with stories of how he'd saved their lives or rescued them from danger. As if they hadn't all done their part at some time or another to keep *his* butt alive.

But Elissa had taken in all their nonsense, glowing up at him as if he were some hero.

Her parents had been there, too, listening to the tributes. Her mother, with eyes very much like Elissa's, cried and hugged him. Her father made a toast, welcomed him to his family and called him his son. Warm, unfamiliar sensations had crowded Jesse's chest.

His own mother had been at the reception, although he doubted she heard the speeches. She'd been silently daydreaming in the chair beside him. At one point, though, she had noticed his dress uniform with all its ribbons and medals—the uniform Colonel Atkinson insisted he wear—and whispered, "You look like your father. He had a uniform, too. Air force, I think." Sadly, she added, "He was killed in the war, you know."

Jesse had stared at her, astonished. She'd never spoken about his father before. Even more surprising was the fond, reminiscent look on her face. "You kept in touch with him?" he asked, disbelieving.

"He wrote me letters. Asked for pictures of you."

A sneak attack by a stealth bomber wouldn't have surprised him more. "But I thought... Hadn't he... hadn't he hurt you?" Another first—Jesse had never asked her about the rape his aunt had so often mentioned.

His mother's forehead wrinkled and her eyes glazed with confusion, as if she weren't quite sure what he meant.

Gently, he persisted, "Didn't he force you to...to *do* something you hadn't wanted to do?"

"Oh, no." Her childlike blue eyes widened. "Robert would never make me do anything I didn't want. He was always nice to me."

Jesse frowned. "He didn't rape you?"

She blinked, still looking confused. "Muriel said he did. She said Robert should have known better, even if I didn't tell him no. She wouldn't lie to me...would she?"

It had, indeed, been a surprising day. Looking back, Jesse reflected that his Aunt Muriel had been wise to stay away from the reception. She wouldn't want to hear the things he had to say to her.

His cousin Dean had also been noticeably absent. Not that this surprised or bothered Jesse in the least. He hoped his boot was still imprinted on his pompous backside.

Jesse's mother had shared one more bit of news: because she was going to marry and live with that nice preacher who spoke at his funeral—a lovely funeral; Jesse should have seen it—her sister Muriel planned to sell her town house in Savannah and move in with her son. To help get Dean's life in order, Muriel had told her...

Jesse couldn't help a satisfied grin as he turned off the shower. Muriel and Dean deserved each other.

As he pushed aside the vinyl shower curtain, he heard it—soft murmurs issuing from the bedroom. Disappointment drew his mouth down into a frown. Was someone here? Whoever it was, he'd throw them out. Shove 'em right out the door. This was *his* night with Elissa, the start of their honeymoon, and he meant to monopolize every second of it.

A year, two months, and too many weeks had gone by since this body of his had taken hers. He needed that now. Needed the passionate insanity that somehow made his spirit soar. Needed to know that after all he'd been through, he could still make her tremble in his arms and cry out his name....

It was Elissa's voice he heard, he realized as he slung a towel around his hips. Soft, loving sounds. Who the *hell* was she talking to? Bewildered, he pushed open the bathroom door, his hair dripping in little rivulets down his neck and shoulders.

She lounged against a mound of pillows, her long, sable dark hair flowing loosely around her slender form, with some black, wispy little lace thing doing nothing at all to hide the feminine curves and valleys that so intrigued him. Where the black lace ended, her golden legs stretched for miles along the bedspread, from thighs to shapely calves, crossed with seductive allure....

A telephone receiver, he belatedly noticed, was pressed against her ear. "I love you, baby," she murmured in a low, fervent voice into the mouthpiece. "I miss you. Do you miss me? Don't worry, we'll be together soon...."

Every muscle in Jesse's body froze. For an instant—the briefest, blackest instant—the euphoria of the day evaporated, and he was once again the outsider, battle-scarred and deformed, pressing his nose against the window and peering in at a warmth he'd never know....

But before his heart had even missed a beat, a new, awesome certainty embraced him. *He could believe in her.* If he trusted his heart to pump his blood, if he trusted his lungs to draw in breath, he could trust this woman to love him; she'd been far more constant than either. When his body itself had failed him, she had not. She never would.

As though sensing his presence, Elissa lifted her gaze. She smiled a warm, dazzling smile that blazed a path of love straight through his heart. "Know who else is here?" she murmured into the phone. "Your old pa."

And she handed the receiver to Jesse.

He took it by rote, overcome by awe that he, of all men, had been blessed with her. And though he had no idea why she'd be talking over the phone to Cody—he wouldn't understand her; couldn't even *talk* yet, let alone answer questions—Jesse dutifully lifted the receiver to his ear.

"Hey, there, boy," he heard himself say, his voice too deep and rusty. Before he knew it, he found himself listening closely for the slightest gurgle. Clearly he imagined a phone being held against that little rounded cheek; saw his son's bright gaze, maybe teary-eyed from wanting his mother. "Love you, Cody," he muttered hoarsely. "We'll be home soon, just wait and see."

As he murmured the kind of nonsense he never imagined would come from his mouth, a torrent of goodness, warmth and light flooded him. He was whole. He was healed.

He was loved.

A slender hand swept up his leg and tugged at his towel. "Tell him good night" came the throaty feminine voice that set a thousand flames licking through his veins.

"'Night, son," he breathed. The receiver had barely hit its cradle before he'd tossed aside the towel and lowered himself to the bed.

"I love you, Jesse," Elissa swore in a solemn whisper.

His hands delved beneath the black lace and swept along bare, silken flesh. His arms filled with fragrant, womanly warmth; his mouth connected hungrily with hers. He loved her so much it hurt. She was his, all his, and they'd spend the rest of their lives doing just this—proving, probing, exploring their love for each other.

Till death do us part, she had promised.

But for Jesse, that wasn't good enough.

He wanted longer.

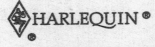

Take 4 bestselling love stories FREE

Plus get a FREE surprise gift!

Special Limited-time Offer

Mail to Harlequin Reader Service®

3010 Walden Avenue
P.O. Box 1867
Buffalo, N.Y. 14240-1867

YES! Please send me 4 free Harlequin Temptation® novels and my free surprise gift. Then send me 4 brand-new novels every month, which I will receive before they appear in bookstores. Bill me at the low price of $2.90 each plus 25¢ delivery and applicable sales tax, if any.* That's the complete price and a savings of over 10% off the cover prices—quite a bargain! I understand that accepting the books and gift places me under no obligation ever to buy any books. I can always return a shipment and cancel at any time. Even if I never buy another book from Harlequin, the 4 free books and the surprise gift are mine to keep forever.

142 BPA A3UP

Name	(PLEASE PRINT)
Address	Apt. No.
City	State	Zip

This offer is limited to one order per household and not valid to present Harlequin Temptation® subscribers. *Terms and prices are subject to change without notice. Sales tax applicable in N.Y.

UTEMP-696

Free Gift Offer

With a Free Gift proof-of-purchase
from any Harlequin® book, you can receive
a beautiful cubic zirconia pendant.

This stunning marquise-shaped stone is a genuine cubic
zirconia—accented by an 18" gold tone necklace.
(Approximate retail value $19.95)

Send for yours today...
compliments of 🔶 HARLEQUIN®

To receive your free gift, a cubic zirconia pendant, send us one original proof-of-purchase, photocopies not accepted, from the back of any Harlequin Romance®, Harlequin Presents®, Harlequin Temptation®, Harlequin Superromance®, Harlequin Intrigue®, Harlequin American Romance®, or Harlequin Historicals® title available in February, March or April at your favorite retail outlet, together with the Free Gift Certificate, plus a check or money order for $1.65 U.S./$2.15 CAN. (do not send cash) to cover postage and handling, payable to Harlequin Free Gift Offer. We will send you the specified gift. Allow 6 to 8 weeks for delivery. Offer good until April 30, 1997, or while quantities last. Offer valid in the U.S. and Canada only.

Free Gift Certificate

Name: _____

Address: _____

City: _____ State/Province: _____ Zip/Postal Code: _____

Mail this certificate, one proof-of-purchase and a check or money order for postage and handling to: HARLEQUIN FREE GIFT OFFER 1997. In the U.S.: 3010 Walden Avenue, P.O. Box 9071, Buffalo NY 14269-9057. In Canada: P.O. Box 604, Fort Erie, Ontario L2Z 5X3.

FREE GIFT OFFER   084-KEZ

ONE PROOF-OF-PURCHASE
To collect your fabulous FREE GIFT, a cubic zirconia pendant, you must include this original proof-of-purchase for each gift with the properly completed Free Gift Certificate.

084-KEZ

COMING NEXT MONTH

#629 OUTRAGEOUS Lori Foster
Blaze

One minute, a sexy-as-sin cop is rescuing Emily Cooper from drunken hoodlums. Five minutes later, he's tearing his clothes off in front of a group of voracious women. What kind of man is he... and why can't Emily keep her hands off him? Little does she know that Judd Sanders really *is* a cop, whose "cover" leaves him a little too *uncovered* for his liking!

#630 ONE ENCHANTED NIGHT Debra Carroll
It Happened One Night...

Lucy Weston doesn't believe her aunt can conjure up a man from her dusty book of love spells, but she agrees to help try. Soon after, there's a knock at the door, and a gorgeous, unconscious man falls into her arms. Before long the sexy stranger has also fallen into Lucy's bed. But no one, not even her fantasy lover, knows who he is....

#631 TWICE THE SPICE Patricia Ryan
Double Dare

Meet shy, studious Emma Sutcliffe and her flamboyant identical twin, Zara. And see what happens when Emma reluctantly takes on her sister's identity, her daring clothes and a risky adventure with the sexiest man she's ever met. And then, next month, don't miss Harlequin Intrigue #420, *Twice Burned*, for Zara's gripping story.

#632 THE TROUBLE WITH TONYA Lorna Michaels

Tonya Brewster is a walking disaster area. She can't hold a job, isn't capable of driving within the speed limit and hasn't had a date in who knows how long! But when she sets her sights on rugged, hunky Kirk Butler, he doesn't stand a chance. Because Kirk has no idea just how *much* trouble Tonya can be....

AVAILABLE NOW:

#625 THE NEXT MAN IN TEXAS
Kristine Rolofson

#626 AFTER THE LOVING
Sandy Steen

#627 THE HONEYMOON DEAL
Kate Hoffmann

#628 POSSESSING ELISSA
Donna Sterling

You're About to Become a *Privileged Woman*

Reap the rewards of fabulous free gifts and benefits with proofs-of-purchase from Harlequin and Silhouette books

Pages & Privileges™

It's our way of thanking you for buying our books at your favorite retail stores.

PROOF OF PURCHASE

Offer expires March 31, 1997

HT-PP23

**Harlequin and Silhouette—
the most privileged readers in the world!**

For more information about Harlequin and Silhouette's PAGES & PRIVILEGES program call the Pages & Privileges Benefits Desk: 1-503-794-2499

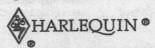

HARLEQUIN ®

HT-PP23

Half-Hearted Detective

Just then the whole wall of glass shattered, and pieces were flying all over the room. I grabbed Mrs. Pardo by the shoulders and pulled her to the floor, covering her body with mine as best I could. Tony was still standing there.

"Get down! Get down!" I yelled at him, until he dropped alongside us. His face was white and I could sense the fear coming out of him. Men's voices were shouting somewhere outside, but otherwise it was so still that I could feel Mrs. Pardo's heart pounding under mine. Or was it my heart pounding? My bunged-up heart! Jesus! No bullet had ever been fired at me in all my years on the force. There was a slight pressure on me, and I looked down at Mrs. Pardo's face about an inch from mine, her eyes staring right into me, and along the whole length of my body there was a hotness where her parts mashed into mine. . . . I looked back into her eyes, and I could swear she was laughing at me. . . .

THE
Half-
Hearted
Detective

A VINNIE ALTOBELLI MYSTERY

Milton Bass

POCKET BOOKS

New York   London   Toronto   Sydney   Tokyo   Singapore

An *Original* Publication of POCKET BOOKS

POCKET BOOKS, a division of Simon & Schuster Inc.
1230 Avenue of the Americas, New York, NY 10020

Copyright © 1993 by Milton Bass

All rights reserved, including the right to reproduce
this book or portions thereof in any form whatsoever.
For information address Pocket Books, 1230 Avenue
of the Americas, New York, NY 10020

ISBN: 0-671-74242-6

First Pocket Books printing February 1993

10 9 8 7 6 5 4 3 2 1

POCKET and colophon are registered trademarks of
Simon & Schuster Inc.

Cover art by Ben Perini

Printed in the U.S.A.

For RUTHIE
(Who) (Whom) I love more

THE

Half-Hearted Detective

1

Brady not only lost his grip on the kid but fell on his ass at the same time, so I was the only member of the posse tearing up the stairs after the perpetrator. He was short, zit-faced, acned, and bony-kneed, so he was almost to the first landing before I took off after him. By the third flight I was gaining on the bastard, but I could feel my heart pounding faster as my breath grew shorter, and the taste of the fried eggplant grinder was working its way up my throat. Right then I wouldn't have taken odds I wasn't going to see it on the stairs ahead of me all chewed up and mixed with the marinara sauce.

For a second I considered giving up the chase, knowing he would be over the roofs and away once he made it out the steel door into the open. But I take it personally when punks rip off Social Security checks from mailboxes, and there was also the matter of this scrawny little shit outrunning me in the race of good guys versus bad. When I was in high school I would have been dancing up the stairs ahead of him by now, maybe even backwards, but that was fourteen years and thirty-five pounds ago, and I was losing the desire with each step.

He ran out of breath on the fourth floor landing and was hanging over the railing as I came up to him, his chest heaving and the spit running down the side of his mouth. But just as I was reaching out to grab him by the shoulder, he hauled off and belted me one in the middle of my breastbone that hurt more than anything I had ever felt in my life, including the time the two linebackers from Montrose High blindsided me both high and low.

Just before I went out, I couldn't help but wonder how such a piece of slime could get off a punch like that without me even seeing it. He had to have a piece of pipe somewhere on him. I was looking him right in his rat-face and I could hear Brady pounding up the stairs behind us, but then I didn't see any more and didn't hear any more. As far as I knew, there wasn't any more.

2

The voices came first, mumbling so low that I couldn't make out what they were saying, but I was too tired to even open my eyes. I knew I wasn't home, because I lived alone and there wouldn't be anybody in the apartment unless I had invited them there. It was all very peculiar. If I opened my eyes, I would know where I was and who was with me, but it wasn't that important; I wasn't that interested.

My ears were working, though, and I could hear a beeping and a humming and something was squeezing

2

my left arm—squeezing, squeezing, squeezing—and then it stopped cold, and I felt the muscle go soft again. Somebody put a wet cloth on my face and rubbed, not hard, and it felt good, good enough so that I tried to shove myself up on my elbows, but this woman's voice said, "Whoa, boy, whoa," and I fell back on what had to be a bed. Who was it that yelled, "Whoa, boy, whoa," when we rode into the sunset together? Mimi Barnes yelled, "Deeper, deeper!" and Sally screamed, "Harder, harder!" and . . . and . . . the squeezing started on my arm again, and I wanted to reach over and rip the hell off whatever was doing it to me, but right then I couldn't tell which arm was which, so I decided to just lie there until things figured themselves out.

There wasn't any two ways about it. I was going to have to open my eyes.

3

She was worth opening your eyes for. Somewhere in her late twenties, brunette, blue eyes with dark circles under them, not enough makeup to decide whether or not there was any makeup at all, full red lips. . . . Jesus, a real beauty.

She was looking down at me and I could see the washcloth ready to go to work again, but she had stopped when she saw my eyes open.

"How we doing, Sergeant?" she wanted to know.

"What are we doing, and why are we doing it?" I wanted to know.

My voice came out all cracked, and my mouth was so dry that I couldn't make my throat work to swallow. It was a hospital, that was for sure. The little prick had really done a job on me. I could already hear the ribbing from the guys in the squad. "Did you hear about Altobelli? Got taken down by some junior high school kid. Hey, Altobelli, is it true they made him stay after for detention?"

The thing on my left arm was a blood pressure cuff, and in my right wrist was one of those I.V. things, and I could see four different bottles hanging from the rack above me. What the Christ did he hit me with?

"Are you feeling any kind of pain?" she asked, and I stared straight up at her because she was better than any of the other stuff I'd been looking at.

Pain? No, there wasn't any pain. I couldn't even feel anything where the little shit had belted me. Had to be some busted ribs there. No way I could've gotten off without any busted ribs. But there wasn't any pain. I just felt lousy all over.

"What did he hit me with?" I asked her.

"What did who hit you with?"

"The kid. The kid I was making the collar on. He hit me in the chest with something. Had to be a pipe. It hurt too much for just wood."

"Nobody hit you with a pipe. Nobody hit you with anything. You had a heart attack."

I could sense the tears filling my eyes, all the water that had been drained from my throat, and a feeling went over me like they were closing the coffin lid on my head. Heart attack! That couldn't have happened. I was thirty-two years old. People died from heart attacks in my family all right. But they were between ninety and a hundred when they did it. I had an uncle in Italy who was a hundred and eleven years old, and young girls were afraid to be in a room with him. Christ, in my family, thirty-two was just going into puberty.

"Who said I had a heart attack?" I asked her, trying to use my interrogation voice, but the croak was still there.

"Along with all the other symptoms, the enzymes said you had a heart attack," she answered.

"Who are the Enzymes?"

She put the washcloth on my chin and rubbed gently. "The enzymes are the things that show up in your blood after you've had a heart attack. It's a lot more technical than that, but there is no doubt that you had a real, honest-to-God heart attack. You must face the fact that you are in the Intensive Care Unit of the San Bernardino Medical Center."

"But how can you . . . ?" I began, and she moved the washcloth so that it covered my mouth and I stopped trying. I didn't have the strength to fight even a washcloth.

"Look," she said, "I've already told you more than I should. You'll have to ask Dr. McMurty about anything else. Your mother, father, and all four grandparents are waiting outside to see you. They can only stay five minutes, but they're driving everybody crazy out there. So I'm going to bring them in."

My grandmother Nano was carrying a bowl covered with foil, and I knew it contained some variation on minestrone soup, tailored to meet the needs of a heart attack victim and make him, as my grandfather Angelo would say, "one hundred per cent" again. When they first came in, they all looked at me like I

5

was already laid out at Bencivenga's Funeral Parlor, but once my mother broke the silence they all started jabbering away. The questions were coming at me at a rate of about fourteen a minute in the regular mixture of Italian and English, but after I mustered the strength to smile, I pooped out again and had to fight to keep my eyelids open.

That was when the nurse came in and shooed everybody out. Nano tried to hand her the bowl, but she dodged nicely and told them they couldn't peek in again until the late afternoon.

"What time's it now?" I asked her as she started filling in the chart that she pulled from the alcove over the chest of drawers set in the wall.

She glanced at her watch. "Two P.M."

"I've been here four hours?"

"What four hours?"

"It was ten A.M. when we tried to make the collar on the kid, and you say it's two now. That comes to four hours."

"That comes to four hours and two days," she said. "You came in here on Tuesday. This is the first time you've been with it since they brought you in. You're lucky they had paddles in the ambulance."

Paddles. Those things they used to shock people back to life. I was dead and they had brought me back to life. Two days. Two days and four hours. I tried swallowing, but there wasn't enough spit. "Could I have a drink, please?" I asked her.

"What's your pleasure? Bourbon? Scotch? Perrier? Water?"

"The water will do."

"Okay, but not too much. Just a couple of sips. And your partner's outside and says he's going to shoot his way in if I don't let him see you."

6

"Brady?"

"He looks like a Brady ought to look."

But Brady didn't look like he ought to have looked. He looked scared. I tried another smile. It felt better.

"Jesus," said Brady, "what kind of shit is this?"

"Did you get the punk?"

"What punk?"

"The kid. The mailbox kid. You got him, didn't you?"

"Nah. He went up to the roof and disappeared while I was trying to take care of you. I thought he'd hit you with something, the way you were slumped on the stairs. I couldn't believe it when they told me you had a heart attack."

"You couldn't believe it? I still can't believe it. There's got to be some kind of mistake. I'll never buy another eggplant grinder at Angelina's, I'll tell you that right now."

"Okay," said the nurse, "you've seen him. Now get out of here and don't come back until he's in a regular room. Tell all his other friends too."

"Can you take this fu . . . this machine off me," I asked, nodding toward the blood pressure cuff on my left arm. "It hurts like hell every time it blows up."

"It automatically takes your pressure every fifteen minutes," she said, "and it won't come off until the doctor says so."

"When am I going to see this doctor?"

"He'll be in about six."

"Nurse?"

"My name is Betty."

"Betty, am I going to die?"

"No, you're not going to die. I won't let you die. No matter how hard you try, I'm not going to let you die." She came over to the bed and took my right hand in both of hers and pulled it up against her chest. As lousy as I felt, I could still feel the softness molding into the back of my hand.

"Nobody dies on me," she said. "Nobody."

4

The doc was young, somewhere in his early thirties. Tall, maybe two inches over my six one. Ruddy-faced. Nice-faced. "Ah, Mr. Altobelli," he said, "you're finally with us again."

He went to the wall and pulled out the chart, checked it over, took hold of my wrist for a few seconds. Then he put the ends of the stethoscope in his ears and listened to my chest in four different places. "Had you been feeling ill in any way?" he asked.

"Just some indigestion," I told him. "But we keep crazy hours, and I eat a lot of crap while I'm on the job. I had a fried eggplant sandwich just before . . . just before this happened, and that wasn't sitting too good when I ran up the stairs after the kid."

"Yes, your friend Mr. Brady told me what happened. What would you like to know?"

"What happened? Am I going to die? If I'm not going to die, what's my life going to be like? I don't feel any pain. Just tired. If I'm not going to die, when do I get out of here, and what happens after that?"

"You've had a heart attack, but you're not going to

die. Your life is going to be different. If your signs keep improving, you should be down in a regular room in two or three days. As soon as possible, you're going to have a catheterization in which we thread a wire into your heart and learn how much damage has been done. I think there's been only moderate damage, because your pumping ability seems unimpaired. But we won't know exactly until we do the angiogram. Having a heart attack is not the end of the world. There are all kinds of remedies and alternatives. Nature works a lot of miracles on her own. Lie back and let her do her work. I'll see you tomorrow."

"I liked him," I told the nurse.

"He's good," she said. "Maybe the best. Do you want to sleep for a while? You can have a little more to drink. What do you want?"

"I want to get cleaned up and brush my teeth and maybe have a shave. I think I'll feel a lot better if I do."

"We've got to take it slow," she said. "You've still got a long way to go. But I will clean you up and brush your teeth. The shave we'll talk about later."

I've had a lot of women's hands all over my body, starting with my mother right up to . . . right up to . . . The last one was . . . the last one was the piano player at Nickleby's bar. She had good strong hands. But never, never have I felt hands like that nurse had as she cleaned me up with her major weapon, the washrag. She wouldn't let me raise my head to rinse out the toothpaste. I had to turn my face sideways and spit into the metal pan. Some of it went on her hands, but it was as if she didn't even notice. Then she wiped my mouth, smoothed out the covers, and told me to close my eyes. I must have fallen asleep while the lids were still on the way down.

5

McMurty came into the room with another doctor in tow, another young guy, but this one was blond and wore glasses and had what looked like dried blood on the front of his full-length white coat. They looked around before they said anything, but my roommate was taking his ten turns around the corridors to start getting his heart in shape again. I was doing it five times a day before I pooped out, and he was almost forty years older than me.

"This is Dr. Englund," said McMurty. "He's the chief surgeon in the cardiology department."

The Swede wasted no time. "I just looked at the films of your angiogram, Mr. Altobelli," he said, "and I have recommended to Dr. McMurty that a bypass is indicated. You have one artery completely closed off and another with nearly fifty percent blockage. Consequently I feel an operation is the right course to take. I have a tight schedule, but I can fit you in exactly one month from today."

"Wait a minute," I told him. "One of the guys on the force had a heart attack, and all he does is take pills. Am I going to die if I don't have the operation?"

McMurty wasn't saying anything, but he was looking funny.

"No," Englund said, "I wouldn't say you are in immediate danger of dying, but I can promise you a better and longer life after the operation. Of course, all of my patients go on a strict diet—no red meat and no dairy—but that is something we can discuss in the future."

"Dr. McMurty," I said, "how do you feel about the operation?"

His face got a little red, and he shuffled his feet. If we were in the interrogation room I would know that the guy had something to spill, that he was holding back, that he was caught in a bind. "Dr. Englund has done this operation innumerable times," he said, "and with great success."

"What if it was you?" I asked him. "What if you were in my shoes? What would you do?"

He thought about it. "Well," he said, "I am a very active man and would want the maximum available. I guess I would have the operation."

I wondered what he would say if I put Brady on him. Brady was good at making strong men cry.

"I'm going to hold off on this," I told them. "Think about it. Maybe get some more opinions."

"If I don't make the appointment for you now," said Englund, "I don't know what my schedule is going to be like a month from now and may not be able to work you in for several weeks or even months."

"I'll take my chances on that," I told him.

He looked at me and then at McMurty, and without saying another word he left.

"When am I getting out of here?" I asked the doctor.

"You've got to stay on this medication another week before you can take the stress test again," he said. "You didn't do well enough on the first one, and we've got to see how effective the medicine is."

"Am I going to die?" I asked him.

He laughed. "Someday," he said, "but I don't see it

happening too soon. You're young; you've got a lot of years ahead of you."

"Do you really think I should have the operation?" I asked him.

"Why don't we see how the medicine works?" he said. "We have some good ones now, and there are better ones coming out all the time. You can always get the operation later if the medicines don't work."

"Doc, you are leveling with me on all this, aren't you?"

He got that strange look again. "I always level with my patients, Mr. Altobelli," he said. "I find it works best in the long run. Let's see how the medicines work."

My roommate came back. "Twelve times," he said. "I'm almost ready for some stairs."

6

I've been on stakeouts that lasted so long I thought I'd died and this was what hell was like, but that week before the stress test made everything before it seem like a vacation. It wasn't that I lacked for company. Along with everybody else in the family, Nano showed up every day with a bowl of something or other. At first the nurses complained about having to get rid of it, but one day somebody took a chance and tasted whatever the hell it was, and from then on they fought each other over who was going to "get rid of" Nano's bowl.

Since I was the "baby," my five brothers were also there every night after they had eaten their supper, and they brought wives and kids and several people who were strangers to me. Everybody on the force, including the chief and captain, made at least one appearance. I asked them both the same question and got approximately the same answer. After they told me not to worry about anything and just get my health back, I said, "I can't wait to get back to work," and they both answered, like fucking parrots, "Don't even think about that now. Take one thing at a time." I was also visited not only by the girls I had been going out with but also several who popped out of the past to see how I was doing. There was one I'll swear I'd never met before, but she acted like we were engaged or something. She wasn't bad looking, either. Two of my snitches showed up, and one of them hit me up for twenty bucks as he was leaving. Some things never change. Everybody else brought food or books or magazines, and we racked up enough chocolates to keep the kids' ward in supplies for a year. I had no idea what happened to all the flowers. My mother took the plants home to keep company with the two hundred she already had.

All the men had the same question when they could get me alone for a second. "You still going to be able to do it?" they asked, their faces screwed up like they were watching a horse being gelded. The women didn't say anything, but I could see it in their eyes. Thirty-two years old and everybody thought my fucking life was over.

One of the booklets they gave me to read had to do with sex. "The physical energy required for intercourse," it said, "is the equivalent of climbing two flights of stairs. If you can climb two flights of stairs, and with your doctor's permission, you are ready to resume sexual relations. If you wish to start by keeping physical effort to a minimum, one way is to sit on a chair and have your partner mount you."

I had done that once with a girl named Judy something-or-other, but at the time it had nothing to do with saving my physical energy. I threw the booklet at the wall, but it was only eight pages and didn't have the weight to carry so it just fluttered to the floor. That was appropriate to the situation.

I had always bragged that I could sleep through anything, but the hospital cured me of that notion. It wasn't just the nurses talking to each other in the middle of the night like everybody was deaf, or them coming in with pills for my mouth and Fleet syringes to stick up my ass, or the interns and the residents practicing on me day and night.

What was keeping me up was wondering what the hell I was going to do for as many years as I had left to live. The chief and the captain didn't say anything about me maybe coming back even in some kind of desk job. You could tell by their eyes that I was off the roster. A sergeant named Donovan brought in some papers for me to sign and said I would get three-quarters of my salary for a service-incurred disability.

"Goddamned politicians don't want to count heart attacks," he said. "Fucking idiots have no idea what pressure we're under."

In his job he was under about as much pressure as President Reagan used to have, but I just nodded like we both needed the bulletproof vests even when we went to the crapper.

I had never thought about dying, even when we went into a crack house or an alley or a cellar or a warehouse or any of those places. Nothing had ever bothered me before, and I'd never met a man who scared me. But this was heavy stuff I was carrying now. Mr. Death was sitting on my shoulders, and no matter what I was doing, day or night, I could feel his weight pressing down.

They told me I couldn't eat anything from midnight until three hours after my test the next day because they were going to inject something called thallium into me while I was taking the test.

"What's thallium?" I asked the nurse.

"It's radioactive something-or-other," she answered, and pumped up the blood pressure cuff.

"Hey," she said, "we're a little high today. Something bothering you?"

She tells me they're going to turn me into a moonglow, and then she asks if something is bothering me.

Even though I wasn't going to be able to eat again for something like twenty-one hours, I ordered my usual tuna fish sandwich, mashed potatoes, and canned peaches for dessert. I'd tried eating the cooked dishes, but I couldn't take it after the third day, and I stuck to sandwiches. I knew that Nano's bowls were not low fat, low sodium, but they had one thing the hospital dinners didn't—taste. Eleven pounds had dropped off me since they had carried me in, and the doc said I should get back to my high school weight. It had to be by diet because you didn't lose weight by taking a turn or two around the hospital hall.

The other bed in the room was empty because the guy who was in it had complained of chest pains and they had hauled him back to coronary. He was a heavy smoker, in after his second heart attack, and they had sent a three-man antismoking team to give him religion. That was one way to keep hospital costs down—

three-man nonsmoking teams, one member of which was a doctor. They asked the guy if he had ever given up smoking, and he told them he had stopped for one week a couple of years before.

"Why did you go back to it?" asked the doctor.

"Because I got out of intensive care," said the guy as if he was explaining it to a dummy. Maybe he was.

I almost asked the nurse to give me one of those Halcion tablets about three o'clock in the morning, but then I thought it might slow me down in the stress test, so I just lay there staring at the ceiling, wondering when that pain in the chest was going to come back and waste me permanently.

I must have dozed off sometime, because the orderly had to shake me to show me that the wheelchair was there.

7

The sweat was pouring off me in buckets, and I could feel my heart pounding away like it was going to take off somewhere on its own. My legs were made out of solid lead. But I had to stay in there because I was running for my life.

I don't know how many minutes we had been going when the doctor asked me for the hundredth time, "Are you feeling any pain?" and I told him, "No, no pain," and he said to the nurse, "Okay, give it to him," and she stuck a needle full of stuff into the doohickey on the back of my wrist, and the doctor said, "One more minute. Hang in there for one more minute," and the nurse stuck another needle full of stuff into the thing and said, "Saline solution," and I kept pounding away until I felt the treadmill slow down, and it finally stopped.

The nurse put her left hand on my left shoulder and her other arm around me, and led me to the table, where I sat down with my chest heaving and the sweat running down into my eyes. The doctor wasn't even paying me any attention; he was checking the narrow piece of paper that was peeling out of the machine.

Finally he turned and looked at me. You learn to read people when you're a detective, when you're any kind of cop, I suppose, and I wasn't sure about the look he had.

"Okay," he said, "you had a good run. It looks pretty good. We're going to take some pictures now, and then some more three hours from now. But from what I've seen, I'd say the medicine is working. I'll talk to you tonight."

When I got back to the room, my cousin Alfredo was sitting there picking out horses on his sheet. I could see he was set for the day, so I told him I had more tests to take and I wasn't allowed any company. When I lay down on the bed, I felt pretty good all in all. "It looks pretty good," he had said. Here I had run as hard as I could going after that kid up the stairs, and there had been no explosion in the chest, and the doctor said, "It looks pretty good."

I was asleep when they came for me three hours later for the final pictures, and when I came back, the nurse got me some scrambled egg substitute with rye toast and a scoop of mashed potatoes and some decaffeinated coffee. It was the first meal I had enjoyed since I came into the hospital.

The doctor came in about nine P.M. He looked like hell, eyes all red and skin a little gray. I don't know why, but it made me feel good to see him that way.

"The pictures look stable," he said. "I just went over them with the radiologist, and he agrees. So you can go home tomorrow. When you get there, call my office and we'll set you up for an appointment. The nurse will give you a list of instructions to follow until I see you again. Take care."

He stuck out his hand and we shook. I liked that guy. If he ever wanted anybody's kneecaps shattered, I was his man. Provided he said it was all right for me to swing a bat.

8

My mother insisted that I get my strength back at her house instead of going back to the apartment. To tell the truth, I was still shaky enough so that I didn't debate it with her. I didn't even argue when the nurse said I had to be wheeled to the main entrance instead of walking like real people. Brady was waiting outside at the wheel of a squad car, and a young uniformed cop was standing by the door, ready to help me in. It's the kind of thing these clowns would think was funny.

Just before we went out, my intensive care nurse, Betty, came out of a side corridor and walked over to stand beside me. "I've been keeping tabs on you," she said, "and they tell me you're okay."

"I asked about you," I told her, "but nobody ever answered me."

"You're going to be fine," she said, patting me on the shoulder. "Here's my phone number. If you need someone to talk to, I'll be there."

I felt my throat go tight and my eyes started to fill up when she said that, and as I took the note from her, I tried to tell her how much I appreciated what she had done for me, but the words got stuck.

"Hey," she said, giving my shoulder a squeeze, "nobody dies on me."

I was still thinking about her when the car stopped in front of my mother's house, and both Brady and the cop—Connors was his name—got out and walked with me up the stairs. I thought for a minute one of them was going to take my arm, but not even a comedian like Brady would have the balls to do that. The door opened before we got to it and there was my mother. And behind her was every relative I had, dozens of them crowded into the hall and spilling into the side rooms. It was Sunday so everybody had the day off to welcome me home.

My mother pulled Brady and the patrolman into the house, insisting that they had to have something to eat before they returned to work. There was no doubt that everybody was going to have something to eat, because the whole place was set up like for Christmas with tables stretching from the living room around through the dining room and even places for kids in the bedrooms.

I had the seat of honor in the dining room, and before me were mounds of hot and cold antipasti and fresh bread, and from the kitchen came aromas that indicated it was an all-out, no-holds-barred, praise-God-and-pass-the-hot-peppers feast.

There were so many people around me, laughing,

slapping me on the back, hugging and kissing, that the air seemed too hot to breathe, and I could feel the sweat breaking out under my armpits. I was tired, really tired, and what I wanted was to get into some clean shorts, lie down on a bed in a cool room, and sleep. I knew that now I was home I would sleep again, but the question was whether or not these people were going to kill me off before I had a chance to find out.

The women started to come out of the kitchen with huge platters filled with every specialty my mother and aunts had ever mastered. Plunked down right in front of me was Aunt Clara's *pièce de résistance,* coniglio al forno al sugo de cinghiale—roast rabbit with wild boar lard. Aunt Clara's connections made the Colombian drug cartels look like the Epworth League in Kennebunkport, Maine. The recipe called for a pound of wild boar fat, but if others in the United States made the dish, I'm sure they used either fatback or prosciutto fat as a reasonable substitute. But not my Aunt Clara. I have no idea who or what shipped it in from Italy for her, but you could be damn sure that what you were tasting was real wild boar fat. Sitting next to it was a plate of bruschette, thick slices of whole wheat bread grilled with melted sweet butter and fresh ground black pepper. The men started spooning the melted fat onto the slices of bread, and one of them was shoved into my left hand.

In my pocket was the list of instructions from the doctor, and the part about diet would be as foreign to these people as if it had been written in Mongolian.

There was my own mother's risotto pasticciato—messy rice—that contained sweetbreads, veal, chicken livers, butter, meat sauce, and fresh grated Parmesan, among other things. At least two olive trees had to have been sacrificed to furnish the oil for all the dishes, and there were four kinds of sauces to go on the different pastas, and roasted eel, and Nano's tripe Genoa-style, and salads and fruit and cakes and pastries and pitchers of wine, some with fresh peaches soaking in the bottom, and beer for the younger men.

People kept dumping this and that on my plate, and I would push the food around with my fork, but I wasn't able to lift even one bite to my mouth. I could feel my body trembling even though I was sitting down, and the sweat was drenching me all over. The men sitting near me were concentrating so hard on the food that they didn't seem to notice I wasn't eating, but all of a sudden my brother Pete, the accountant, was sticking his head over my shoulder. "You all right?" he asked.

"I'm not very hungry," I told him, "and I'm feeling kind of shaky."

"You're out of here," he said, and a minute later he was walking me up the stairs to my old bedroom.

My mother appeared at the bottom before we reached the top. "You all right, Vincent?" she called up. "Is he all right, Petey?"

"He's fine, Ma," he told her. "He's just a little tired, and the doctor said he had to rest a lot. He's going to take a little nap, and then he'll come down again later."

I turned to look, and her face showed some indecision as to what she thought was going on, but there were forty guests to take care of and Pete could be depended upon in any situation.

There was a suitcase full of stuff that my brother Dominic had picked up at my apartment, and Pete had me into pajamas in no time. I usually slept in a T-shirt and undershorts, but someone must have given me a pair of pajamas once and Dom had probably found them buried in a bureau drawer. The bed felt good, and when Pete pulled down the shade, I let my eyelids drop from their own weight, and that was all I remembered until I woke up in the dark.

The house was silent and it took me a few seconds to figure out where I was and how I had gotten there. I felt better—pretty good, in fact—and I could feel my belly gurgle with hunger.

"You awake, Vincent?" my mother called softly from the doorway.

"Yeah, Ma."

"You feeling all right?"

"Yeah. I'm fine, Ma."

"You want something to eat?"

"Yes, I do, but first I want to take a shower."

"The green towels are for you."

"Thanks, Ma."

She came into the room and sat down on the edge of the bed, then touched my forehead with her right hand to make sure I didn't have a fever, just as she had done with all of us right through high school and I'm sure would do as long as she could lift her hand.

"What's going to happen, Vincent?" she asked.

"It's going to take me a few weeks to get my strength back, Ma, and then I'll move back to the apartment."

"You going to be all right alone? What about your job? When are you going to be able to go back to your job? I don't like you being a policeman, Vincent. No one in the family has ever been a policeman, here or in the old country."

"I don't think I'm going to be able to be a policeman any more, Ma. I'm going to have to do something else. But my pension will be pretty good, so I won't have to worry about that too much."

"Alessandro said you could come work for him."

"I don't know anything about the construction business, Ma."

"Your other brothers, they can help you, too. And

22

we'll leave you the house. The other boys have houses of their own. We'll leave the house to you."

"Ma, I'm going to be fine. You don't have to worry about me. The boys don't have to worry about me. I'll be fine."

"Sure you will," she said, standing up. "You'll be fine. I'll go warm up Nano's soup while you're taking your shower. She said she put something special in it to help you get back your manhood."

I lay there a minute after she went down the stairs, wishing I was back to the time when my mother would give me a hug and everything would be all right. But everything wasn't all right. The doctors said I had only half a heart left to do the job. And my grandma was putting something extra in my soup to make sure I could get a hard-on again. You couldn't have sex with only half a heart, could you? I didn't think even Nano's magic soup could help you with that.

9

My brother Frankie sent over one of his vans to move me back to my apartment, and my mother stood at the door looking like I was going off to war and was already as good as dead. She had been trying to get me to give up the apartment and move back home, and the scary thing was that sometimes it almost made sense. There were mornings when I woke up feeling shaky, and whenever I took a pill, six times a day, it reminded me that these were what were keeping me going, that I couldn't make it on my own anymore. And whenever I stuck my hand in my right pocket, I felt the little bottle of nitroglycerin tablets that were there for emergencies.

Frankie must have given the guy strict instructions, because when I started to bring my suitcase down the stairs, he ran up and grabbed it from me so hard that he almost knocked me down. He opened the car door and stood there to make sure I could get in all by myself, like a mother putting her kid on the school bus, and when we reached my building, he insisted on carrying the bag all the way to my bedroom.

It was about four in the afternoon when I got there, and after I unpacked the bag and put away the clothes, I wandered into the living room and turned on the TV. I switched from channel to channel, checked HBO and SportsChannel and all the rest of them, clicking them off one by one, but nothing grabbed me, there was nothing I wanted to watch.

What I wanted to do was go back to being a cop. Someone had once pinned up on the bulletin board in the squad room a clipping that had to do with a Massachusetts cop suing and winning to get back on the force after he had a heart bypass. We had all said at the time that the guy was nuts, and that we'd never do anything like that. All we talked about was the day we could hang up the badge and lead normal lives. Maybe some of the guys meant it. I had said it at the time and I thought I meant it. But now that it was too late, I knew. All I wanted out of life was to do what I did best—be a good cop.

Clicking off the TV, I looked around the room. I had read the paper at my mother's house and walked my laps around the track after breakfast. It was a

Thursday. People were getting ready to quit work for the day. What was I getting ready to do?

Supper. I would have to do something about supper. I opened the refrigerator door, and it was packed solid with food. For the first time I noticed that the apartment had been cleaned and that somebody—one of my brothers' wives, or two or three of them—had also bought groceries. There was milk—whole milk—and cheeses and bacon and Genoa salami and ice cream and a dozen other things that I wasn't supposed to think of, let alone put in my stomach.

I wasn't hungry, but I needed something to do, so I continued to rummage through the refrigerator's contents. Of all the things there, the only one that would have made my doctor happy was an apple. I took a bite and went back to the couch, turned on the TV, and started looking at the people on the screen. The apple was dry and mushy, so I put it on the coffee table and leaned my head against the pillow. I felt so tired.

The first ring of the telephone scared the hell out of me, and I tried to jump up but couldn't move. It took me a couple of seconds, but I finally realized I was home. The bright spot was the television screen. Everything else was dark. I figured out I must have fallen asleep. So far so good. The light from the screen was enough to let me reach out to exactly where the phone was, and I picked it up.

"Hello," I said.

"Vinnie?"

"Hello, Ma."

"You all right, Vinnie?"

"I'm fine, Ma."

"Did you eat something?"

"Yeah. The refrigerator was full of food."

"Angie. Angie and Lorraine did that." My mother liked Angie better than she did Lorraine.

"That was nice of them."

"You want to come over?"

"No, not tonight, Ma. I'm going to bed early."

"You call me in the morning, you hear?"

"Yeah, I'll do that. Good-bye, Ma."

I had barely hung up when it rang again, and this time it was my brother Petey. He said about the same things my mother did, and then he said he'd talk to me tomorrow. Within the next half hour the rest of my brothers called and then Brady, and I should have put a message on my machine that I was all right, and no, I didn't want to eat at their houses, and yeah, I would call them tomorrow. But instead of that, I answered it each time because they all cared so much and meant so well. There was one other thing. I was lonely, and it felt good to talk to somebody. There was another one other thing. It was still fairly early and I didn't know what to do with myself. I couldn't sit still enough to watch television or read anything. I could have gone to somebody's house or called a girl and gone for a drink or maybe a movie or just sat and visited, but I realized it would be tough to try and make conversation with anyone—my brothers, Brady, a date. And one final thing. One final thing that I had to face up to. Mr. Death. He was still sitting up there on my shoulders, and I was scared. I had to say it aloud.

"I'm scared," I told the room, then flipped on the light switch. "Me. Vinnie. Vinnie Altobelli. I'm scared."

Saying it didn't make it go away or cause me to feel any better. But at least I wasn't trying to hide it at the back of my head anymore. In school, if I thought I might be afraid of somebody, I usually picked a fight with him. It wasn't that I wanted to show everybody that I was king of the hill. It was just something I had to prove to myself. And even the two times I got beat up real bad did some good. Because even as I was getting trashed, I realized that I wasn't afraid, that the guy could kill me but I wasn't afraid of him.

But Mr. Death was a different matter entirely. There was no way to fight back. He just sat up there on your shoulders until the weight brought you down. And then you weren't there anymore. In the hospital I had looked out the window one day, and I could see people walking down the street going about their business, and I realized that if I died it wouldn't make any difference to them one way or another. It would hurt my family, but even for them life would go on without me. I thought of all the people who had died before me, who I had felt bad about, but my life had gone on. And now it was my turn to disappear, and life would go on.

I went into the bedroom to the closet and took the shoe box from the closet shelf. Brady had said that's where he had put my piece, and there it was. I pulled it out of the holster and walked back to the living room, where I turned off the TV and sat down on the couch. Brady had unloaded it, so I picked up the magazine and slapped it in, pulled back the slide, and fed a bullet into the chamber. Three times in my years on the force I had walked into a room where a guy was sitting on a couch or in a chair with a gun on the floor and half his head blown away. "Poor bastard," I had said, and I could hear my own voice echoing in my ear. "Poor bastard."

Was that what I had become—a poor bastard? I clicked the magazine out of the gun and ejected the cartridge. I might be a lot of things and I didn't know what I might become in the future, but nobody was ever going to stand over me and say "Poor bastard."

I tossed the gun on the couch. I would need a permit for it if I wanted to carry it from now on. What the hell did I need a gun for now? I'd never shot at anybody while I was on the force. Why would I need a gun now? The only reason was that I would feel naked without it hanging on me somewhere.

Twenty minutes past seven. It was twenty minutes past seven. Too early to go to bed even if I was sleepy. I went into the bathroom and washed my face with cold water and could feel my hands shaking as I picked up the towel. The funny feeling was gurgling inside my stomach, and I felt just a little dizzy. Twenty minutes past seven. Christ, I had missed my Isosorbide pill. I stood there a moment, thinking about not taking any more pills, letting whatever was going to happen just happen. Then I went to the kitchen and drew some water and swallowed the pill. I could feel my eyes getting all wet, and the feeling in my stomach was becoming colder by the second, and I picked up the phone to call my mother or one of my brothers or Brady or the doctor, and then I put it down again. What was I going to tell them? How could any of them understand who didn't know what it was like inside?

I shook my head the way a dog does when it gets out of the water, but that didn't change anything. One of the residents at the hospital had talked to me about post-cardiac depression, and I had half listened as though I was interested, but it hadn't meant anything to me. Was that what I was going through? I tried to remember what the guy had said, but it wouldn't come back. I hadn't listened. Maybe I should sign up for one of those groups the doctor had mentioned.

There were a lot of other people with heart attacks. They were probably going through the same thing. But what if they were? It still wouldn't do anything to get me back on the force. If only I had somebody to talk to who would understand without the whole fucking world being involved. If only I could go back to where I had been. I looked up at the ceiling as though I expected God to be there to explain it to me. But there was just the ceiling. Nothing more, only the ceiling.

10

Everybody was still checking on me, but people had their own lives to live, even my mother and father, and I had a lot of time to myself. The doctor said I could go back to work whenever I wanted as long as it was something within my physical capabilities, as he put it, but the only work I did was jogging around the track and opening the disability checks from the city. Being a cop was what I did. What the hell else did I know how to do? I stopped in to see the boys at the precinct one day, and everybody was nice as hell, but after a couple of minutes we ran out of things to say to each other.

The captain was in his office, so I said what the hell and went in to see him.

"How are you doing, Altobelli?" he asked

"Fine," I told him. "I'm doing good. I was just

29

wondering if there was some kind of job I could do until I get my full strength back. I'm going nuts on the outside, Captain. There has to be some way in which I can be of service to the department. I know everybody out on the streets, I could still do interrogations, there's nobody better at interrogations, Captain, and . . ."

"Vinnie," he said, "Vinnie. If it were up to me, you'd be back in your old job right now. You were the best detective in the city. If they gave the okay, you'd be at your old desk this afternoon."

"Who's they?" I asked him.

"They?" It took him a few seconds to round them up. "The police surgeon. The medical board. The chief. He has the final word. Why don't you go see the chief, and I'm sure he'll take care of you. Let me call and see if he's in."

The captain usually wasn't this accommodating. But he wanted me out of there and in somebody else's hair. So five minutes later I was up in the chief's office, where I had been only twice before, once to get commended and once to get yelled at. His hello was bigger than even the captain's had been.

"Vinnie," he said. "Vinnie, Vinnie. It's good to see you up and around. You look great."

"I feel great, Chief," I told him, even though I was stretching it a bit. "I was just talking to the captain about coming back to work, maybe starting at a desk until I got my full strength back."

That wiped the welcome-home smile off his face. He started off the same way the captain had begun.

"Vinnie," he said, "if I had my way, you'd be back in here tomorrow." That wasn't as good as the captain, who had wanted to get me back the same afternoon. "But we've got to face realities, son.

You've got a damaged heart, but that's only part of the story. You know who they're replacing you with? Nobody. The budget is so tight that we can't bring in even one academy graduate. The next three guys that retire will not be replaced. Here they keep yelling that we need more cops, and at the same time they cut the budget by a third. You know what, Vinnie? I envy you. I can't wait until my retirement so I can get out of this rat race. You're lucky, Vinnie. You've got a nice pension and no worries. You're a lucky guy."

I was so fucking mad that I don't know what I would have done or said if his phone hadn't rung before I could open my mouth. He picked it up and listened, instructed whoever it was to wait, and then told me to drop in any time. I sat for a moment, the anger burning in me, but there was nothing else to do but leave. What the hell could I do anyway? Punch him out? He had some blubber on him, but he would have given me a hard time of it even before anything happened to me. Yell at him? He could outyell a typhoon. I didn't go back into the squad room, although I could see the back of Brady's head at his desk. They were all working away, writing up reports, talking on the phone, asking questions of somebody or just yakking. I could never be part of that again. The final nail in the coffin was the one time I answered a newspaper ad that said this company had several security posts open. The head of security, an ex-cop named Dougherty, was all excited about my credentials until he asked why I had left the force. Then a curtain fell over his face. "I'll be frank with you, man," he said. "The company wouldn't let me take you on for a minute."

"I'm all right now," I told him. "My doctor says I'm in great shape."

"That may be, but if something did happen, there could be a lawsuit, and they want no part of anything like that."

"Suppose I signed a paper releasing them from any liability?" I asked. "Then they'd have nothing to lose."

"Those waivers don't mean shit," he said. "You or your family could still go to court if something happened. Christ knows I would like nothing better than to have a real cop like you to get all my misfits in line, and I'd be willing to take the chance personally, but the company won't go for it, and there's nothing I can do."

One Saturday I went to watch the guys play ball and stood talking to the wives and girlfriends while my brothers and the others banged each other around. When I asked if I could run a few plays, there was this big silence for a moment and then my brother Don said, "Sure. Come and be quarterback."

Joe Montana never had protection in the pocket the way I did, and I could see that the others were not really trying to get to me before I threw. I heaved one long. When my brother Frankie jumped up to intercept it, my brother Pete whacked him so hard that he lay on the ground for a full minute before he would reach up for Pete's hand. Right then everybody claimed they were pooped and they quit even though they usually play a half hour longer. And when they were standing around swigging beers, they all made it a point to talk to me and tell me how good I looked out there, just like the old days, but mostly they were ragging each other about how lousy the other guys played. I looked at them standing there all sweaty and drinking cold beers, and remembered how it was to take a shower after a workout like that. There's nothing better than taking a long shower after you've worked up a good sweat. Almost nothing better.

Petey's wife, Delores, insisted I come for dinner that night, and there was a girl there, a really nice, as well as nice-looking, girl they thought might be just the ticket for me. But in the middle of eating it was time to take one of my Cardene pills, and when I looked up they all had their eyes on me. So I told them I was tired and went home early. The one good thing was that nobody argued with me about anything for too long. And if they forgot and did argue once in a while, I could just put a look on my face and they would freeze.

"You all right?" they would ask.

I stopped making those faces because I realized what my nurse would say about it: "Cut that shit out, Altobelli. You'll be a full time invalid if you act like one."

What did I want to be full time? The pension check was enough to keep me going, but it wouldn't get any bigger. A guy had come around once with an insurance policy that would have taken care of the very situation I was in, but it had sounded too expensive. Too expensive. I should have rolled the dice. In any case, I had to do something if I wanted to get a new car once in a while or take a vacation from my permanent vacation or buy Christmas presents for my family. I started feeling the scared thing in my belly again, and I shut my mind off. My mother would have said that God would take care of it, and if I started going to church again, something good would happen.

"What Mass do you want to go to?" I asked the television set. "Afterward, God will provide."

There was a knock on the door, and I looked at the clock. Too early for one of my brothers to be off work.

Maybe Brady was dropping by for a break from the routine. I opened the door and three guys were standing there. Jesus, that was smart. I should put a sign out for all robbers and muggers that former detective Vinnie Altobelli was now open for business with no questions asked. All you had to do was knock on the door. They didn't act like they meant me harm, but the two big ones on each side of the dapper guy in the middle looked like they could bend steel bars with their pinkies.

"Vincent Altobelli?" the aforesaid guy inquired.

I nodded.

"Tony Pardo," he said, sticking out his hand.

Jesus! I suppose I should have recognized him, but all I'd ever seen were pictures. Tony Pardo. Mr. Mob. Mr. Mafia. Mr. Nobody Never Proved Nothing. Often questioned, sometimes by policemen, sometimes by federal grand juries, sometimes by congressional committees, but never indicted even once in his whole life. Great giver to charities, great attender of social and sports events, great dresser. But biggest laugh of all: graduate of the Harvard Business School. I wonder what the president of Harvard said to the dean of admissions when their Tony bloomed into full flowerhood. Led the quiet life until his father died, and he took over the empire. His two goons would have clean records also, and permits to carry weapons because they were "occasionally trusted to convey large sums of money" for one of Pardo's multitude of corporations. This guy didn't miss a trick. If one of his goombahs was ever arrested for anything, including speeding, the guy disappeared, sent off somewhere else to work for the company. Reportedly, if they got caught doing something a second time, they disappeared again—permanently.

I instinctively stuck out my hand to shake his, and said, "What do you want with me?"

"May I speak with you privately?" he asked, indicating with his hand that we should go into the apartment.

I hesitated.

"Just the two of us," he said. "My friends will stay out here."

I backed off and let him in. Our paths had never crossed before, and I had never worked on a case that might have had anything to do with his operations. I did feel a little uneasy, but if he had wanted me killed or worked over, it wouldn't have been done like this. It would have happened someplace else, and he and his guys would have been in Madagascar at the time.

Pardo inspected the apartment, his face a mask. It must have looked like a dump to him, but he showed no disrespect. While he inspected the apartment, I inspected him. He had to be pushing forty hard, but his face was unlined and pink skinned. Mother Nature doesn't care one way or another if you're not a good person. There was nobody God would approve of more than my brother Petey, yet his thirty-seven-year-old face was swarthy and filled with wrinkles. Pardo was about as short as the actor who played in all the "Godfather" movies, Pacino, and yet I would bet the two hulks with him wouldn't dare breathe if he gave them a look. All in all a nice-looking man, but all-in-all not a nice man. The kind of man I despised, yet I showed him no disrespect.

"What do you want?" I asked again, feeling the dampness come out on the palms of my hands.

"I'm here to make you a business proposition," he said.

"A business proposition?"

"Yes. One that I think you won't refuse. I want to hire you to be head of security for all my corporations. A lot of my businesses are cash operations that invite stealing by employees: some of them deal with merchandise that can be misappropriated; others involve buildings and stores that must be adequately guarded and have employees protected. I need someone who can oversee the whole operation, train people, build up employee loyalty and dedication, protect our enterprise from any outsiders who might do us harm of even the smallest nature."

He sure talked like Harvard.

"Why me?" I asked. "How did you get my name in the first place, and how do you know I'd be right for the job?"

"I know about you," he said. "I know you were an honest cop and a first-class investigator, a man who took pride in his work, and gave the best he had every day."

"But do you know why I'm not a policeman anymore, what happened to me?"

"You had a heart attack," he said, "a moderately severe heart attack. But you've recovered nicely, you have the right credentials, and you are capable of handling responsibility. You're the man I want."

"But why me?" I asked again. "How do you even know about me?"

"We're related."

He so caught me by surprise that I almost laughed in his face, and then he would have invited in the two goons. I told myself to calm down. "What do you mean we're related?"

"My aunt Clara is cousin to your grandmother Concini."

"My grandmother never said anything about being related to your family."

"There's bad blood. My aunt Clara never says anything about your grandmother Concini."

"How do you know about this if nobody talks about it?" I asked him.

"I hired an expensive genealogist to do a family tree for me, and it's all there."

I almost cracked that he could have gotten it done cheaper by getting copies of the police files, but by that time I was feeling easier and in better control.

"What you want done," I told him, "is something that the big detective agencies specialize in. I haven't had any real experience in organization or administration. You want to talk to guys in sharp suits who carry briefcases."

"I've used those in the past," he said, "and found them to have no real understanding of the kinds of problems we have. I want a real cop whose nose quivers when something's wrong."

"I don't know," I told him. "It sounds interesting, but my specialty is going after one piece of slime and tracking him to the ground. What you want——"

"The pay's good," he broke in. "You're going to find things tight if you try to get by on just your pension."

The son of a bitch knew everything about me. He even knew what I was thinking.

"I don't know," I said again. "After all, I was a cop, and you . . . you are what you are, and I don't know if I'd feel comfortable working for you even if I could do the job."

"I'll pay you a million dollars," he said, "and there are perks that go along with it."

I felt my heart skip a beat, and I wondered if this crazy man was going to drive me into a heart attack.

Slow and steady. Slow and steady was the course. A million bucks! Did he take me for a fucking idiot?

"I don't know what the hell's going on here," I told him, "but it's not doing me any good. I do have a heart condition, you know," and I tried putting that look on my face that froze off my family and friends. I just wanted him out of there.

"I know all about heart attacks," he said. "My father died from one, and it's in my family. The genes. There's nothing you can do about the genes."

"There's no way you can be offering me a million dollars for any kind of a job," I said, getting a little pissed off. "There's got to be more to it than what you've told me, and considering who you are, it's got to be something outside the law if you're at all serious. What the hell would I tell my family and friends if I started working for you, and I was knee-deep in money all of a sudden? Knee-deep in shit is where I would be, and over my head is where I would end up. I think we've talked long enough."

"Okay," he said, "you're a good detective. I have been holding out on one thing. The offer is legitimate, and I'm sure you can do the job, but there is one more thing that has priority over all the others."

I waited, in complete control of myself this time.

"Somebody in my family is trying to kill me," he said, "and I want you to find out who it is."

11

Why would anybody in your family want to kill you?" I asked, and for the first time I broke through the evenness of his face. It twisted into the kind of look you expect from a gang boss instead of a Harvard man, and his voice took on the harshness of a snarl. His hands clenched into fists, and I thought of the two guys standing outside in the hall, and how all it would take would be one yell, and I'd be dead before I could reach the telephone, let alone the unloaded gun in the shoe box in the closet.

"I keep asking myself that," he said, his voice quavering just below a shake. "I give them everything they want, everything. I take care of all the problems, all the worries. Everything. I give them everything. And yet somebody, or maybe more than one somebody, is trying to waste me. I want you to find out who they are."

"What kind of family are you talking about?" I asked. "Are you talking organization family or family family?"

"That's for you to find out," he said, his lips barely open as he gritted the words out.

"And what happens if I do take the job and do find out?" I asked. " Am I supposed to take them down? Is that why it's a million bucks? Do they get rubbed out in front of me? Are we talking about blood money here?"

"We're talking about being hired to do a job, doing it, and then going on to something else," he said, the normal tone returning to his voice. "When you were on the force, that's what you did. You did the job and then the other people took over. I'm not thinking of rubbing somebody out. I'm thinking of protecting my own ass so that I don't get rubbed out. I'm talking about self-preservation, which every man is entitled to."

"What would I have to do?" I asked.

"Come out and live in the house with us. Snoop around. Do whatever the hell a detective does. Find out who's trying to kill me."

"What do you mean when you say that somebody is trying to kill you?"

"What do I mean? Twice I've been shot at while standing on my own terrace, and once the bullet came this fucking close." He held up two fingers about an inch apart. "Twice there have been bombs. Once in the car and once in the desk in my office. Once somebody doctored a bottle of wine. If I wasn't as lucky as I am smart, I'd be up there bullshitting with my father."

Down there, I thought. Down there bullshitting with your father.

"I don't know," I told him. "First of all, I don't know if I'd want the job. Secondly, I don't know if I could do the job. Thirdly—"

"Wait, wait," he said, holding up his hand. He went to the door, opened it, and said something to one of the guys outside, who handed him one of those leather cases that businessmen carry around. He closed the door, took the case over to the table and unhooked the catch. With flicks of his thumbs, he pushed up the cover, and inside were stacks of bills, all neatly packed together. It was straight out of "Miami Vice."

"There's a hundred grand in there," he said. "Consideration money. You consider everything I've told you for a couple of days and then decide what you want to do. Whatever it is, yes or no, the money is yours free and clear. No questions asked, no hard feelings. I just want you to think it over and know that there's another nine hundred thousand waiting."

"What am I supposed to tell the income tax people?"

"You can tell them nothing, or we can set it up that you're on salary as head of security for my umbrella corporation, and you pay your taxes like the next honest man."

"Does this money have cocaine dust all over it?"

"Look," he said patiently, like he was explaining the way of the world to a high school social studies class, "at this stage of the game there is no money in the United States, not one fucking dollar, that doesn't have cocaine dust sprinkled over it."

"Suppose I tell you to take it with you, that I don't want anything to do with it?"

He gave me a long look, measuring me. "Then I take it with me," he said, "and that's the end of it."

"All I have to do is think your offer over?" I asked. "It's mine whether or not I take the job, and there are no strings attached, nothing happening to me on a dark night?"

He smiled. "Hey," he said, "do you know what a hundred grand means to me? Do you know what a million bucks means to me?"

The ripped envelope from my pension check was on

the table beside the case with the money. He'd made his point.

"I'll think about it and let you know," I said.

He smiled again. "I'll call you in two days," he said, sticking out his hand again, which I shook. "That is, unless the sons of bitches get me first. I'm living like a fucking monk, afraid to go back to my own house. A million bucks. Think about it."

I didn't move for maybe five minutes after he went out the door, listening to hear if anything was going on outside. Then I went over to the case and lifted out one of the packets. Tens, twenties, and fifties. All a little bit used and none in sequence. Unless there was a hidden dye or something, untraceable. You couldn't believe what a man like him said. There had to be something else. But I'd let him leave the money. That was an agreement of some kind. I could always give it back to him, say, Take your money and leave me alone. But I already was alone. A man with a bad heart is all alone no matter how many people are around him. What the hell was there to lose except my life? And that was already up for grabs.

I put the stack back in the case and ran my hand along the lid. Real leather. Those Harvard guys had class. A hundred thousand dollars. I could feel a smile work its way onto my face, and I did nothing to stop it.

12

To hell with it," I told the world, and broke into a trot. It was a quarter-mile track, and I had worked myself up to eight laps in twenty-six minutes without going into a heavy sweat or having anything hammering at my chest from the inside. The doc had said to increase the distance and the pace gradually, not to push it, but I had already been home four weeks, and the inactivity was beginning to get to me.

Two times when I had eaten dinner with my folks and had let my ma talk me into tasting something that was dangerous even for my uncle Pietro, who could chew concrete and digest it, my stomach had kicked back, and there had been pains. The question you ask yourself each time is what kind of pains?

"You're doing fine," the doc had said. "The medicines are working, your pumping action is normal, your cardiograms are consistent. If I didn't know you had the heart attack, I would have trouble picking it out on the graph."

He stopped talking for a moment and looked me straight in the eyes, straight enough to make me sit up and square my shoulders. "But don't delude yourself," he finished. "You had a heart attack, and the damage, though minimal, is there."

"What about marriage?" I asked him. "What about getting married and having kids? What about . . . ?"

He put his hand up in the air and stopped me. "The only word you need in your life is 'moderation,'" he said. "Moderation in everything. Whether it be exercise or eating or marriage or having kids makes no difference as long as you don't extend yourself beyond your heart's present capabilities. You can't let yourself get excited or upset or any of the other luxuries available to the average citizen."

"What about my job? Suppose I handled it the way you suggest, taking it easy and . . ." His smile stopped me.

"I've already talked to the police surgeon," he said. "They needed a full report on your condition. I don't know what the policy is at the police department, whether they can give you some kind of duty away from danger or strain, but I would not advise your getting in a situation where your life was endangered. There are all kinds of opportunities for a man of your experience and capability. But running up several flights of stairs to grapple with a criminal is not one of them. There are all kinds of support groups for people like you. I suggest you enroll in a cardiac-fitness program—we have an excellent one at our hospital—to find out how far you can go with your body, and that you find a good therapist who conducts sessions in this kind of problem. You're not alone, you know. You are definitely not alone."

But I was alone. I was definitely alone. Nobody at the department had bothered to tell the doctor that his report had forced me on pension. There was no sense hassling him about it, but I wasn't going to take part in any fitness class with all those middle-aged and even old guys who had suffered heart attacks. They'd had their shot at life and just wanted to coast comfortably the rest of the way. I was a good cop and a better detective, and I'd been on my way up on the force. There was no reason why I couldn't have been the first Italian chief. No reason at all. Until now. Until this.

But mostly what was bothering me that day on the track was Mimi Barnes. I had taken her out to dinner the night before, my first real adventure on my own, and afterward we had gone up to her apartment and were sitting around watching some TV and she smelled awful good and she was wearing a sweater with a deep V cut, and I turned her face toward me and kissed her on the lips and slipped my hand down her front and felt that rubbery smoothness that's like nothing else in the world, and I started to move my hand between her legs when she pushed me away with the sides of her arms and gave me a strange look.

"What's the matter?" I asked her.

"Do you think you should be doing this kind of thing?"

"Christ, we've done it a hundred times before."

"But this time it's different."

"You mean you don't want to do it?"

"It's not that, Vinnie. But suppose something happened to you. I mean, while were doing it."

Jesus! How dumb can I be?

"You mean suppose I had a heart attack while we were doing it?"

She didn't answer. Didn't need to answer. I was so mad I had to clench my fists not to reach out at her. I could feel my heart start to pound. Moderation, the doc had said. I couldn't let myself get excited or upset. Or mad. Jesus, I was all three right then. She was worried about what she would do, how it would look, how inconvenient it would be if I croaked while I had my prick inside her.

I stood up and started for the door, wanting to get

out of there before I said or did anything that I couldn't handle later.

"You'll call me?" she asked as I reached the door.

I didn't answer.

I lay in bed all that night wondering, wondering if a piece of ass would kill me. Not a bad way to go, I kept telling myself, not a bad way to go. But I didn't want to die. I wanted to get old like my parents and get married and have kids and play pool with my brothers and drink beer and eat pasta and have a boat and stop all the scrimy bastards of the world from picking on decent people. I had enjoyed being a cop, and I was a good one. Whenever I made a collar, I came home feeling something special inside me, as if I was a doctor or a priest. My mother had wanted me to be a priest, she'd wanted all of her sons to be priests, but she really brought the pressure on me because I was the last one she had a crack at. She wasn't only disappointed in that; she had never understood my becoming a cop. "We've had plenty of crooks in our family," she used to say, "but never no cop."

She did insist I go to the community college, though, and I now had an associate degree in criminology. My brother Petey was the only other one who had gone to college, and he had an honest-to-God diploma from Notre Dame and a master's degree from Wharton. My other four brothers had their own businesses and made as much or more than Petey. I had been the low man on the pole, and now I wasn't even on the pole.

So that's why I broke into a trot after I had fast-walked the first eight laps. If I'd gone to that cardiac class, they would have had me hooked up to all kinds of monitors to make sure I didn't go beyond the limits, but here I just had me. The first lap didn't feel too bad, so I started in on the second lap at the same pace, and that's when the pressure started pushing on my left side and I could feel it moving up and over to the middle and there was a sharp pain, and I stopped, standing there all sweaty, waiting for the big one, the good-bye, goombah.

Two seconds after I stopped it was all gone, nothing, just normal, with my pulse starting to ease off. I must have taken my pulse twenty times a day since I'd been home, and it was always nice and steady and slow. Some of this was because of the medicine, the doc had said.

The sun was drying the sweat on me, and a chill passed over my body so quick that it was almost as if it hadn't happened. Someone walking on my grave. I looked down at my right hand, which was beginning to go into the sign to ward off evil that my grandma Bella had taught me when I was five years old. Go away, Mr. Death.

I walked over to the bench where I had left my sweatshirt and took several deep breaths before sitting down. No pain. No pressure. But they had been there. They had been there. Mimi Barnes had been right. A guy who couldn't run two laps was nobody to fuck with. I thought of a hundred thousand dollars sitting on my closet floor, and nine hundred thousand more waiting to squeeze out the rest of my shoe space. There was no way I could take on Tony Pardo's problem. I had enough of my own.

13

Things didn't look any brighter the next day, and I didn't get dressed until almost noon. Every morning I had taken my walks or runs at the park, but right then there was no strength in me, and I didn't eat anything, or take a shower, or want to leave the house. Mostly I sat and stared at the television screen even though I hadn't turned it on to watch anything. I knew that if I clicked the remote, I would bring people into the room with me, and even though they wouldn't know I existed, they would be more than I could handle. The problem was that there was nobody in my life who really understood what it was like to have your legs cut out from under you—not my brothers, not Brady, not anybody. It was like they were from one planet and I was from another. If only there was somebody from my planet who would be able to understand what I was going through. If only . . . I banged my forehead with the palm of my hand just like my grandmother Nano did when she forgot to serve the vegetable she had cooking on the stove. How stupid could you be? I dug into my left-hand pants pocket. Nothing. These weren't the pants I had worn home from the hospital. Which ones were they? The gray ones. Frankie had brought me the pair of gray ones. I rushed into the bedroom and pawed through the stuff that had been in the suitcase. The gray ones. I put my hand in the pocket and felt some paper. Kleenex. I put my hand in the other pocket and felt paper again. Pulling it out made my heart pound. It was all balled up, but when I unrolled it, there it was. Betty Wade. I punched in the numbers and listened to it ring—three, four, five. Just listening to it ring made me feel better even if she wasn't there, and I don't know how long I stood just listening, barely hearing it in the distance.

"Hello," a voice said. "Hello." It was a woman's voice. Husky. "Hello," it said again.

"Hello," I answered.

"Who is this?"

"It's Vinnie."

"Vinnie?" There was a pause. "Vinnie? Altobelli? Is it Altobelli?"

"Is that you?" I asked her.

"Of course it's me. I was taking a nap. That's why it took me so long to recognize who it was."

"It's me," I told her. "It's Vinnie."

"Are you all right? Are you having pains?"

"No, I'm not having pains. But I don't think I'm all right."

"What's bothering you?"

"It's . . ." I couldn't talk for a minute, but she didn't say anything, just waited. "It's that I'm . . . that I'm . . . I think I'm . . . scared."

"Where are you?"

"I'm at my apartment."

"Is anybody with you?"

"No."

"Do you want someone from your family there? Or a friend?"

"No."

"What do you want?"

"I don't know."

"Can you drive? Did the doctor say you could drive?"

"Yes, I can drive."

"Do you know where Burger Lane is, off Seventy-sixth Street?"

"I know that area."

"I'm at number seven-thirty, apartment seven-I. I'll tell the doorman you're coming. Give me a half hour. I have to shower."

"Betty?"

"Yes?"

"Do you know what's wrong with me?"

"I think I do. But when you get here, we'll talk about it and find out."

"Should I call the doctor?"

"Are you having pains?"

"No. No pains."

"Then come over here first. I'll see you in a half hour."

She clicked off. I held the phone for a long time before putting it back on the hook. I felt better. Just hearing her voice made me feel better. I switched on the tape and said, "This is Vinnie. I'm over visiting a friend. Leave your name and number and I'll get back to you."

14

She was wearing one of those shabby hospital bath-robes and a small towel wrapped around her head. Her face was pink and shiny and wet, and the circles under her eyes didn't seem as dark without any makeup to set them off.

"Altobelli," she said, grabbing the sleeve of my sweater with her left hand, "come on in."

It was a nice apartment except for one thing: there wasn't any furniture. Not any real furniture. There was just a small table and two folding chairs, a beat-up floor lamp and a trunk with the lid open.

"You been robbed?" I asked her.

"No." She laughed. "I'll explain it all later. Come into the bedroom. The bed's the only soft place in the whole apartment."

That's all there was in the bedroom—a bed. That is, if you didn't count the big cardboard boxes and milk crates scattered around. The closet door was open, but there wasn't much hanging in there. Clothes were scattered around the floor, some spread out and others just balled together or thrown down any which way. It was so different from the hospital room. She swung onto the bed, crossed her legs like one of those yogas, and patted a place near her to show where I was supposed to settle.

"Take off your shoes," she ordered, "and then you

51

can sit comfortably like I am." I did as I was told, but I sure didn't feel comfortable. It was so different to be with her like this instead of me lying there with tubes sticking out and machines hitched up, and her all neat and clean and sure, moving around me continually.

"It ain't much," she said, reading my mind, "but it's sure better than being tied down in ICU."

It took me a second. ICU. Intensive care unit.

"So," she said, "are you back in your own apartment? Are you taking your pills? Are you doing your exercises? Are you watching your diet? Are you keeping calm and steady?"

Just listening to her talk made me feel better, and I knew if I could have her around me all the time, there would be no problems, I would be the Vinnie of old. No, I was never going to be the same Vinnie again. The guy who had come out of ICU was not the same one who went in. "Don't delude yourself," the doctor had said. Once your body crosses the line, there's no going back.

"I'm doing okay," I told her.

"You didn't sound okay when you called," she said. "You sounded pretty unfucking okay."

She caught me by surprise with that. I was used to hearing girls swear, and not just the ones who were dragged into the station. On some of my collars the language of the women, the names I was called, made me feel nervous. The drug dealers' women were the worst. They would tell you to do things that made a simple "fuck you" sound like a priest giving you a blessing. And you couldn't walk down the street without hearing some fourteen-year-old girl yelling swearwords exactly like those you heard in the police locker room. A couple of the girls I had dated thought it smart to say "shit" and "fuck," but it never rang right in my ear.

So I was having trouble understanding why my nurse would use a word like that. I didn't swear once while I was with her in the hospital, and even Brady, who can't say a long word like "Mediterranean" without sticking a "fuck" in the middle of it, had been a choirboy whenever he visited me.

There must have been a strange look on my face because she cocked her head to one side, took my chin in her hand, and looked me straight in the eyes. "What's the matter, Altobelli?" she asked. "Did you get a sudden pain? Are you dizzy? Do you feel all right?"

"I'm all right," I mumbled.

"No, you're not all right. What just went through your body or your mind?"

"Nothing. It's nothing."

"Is it because I'm not like I seemed to be in the hospital? Do you miss the uniform? The cool, clinical manner? I'm just a woman, Altobelli. I'm not some angel that God sent down to man the ICU. I've never been as constipated as you were, but I use the bathroom for the same things you do."

"What are you trying to do?" I asked her.

She stopped and gave me a long look. "I guess maybe I'm trying to show you that the world hasn't changed because you've had a heart attack. That people are people, and outside of some physical restrictions, you're still people too. Now, something is bothering the hell out of you, and I want to help. But before I can help, I've got to know what needs helping. The problem right now is in your mind, not your body. But you're the kind of guy who would rather suffer than talk to somebody like a psychologist or a social worker. So you call me up in hopes that I can reassure you, can answer questions you're afraid or ashamed to ask anybody else—the doctor, your brothers, that big ape who was your partner. As my father used to say, am I right or am I right?"

She didn't just look pretty, she looked beautiful, and I wanted her to wrap her arms around me and hold me on that bed forever, not thinking, not worrying. By the second day in the hospital it wasn't the tubes or the monitors that were keeping me alive—it was her. She was connected to my body and mind in a way that let her know everything that was going on inside there, and she was the one who brought me back, who kept me breathing, who pumped the life back into me.

"You're right," I told her.

"Okay. Now that we have that settled, tell me what's bugging you."

I wasn't sure where to start. Things were bugging me all right, but it was hard to talk about them with another person. Except this wasn't just another person. This was The Nurse.

"I don't know what I'm going to do with my life," I finally confessed. "I can't be a cop anymore. I can't play basketball or football or softball with the guys on Saturday morning anymore. I can't eat this and I can't drink that, and I'm not supposed to lift anything heavy higher than my waist, and I'm not sleeping right, and everybody treats me like I'm an egg with a cracked shell . . . and I can't . . . I can't . . ."

I looked at her, and I could feel my throat tightening up so that I couldn't talk.

"You were a pretty lusty guy, weren't you, Altobelli?" she broke in.

That cleared my throat in a hurry, but I didn't know what to say.

"What did the doctor tell you about sex, Altobelli?"

"I didn't ask him."

"Did it cross your mind?"

"Yeah. I almost asked him, but I didn't."

"You wondering if and when you can get laid again, Altobelli?"

It was as if she had hit me in the head with a brick, and I was too shook up to talk. I just looked at her some more. Christ, I didn't know what to do. So I looked at her.

"There's no reason you can't have a normal sex life, Altobelli. I'm not talking about taking on a Turkish harem, but as long as you're all right down there, you don't have to worry about here."

She touched my crotch and then my heart while she was saying this. I looked at her.

"Have you been afraid to try it?" she asked.

"I think I was going to, but the girl . . . the girl . . ." I couldn't get out any more.

"The girl was afraid you might drop dead on her, right, Altobelli? And that made you think about it. You're wondering if you might drop dead while you're doing it. Well, you won't, Altobelli. You won't."

"Yeah. Okay." I didn't know what to say. She was getting me all confused. I had wanted her to say something nice, something reassuring, something medical that would show me I was going to be all right. I didn't know what to say to this kind of thing.

"Yeah. Okay," she repeated, deepening her voice to sound like mine. "You don't believe me, do you, Altobelli? Take off your clothes."

I could only look at her.

"Come on," she said, slipping the bathrobe off behind her and pulling the towel from her head. Her hair tumbled down all damp and glossy, and I sat there, unable to move or think, looking at this beautiful woman naked from the waist up unable to move or think.

She stood up, and the robe fell away, and there she

was a foot away from my face, and I could feel myself stirring. Grabbing my sweater, she started to pull it up over my head, and I lifted my arms, and she helped me to stand up on the shaky bed, and in two minutes I was as naked as she was. Then she sank to her knees, dragging me with her, and we went down on our sides, and she put her arms around my neck.

"Don't panic, Altobelli," she said, and she was almost crooning, her voice soft, her arms moving around my neck. "Just let it all happen as it happens," and she kissed me, soft at first, then harder and harder, and she pulled backwards, and somehow I was in her and riding as hard as I could, but this time she wasn't saying, "Whoa, boy, whoa."

It didn't take long, maybe less than a minute, but it was as good as I've ever had, maybe better, and I could feel my heart beating steady as a drum, and I wasn't dizzy, and I didn't feel strange.

"There, Altobelli," she said. "I hope you were as good as you ever were, because I thought you were pretty damn good. And you're alive and well. Piece of cake. Your life can be a piece of cake the same way if you just go into everything thinking positive. My only word of caution is that you wear a condom if you don't know the woman's background. We didn't need any because I know what your blood tests were, and I know my own. But you be careful with other people."

I started to push up on my elbow, but she still held me around the neck and I relaxed into her again.

"Don't go away yet, Altobelli," she said. "I'm going to take your blood pressure, and then in a little while we're going to do this again. I wouldn't advise it with just anybody, but I'm a trained nurse so we're doing it under controlled circumstances."

My blood pressure was one sixteen over seventy-four.

"I can't understand why you had a heart attack, Altobelli, but sometimes these things happen without any good explanation. With the parents and grandparents you have, you could still live to be a hundred. Now let's see if we can get that blood pressure up again."

This time it was slow and easy because I was making love to a beautiful woman, and I wasn't scared, and she was making love to me in a way that had nothing to do with sex, and if someone had asked me at that moment if I would have given up what was happening in exchange for not having had the heart attack, I'm not sure what I would have answered. Probably not to have the heart attack, but I wasn't sure.

"Now I'm going to have to take another shower," she said, "and there's so much I still have to do."

"Do you want to go out and get something to eat?" I asked her.

"No, I don't have the time."

"What about tomorrow? What do you want to do tomorrow?"

She looked at me and then reached out and pulled me to her and gave me a long slow kiss.

"There isn't going to be any tomorrow for us, Altobelli," she said. "I'm leaving town tomorrow."

It was like when I thought the kid had hit me in the chest, that's how shocked I was.

"I don't understand," I told her.

"I'm moving to Tucson, Arizona, tomorrow, Altobelli," she said, "to work as a pediatric nurse. I'm burned out from ICU. I've got to recharge my batteries."

"But . . . but . . ."

"I like you, Altobelli," she said. "There was something different about taking care of you, bringing you back, making you whole again. Of course, it didn't hurt that you look a little like Rambo. You've got a bunged-up heart, but you're whole again. If you take care of yourself, there's no reason why you can't get married, have kids, do the whole bit."

"But I want you to . . ."

She put her hand over my mouth. "I've got to leave," she said. "I was supposed to go last week, but the hospital held me to my contract to the last day. Maybe if I was staying, something would have worked out between us. I don't know. Right now I just like you a hell of a lot, and I wanted to help you as much as I could. Why don't we leave it at that for now? Write down your address and your telephone number, and I'll send you mine, and who knows what might happen in the future? But I'm going tomorrow, Altobelli. I'm going."

She buttoned my shirt for me and folded the blood pressure machine into its case while I tied my shoes and pulled on my sweater. She took my arm and walked me to the door, then stopped and gave me a long kiss and hug. Finally she opened the door and gently pushed me through it. I stood there looking at the closed door for a minute, but as I turned to leave, it opened again.

"Remember, Altobelli," she said, "nobody dies on me. Nobody."

15

Even though I knew she wouldn't be there, I spent the whole next day calling Betty's number every half hour, but nobody answered no matter how long I let it ring. One time I laid the receiver down on the couch and didn't go near it for fifteen minutes, but it made no difference. Nobody answered. She was gone. To Tucson, Arizona. Hell, I was a cop . . . a former cop. I could track her down in Tucson in ten minutes. How many hospitals could they have in that city?

But she'd told me she'd get in touch with me when she was ready, and she was the kind of person who told it like it was, who laid it out exactly the way she wanted it. So if I went chasing after her before she was primed for it, the whole thing might go down the tubes. I had to be something special to her or she wouldn't have done what she did. She didn't do that for all her heart patients, I was sure. I started to think on that a bit but stopped cold. It was a place I didn't want to go.

I didn't know which was worse, knowing what I'd had or not knowing if it was ever going to happen again. She had brought me back to life twice. I would lie on the bed or sit on the couch thinking about it, not getting all hot or frustrated or angry, but like it was a nice dream that you weren't sure was really happening.

The phone rang. Two days. He said he'd call in two days. Get it over with; get it over with now.

"Yes," I yelled into the phone.

"Vinnie, it's Petey," my brother said.

It took me a few seconds to make the shift, but then I was all right. "How's it going?" I asked.

"I'm fine, but Frankie's got some trouble."

"What kind? What kind of trouble?"

"With the banks. I told him he was expanding too fast, putting too much money into heavy equipment, and now the construction business is down and he's got all this machinery sitting around doing nothing, but the loans are all doing something. I'm trying to raise a hundred thousand to help him out, but I need a few people to co-sign notes, and I wondered if you'd be able to come to the Home Bank this morning and sign one of them. Dominic will sign one, too. I don't want Pa and Ma knowing anything about this, but the bank is putting on a lot of pressure, and we have to do something fast."

"How much does he need?"

"The hundred thousand will hold him until he's paid by the state for the work he did on the highway, and then I think he'll be all right. He wouldn't be in this mess if the fucking state didn't shaft him like this. They keep saying there isn't any money, but they don't want to raise taxes to get the money, so what they do is fuck all the little guys they owe money to. They'll finally get around to it, but it won't do Frankie any good if the bank has closed him down."

I looked up at the ceiling to see if God or the Devil was looking down on me. This kind of coincidence couldn't have happened by chance. My brother Frankie needed a hundred thousand dollars, and I had a hundred thousand dollars in a briefcase in my closet. I could feel my blood pressure going right up through my head. The doc had said to keep the blood pressure down, to stay calm, relaxed, cool. But my brother Frankie needed a hundred very big ones.

"I've got a hundred thousand dollars I can give him," I told Petey.

It took him a few seconds to try to make an adjustment.

"What the hell are you talking about?" he finally managed.

"I didn't tell anybody about this," I said, "but I took out this insurance policy two years ago that paid me a hundred thousand dollars if I got disabled on the job. I notified the agent, and he says he can have the money for me this week. I'll just transfer it over to Frankie's account."

My brother Petey is a smart guy. I could hear him trying to sniff out what was going down right over the telephone.

"A hundred grand?" he said. "You had a policy for a hundred grand? Jesus Christ. But Frankie wouldn't take your money. You've got a . . . You need it for yourself. . . . Frankie wouldn't take your money."

You've got a heart condition, he almost said. Frankie wouldn't take the money from his crippled brother even if his business was flushed right down the toilet. I could feel myself getting hot and a little mad. Even if my family no longer felt I could take care of myself, one of the most powerful men in the whole fucking area thought I could still do a job.

"You said it was just a temporary thing," I told him. "He can give it back as soon as the state pays him off."

"He'd want to pay you interest," said Petey. He'd grabbed at the offer so quick that I wondered if it might not have been that easy for us to get loans from the bank. Petey had a wife and kids and a business. He would have been putting his own ass on the line.

"Forget about all that," I told him. "The main thing is to get Frankie out of the jam. You find out where the money should be paid, and I'll tell the insurance guy to deposit it in there."

"Jesus," said Petey, "a hundred grand and you never said boo. All these years I've been worrying about you spending all your money and ending up without a dime to your name. I've got a doctor client who had one of those policies, and he's going to be sitting on his ass as long as he lives making as much money as he would have if he'd kept working. I looked into it, but they're so expensive. And here I was worrying that you were blowing all your dough on booze and broads. *Salud,* Vinnie, *salud.* I'll call you later today and tell you where to send the money."

I was still looking at the phone I had hung up when it rang again. Another disaster? Or maybe Betty this time.

"Hello," I said, hoping the voice would be sweet and steady.

"It's Tony Pardo, Vinnie. I know I said I'd get back to you in two days, but this is driving me crazy. What I want is—"

"I'll do it," I told him.

"What?"

"I'll take the job. But there's something I want . . . something I'd like you to do for me."

"What's that?"

I told him about my brother's problem and what I wanted to do. "But I can't walk into the bank with a hundred grand in cash," I said. "I'd like you to take the cash back and deposit a hundred thousand from one of your businesses into my brother's account so that everything looks kosher."

There was silence for a few moments.

"I'll tell you what I'm going to do," said Pardo. "You keep the hundred grand you've got, and I'll transfer another hundred K for your brother. That will make a two hundred grand retainer, and if you do the job, there will be another eight hundred thousand for you at the end. You can see how serious I am about this. Where do we send the money?"

"I'll know that later today," I told him. "Give me a number to call."

"Okay. When you get it, you call this number and give the information to whoever answers." He read off a phone number and then said, "He'll know what it's about. And at five o'clock I'll have a car pick you up and bring you out to my house."

"Tonight?"

"Yeah, tonight. I help your brother fast, you help me fast."

"What do I tell my family?"

"Your family? Tell them a friend invited you to his place to rest and recuperate, and it's up in the woods and you'll call them as soon as you can."

"I don't know if I can sell them on that," I told him.

But I could and I did, and at five P.M. I was sitting in the back seat of a black BMW being driven by a guy wearing an honest-to-God chauffeur's outfit. He never said one word picking me up or driving me out to Pardo's place, but his gray suit and peaked cap were so like the ones that you see in the movies that I wondered if he spoke with an English accent. With Tony Pardo you never could tell.

16

Pardo's house—or castle, or whatever you should call a place that big—lived up to the promise of the chauffeur's uniform. As might be expected from a man who knew for a fact that somebody was trying to kill him, the entire area was well lighted, and you could see that the grounds were kept up by an Italian or a Japanese or maybe both. A guy in uniform in a little guardhouse pressed the button to open the gate only after the chauffeur and I got out of the car and stood there under the spotlight. It was the first time the chauffeur had talked to me, and his "Get out" didn't sound very English. That was okay because I knew cops in uniform who weren't really real cops. There was a guy with two German shepherds roaming the grounds as we circled up the long driveway. It all looked like one of those ritzy movies, and I wondered if we were going to be riding to hounds before breakfast.

But I wasn't prepared for the inside of the house after we came through the door. A middle-aged man in a dark suit had been waiting for us at the bottom of the porch steps, which were made out of some kind of fancy colored stone, and the chauffeur handed him my bag from the trunk of the car. I had brought a sports jacket but no ties. The only formal clothing I owned was the dress uniform that I had worn at funerals when I was on the force. I still had trouble getting that straight in my mind. Everything now was in terms of "when I was on the force."

The front hallway looked like the lobby of one of those hotels with a garden in the center and elevators shooting up the outside of the building. The floor had to be real marble, and the furniture could have been genuine antiques for all I knew. Once an investigator for the IRS told me about the guys who owned small businesses and restaurants and skimmed cash every day from the till. They couldn't spend it out loud because someone would squeal to the IRS about extra money coming out of nowhere, so they would go on lush vacations, paying for everything in cash, including diamonds for their wives' fingers. I always wondered what the mob guys did with all the millions that were supposed to be coming in to them every day. If the sixteen-year-old dealers on the street had money to burn, what was the take of these people? How many millions did they have to sit on? They couldn't spread it around too thick or the government would be on them like my uncle Annunzio's bees. Pardo probably took enough from his legitimate businesses to build a place like this and stay within his tax limit, what with mortgages and whatever, but he could put a billion inside his house without anybody knowing the difference. A man's home was his castle, and that was exactly what he had here.

"My name is Jefferson," said the guy in the dark suit. "Mr. Pardo left instructions that you were to be taken to your room, and he will phone you there after you've had a bath and a rest."

A bath and a rest? We were back to Harvard talk. I walked with him to the stairs, but when we got there he turned left and opened a door, which turned out to be an elevator that could hold maybe three people.

"I will show you all the elevator locations so you won't have to climb any stairs," said Jefferson, "and if you will tell me what you are allowed in your diet, I will inform Cook."

"Whatever anybody's eating is good enough for me," I said, a little pissed that Pardo had spread the word on my condition. I wanted to be like everybody else, for Christ's sake, not like an invalid.

"They all eat something different at meals," said Jefferson, "and the kitchen is set up to provide whatever each person wants. Also, if you get hungry during the night, you can call down to the kitchen, and they will prepare anything you desire."

"Twenty-four-hour room service, eh?" I said. "Is there a TV in the bathroom, and do I get mints on my pillow?"

"There is a TV as well as a telephone in your bathroom," the guy said, as cool as my mother's treatment of my brother Dominic's wife, who is a Protestant, "and you can, of course, have mints on your pillow each night if that is what you desire."

There was no way I was going to beat this guy at his game, so I just shut up and followed him down the hall of the second floor until we came to a door at the end of the corridor, and he opened it and waved for me to go in ahead of him. Brady once told me how he had gone on a gambling junket to Las Vegas and they had given him a suite because they knew he was a cop. Brady's setup had sounded like the kind of castle Tony Curtis lived in when he was playing a prince of Baghdad in one of those old movies, but it had to be nothing compared to the mother I was standing in right then.

The bedroom was twice the size of my whole apartment, and the bed looked like one of those that the guy who owned *Playboy* used to exercise bunnies on. There were two corners where three or four chairs were grouped like in somebody's living room, there was wall-to-wall carpet so thick that you sank a little bit into it, there was one of those fifty-six-inch TV sets against the wall opposite the bed, and thirty-inch ones where the chairs were bunched together, and a shelf of videos, and another of compact discs for the stereo hookup, and on the table to the left there was a bottle of white wine in a cooler, and all kinds of little sandwiches and pastries on plates with glass covers.

My mother had asked me who the person was that I was going to visit, and I had told her it was a San Diego cop I had become friendly with at the police convention, and she asked me what kind of place he had up in the mountains, and I had told her it was nice but nothing fancy. I had lied on purpose to my ma plenty of times in my life, but I had never told her this big a lie by mistake.

Jefferson opened the door to the bathroom, which turned out to be three separate rooms instead of one—a little one where you shit, a bigger one with a giant glass shower stall that you could change into a sauna if you wanted, and the main part with a round tub in the middle with air jets inside it, and two wash basins against a wall of solid mirrors. Jefferson showed me where you could stand to have a jet blow warm air all over you to dry you off, just like you could do with your hands in a public toilet that didn't want to bother with paper towels, and how to turn on and off various things, and how you could set the bath and the shower to the exact degrees you wanted the water to be, and it all made me think of the old joke where the guy tells you not to push the third button on the toilet bowl while you were on the seat.

After Jefferson backed out of the room, I strolled around a little to loosen up after the ride in the car. I hadn't had a chance to do my two miles in the morning, but who would have ever thought you could get your exercise just by strolling around a goddamned bedroom? I was tired, what with working myself up to take this thing on, then having to make up the story for my mom, then calling the guy to tell him where Petey said to put the money. I hadn't told Petey about going away because he would have asked a lot more questions about it, and my imagination—or lying, whichever way you looked at it—wasn't that good where a smart guy like him was concerned. Ma would tell him and then it would be too late for him to do anything until I got back. I could hear him now yelling at her that she should have got an address or a phone number, and then her finally shrugging her shoulders and walking away from him. On my tape machine I had just left a message that I was out and would get back to whoever it was as soon as possible. Right then I just didn't want anybody to know I was working for Tony Pardo.

I thought I'd lie down on the bed for a while and rest my eyes, and the next thing I knew the phone was ringing. The grandfather clock in the corner said it was fifteen minutes to eight, and I had to have slept at least a half hour.

"Hello," I said into the phone.

"Vince," said Pardo, "is everything all right? Do you need anything?"

"No. I'm fine."

"Look, we usually eat about eight-thirty if that's okay with you."

"Sure."

"You sound sleepy. You all right?"

"Yes. I'm fine. I fell asleep."

"Oh, sorry I woke you. Take a nice shower and then

you'll wake up. Did you tell the cook what you wanted to eat?"

"Yeah, it's all taken care of. Everything's fine."

"Look," he said, "time is of the essence here. I'm nervous just being in my own goddamned house! You can go nuts wondering who's trying to knock you off when you're in the middle of your own family."

"Maybe it's someone in your own family," popped out of me.

There was a silence. "Jesus Christ," he finally managed, "what are you talking about? That's unbelievable. This is my family, for Christ's sake. I'm the one takes care of them. They all depend on me. If something happened to me, the whole place would turn into shit."

"Look," I said, "the fact that somebody is trying to waste you, or at least scare the hell out of you, is a given. You hired me to find out who that somebody is, and I'm going to earn my money. That means that nobody and nothing's off limits during the investigation. I'm not saying that somebody in your own family is trying to kill you. All I'm saying is don't count out anybody until I find the right somebody. Does your family know everything that's going on or have you kept it from them?"

"They know all right," he yelled. "Christ, my sister Theresa was standing right by me on the terrace the first time it happened. And it was Florence who told me that the wine smelled funny. We could be dead right now if her nose wasn't so big."

"How do you know that somebody isn't trying to kill them instead of you?"

"Why the hell would anyone want to kill them?" he asked. "The bombs were in my car and my desk."

"Did you have the wine analyzed?" I asked.

"No. We dumped it out."

"Then you don't really know if it was poisoned. It could have just turned sour."

"Listen, it smelled like poison. It had to be poison. What with the bullets and the bombs, what the hell else could it have been?"

He had me there.

"I'll be down at eight-thirty," I told him. "How will I know where the dining room is?"

"I'll have one of the maids come up and show you where it is. Listen, did you bring your gun?"

The gun. I hadn't even thought about a gun.

"I don't have a license for it yet."

"There's a gun in the top drawer of the table by your bed," he said. "If you don't like it, we'll get you another one. See you at dinner."

The gun in the drawer was a brand-new Beretta with a full clip lying beside it. A nice gun. There was both a shoulder holster and another rig so you could wear it over your ass if that was your style. I figured I'd be wearing my jacket to dinner in a place like this so the shoulder harness would work fine. What the well-dressed man should wear at Tony Pardo's house.

17

When I opened the door to the soft knocks, a young, attractive bottled blonde was standing there in one of those skimpy black maid's uniforms. We once raided an East Side whorehouse that specialized in costume stuff. The client could have whatever he wanted—a schoolgirl in see-through lingerie, or Little Bo Peep, or even an Amazon dressed in an SS uniform. Brady and I had gone back the next day on some phony reason or other just to rummage in the walk-in closet. This girl could have walked right out of that closet.

"Mr. Altobelli," she said, "I'm here to take you to dinner."

Ordinarily I would have made some wise-guy crack to a dish like this, but I was so surprised to see someone dressed like that in this particular house that I just nodded and followed her to the elevator. She made no pretense of squeezing against the side of the opposite wall, and we stood practically toe to toe all the way up. One more inch and I would have had nipple marks on my jacket.

She didn't say anything or even smile, but the waves that were coming off her would have made a surfer scream with ecstasy. I couldn't understand why we were going up instead of down, but it turned out that the dining room was on the third floor. It seemed to take up half the floor, and I wondered what a place like this would charge to cater my niece Carmen's confirmation party.

There was a table that they had to have bought from the Queen of England. Something like sixty chairs were around it, nine of which had people in them. The maid pointed toward the bunch of them, and then in this soft voice she said, "I'll be back to turn down your bed later." I shifted to look at her, but she was already on her way back to the elevator.

They didn't need her in the dining room because there were three guys in tuxedos and two girls in regular black uniforms waiting on the people who were sitting there. Everybody was clustered at the far end, and Pardo, who was in the place of honor at the head, was the first to notice me.

"Hey, Vinnie," he yelled, jumping up and coming toward me with his hand outstretched. We shook as though we were being introduced for the first time, and then he took my elbow and led me back to the group, where he sat me down beside him.

"Hey, everybody," he yelled, as though all of them already didn't have their eyes pasted on me, "this is my friend Vinnie Altobelli, who was one of the top detectives in the San Bernardino police force before he retired. He's the new head of security for Pardo Enterprises, and he's here for a few days for an orientation session."

Orientation session? I didn't know which was worse —when he talked mob or when he spoke Harvard.

There was an old lady dressed in black on his right, and he introduced me to her first.

"Mama," he told her, "say hello to Vinnie."

"My husband died from a heart attack," she said, with a little bit of an accent and a lot of sob in her voice.

Great. Pardo must have put out an all-points bulletin on my condition. The maid couldn't have known it because she had done her best to put me into shock on the elevator, and I still had her perfume in my nose. But everybody else was staring at me as though I might drop dead on them any minute, and the four men looked willing to do it to me if my heart let them down.

I met Tony's two older brothers, Aldo and Cistercio; his two older sisters, Angelina and Florence; and his two younger sisters, Theresa and Constanza. The other two men, both of them somewhere in their forties, were introduced as José Gonzalez and Sancho Esteban, business associates from South America who were visiting for a few days. I wondered if just by chance they might be from Colombia.

Aldo and Cistercio were also somewhere in the middle forties, maybe four and five years older than Tony, and the two senior sisters looked five or six years beyond that. None of the four was attractive, all of them swarthy, with big features. The two younger sisters, who ranged somewhere between twenty-five and thirty, looked like Tony and more than made up for the ugliness of the others. They were the only two who gave me a smile when Tony mentioned their names. The two older sisters lowered their heads a half inch in turn to show who was who, but the four men looked at me as if I knew where the bodies were buried, and that I might soon be joining them.

Some of them were eating shrimp cocktails and others were spooning up soup, and when I looked down at my plate I saw a menu there, the kind that a restaurant prints out each day to stick in the regular bill of fare. There were five appetizers and three soups and maybe seven entrées and four kinds of pasta and a couple of salads and things like potatoes and vegetables and a whole list of desserts. It didn't just say ice cream in the desserts; it said Ben & Jerry's and Häagen-Dazs and one called Fabulous Phil's, which I'd never heard of before. At the bottom was a list of sandwiches with names—the Tony Pardo, Mama's Favorite, Gretchen's Gruyère, and a whole lot of others—with all ingredients listed. Tony's sandwich had turkey, Genoa salami, sliced mozzarella, bacon, and hot peppers. Sounded good.

A waiter in a tuxedo was standing beside me, but at least he didn't have a pad in his hand. When somebody ordered something at Tony Pardo's house, the waiter had better goddamn remember it.

"Whatever you choose," said Tony, "the chef is

going to keep it low in fat and sodium. It's too bad, because he's got some beauties I wish you could try, but they're all loaded with butter and heavy cream."

I was so mad that I could hardly speak. These people seemed more concerned about my welfare than my own mother. But I finally was able to come out with "Shrimp cocktail, chicken venetio, baked potato, peas, and green salad."

"Sour cream with the potato, sir?" asked the waiter, and Tony Pardo went nuts.

"Jesus Christ," he screamed at the waiter, trying to shove back his heavy ornamental chair, maybe the same one King Arthur had sat in, "didn't I tell you this man gets a low-fat diet? What the fuck is the matter with you, Anastasio?"

The man cringed back about two feet, his face pale. "Yogurt, sir," he yelled in my ear. "I'll bring some yogurt."

Tony gave up the fight and sank back in his chair, but his eyes followed the waiter out of the room. I hoped the poor son of a bitch wouldn't spill anything on anybody.

The Pardo version of a shrimp cocktail consisted of a dozen giant shrimp spread out on a plate with three kinds of sauce. I wondered how I was going to be able to eat a whole chicken. There wasn't much conversation at the table, so I concentrated on the shrimp, but as I was chewing my way through the third one, the noise of a helicopter filled the room, so loud that I thought it might be coming in the window. I tensed my legs against the chair, ready to push back and take off in the opposite direction, but then the roar stopped as suddenly as it had begun.

The rest of them, including Tony, kept on eating as though they hadn't noticed the glass rattling, and I wondered if the house was on a direct line to an airport. I threw in the napkin after six shrimp and was waiting for my chicken when a very tall good-looking blond woman breezed into the room. She was carrying a brief case that looked like the very one Pardo had brought my hundred thou in, and she dropped it on the floor with a thud as she came up to Pardo's chair, leaned over, and gave him one of those movie kisses that usually take place in a bed and seem to go on forever.

When she finally pulled away, she straightened up and took in the table. "Hello, everybody," she said. "You must be Mr. Altobelli," reaching her hand out in front of Tony's nose. It felt funny to be going up and down two inches from the guy's face, but she had a strong grip, and it was like she was testing me the way a guy sometimes does to demonstrate to you that his balls hang heavy.

Nobody else, including Tony, stood up when she came to the table, so I didn't even try to shove back the heavy chair, just smiled and nodded.

"I'm Gretchen Pardo, Tony's wife," she said, and she turned and gave the whole table a fuck-you look when she said it. The mother, the brothers, and the sisters were staring at her with the real Italian death wish in their eyes, the kind of look my aunts get when they are forced to deal with Protestants. Gretchen Pardo looked Protestant all right, about as Protestant as anybody could get. How the hell had she broken into the circle?

"Sit down," said Tony. "Have something to eat."

"I had a sandwich on the copter," said Gretchen, putting the palm of her hand over his lips, "and anyway I have to see you right away on something most important."

This time as he started to stand up there were two

waiters ready to pull the chair back, and without another word he went with her to the doorway. Just before they disappeared, Mrs. Pardo turned, looked at the watch on her wrist, whose diamonds sparkled even in the dim light, and said, "Mr. Altobelli, why don't you meet us in the office in exactly one hour?" She was gone before I could even nod.

There was about ten seconds of silence and then the youngest sister, Constanza, said in a fairly loud voice, "How can you expect the schmuck to think straight when she's always fucking his brains out?"

Nobody said anything. And nobody laughed at her joke, if it was a joke, including her sisters. I looked over at the mother, expecting her to tell her daughter not to have such a dirty mouth, but it was as if she hadn't heard a thing. Neither the older brothers nor the two South Americans had said a word the whole time I had been there, and the two older sisters had just mumbled to each other a bit. The two younger ones had been giving me the eye all during my shrimp cocktail and then whispering in each other's ear while giggling. Christ, it was like we were back in the high school lunchroom.

The chicken was pretty good, but I wasn't really very hungry so I only ate part of it and refused the offer of salad and dessert. The waiter brought me coffee without my asking for it, and as he poured it he informed me in a low voice that it was decaffeinated. They were more careful of me here than when I was in the hospital. Which made me think of Betty Wade, and I felt this sadness go through me. No other woman had ever made me feel like she had, but now she had gone away, and who the hell knew if I would ever see her again.

I couldn't remember whether or not I had taken my aspirin that morning, so I downed one with the rest of my water and asked if anybody could give me direction to the office. It was probably about ten seconds, but it seemed like forever before Constanza finally volunteered. "Take the elevator to the second floor," she said, "turn right and walk till you get to the double doors. You're a detective. Even you should be able to find it."

She didn't say it with a smile, so I just nodded my head toward her, asked the mama if I could be excused, and left when I realized she wasn't going to answer. Nobody said a word as I walked out of the room. The dinner had been about as much fun as the time Internal Affairs called me in to find out if the pimp, who was about five feet four inches tall, had really tried to assault Brady.

18

Finding the office was not as easy as Constanza had made it out to be because there were two right turns instead of one, and I, of course, former top detective of the San Bernardino police force, had tried the left corridor first when I came to the wall. Constanza had put me to the test, and I had failed.

"Vinnie Altobelli owes you one, you little bitch," I muttered as I turned to go the other way.

Even though it was scarcely forty-five minutes since she had left the dining room, Mrs. Pardo, wearing giant horn-rimmed glasses that focused your attention on the blueness of her eyes, was already sitting at a huge desk on the left side of the room. She was talking on the telephone, and it had to be important because even though she seemed to be looking right at me, there was nothing on her face to show she knew I was there. A good-looking lady. Her face reminded me of somebody, but I couldn't nail it down. Some movie actress? A model? Or was it just that all natural blondes look alike? But her blondness didn't fit in with Tony, the family, the house or any part of it. It was like she was from another planet. Tony came in while I was looking at her, and you could tell that he'd just had some kind of physical workout because his face was flushed and he walked like he'd rather be lying down somewhere and smelling the roses. He'd changed from his suit to brown slacks and a tan cashmere sweater, and when I looked back at his wife, I noticed she was in a green warm-up suit. She didn't look tired at all. My brother Sandy, who my brother Petey called "the whorehound from hell," had a little trick he kept doing even though we had all seen it a hundred times. He would stick his middle finger into his glass of beer and say, "See, no matter how many times you stick this in there, when you pull it out, it doesn't leave a mark. That's how it is with screwing. If a woman wanted, she could kill you.

There's an old joke about a guy trying to love his wife to death, and she blooms while he's fading away. "Look at her, the dumb bitch," he tells his friend. "She doesn't know she's going to die." I studied Pardo's flushed face again and wondered if maybe he might be killed off in other ways than bullets, bombs, and poison.

The office was almost as big as the dining room, with one whole wall of solid glass looking over the flood-lit lawn and trees. Tony led me over to his desk on the other side of the room, and I sat down in a heavy leather chair across from him. We didn't say anything, just waited for her to finish on the phone.

When she finally put down the receiver and looked at us, a big smile lit up her face. There was no doubt that whatever had happened between the two of them after they left the dining room had given her the energy he had lost. Carlotta was the only woman who had ever done that to me. I'd be lying on the bed, the floor, in the bathtub, wherever the hell I had been when the mood hit her, and she would be bouncing around the room like she was on springs. Sometimes I ached so bad for Carlotta that my bones grated.

"That was my mother," Mrs. Pardo explained to Tony. "My father won't listen to her or the doctor, and says he's going to preach on Sunday, and I quote, 'come hell or high water.'" She turned to me.

"Hi again, Mr. Altobelli," she said. "My father's a Congregational minister in Durham, New Hampshire, and he thinks God's message can't be delivered on Sunday unless he's the one to do it."

A minister's daughter! Don't let anybody ever tell you that God doesn't get a kick out of screwing things around sometimes. I'd have picked some dark little Italian thing or maybe a peroxide blonde like the maid for Pardo's wife. What mixed-up Cupid had shot the arrows into this particular pair?

"Okay," said Pardo, "we're up to our ass in work here. What do you want to know?"

"Outside of your regular competition, who would want to see you dead?" I asked.

"What the hell do you mean, 'regular competition'?" he yelled, standing up so hard that he knocked the heavy chair back three feet on its rollers. "Do you think you're dealing with a street gang here? We own enough legitimate businesses to be in the Fortune 500, for Christ's sake. Do you think—"

"Tony," said his wife, catching hold of his right arm with both hands, "Tony. We brought Mr. Altobelli here to find out who is trying to kill you. If you fly off the handle every time he asks a question, he's never going to be able to do his job and help us. We agreed that we would cooperate in every way."

"If you want me out of here, I'm gone," I told him. If at that moment I could have given back every dime he had paid me, including the hundred to my brother Frankie, and returned to where I was before I tied in with him, I would have thanked God for the favor and surprised the hell out of my mother by going to Mass with her on Sunday.

Mrs. Pardo's hands must have been like somebody who pats his dog on the head when he's frothing at the mouth, and the mutt shuts up and wags his tail. Tony was still shaking a little, but he relaxed his body a bit. I wondered what he was like when he lost it completely. Then I decided I never wanted to know.

"Okay," he said, "okay." He pointed his finger straight at my head, and it was the same as if it was a gun. "Just remember who you're talking to. What do you want to know?"

"It's obvious that it's an inside job," I told them. "I don't know what all your security arrangements are, but from what I've seen and heard it would be next to impossible for anybody from the outside to get in here and do the kind of damage that's been done. On the other hand, either you've been lucky, or maybe they were just trying to warn you or maybe they're not very good at this kind of thing. Whatever it is, if it has nothing to do with business, then it's got to be personal, and if it's personal, who has something to gain or who hates you so much they just want you dead no matter what happens afterward?"

The two of them exchanged a look, the kind that married people drive you nuts with when they're giving each other a message that shows they know something you don't, and hell could freeze before they'd bring you into it. How much of what Tony Pardo had told me was true, and how much had to do with something else than people trying to kill him? A million bucks. He was paying me a million bucks. A quarter of a million would have caused me to get as excited as the million did because that was as high as my dreams would go. He had to know this, so why did he make the stakes so high? As Carlotta was always saying to me, "Just who is doing what to whom here?"

"Mr. Altobelli," said Mrs. Pardo, "Tony tells me we can have faith in your integrity and that like all private detectives you will consider everything you learn here to be confidential."

"I'm not a private detective," I told her. "I'm just an ex-cop. I don't have any kind of a license."

"Well, as a matter of fact you do," she said, going back to her desk and returning with two plastic cards. She handed one over, and there was my picture on an official California license naming me as a private investigator. The other one was a permit to carry a pistol.

"As head of security for Pardo Enterprises," she said, "you should have these permits, and knowing how busy you have been, we took the liberty of saving you the paperwork."

Yeah. Busy sitting on my ass in my apartment and waiting for the "Cheers" reruns. That was probably the real reason I had taken the job so quickly. The million bucks was *lagniappe,* as my uncle Ferdo used to say about the money he made handling the numbers in his variety store before the lottery killed that business off. Pardo was the first guy to make me feel like my life wasn't over yet, and he could have been talking about going to the moon and I would have hopped aboard.

"You must have some really good friends downtown," I told her, slipping the cards into my pocket. Two licenses, one with my police department picture on it, in one afternoon. I doubted if the mayor could have done it so quickly.

"We do a lot for the city," she answered. "Our company has been the primary force in revitalizing the downtown area. It is true that in the past Pardo Enterprises has been connected to organizations that are on the thin edge of legitimacy, but we are trying to phase out that aspect of our business. Which is why it is so important that we find out what the present problem is and neutralize it."

Thin edge of legitimacy. That was a good one.

"Is it possible that the people behind this don't want to be phased out?" I asked her.

She gave me one of her big smiles. It made me feel like maybe I was as good as they thought I was.

"You're a very intelligent man, Mr. Altobelli," she said. "When Tony came up with your name, I wasn't sure that you would be able to do what was necessary, but you seem to be a real detective, one who quickly grasps situations and knows how to look for solutions. What do you need and what do you want in order to get on with the job?"

I wondered what it would be like to be in bed with her, to have this ice-cold-looking blonde strip down and go at it. According to Constanza, the wife put

Tony to the test every day. You could feel the energy coming off her—"the beast," as my brother Sandy called it. He was the family authority on the dirty deed, and he always said that only a few men in their lifetimes are lucky enough to go up against "the beast."

"First of all, I want to tour the place," I said, "and meet all the people and talk to them, especially the ones who were around when these things happened. Do you have background on everybody?"

I winced as I thought back on that last question. The background sheets on some of the punks on the place would probably read like the police blotter. This was crazy. Crazy.

"Tino Barzatti is in charge of personnel," said Mrs. Pardo, "and we will have him take you on a tour of—"

Just then the whole wall of glass shattered, and pieces were flying all over the room. The whine of the bullet had gone maybe an inch past the lobe of my right ear, and for that one moment I was frozen in time and space, waiting instinctively for the next one to go into me. But then I grabbed Mrs. Pardo by the shoulders and pulled her to the floor, covering her body with mine as best I could. Tony was still standing there, his mouth open, and I saw a dark stain blossom on the front of his pants. "Get down, get down" I yelled at him until he dropped alongside us. His face was white, and I could feel the fear coming out of him. The noise of the glass falling seemed to go on and on, but it couldn't have been more than a few seconds before it stopped. Men's voices were shouting somewhere outside, but otherwise it was so still that I could feel Mrs. Pardo's heart pounding under mine. Or was it my heart pounding? My bunged-up heart. Jesus. A bullet had never come that close to me in all my years on the force. There was a slight pressure under me, and I looked down at Mrs. Pardo's face about an inch from mine, her eyes staring at me, and along the whole length of my body there was a hotness where her parts mashed into mine, and crazy as it was I started getting hard. I looked back in her eyes, and I could swear she was laughing at me.

When I rolled off her, onto the floor, a sliver of glass stuck in my neck, and I pulled it out as I got up, cutting the palm of my hand a little. I reached down and pulled her up to a sitting position, and when she took her hand away, she noticed the blood from my cut on her own hand, and she opened her mouth and licked it off, staring at me all the while. Tony had gotten up to his knees by then, but he didn't seem to have the strength to haul himself any farther, so I reached down and hauled him up.

"Stay away from the window," I told them. "Stay back here where they can't see you from the outside."

Two guys came tearing into the room with their guns out, and Mrs. Pardo told them to put the guns away. The older guy was in his fifties and had the mobster look on his face, the kind of look you can smell before you even see it.

He ran up to the wall, leaned out the broken window, yelled down that the whole place inside the fence should be searched, and then came back to where Pardo was standing.

"What happened, boss?" he asked. *Boss.* Now we were getting down to basics. Nobody shoots at one of the leading businessmen in the area. It's bosses who get shot at.

"Mr. Altobelli," said Mrs. Pardo, getting to her feet and speaking in the kind of formal voice you use to introduce somebody at a class reunion, "this is Tino Barzatti."

The guy didn't look at me like we were going to be buddies, so I didn't bother to nod at him. He was the man in charge of all the soldiers, and having me around to pick up the pieces he couldn't even find was not good for his image.

"What happened, boss?" he asked again.

Pardo's face turned from white to red. "What happened?" he yelled. "What happened? Somebody shot at me again, that's what happened. You said you needed more men, I got you more men. Are you getting too old for this? Maybe somebody else should take over. Yeah. Somebody else should take over." He turned to me. "You're the head of security for Pardo Enterprises. From now on you're in charge around here." He turned back to Barzatti. "You hear that, goombah? Altobelli's in charge. Whatever he says, you do. *Capisce?*"

Barzatti didn't even bother to answer. Here I was on my first day, and I already had morale problems among my staff. I'd gone from sergeant to chief. Might as well start in.

"Tino," I said, "get a screwdriver and pry that bullet out of the wall."

"What? What bullet?"

"The one over there," I said, turning and pointing to a small black hole about six feet up the wall in back of us. Both the Pardos turned to look where I was pointing.

"See?" said Pardo to Barzatti in the so-there kind of voice that kids used to use in elementary school. "He's already got a clue."

A spent bullet wasn't going to be much use without a laboratory to analyze it, but what the hell. At least it would give me an angle of fire. I could feel that little tickle in my belly that I always got whenever I took on a new case. It was time to start earning my million bucks. Which, under the circumstances, might not be such an overpayment after all.

19

The bullet was a .22 long, but that was all the good I could get out of my detecting. There are guys in the department who can figure out where a shot was fired from by measuring the trajectory from the bullet hole, but I could only guess that it was from a stand of trees nearly a thousand feet away.

I left Pardo yelling that he wanted the office cleaned up and new glass installed as soon as possible. *Bullet-proof glass.*

"I'm getting out of here and going back to the city," he told me. "You find out what's going on here, and as quickly as you can. I'm giving you another advance on your fee, and the quicker you get the son of a bitch, the quicker you get the whole boodle. I've passed the word that you're running the show, and anybody who gives you any shit will have me to answer to. Any questions?"

"First of all," I said, "we don't know whether it's one person or several. Secondly, why do you feel safer in the city than you do here?"

"I don't," he answered. "But in the city I can move

around to different places, and it's worked so far." He hesitated a few moments, making up his mind. "I take a suite in a different hotel every night," he said. "I've got five guys around me who have been with the family for years. Here there's too much space to cover. In the city we can keep things under control."

"I'll see if we can do the same thing here," I told him.

"You're a good boy," he said, "and I'm counting on you. I have to go out of the country for a few days, and I know you'll have it all straightened out before I get back. But until then, I'm out of here."

That he was within the half hour, the helicopter making one pass around the house before it pushed off for the city. I listened to it go as I watched four men sweeping up glass, and as the sound grew fainter and fainter, so did I. Because just before the noise whispered off into nothing, it suddenly occurred to me that the sniper might not have been going for Tony Pardo at all. It was my ear the fucking bullet almost nipped. Maybe somebody didn't want an outsider prowling around.

"Jesus Christ," I said out loud. And I wasn't swearing.

When I got back to the room and closed the door behind me, the first thing I did was check to see if the curtains were drawn. Whoever was out there with a rifle could have shifted to my side of the house. I wondered again if it was me or Pardo who had been the target. He had flown away; I was still here.

The only difference in the room from when I had left was that another leather case was in the middle of the bed. How the hell had he done it? Did he say "Scotty, beam another hundred thou to Altobelli"? But there it was, all the bills neatly stacked when I lifted the cover. He was my golden goose, and I would do my damnedest to see that nobody killed him while I was still collecting eggs. In the long run, it might be better for society in general if Tony Pardo bought the farm, but definitely not for farmer Altobelli.

I was tired but I knew I wouldn't sleep, so I switched on the big TV set and clicked through the channels. The only sports being shown were wrestling and a ping-pong tournament on tape delay from China. I turned it off and went into the bathroom to brush my teeth. While I was doing it, I pulled open the medicine cabinet door with my left hand, and the inside so surprised me that I stood there letting foam dribble down my chin.

The cabinet held every goddamned thing you could ever think of, including a brand-new electric razor still in its plastic wrapping, and deodorants and after-shave lotions and stuff to gargle with and aspirin and Tylenol and toothbrushes and a whole box of Trojan lubricated rubbers. There had to be five hundred bucks' worth of stuff in there. Pardo had spoken the truth. Money meant nothing to him. The guy could buy anything he wanted. Except for one thing. Somebody was trying to kill him, and the one thing you couldn't buy off was Mr. Death.

I went back into the bedroom, and my heart gave a jump that almost lifted me off the floor. I stood there listening to it pound away in my chest so fast that I couldn't make out the separate beats. How many heart patients died from somebody yelling "boo" or maybe just being there where nobody was supposed to be? First a bullet in the ear, and now her.

She had come in without a sound, and I realized I had been so upset that I had forgotten to lock the door behind me. On her left arm there hung a wicker basket like the one Red Riding Hood was taking to her grandmother, and on the other was a stack of towels.

"You all right?" the maid asked. "You're white as a ghost."

"I'm all right," I told her, feeling the sweat chill on my skin. "I just didn't hear you come in."

"I didn't know you was here yet," she said. "I came to set you up for the night."

"Go right ahead. I'll stay out of the way."

She went into the bathroom and busied herself there for a couple of minutes, threw the wet towels into a hamper chute in the wall, came back, and began folding the spread off the bed. I moved over to the shelves and started checking out the videos. *Lethal Weapon III*. One of my favorites. I never would have admitted it to anybody, but when I was working, sometimes I would ask myself what Mel Gibson might do in the situation I was in. Crazy, huh?

She finished with the bed, tugged the sheet back a quarter turn, and walked over to the dressing table where she stood in front of the mirror. When she raised her hands to the little white cap on her head, her tits pushed out like they would never stop, and I could feel my face getting all flushed. Blood pressure. This couldn't be good for my blood pressure.

She undid a couple of hooks or buttons and her whole damned outfit fell to the floor, showing that she wasn't wearing a bra or panties underneath. She carefully stepped away from her uniform, and kicked off her high-heeled shoes before turning to me.

"Do you want me to take off my stockings, or do you want to do it yourself?"

That was a question I would match alongside When did you stop beating your wife? I could feel my pants resisting the pressure.

"Wait a minute," I instructed her. "What's going on here?"

She looked at me narrowly for a moment, and I

could see she was trying to puzzle out what the problem might be.

"Do you want something special?" she asked. "I do most things, but if it's real kinky, I'll have to get Claudine."

"Who the hell's Claudine?"

"She's the other maid."

"What do you mean you'll get her?"

"She's supposed to do the other two guys tonight, but they don't quit drinking until late, and she's still in her room. I'd rather do you myself, but if you want, I'll get Claudine."

"What's your name?"

The question seemed to surprise her. It was almost certain that most of the people she serviced couldn't have cared less what her name might be.

"Renee," she finally managed. "Did I do something wrong? You ain't going to tell Mr. Tony that I did something wrong, are you?"

The fear was so great that it had brought out little drops of sweat on her face, and I could see the streaks in her makeup.

"No, I'm not going to tell anybody anything. I take it you're supposed to lay down for me?"

She didn't seem capable of answering, just stood there looking at me dumbly.

"I'm supposed to make you happy," she explained. "When Mr. Tony asks you how I was, if you say I made you happy, then I get a thousand bucks extra."

"What if I don't?"

She tried to figure that out.

"I don't know," she said. "Up to now I've made everybody happy."

"You put your clothes back on," I told her, "and tomorrow I'll tell Tony that you made me happy, and you'll get your thousand bucks without anybody being the wiser."

"If I don't stay awhile," she said, "somebody will tell him. He knows everything that goes on. That Jefferson is out to get me because I wouldn't French him yesterday, and he'll tell."

"Look," I said, "I'm very seriously involved with a girl and . . ."

"Oh, that's all right," she broke in, relief in her voice. "She ain't never going to know. Me and Claudine have done guys while their wives were downstairs talking to Mrs. Pardo, and they never even knew."

"No, it's not that. It's just that she's the only one I want to do it with."

Her face broke into a big smile, the kind that true believers make when they are exposed to a religious shrine.

"Jeez," she said. "You're something else."

"So why don't you put your clothes back on, and we'll talk for a while or watch TV, and then you can leave and you'll be all set."

"Listen," she said, taking charge. "He's got people who check on everything that goes down here. Including me. If it looks like we didn't make it, he'll do something to me. So why don't you take off your clothes and we'll get in the bed, and then if somebody comes in we can make believe we're resting up before our second one."

She was as logical as Mr. Spock. She wanted Tony to think she'd earned her thousand bucks, and I wanted him to think I was like all the other guys who had enjoyed his hospitality. Didn't want him to think I didn't like girls. So there we were in the bed, both buck naked, her eating a nectarine that was dribbling juice between her tits, and me—my erection diserected because of all the conversation—leaning against the two pillows and watching Mel Gibson blow fourteen guys into gristle. Then it hit me.

"Renee," I said, turning the volume down, "tell me about this place."

"What do you mean?" she asked, sucking little strands of fruit off the pit. I could feel myself getting hard again. What I had to do was concentrate on business. I had been hired to do a job. Here was a primary source of information to be interrogated.

"What's it like here?" I asked her. Do you know why Mr. Tony brought me here?"

Jesus. I was now calling him Mr. Tony. Except for the difference in price, I wasn't that much different from this hooker.

"It's okay. It's the best deal I ever had. The real maids do all the work, and Claudine and I have a lot of laughs together."

"How often do you have to do this?" I asked, waving my hand toward the room in general.

"I've been here three months," she said, "and there's only been one very busy week. Mr. Tony and Mrs. Pardo are away a lot, but then they might be here, and all kinds of people come to see them. Some of them just come and go the same day, and a couple of those I've had nooners with, but the two greasers have been here since Thursday and they don't leave until tomorrow. We each took one last night, but you're special so Claudine has to handle both of them tonight."

"Do you know about Mr. . . . . about Tony's problem, the reason he brought me here?"

"No, I don't know why he brought you here. But if you mean about the bomb blowing up the car, yeah, everybody knows about that. He brought in twenty extra soldiers just last week. They're all over the place. They fixed up rooms in the old horse stable, and they eat and sleep down there."

"Who do you think is trying to kill Mr. Tony?"

"Jeez, I don't know. When that bomb went off, it sure scared the shit out of me."

"What's the family like?"

She wriggled a bit and I could tell she liked that question. The gossip had probably been piling up inside her, and I was a person on whom to unload.

"That Mrs. Pardo," she said, "she's a bitch on wheels. Sometimes I wonder who's hung heavier, her or him. You know, when I first came here, Claudine had already been here for a while, and I asked her if there was anything the boss liked special, and she said we'd never know, because wifie fucked him until his ears were ready to fall off. She treats us like she doesn't even know we was here unless she wants us to do something, and then it's like she's telling the wall to do it. Everybody's scared shitless of her."

"What about the rest of the family?"

"The family." She thought about it for a minute. "The old lady can be a real bitch, too, and Angelina and Florence and just like her. The two younger ones aren't too bad, they joke around with you sometimes, but they never let you forget who you are and who they are."

"What about the brothers?"

"Ain't they creepy? That Aldo had me come to his room the second day I got here and really gave me a going over, but Mr. Tony found out about it, and he told me I was here to take care of guests only, and if anybody else tried anything, his brothers or any of the guys who work here, I was to tell him. He must have passed the word down, because except for Jefferson, nobody's tried anything since."

"Why's Jefferson so brave?"

"I dunno. He's weird."

"Any of the family married?"

"Mr. Tony's the only one of the boys. Claudine told me the two older bitches were married, but they found one of the husbands in the trunk of the Cadillac in Tijuana and the other one just disappeared. Claudine said he was probably visiting Jimmy Hoffa. Do you know who Jimmy Hoffa is? I laughed, because I knew she was making a joke, but I never heard of him."

"What about the two younger girls?"

"They ain't never been married, as far as I know. That Theresa, she's always got something up her nose or somebody in her twat, but I don't know about the other one, Constanza. Mr. Tony acts like they're both virgins, and most of the guys are careful around them. Nobody would be surprised to see that guy who's boinking Theresa end up in the trunk of a Ford Fiesta."

She laughed out loud when she said it, so somebody must have told her it was a joke.

"Does anybody have any idea who's trying to kill Pardo?" I asked, and that stopped the laughing. She wasn't at all surprised by the question, and when she took a deep breath to think about it, she raised the sheet about four inches.

"You know," she said, "I can't understand why anybody would want to whack out a man like that. It's a crazy world, isn't it?"

"Yeah," I said. "Listen, you've probably been here long enough now, and I'll tell Tony how great you were."

"You don't want me to stay?" she asked, turning toward me. "I can go get some coke and we could turn on, and then maybe you'll feel like partying."

"No, thanks," I told her. "I have a heart condition and . . ."

"Oh, yeah," she said. "They told me. You look so great I forgot about it. If you wanted, I could . . ."

"No. No thanks. I'm feeling kind of tired, and I have a lot to do tomorrow."

"It's so comfy here," she said, stretching her arms straight up so that both her trampolines were reaching for the ceiling. "Why don't we go to sleep, and if you wake up in the night and feel like . . ."

"No, really. No thanks. I think you ought to go, and I'll be sure to tell Tony you were fantastic."

She looked at me almost suspiciously, not quite sure in her mind that I would keep my word. You could tell that a lot of people had not kept their word to Renee in the past.

"Okay," she said finally. "But if you change your mind in the night, just dial one-nine-seven and I'll come back. I really would like to make you happy, and not just for the bucks."

"Great," I told her. "That might be great."

She dressed quickly, gave me a smile, and had her hand on the doorknob when she made a small noise and turned around. Going over to the wicker basket that had been left on the floor, she picked it up and carried it to the other side of the bed. She pulled out a box and placed it in the center of the pillows she had been using, smiled again, and was gone. I could tell from the look on her face that she wasn't completely at ease about the way things had worked out, or not worked out. To tell the truth, I wasn't either. Even knowing that one or both of those South Americans had used her the past few nights, and who knew how many others, I still wondered what it would have been like to let my hard-on decide the matter. But I hadn't been lying about being involved with another girl. The thought of Betty Wade had made it easier for me to pass up something like this. I reached over and picked up the box on the pillow. Mints. Chocolate-covered mints. These people were scary.

I switched off the lights with the remote control on the bed table and lay back against the pillows. One hell of a day. A million-buck deal. A bullet past my ear. Me or Tony? I preferred to think it was Tony. But just being around him had its risks. I switched on the lights again, got up, and went to the desk, where I found a pad and a pen. I wrote a million down on the paper and divided it by 365. It came to two thousand, seven hundred and thirty-nine dollars and seventy-three cents a day. But what if I cleared it up in a week? That would come to a hundred and forty-two thousand, eight hundred and fifty-seven dollars and fourteen cents a day. I didn't have to count sheep; I fell asleep counting money.

As I looked at the lawns and the woods the next morning, it occurred to me that it might have been a good idea for me to take a copter spin around the grounds to give me an idea of the lay of the land and where everybody was situated. Since it was too late for that, I settled on a Jeep tour with Barzatti at the wheel.

"How many people working here?" I asked as we set off down a narrow dirt road from the back of the house.

"What do you mean?"

"How many are there? Servants, soldiers, men, women, children, whatever."

"They got a shit load of servants. Jefferson can tell you better about that than I can. I keep ten guys in the house at all times, five on the day shift and five at night. They sleep in the cellar, so there are always ten guys around no matter what. There are eight guys who take care of the grounds, but they don't count. I had six guys checking the outside before the fucking place started to blow up, and then I brought in twenty more. They live down in the old horse barn, and there are nine of them out on the grounds day and night. Aldo and Cissy sometimes have guys visiting them who are personal friends, so they might have five or six extra staying at a time, and they're usually made guys so they can be counted on."

"Who's Cissy?" I asked.

"Cissy? Cistercio. The second brother."

"How come Tony's running the show when there are two older brothers?"

Barzatti braked gently to a halt, turned off the engine, pulled up the hand brake, and stared straight ahead into nothing for a minute. Then he turned and looked me in the eyes.

"Tony said that you're calling the shots while he's away. I don't think that's a good idea, but hey, what do I know?" He shrugged his shoulders almost as good as my uncle Pepi. "He says to do what you want done and tell what you want told. But I'm sure that don't include the family."

"Why don't we call him and ask?" I suggested.

This caused him to think further. He was the one who had been in charge when somebody tried to snuff Tony. It was his responsibility, and he had failed in his job. More than once. The boss had to be pissed about that, and the boss had told him that I was head honcho while he was away. If he called him up and asked about every little thing, or even one big thing, there was always the chance the boss would be more pissed off than ever. If Tino told me things he shouldn't have, however, there was always the excuse that he had only been following orders. One good thing about being Italian is that you know how Italians think. Or at least you think you know, which can be a fatal mistake. He decided he didn't want to talk to Tony any more that day.

"The father, Guido," he said, "was what you would call an excitable man. He could give *agita* to an Alka-Seltzer tablet. He could make you very unhappy. He could also make you disappear. And if he did, even your mother wouldn't dare to ask where you were. The boys did not have a happy childhood. And when the girls were big enough to start showing tits, they didn't have an easy time of it with the old man, either. He scared me so much that my father—his soul should rest in peace—shivered in his grave. The problem was that he would love you one day, and the very next day he could smash you in the face because he thought you didn't show the proper respect when he walked by. I wish I had a nickel for every time he made the boys piss their pants from fear. He could love one and hate the other two, or love two and hate the other one, or hate them all. He made Tony go to college because he said the other two were too dumb. Tony didn't want to go to college, but he was so smart in school that the *padrone* made him go. But when Tony graduated and wanted to keep going to school, the old man told him he had to come back. And then Aldo and Cissy fucked up over something unimportant after Tony had been home a couple of months, and the old man told Tony he could go back to Boston. That's where Tony met his missus. They went to school together in Boston."

I wasn't sure Barzatti remembered I was there with him. He had never been ordered by his boss to talk before, and it was as though he was listening to himself the same way I was listening to him. This happened sometimes when you had a guy in the interrogation room and something triggered him, and all you had to worry about was having enough tape in the machine.

"When they came back here," said Barzatti, "the old man didn't know Tony was coming back with a wife, and he was so pissed that I wasn't sure what was going to happen. But then all of a sudden—and it had to be because he'd never had any woman with her class that close—the old man turned just the opposite. He couldn't keep his hands off her, pulling at her tits or grabbing her ass whenever she slipped up and let him get near enough. She did pretty well keeping him off, laughing like it was a game, but one time— and I only know about this because Jefferson was in the room—she reached out and grabbed the old man right by the balls so hard that Jefferson said he yelled out like God had come to collect the bills, and then he passed out. Cold. Jefferson ran to him and put some water on his head, and all the while Tony's wife just stood there like a rock. When the old man came alive again, she leaned over maybe two inches from his face, and she said, 'Listen, Tony's father, I am Tony's wife, and he is the only one who touches me. If you ever try to touch me again, I won't just squeeze them for you, I'll cut them off.'"

Barzatti started laughing, laughing so hard that he had to wipe his eyes. "He believed her," he managed to say. "Oh, boy, did he believe her. And from then on she and Tony could do no wrong, and he announced that Tony was the one who would take over when he was gone. Except that nobody ever thought he would really go, least of all himself. But you don't fool God.

You can fool everybody else, but you don't fool God. One day he was here and the next day, gone."

"How did the older brothers feel about Tony becoming the boss?"

Barzatti looked at me and smiled, the smile of a patient man talking to an idiot. "How would you feel?" he asked.

"Would they try to kill him?"

This one required some thought.

"Anybody can kill anybody," he said, and I felt he was talking from experience. "But they were with me one of the times somebody shot at Tony, and today they were in the kitchen playing cards with the boys when the glass got knocked out. You can't be in two places at the same time."

"Could they have hired somebody else to do it?"

This didn't take too long. "I've double-checked everybody in this whole fucking place," he said. "They're all family. There's not one bad apple in the bunch."

I was sure that his idea of a good apple was not the same as that of my fourth grade teacher, Sister Ursuline, and what he meant by family wasn't the same as when I talked about my family, but I knew what he meant. "What about the girls?"

"What about the girls?"

"Could they have anything to do with this?"

"Tony's good to them. They can buy any clothes and jewels they want. They travel all over the world. They don't even have to wipe their own asses if they don't want to. Why the hell should they want anything different?"

"What about you?"

"What do you mean, what about me?"

"Are you a happy camper?"

"What does that mean?"

"Do you feel the same way about Tony as you felt about his father?"

"No. No, I don't. No way. I never had it so good with Guido as I do with Tony. He gives me a better cut. He doesn't scare the crap out of me. His father didn't trust anybody. Tony trusts me. He is a true *padrone*. And he's smart. He's got more money coming in than the old man ever dreamed of. I don't want nothing to happen to Tony. I'll kill whoever's pulling this crap. He'll wish he never met up with Tino Barzatti."

I've learned from interrogations that too often the people who seem most sincere can be bullshitting themselves as well as you. But there was something Old World Italian about this guy, in his voice, in his eyes when he looked at me, that made me believe him. I needed someone I could trust, someone to back me up if things got hairy, and so far he was the only one who even came near the mark. Except that it would be stupid to trust anybody there. Might as well trust the two South Americans as this guy talking as though olive oil wouldn't coat his tongue.

"Let's go look at that little clump of trees," I said.

The trees were on the edge of the mowed lawn, so the bushes under them were maybe two feet high. I got out of the Jeep and turned so that I could see the house. The windows, which were being boarded over as I looked, were in plain sight on a direct path, and I moved to where I thought the line of fire might have come from. Barzatti was sitting in the Jeep smoking a cigarette, uninterested in whatever the hell I might be doing. Or at least he was acting uninterested.

Stepping carefully, I pushed my way through the brambles, and two feet in I found it. A whole area was trampled down, maybe six feet long and three feet wide. Plenty of room for a man to have lain down flat and taken a sight on the windows. I knelt and rubbed my hand along the ground as best I could. I almost missed it but on a reverse pass I felt a little dent in the ground, and when I parted the grass I found a hole just the right size for an elbow. This was where the shooter had staked himself out, and if he was sloppy, there should be a shell casing just to the left of me. But though I spent ten minutes running my hands over the ground and parting the grasses and even lifting up stones, there was no casing. It might have been there, but I couldn't find it.

The clump of trees marked the beginning of the woods, and all the guy had to do after he fired was back up about ten feet and he was gone to where nobody could see him. I went in deeper, but although a few twigs were broken and maybe some grass trampled, there was no way of telling which direction he had gone. I needed an assistant who would call me Kimosabe if I wanted to track where the guy had run off. But all I had was Barzatti, and he was about as far from a Noble Red Man as you could get.

He didn't say anything when I climbed back into the Jeep, and I decided to play his game and say nothing about what I had found.

"Show me where the stable is," I told him, and we started back the way we had come, passing by the rear of the house and then over a little hill, and down by a stream that looked too pretty to be real was this giant barn with all kinds of fences around it and maybe a dozen horses munching grass in the green fields. King Tony and his empire. Better than being head of Vietnam or Romania or one of those places.

Four guys were sitting in lawn chairs, all of them smoking, and two with bottles of beer in their hands. They watched us drive up in front of them, but only the smoke from the cigarettes moved. They all had the kind of faces I would come across every day when I was on the force. Fuck-you faces. No use asking them any questions.

Barzatti hopped out of the Jeep and walked over to a cooler that sat behind the chairs. He pulled out a bottle of beer, unscrewed the cap, and took a long pull. He turned to where I was sitting and said, "Want a cold one?"

I shook my head and got out of the Jeep. If we'd been alone, I might have said no, thanks, but that kind of talk would've been like telling these guys I had no balls. Anybody said thanks around them, they would peg him as a queer.

"Boys," said Barzatti, "this here is Vinnie Altobelli, the guy I was telling you about. Mr. Tony said he calls the shots."

Why fool around? "Anybody know who knocked out those windows?" I asked.

They not only didn't answer, they still didn't move. Their eyes were pasted right on me in that tough-guy look that's supposed to make variety store owners cough over the protection each week. I could feel my heart beating faster—too fast?—and a sadness came over me that almost made my eyes wet. Was I never again going to be able to grab one of these guys by the shirtfront, knee him in the balls, and wipe that look off his face? I had the fear, but it was from inside rather than out. These guys didn't scare me one bit. But on the other hand, I wasn't going to be able to scare them one bit either. I was a former cop with a heart condition who was doing some investigative work for a mob boss. What would Brady think? What would my family think? What did I think about it? Was I dead or was I alive?

I walked over to where they were sitting. "Look," I said, "someone is trying to kill Mr. Pardo. It could be any one of you. I asked you in a nice way to cooperate, and you're giving me bullshit. So I'm not going to ask you any more. And when he comes back, I'm going to tell him exactly what happened, and Barzatti here will give him your names. So then we'll see if you answer the questions when he asks them."

I turned around and headed for the Jeep.

"Hey," somebody yelled from behind me, "what do you want to know?"

I turned back and looked at the five of them. One was standing up, so I figured he was the one who had yelled. I spoke directly to him, as if the others weren't there. "I want to know if any of you people know how somebody could take a shot like that and then disappear into thin air. I want to know if any of you have access to twenty-two-caliber target rifles. I want to know why you people aren't doing your job of protecting him. I want to know if you have any idea who's doing this, and how he's getting away with it."

"We can't figure it out," broke in Barzatti. "We've talked it over and over. There ain't no twenty-two anywhere that we can find. Pieces, AK-forty-sevens, things like that we've got. We've all got. But nobody has a twenty-two-caliber rifle, for Christ's sake. This ain't a Boy Scout camp."

"Then how do you read it?" I asked. "How can somebody be pulling all this stuff without you guys figuring out who it is or catching him at it? It doesn't add up. My job is dealing with things that don't add up, and I'm going to find out who or what is wrong here. Things will be a lot easier on everybody if somebody can come up with an answer before it's too late—too late for Tony or too late for one of you guys.

If anybody has anything to tell me, you can call my room at the house. I saw the number four-one-one on my phone, so I figure that's the right one. All information will be strictly between whoever calls and me. Or I'll meet anybody anytime anywhere, and that will also be confidential."

Because he's so big and because he enjoyed it, Brady always played the bad guy to my good guy. But here I had to be both good guy and bad guy at the same time, letting them know I was ready to listen but also ready to put the finger on whoever might be holding out. I turned again, walked over to the Jeep, climbed into my seat, and looked straight ahead. After a few seconds I could hear Barzatti walking toward me, but I didn't turn my head. He got in, started up the engine, took off, and drove slowly back to the main house.

"Where you wanna go now?" he asked.

I was feeling tired and a little sweaty. One of my pills was an hour overdue, and I could see my hands shaking a little where they were resting on my knees. I wanted to curl those hands up and pound them on my knees and yell, "Why me, God? Why me?" I had an appointment with the doctor in five days, and maybe I should go back to the city and take it easy before I saw him. Was I overdoing? He said to be careful not to overdo. What good was the money if you were too dead to spend it? Cops are always thinking that maybe today is the day you catch a bullet. You never know who might kill you. But I was the one I had to watch out for now. I was the one who could kill me.

"Take me back to the house," I told him. "I've done enough damage for today." I don't know who he thought I was talking about. But I was talking about me.

20

The Jeep had no roof on it, and my scalp was crisped tight from the sun. I was all sweaty under the arms, and my head felt a little light, so that I was putting each foot down in front of me very carefully. I looked at the stairs and then walked over to the elevator. There was nobody around, and the house was so quiet that I could hear the lawn mowers working outside somewhere but nothing else. I was so tired that I sat down on the bed and just stared at the striped wallpaper until it seemed to be moving up and down. A few minutes' rest might be just what I needed, but as I moved my head to the left I caught sight of the telephone on the bed table. I dialed my mother's number. The recorded voice came on, telling me that this was not a local call and I should try again. So I hit "one" before the other numbers, and in a second the phone was ringing.

"Hello?" asked my mother.

"Ma, it's me. Just checking in. How's everything?"

"Everything is fine. Petey yelled at me because I don't know where you are. You all right, Vincent?"

"I'm fine, Ma. I'm having a good time."

"Where you calling from?"

"From a pay phone, Ma. My friend doesn't have a phone in his cabin."

"What you doing there?"

"We're fishing, Ma. I'll bring you some."

"Petey says he wants you to call him."

"I'll do that, Ma. But I'll be home in a few days. Tell Petey I'm having a good time."

"You take care of yourself, Vincenzo."

"I will, Ma. I'll see you in a couple of days."

Suddenly I felt very hot and sticky, so I stripped off all my clothes, lay back on the bed and closed my eyes. Why wait a couple of days? I should get the hell out of here today. I had a bad feeling in the middle of my stomach. Best to go home to my mother and the family and my apartment and my pension. I thought of the briefcase at home with the hundred thousand and the briefcase in the closet with another hundred thousand, and my brother getting another hundred thousand, and seven hundred thousand still to go. Go home, my stomach was telling me. But the only time your belly makes real noises is when you're hungry, and I was hungry for the money.

One time Brady and I arrested a Gypsy woman who had conned an old lady out of thirty grand by telling her she was channeling the money to her dead husband who was having trouble making ends meet in heaven because things were so expensive there. People wonder why cops get so they don't believe anything you tell them, but it's because we're dealing with stuff like this all the time. Anyway, the Gypsy lady went through all the motions, including that she was putting a curse on us.

"Some night you'll be asleep," she said, "and in your sleep you'll feel beings in the room with you, strange, terrible spirits that will rip the soul from your body and condemn you to hell forever. I can do that to you. I can do that. That is what I'll do to you if you don't go away and leave me alone."

They never found the money and the Gypsy got two

years for her scam, but the day after she was sentenced, Brady came in and swore that there were evil spirits in his bedroom the night before.

"They kept grabbing me by the dick," he said.

"That was your wife, dickhead," I told him. "It's been so long since you've been able to do it that you can't tell the difference between a woman in heat and an evil spirit."

"Believe me," said Brady, "when my wife wants it, she's an evil spirit."

It was somewhere around then that I must have fallen asleep, because I could feel the evil spirits in the room with me, and I wanted to get up and run away, but I couldn't move, I couldn't wake up enough to yell for my mother to come make the sign of the cross in front of me or for Brady to pull out his dick and wave it at them, and I could feel my chest getting tighter and tighter like it was going to explode, and I yelled, "Betty, Betty," and sat up in the bed feeling like I was going to puke all over the place.

There were evil spirits all right. At the foot of the bed, staring at me. Six of them. No, seven when the old lady came zooming from around the back of them in her electric wheelchair.

The two brothers, the four sisters and the old lady were staring at me, and I looked down to where their eyes were focused, and I was wearing nothing but a hard-on that stuck out like a sore thumb. I dropped my hands to cover up, but it was like trying to hold back the tide until suddenly it collapsed from its own weight. The only time I was ever this panicked was when I forgot to lock the bathroom door, and my mother walked in with my aunt Florinda. Florinda had bought us a present of one of those cushiony plastic toilet seats, and they were up there to replace the hard old white one with the fancy purple one.

Florinda, who had left the nunnery after only one year, always gave me a squeeze on the arm and a funny little smile after that.

"What the hell do you want?" I yelled at the Pardos. "Get out of here. What do you want?"

"We want you to go," said Aldo. "Go back to the city. Leave us alone. We don't want you here. You'll only cause trouble."

Constanza had a little smile on her face, kind of like the one my aunt Florinda specialized in, but the rest of them looked as mean as they were ugly.

"Go away," yelled the old lady, waving her arms at me. "You are evil. You bring evil into this house. Go away."

Jesus. What was happening to my life? First a fifteen-year-old kid gave me a heart attack. Now seven crazy Italians had me pinned naked on a bed. The Beretta in the drawer flashed through my mind, but I would have to remove my hands in order to get it. Then what would I do? Shoot them? *Basta!* I'd had enough. I lifted my hands and pushed myself off the bed, walked into the bathroom, and slipped on my Jockey shorts. I thought about getting completely dressed, but I was too pissed off for that. They were still standing in the same spot when I returned, like a septet from one of the operas my uncle Rodolfo dragged me to when I was a kid. Except I didn't like the songs these people sang.

Constanza's smile got a little bigger when I walked into the room, and Theresa's face turned a bit softer, but the mother, the two brothers, and the two older sisters were still like rocks.

"Listen," I said, "the head of this family, Tony Pardo, hired me to come out here and find out who is trying to kill him. It would seem to me that you people, of all people, would be just as interested in getting whoever it is. How do you know you won't be next? Tony's the one who brought me in, and he's the only one who can throw me out. And now I'm telling you to go—and never come in here again without knocking or calling me on the phone first. Tony told me to ask questions of anybody I want, and I'm going to get around to all of you. So you wait until you hear from me. Now get the hell out of here before I call him in the city and tell him what you've done."

They all stared at me for a few seconds, uncertain now that I had yelled back, and then the two older sisters started turning away.

"Wait a minute," I said, and they all stopped whatever they were about to do or say. "As long as I've got you all together, is there any one of you who knows why someone is trying to kill Tony, and is there any one of you who thinks he knows who might be the perpetrator?

They stared at me for almost a full minute.

"Fuck you," said Aldo, and turned and left the room.

"Fuck you," said Cissy, and followed his brother.

The old lady put her machine into gear and buzzed out. Three sisters left without a word, but Constanza lingered a moment.

"I was going to tell you at supper that I would like to see more of you," she said, "but now I don't have to say that. What we've got to do is arrange for you to see a lot more of me." And she was gone, closing the door behind her.

I went back to the bed and sat down, thinking it was time to start thinking. The phone rang and I picked it up.

"Any progress?" asked a woman's voice.

"Who is this?"

"It's Gretchen Pardo."

"Oh, Mrs. Pardo . . ."

"Call me Gretchen. Have you found out anything yet?"

"The only thing I've found out is that it's going to take a lot more than me nosing around to get anywhere. These people aren't going to tell me anything at all, and I don't have the power to make them. I don't have a badge or other cops or subpoenas or district attorneys or any of the other things you use to conduct a proper investigation."

"You've got something better than all of them," she said.

"What's that?"

"You've got Tony Pardo," she said.

"But he's not here, and they couldn't care less."

"I care, and that's all you need."

"Maybe I'm not the guy to do this job," I told her.

"I think you are. I think you may be just the guy for the job. I for one am ready to put myself completely in your hands," she said. "Why don't you come to my room at ten-thirty tonight and we'll discuss strategy."

The way she'd said that made me twitch a little bit. It was the same tone Constanza had used, except it was different. One was a smoldering fire, and this one was a goddamned lightning bolt. I wanted no part of either of them. I had to use my head both to solve the case and to keep Tony Pardo from wasting me because of his sister or his wife.

"Ten-thirty?" I asked.

"Yes," she answered. "I can't break free until then."

"We could talk about it right now if you've got a few minutes."

"No. Ten-thirty." And she broke the connection.

I went into the bathroom and started running water into the tub. When it was full and the air jets were going all out, I slipped into the water and lay back, letting the jets float me near the top. The roar of the motor and the swishing of the air bubbles were loud in my ears. I had to think. I had to put everything but this noise out of my mind. How was I going to find out anything? What would a private eye—a guy who had to work without backup from a police department— do? Their rooms. While they were all eating supper, I would toss their rooms. It was a long shot, especially since I didn't know where any of their rooms were, but at least it was better than sitting in my room eating chocolate mints.

I dried myself off with the towels and then the warm-air blower. A guy could get used to this life-style. No lunch. I hadn't had any lunch. And there was going to be no dinner unless I used room service. The hell with all that. I took the glass covers off the sandwiches and ate three halves. One tuna and two Genoa salami. There were éclairs under one of the covers, and I looked at the dish for about three minutes before I uncovered it. My shoulder didn't hurt anymore. The limit was going to be one éclair, but I ended up eating three. Then I brushed my teeth so I wouldn't be tempted to eat any more. Then I watched *Terminator IV* and *Rambo V,* falling asleep some of the time, and all of the sudden it was twenty minutes past eight.

21

I was so nervous waiting for the clock to show eight forty-five that I barely realized how many guys Stallone was killing with what looked like a nuclear-powered slingshot. At one point I had the bottle of Valium out of the case and the tablet shaken into the palm of my hand before I pulled myself up and said, "Whoa, boy." It was amazing how many times I could hear Betty saying, "Whoa, boy," in my mind. It would be easy to become as much of an addict on Valium as you could on coke, and since I was forbidden to do the kind of workouts that would make my body tougher, I had to learn to make my mind tougher. Strenuous mental exercise was all I was to be allowed for the rest of my life. I would have to read books and maybe take more classes at the community college and learn all the things that would help me get the rest of the way through whatever years I had left without going crazy. I thought of the times I had put on the gloves with the guys at the police gym. What I would have given to be in the ring with somebody, feeling the sweet shock through the arm when I landed one, and shaking off whatever pounded into me. The therapist at the hospital had told me about things like yoga and transcendental meditation and biofeedback to calm me down, but I now realized there was nothing like a good punch to cool off your mind.

I almost took off at eight-thirty, but I knew that would be stupid. These people didn't care if they kept somebody waiting. They could be as late as they wanted and might not get to the dinner table until nine. Or they might be staying in their rooms and having the food brought to them. What the hell did I say if I walked in on Aldo with his mouth full of pasta? Or Constanza parading around without any clothes on? I thought about that for a minute. Then I thought about it for another minute. She sure was a *bellezza*. My brother Frankie, who was an old-style Italian macho man, would have gone nuts over her kind of looks. His wife, Bella, was a lovely person, but she was dumpy.

Eight forty-six. I had forced myself to wait an extra minute to prove something, although I don't know what the hell it could have been. When I came into the hall, I looked at the line of doors ahead of me and wondered in what order to handle them.

"Start at the beginning and go to the end," I whispered to myself.

The first room was that of Angelina, the oldest sister. When I opened the door, the only light was coming from a candle burning on one of the bureaus. It was one of those fat, short votive candles that you see in church, and it was lighting up the picture of a mean-looking son of a bitch. The whole business was sitting on a gold tray, and it was like a small shrine with some dried flowers in a little vase and tiny gold statues of saints. I knew it was Angelina's husband because the room was filled with photographs of the two of them together, his arm clamped around her like he was telling the world "Hey, this belongs to me."

Underneath her underwear was a Beretta just like the one I had been given, but that was all the place had to offer, and I scuttled out of there after a couple of minutes.

The next room belonged to Florence, and it was exactly the same as Angelina's, except that the guy's picture in the shrine was different, and the tray and saint statues were silver instead of gold. The only weapon in the place was a silver dagger on the table, and it could have been a letter opener, except that I doubted she knew anybody who could write.

The third room definitely belonged to Aldo. There were pictures of him with fighters and famous comedians, everybody laughing like hell, and all shot at some gambling casino or nightclub. The drawers were stuffed with silk shirts and silk underwear, and I wondered how he kept from sliding out of them all day. The closet held the bonanza—a .22 target rifle, five pistols, an AK47, a grease gun, two shotguns, and a drawer full of ammo. When the revolution came, Aldo was going to be ready. A .22 target rifle. I smelled the bore, and it had been fired recently. But Aldo had been in the kitchen, playing cards. Would Barzatti have told me if he knew Aldo had a .22 in his closet? Doubtful. Extremely doubtful.

The room across from Aldo's was Cissy's. Cissy! There had to be another nickname for Cistercio. My brother Alessandro was called Sandy, which bothered my grandfather Angelo because he said it didn't sound Italian enough. The same kind of pictures were on the wall as in Aldo's room, except that Cissy had encountered a few famous actresses, and you could tell from the photos that he was practically coming in his pants at the time. Cissy didn't bother to hide anything. There was a .22 target rifle on the bureau, with a revolver on either side of it, and there were shotguns and automatic weapons in the closet, along with a drawer full of ammo. The .22 had the same cordite smell as Aldo's, but Cissy had also been in the kitchen, playing cards. According to Barzatti.

Despite what Pardo had said, these people weren't going to talk to me. "Were you in the kitchen playing cards with the brothers?" I would ask. "Whatever they say," would be the answer.

The room across the hall was dark when I opened the door, and I carefully closed it behind me before trying to locate the switch on the wall. My hand took a hard hit from the edge of a picture frame as I was scrabbling for the button, and when I grunted, there was a small scream from somewhere in the room. What the hell? I flicked the switch up to find myself in a spare bedroom of some sort, and kneeling on the bed was a maid with her uniform pulled up, and standing in back of her was one of the waiters with his pants dropped on the floor. They were so scared that I became cool after that one quick jolt of surprise.

The girl was not Renée, and she didn't look like a Claudine ought to look, so it had to be one of the regular maids. The guy's hands were shaking so bad that he could have whipped up a great cocktail, but the girl was just slack-jawed, her eyes big and round, and she started to sob.

"Look," I said, waving my arms in a circle to indicate that I meant no harm, "I heard a noise so I came in to see what it was. As far as I'm concerned, I didn't see anything. Nothing. Nobody. *Nada.* Nobody will ever know a thing. I'm sorry I disturbed you. I'm going to put out the light and leave now, and I won't be coming back. Excuse me. *Scusa.*"

"Signore," said the waiter, as I was reaching for the switch. I stopped and watched while he waddled over to me, took my hand, and kissed the back of it the way

Italians do with priests or godfathers. I put out the light and left as quietly as I had come. It was only when I was halfway across the hall that I realized I had left him in the dark with his pants down, and getting back to the bed might be a problem. It was a toss-up as to whether they continued or called it a night. It would be nice to think that he had the balls to continue.

The maid had not yet been to Theresa's room, and it was a mess, with clothes and towels and sandwiches with one bite out of them scattered all around on the bureaus and tables and floor. Her drawers revealed a dildo and several containers of high-grade coke. There were no weapons. I got out of there fast because the maids had to be on constant red alert to keep her place straightened up. There was a mean look to her eyes, and I figured it was no fun being her picker-upper.

Constanza's room was neat and tidy, and the walls were covered with pictures of her with good-looking guys of all types and sizes. Most of them were blonds with surfer tans, but there were a couple of dark, romantic types like me. She sure was good-looking, whether she had all her clothes on or just a bikini. There was one small bottle of coke in one of her drawers, but that was all that was out of the ordinary.

The big surprise came in Mama's room, which also had a shrine on the bureau, and this had to be the father, Guido the Terrible, and you could see where the older children had inherited their ugliness. There was a painting of the Crucifixion on each of the four walls, and three-foot statues of saints scattered about the room.

One of the bureaus had about twelve bottles of pills on it, and this is where I got the shock. Before my heart attack, the last thing I would have done was check the labels to see what she was taking. Two of them, Cardene and Isorbide, were on my list, so I shook out a tablet of Cardene and swallowed it dry. This one was on her, the old bitch. The very last bottle contained liquid. Someone had taped a piece of paper to the front of it and written "Strychnine, Be Careful" on it. The best place to hide something was out in the open. But would she have tried to poison her own son? I wished I could have it dusted and check out some fingerprints, but that was out of the question. After wiping the bottle off with a handkerchief, I put it back on its exact spot.

I had maybe taken two steps outside the old lady's room when Aldo came around the corner, giving my heart another lurch. This couldn't be good for me in any way.

"Hey," he said, "ain't you going to eat any supper?"

Altobelli's whereabouts had obviously been discussed.

"I ate something in the room," I told him. He grunted and went to his own room.

The sweat broke out on me like the snap of your fingers, and I suddenly felt a little dizzy. I had asked the doctor about the sweats, and he had mumbled something about their not being uncommon after a heart attack, but it still shook me up to get sweaty when I wasn't doing anything strenuous. I walked back to the room, and found that the bed had been turned down and a new box of mints was on the other pillow. The clock read nine fifteen, which meant there wasn't time for another movie.

My pulse was still fast from my nervous jaunt around the room, so I sat down on the bed to relax a minute and think about what video I wanted to watch after I finished with Mrs. Pardo. There was a tap on the door and before I could say come in, it opened up to reveal two visitors. The redheaded woman with Renée was older than she was, but her body was even more spectacular. It was easy to compare them because they were both wearing string bikinis.

22

In addition to the bikinis, they were wearing the kind of grins I would find on the faces of arrestees who were suspected of snorting a couple of lines of coke and possibly disseminating same. After a while you get to know just how much coke a perpetrator ingested before doing something that brought him to the attention of the police.

"Claudine said she wanted to meet you, so we came straight here from happy hour." Renée giggled.

"Oh," I told her, "I thought you were just home from the beach."

"There's no beach around here, silly," said Renée. "We were just having a bathing-beauty contest, and we want you to be the judge."

Tired as I was, I found this to be a not unreasonable idea. Here were two hookers who had undoubtedly participated in every sexual deviation listed in the police manual, who had been exposed to crabs, herpes, gonorrhea, syphilis, AIDS, and a couple of diseases that the government was still keeping under wraps. But they were also good-looking as hell and friendly in a kid's sort of a way, and they made my heart beat a little faster and my *piccalino* blossom into flowering manhood. It had been one thing to do it with Betty Wade, a trained nurse with a stethoscope on the bed table, but what would happen if I took on these two pros? The acid test. If that was the way I went out, my brother Frankie would smile at the funeral.

"First thing we have to do," said Claudine, "is get wet in the water. Then we can lay down on the beach and get laid."

I figured there was not going to be any formal introduction, that Claudine knew about me and I knew about her, and why screw around with formalities when there was real screwing to do? I'd been around these people too long to think they were attracted to my good looks and manly physique. Maybe I was more appealing than most of the goombahs they had to deal with, but if Pardo told them to, they would take on Freddy Krueger. And make him smile.

"Ladies," I said, knowing that it was going to take more than polite requests to send two cokeheads on their way, "I have had a long and tiring day, and I am afraid I will not be up to your contest."

"Don't worry about that, honey," said Claudine. "We'll get it up for you. Renée here's got the best tongue in the business."

Little tickles of sweat were breaking out all over my skin. What kind of shape was my body in if I started sweating whenever anything exciting passed before me? There had been sweat when I braced those guys down by the stables, sweat when I was going through the rooms. The only time I had ever sweat before the heart attack was when I was working out or chasing some juvenile up a flight of stairs.

"Okay," said Claudine, taking charge, "here's the plan. We'll go in and start putting the ocean into the beach. Then we'll turn on the waves, and then you come in with us, and we'll start the contest."

Without waiting for an answer, they went into the bathroom and closed the door, and I could hear water splashing into the tub. It was big enough to hold three people, that was for sure, but I didn't want to be one of them. Renée could swear she got checked by doctors all the time and all that crap, but the odds were that with the number of guys the two of them had taken on, somebody among them had to be a needle user or a closet gay with the virus in him. I couldn't see either of the two arguing with some killer who didn't want to wear a condom.

Just as I was about to get off the bed and go into the beach area to put the Wrigley's chewing gum twins under a cold shower, the door of the room opened and in came Constanza carrying what looked like the jar of coke that had been on her bureau. Was she also coming from happy hour? She was wearing some kind of robe, a lounging robe maybe, and it was open wide at the top to show that there was no nightgown under it.

"You didn't come to supper," said Constanza, "so I thought you might be hungry for something else."

You know, if the old lady had come rolling in on her wheelchair bare-ass naked it wouldn't have surprised me a bit. I was living out my high school wet dreams, but I wasn't enjoying it as much as I had thought I would. There was a bit of jerkiness to Constanza's movements that showed she was strung out a little too thin, and I never forgot the fact that she was a full-blooded Pardo, which meant that there was always the temper that could explode at any moment.

"Take off your towel," she said, "and let me see what an ex-dick looks like."

She had a sense of humor. That was pretty clever.

"All you have to do is drop it," she said, "just like this." The robe was so light that it fluttered to the floor.

She was skinny compared to my two mermaids in the bathroom, but she was filled out in all the right places, and her skin looked like it would glow in the moonlight. I wished my brother Frankie could have been with me. Right then he would have been walking on the ceiling.

"You know," she said, strolling my way, "I don't usually get interested in dagos"—I thought about all the blond men in her pictures on the wall—"but I might make an exception of you. My mother's always saying 'Get an Italian boy,' and tonight might just be the night."

She had good lines. I wondered who wrote her stuff. I stood up from the bed, not knowing what the hell to do, when the bathroom door opened and Renée and Claudine, their bikinis gone, started toward me with their arms stretched out.

"Vinnie," yelled Renée, "tell the truth. Is my ass . . . ?"

She caught sight of Constanza before Claudine, who was whirling around with her finger pointing at her own rear end.

"I'll give you cards and spades, baby," she was yelling, when her turn brought her to where she, too, could see Constanza standing there with only a bottle of cocaine for cover.

"Jesus," Claudine said, "is Constanza in the contest, too?"

Without bothering to pick up her robe, Constanza

whirled around and ran out of the room, and as her ass vanished just before the door slammed, I decided that she wouldn't have come in less than second if the competition had gone forward.

"What the hell was she doing here?" asked Claudine, unfazed by what had happened. "She knows we're supposed to take care of the guests. Did you ever, Renée? Did you ever see anything like that? How are we going to make a living if she starts giving it away for free?"

Renée shook her head sorrowfully. They were not the least bit disturbed that they had upset Tony's baby sister or that she might seek revenge against them. That was because neither of them was Italian. Right then I was worried about her seeking vengeance against me.

"Hey," yelled Claudine, grabbing my towel and pulling it all the way off, "let's not let her spoil the party."

"Hell, no," echoed Renée, grabbing me where the towel had been and pulling me along as gracefully as I could move until we came to the edge of the bath pool and dropped in. Claudine flicked the switch, and the air jets started to bubble before going into full eruption.

"Okay," yelled Claudine, "the contest is about to begin. First we check out what floats best, and you can be in on this, too, Vinnie, except that Renée has a big advantage over both of us."

Renée smiled coyly and put her hands on the bottom of the tub so that she was bobbing twin mountain peaks and a rain forest above the surface of the water. All the right things flashed through my mind—Betty Wade, my heart, Constanza coming back with a shotgun, the old lady dropping strychnine into the tub, Aldo, Cissy—but my thinking was being done in the area way below my brain, and I was saying, What the hell. Let it happen as it happens.

"Okay, baby," said Claudine, "you're about to enjoy something you've never had in your life before."

And that was the last thing I remembered.

23

The first thing I saw was Renée, wearing only a tiny frown, sitting on the edge of the bed.

She had obviously been watching me closely, because as soon as my eyes flickered, she said, "Are you all right now, baby?"

"What happened?"

"I don't know. We thought for a minute you'd died. You've got a bad heart, you know."

I knew.

"When you went under the water," Renée continued, "we thought you were clowning around, but after a while Claudine figured something was wrong and we pulled you out. You weren't breathing or anything, so Claudine hit you one in the middle of your chest, and you started breathing. Then we dried you off and put you in the bed."

"How long ago was that?"

"It was nearly an hour ago. Claudine broke a nail

dragging you out of the tub, so she had to go to her room, but I was worried about you, so I stayed."

I listened to my body, then moved two fingers of my right hand over the pulse on the left. Nice and slow and steady. I breathed deep, but there was no pain. It felt good under the covers, and I wiggled my toes to see if that part of my body was still operating. Everything was checking out. Had I had another heart attack? They'd have to do a blood test and check the enzymes. That seemed to be the big deal—checking the enzymes. But I didn't want to go through all that crap again. Better to die and just get it over with. No more hospital, tests, people looking at you funny. People feeling sorry it was you and happy it wasn't them. Even my own brothers.

"Can I get you anything, honey?" asked Renée.

"No, thanks, Renée. I'm pretty tired, and I think I'll go to sleep."

"Claudine's gone, but I could still give you a—"

"No. No, Renée. Thanks."

"Jeez, honey, every time we go to do it something happens. It's like we was jinxed."

"Don't worry about it, Renée. Everything's cool."

"Are you sure I can't do anything for you?"

"No, nothing, thanks."

"I guess I'll scoot along, then," she said, standing up and going into the bathroom. When she came out again, she had put on her own bikini and was carrying the other one. "Claudine went without hers," she said, "but I don't want to bump into Jefferson with my tits hanging out."

Since the difference between wearing that bikini and nothing at all was practically zilch, I didn't quite get her point, but she knew Jefferson better than I did.

"Good night, honey," said Renée, coming over to

the bed and bending down to give me a kiss on the lips. She lingered there a few seconds so I could indicate if I wanted anything to develop, but then she stood up again and left without another word.

The fear hit me so hard that I started to shake. What if I had been taking a bath all by myself and gone under? What the hell had happened? Another heart attack? A stroke? Should I go see a doctor? My pill. I hadn't taken the Cardene. The case was on the bureau, but I didn't have the strength to get out of bed. I didn't care. Right then I didn't care. Time to pack it in. *If they let me.* Time to go home. *If they let me.* They had better be careful, though. If they weren't careful, I would die on them, and then where would they be? As well off as before I had come. So far I had done nothing to earn a dollar, let alone a million.

My eyes were growing heavy, and I could feel myself drifting off to sleep. Just as I was about to let myself go, I remembered. Mrs. Pardo. I was supposed to meet her at ten-thirty. My watch said it was ten past ten. I jumped out of bed and began throwing my clothes on, looking at the telephone all the time, waiting for it to ring. Would she dock me a hundred thousand for being late? I started laughing. Couldn't help it. The whole thing had become so ridiculous. What if I was late? So what? I tied my shoes slowly and carefully, put on the sports jacket, checked my hair in the mirror, and was almost to the door when the phone rang.

24

For a moment I considered just going out the door and explaining when I got there, but then I figured it would be easier to say that I was on my way.

I went back, picked up the receiver and said, "Sorry, but I'm on my . . ."

"Vinnie?"

It didn't sound like Mrs. Pardo.

"Yes?"

"I called to apologize."

"Constanza?"

"Yes?"

"You don't owe me an apology. It's all right."

"No, it's not all right. You're trying to do a job for my brother, and we've been giving you a hard time about it. I want to be friends again."

"We never weren't friends, Constanza."

"I mean real friends. I never see anybody here, and you're a cool guy, and I want to get to know you better. You don't need those hookers for company. There are a lot of things you and I could do. We could go bowling in the basement or watch a movie in the screening room or dance. There's a nice dance floor on the third floor with a great stereo. Or we could swim in the indoor pool. Or we could just have a few drinks and sit and talk."

"That all sounds great, Constanza, but I have an

appointment with Mrs. Pardo, and I don't know how long that's going to take."

The sound of her breath being sucked in was loud enough to warn that a storm was in the air. But then there was silence. A long silence. What the hell was she thinking? Or doing?

"Okay, that's fine," she finally managed, but the strain came through. "Business before pleasure. But it shouldn't take too long. Then can we do something?"

"I'm not sure how long it will take," I told her. It was like I was explaining to my eight-year-old niece Dolores why we couldn't at the moment do something she wanted to do. Or why we couldn't do it at all, which was quite often the case with some cockamamie thing she insisted she had to try. My brother spoiled the hell out of her. There was another silence.

"Maybe you're right," I said, caving in a little but not wanting to be even later than I was for the appointment. "It may not take much time at all. Where can I reach you?"

"I'll wait in my room," she said, sounding a bit happier about the whole thing. "You call me when you . . . No, come and get me. Do you know which room is mine?"

That was close to a trick question.

"No."

She gave detailed instructions.

"We can even stay here and watch television or listen to music or just talk," she said.

"You've got a date," I told her, and she gave a little laugh before she clicked off.

Even though I was late as hell, I held the phone in my hand for a moment to think about Constanza. It wasn't only that she was pretty as hell—a smoldering beauty, as my brother Frankie would describe her.

There was also a fire burning somewhere inside her that made me feel warm just looking at her. Renee and Claudine were almost comical when it came to sexual attraction, but there was something about Constanza that made you stand and hold a telephone in your hand when you were a half hour late for a meeting with your boss. I wondered if I would ever see Betty Wade again. But she was wherever she was, and Constanza was there now. And I was supposed to be with Mrs. Pardo. I sighed. Maybe for the first time in my life.

25

When the door opened to her room, you didn't need to be a detective to know that Mrs. Pardo was drunk. A great deal of my professional life was spent deciding how drunk somebody was, and Mrs. Pardo was drunk. Very, very drunk.

She was holding the biggest brandy snifter I had ever seen, the kind that doesn't have a stem and you let it rest in the palm of your hand. It looked like it could hold a keg, and it was about half full.

"Ah," she said, "Vincent." She paused as though wondering what the hell I might be doing there, and then it came to her. "I've been expecting you."

"I'm sorry I'm late," I started to mumble, but then I realized that she had no idea and couldn't care less about whether or not I was late or early or dead or alive. Whatever she had wanted to discuss with me was not uppermost in her mind right then.

"I can come back some other time," I ventured, but she reached out her hand, pulled me in, shut the door and locked it. Now that I was there, that was where I was going to be. She didn't say anything, just stood there taking gulps out of her glass and looking at me like she might be planning to sell me by the pound. I felt if I didn't say something, we could be there forever. The only thing that came into my mind was "When's Mr. Pardo flying in?"

She looked at her watch. "If they're sticking to their schedule," she said, "right now he's sitting in his plane waiting to take off for Rome."

"Rome? How come you're not going with him?"

"We've got too many irons in the fire right now, and most of them need my personal attention. Besides, the people he's meeting don't like to do business with women."

"I guess in the old country old habits die hard," I said.

"In this country, too." She laughed. "You'd be amazed how many times I have to step out of the picture before anything can be agreed upon. No matter how aggressive the women have seemingly become in this country, it's still basically the same as it was. I'm sure that's how it is in your police department."

"My lieutenant's a woman," I told her, for some reason proud of being able to say it even though I had hated the witch from the day she had taken over the squad. Brady and I had hoped that one of us would get the nod, but her *coglioni* turned out to be even bigger than Brady's.

"How do you like working under a woman?"

I never thought a person with her class would pull a line like that on me. My uncle Fabrizio thought he had originated the question, and every time I saw him he would ask it again and then have a laughing fit. Once he started to choke on a veal bone, and so help me I almost didn't bend to help him. But then I realized she was being serious rather than clever. She wanted to know what it was like for me to have a woman as my boss. My reactions had always been from the belly, so I thought about it for a bit.

"She can really pi . . . She can really make you angry, but she knows police work and she puts in fifteen hours a day. Now that I think about it, the guy before her, Lieutenant Mulvaney, he could even make you madder and he barely worked eight hours a day. She's got guts. She's come up against guys who could break her in two, but she never shaded a hair. But sometimes, sometimes, it's all I can do not to snap her bra strap when I go by."

"So all in all, it wouldn't bother you to take orders from a female."

I had to think about that for another minute.

"No, I guess not," I decided. "Now that I don't take orders from her anymore I can see that she's been doing a pretty good job. Why are you asking me all this?"

She smiled, and right then she was beautiful.

"You never know," she said. "There may come a time when I'll ask you to work for me."

That made me think some more. It still bothered me that I had jumped so quickly into Tony Pardo's lap. The money had a lot to do with it, there was no argument about that. Especially with my brother Frankie needing the hundred grand. You see all that cash lying in front of you, and it's hard to think about anything else. But even that wouldn't have been enough to get me to work for a guy who probably caused as much harm in the world as the drug kings in Colombia. I had taken the job because someone wanted me to work. Tony Pardo couldn't have cared less that I'd had a heart attack, that nobody else would hire me, that I was expected to sit quietly in a corner until they put me down. He had given me a chance to do what I do best.

"I guess, in a way, I'm working for you now," I said. "You and Mr. Pardo seem to be a team."

She smiled again, but this time it was a little different. "We look like a team, don't we?" she said. "But Tony's old-fashioned in a lot of ways. Every day I see more and more of his father in him. I'm the one behind all the company acquisitions that have been made recently. But Tony's like that television commercial for investment banking. He likes to make money the old-fashioned way."

"Both ways seem to work pretty well," I said, "because the life-style here is about as opulent as I've ever seen, and that includes the movies.

She laughed a real laugh, one of those that come from deep inside. "You can imagine what effect it had on me," she said, "coming from a small town in New Hampshire and with parents who believed it is better to give than to receive."

"If you don't mind my saying so," I said, "I've been wondering how you and Tony ever got together in the first place."

She laughed again, softer this time. "I'd never met anyone like him," she said. "I had a four-point-oh average at the University of New Hampshire, and I won a scholarship to attend the Harvard Business School. I'd made up my mind that I was going to break the tradition in my family and that I was going to make a lot of money and have a life that was as exciting as possible. Tony was in three of my classes, and one day he asked me if I wanted to go out to dinner. I didn't really know anything about him except that he was attractive and quite different from all the boys I'd grown up with, so I accepted, thinking that we'd eat at one of the little places in Cambridge. Instead we went over the river to the Ritz, and he did the whole bit on me—champagne, caviar, double-thick filets, the works. I'd never experienced anything like it in my life. While we were drinking our brandy, he told me that he had a suite upstairs if I wanted to have a nightcap there. First date. I knew what the drill would be, and I must admit that I was tempted, but you don't knock out all those years of strict Congregational upbringing without a fight, and I said I had to get back to prepare a brief. There was no argument from him. He just smiled and said maybe next time."

"I guess there was a next time."

She smiled again, this time with another little twist in it. "There were many next times," she said. "I made him work for it. But after that we were never separated, and when he asked me to marry him, I said yes. Just like that. I said yes. The day before graduation. I went through all the crap to convert, and we were married in a Catholic church in Cambridge. Then we flew out here, and I met the Pardo clan."

"Did that come as a shock?"

She snorted. One of those loud noises where a woman thinks she's going to laugh, but she's caught by surprise and ends up making the kind of noise that drives the sensitive ones nuts. I find it very appealing.

" 'Shock' doesn't suffice," she said. "I couldn't believe there were people living like this and thinking the way they did and behaving the way they did. It was as if I had landed on Mars."

"Did you have any idea what kind of business the

Pardo family really operated?" I asked, and then I wanted to bite my tongue. For whatever reason, she was talking, and I had to be careful that I didn't push too hard, that I didn't shove her out of whatever mood she was in. She opened her mouth and closed it again, and I could feel my hands shut into fists as I realized I had blown it.

"It took about a week," she said, and I let out my breath so slowly that it was like I was deep under water. "I had never seen so many Italians in my life, and all of sudden one day I said to myself, 'My God, you're living with the Godfather.' Guido was a piece of work, no doubt about that. He frightened me at first. He was in such a rage that Tony had brought home a wife whom he had married without obtaining permission. I don't know what he would have done if he had known I had been a Protestant, but as it was, he wouldn't even see me for nearly a week. Then one day I was hitting balls on the tennis court, using the automatic machine, and he suddenly appeared. 'Tony tells me you a smart girl,' he said. I didn't know what to say, so I just stared at him, having only had a glimpse when we first arrived. Tony and I had been having our meals in our room, where we pretty much stayed to be out of Guido's way. I finally decided that enough was enough and came down to the tennis court while Tony was getting his hair styled in the barbershop."

I couldn't help breaking in. "They have a barbershop here?"

She smiled again. "You'd be amazed at what they have here," she said. "Would you like a drink? We have some hundred-year-old cognac of which I am very fond."

Fond didn't seen a strong enough word, but without waiting to hear my answer, she went to a table and poured out a large jolt in a glass like the one she was holding, and then refilled her own. She walked back and handed one to me, clinked glasses softly after I took it from her, and then sat down in a deep leather lounge chair. I took a short pull of the brandy and felt the warmth slide down my throat until it rested gently in my belly. This wasn't grappa, that was for sure. I tipped the glass up and let the cognac flow down inside me until the warmth was everywhere.

"May I ask you something?" she said.

I nodded at her, hoping the flow of conversation would go back to her after I told her what she wanted to know.

"There's something different about you," she said. "We've done business with all kinds of policemen, but you're not like any of them. You fit in comfortably with this kind of people"—she swept her hand in a circle to indicate the Pardo clan—"but I have the feeling you'd fit in anywhere, including Harvard Yard. Have you had a university education?"

"I went to junior college for two years," I said.

"And what did you concentrate in?"

It took me a moment to realize what she was asking. "Criminal law," I said. "I took courses in criminal law."

"Did you take literature courses?"

"No, not really."

"Then why do I have this strange feeling about your background?"

I thought on that. "It's Carlotta," I finally decided.

"Carlotta?"

"Yeah, I went with Carlotta for two years."

"And how did that affect your life?"

"Carlotta was a high school teacher," I said. "My family didn't like her because she was ten years older than me and she was Spanish, but I went with her for two years, and she made me read books, and she took me to plays and concerts, and she even taught me some Spanish."

"What happened?"

I just looked at her and then took another pull on the cognac. It was sitting nicely.

"Are you still going with her?"

I shook my head.

"Why did you break up?"

"She wanted to get married."

"And you didn't want to marry her?"

"I thought about it, but in a way it would've been like going to school forever, and my family would have raised hell, and she said she never wanted to have kids, and I decided I didn't really like her."

"Didn't like her?"

"Yeah."

"Then why did you go out with her for two years?"

I almost said it, had my mouth open, but then closed it again and took another swallow of the firewater.

"Come on," she said. "There must have been some reason why you went with her for two years."

What the hell.

"The sex," I said.

"What?"

"She could drive me up the wall. Every time with her was like it was the first time. Even after two years. I couldn't get enough of her. We'd be in her apartment or mine, and when I saw her take off her glasses and shake out her hair, I could feel my hands shaking and . . ."

I stopped and finished off the cognac. She went over to the table for the bottle and poured me a medium-sized jolt. I took another drink. It was like I was floating on air, like when I woke up in the hospital.

Mrs. Pardo opened a drawer and took out a bottle, opened it, and shook a couple of pills into her hand. I looked to see if they were maybe like one of mine, but they were both purple and mine were white, green, and orange.

She held out her hand toward me. "These are new," she said, "and they make you feel like you own the world."

"No, thanks," I told her. "I already take enough pills."

She shrugged, popped the pills into her mouth, and washed them down with a slug of cognac. It was amazing that she was talking without any slurs in her voice, and that she seemed steady as a rock. A big girl can handle a lot more booze than a little one, I suppose. But what were the pills?

"Look," she said, "we've got a lot more to talk about, but I'm hungry. I've had them set up a little supper, and we can continue our conversation there." She stood up and walked over to the other corner of the room, where there was a table set with silver and glass, and there were three bottles in ice buckets and one of those warming carts they use in hotels.

Mrs. Pardo checked everything out, kicked off her shoes, turned, and saw me still standing where she had left me.

"Come over here," she said, in a real boss voice.

When I got there, she walked right into me, put her arms around my neck and kissed me for a long time. I was so busy listening for helicopters or knocks on the door or whatever that I froze into position, one arm down and the other holding on to the glass. She finally pulled back.

"We've got a lot to do here tonight," she said, "so let's have something to eat first."

She walked over to the table, lifted one of the

bottles from a cooler, and poured glasses of champagne. In the middle of the table was an iced silver bowl that held a big can of what had to be caviar. I wondered if the warming cart held double-thick filets. The whole schmear. She handed me my glass and then took a long drink from hers.

"What did you say that woman's name was?" she asked.

"What woman?"

"The teacher. The one you couldn't get enough of."

"Carlotta," I said.

"Carlotta," she echoed softly. "Well, remember, my name is Gretchen."

26

I had a buzz on, the first since a week before my heart attack. How long ago had that been? I didn't care. It felt good, my head held up by soft air instead of by my neck. We had champagne with the caviar, which tasted interesting, sort of like an anchovy thing my aunt Filomena used to make. We had red wine with the steaks. I didn't know which was worse for me, the red meat or the red wine, but then I figured they balanced each other out. I ate more cheese than I should have, but it had been so long, so long. The wine we had with the cheese had more bite than the first kind.

Mrs. Pardo popped another purple pill after we finished the cheese, and that reminded me to open my pillbox, and I had forgotten to take the Cardene and the Isosorbide and the aspirin, so I floated all three down at the same time. I think it was with the cognac, but it could have been with the second red wine.

We didn't talk much while we were eating. Mrs. Pardo was a big woman, and she scarfed to fit her size and drank more than enough to wash it down. She had turned on only a couple of the lamps, and watching her chew away, her lips greasy from the meat, was a real turn-on. I kept listening for the sound of the helicopter, because deep down in my gut I knew what was going to happen between us, and all I needed was Tony Pardo's flight to be canceled and him zooming back to find me camped out in his bedroom. There was a line that Carlotta was always reciting when she started harassing me about getting married: "But at my back I always hear/Time's winged chariot hurrying near." A helicopter can do you a hell of a lot more damage.

"Do you like chocolate mousse?" Mrs. Pardo asked.

"I beg your pardon?"

"There's some chocolate mousse in the cooler box."

"I couldn't eat another thing."

"Then let's sit by the fire and drink some more cognac and talk."

There was a fireplace in the right-hand wall, but there wasn't any fire. She took care of that by turning on a gas jet and then pressing a button, which made sparks fly in the fireplace, and boom, we had a fire blazing away.

"Do you know that these people have no idea that most other people burn wood in fireplaces?" she said. "When I asked about it, Florence told me that wood fires would make the room all dirty. I think I'm the only one in the house who uses the fireplaces at all."

I didn't say anything, and she started picking up pillows from all over the room and chucking them in front of the fireplace. She would stagger each time she threw a pillow, and I wondered when the booze and whatever the hell was in those purple pills would send her bye-bye. It looked like a pillow warehouse by the time she quit.

"Come on," she said, "let's get comfortable."

She just sat backward in the air and landed on a leather pillow with a whumpf. Not one drop of cognac spilled out of her glass. She patted a place beside her to indicate where she wanted my rump to land, but I wasn't as good as she was, and I dumped half my cognac onto the back of my hand. She reached over, took my hand, and licked the booze off it, just as she had done with my blood. I almost went for her then, but my ears were still cocked for helicopter noise, and that stopped my other one from rising to the occasion. She leaned against the cushions piled behind her, and I let myself fall back beside her. For the first time since my heart attack I felt warm and comfortable and capable of doing whatever the hell I wanted. What did the doctors know? My heart could have repaired itself and could now be almost like it was. I took another drink of the cognac and let it slide down my throat. It was as if we were in some kind of magic land, and I was there with the princess.

"I have to take a pee," said the princess.

She had trouble getting to her feet and lost the cognac glass in the roll off the cushions to the floor, and then went a little way on her knees before standing up, but she finally made it. I looked into the fire, and I guess I dozed off, because I didn't find out that she was back until she fell across me. She was wearing one of the terry-cloth robes from the bathroom, but she hadn't tied it together with the belt and now I knew half her secrets.

"Vincent," she said, "would you go to my dresser in the bathroom and get me the little gold case?" I rolled off the pillows, walked on my hands and knees until I could push myself up, and went into the bathroom. Her clothes were scattered all over the floor, but the gold case was just where she said it would be. I brought it back to her, and she told me to get the bottle of cognac from the table and bring it to her. She took two of the purple pills from the case, which fell from her hand before she could close it, and then washed them down with a swig from the bottle.

There was a slight pain in my chest that was cutting through the booze, and I felt sweat breaking out all over my body. My pulse was so slow and weak that I had trouble counting it, but it made no difference because I couldn't make out the second hand on my watch in the dim light.

"What's the matter, Vincent?" said Mrs. Pardo. "Why are you standing there? Come on down here, and we'll talk some more about the fucking Pardos."

"My heart's beating a little funny," I told her, wanting to share it with somebody.

"Maybe you need a pacemaker," she said. "That's what they had to put into Guido, a pacemaker. He got his prick up easier than his heart. He almost got me twice, the filthy son of a bitch. The first time, I almost squeezed his nuts off, and I thought that would be the end of it. But then he caught me in the hall some weeks later and pinned me against the wall. He was still strong, and I could feel it sticking into me through my dress, and I relaxed and let him kiss me, and then I bit right through his lip. He would have killed me if I'd stayed there another second, but I was gone. That was when I made up my mind."

Her voice trailed off, and she took another pull from the bottle.

"Tony was the only one in the family who knew the old man had the pacemaker in him," she continued, staring straight up at the ceiling. "Guido had it put in while he was in Los Angeles. Two days in the hospital. That's all it takes. So I told Guido to meet me in the kitchen while everybody was at Mass, told him I would make it worth his while. I got there first and had a cup of coffee in front of me, and he came in and walked over and squeezed both my breasts without saying a word. 'In a minute,' I told him, 'in a minute. First we have to talk.' There was this look on his face, like he already had it in me and was pumping away. He sat down beside me, still without saying a word. With his ego, he thought I had succumbed, that he was too powerful for me to resist. Or maybe he thought that because he had just named Tony his heir that I wanted to cinch the deal so he wouldn't change his mind. I got up and poured him a glass of wine, and on the way back I turned on both microwave ovens. Ignorant peasant. Nobody had told him about microwaves. Maybe the doctors had, but he never listened to anybody. And I sat down and started to tell him how much I admired him and all kinds of other crap, and he got this grin on his face, and I thought, Jesus, he's going to take me right on the kitchen table. What if it doesn't work? Maybe it works only sometimes. Or maybe not at all. And he started to reach out to me, going for my left breast, when he got this startled look on his face, which lasted maybe ten or fifteen seconds, and then he fell over, his head bouncing right on top of his glass. I got up and spilled my coffee in the sink and put my cup in one of the dishwashers. Then I turned off the ovens. I watched him for a few seconds to see if he might revive, but you could tell, you could tell that there was no life there. And I went back to my room and drew a hot bath and just stayed there until Tony came rushing into the room yelling that his father was dead. So I know about heart conditions. I know all about them. And I could kill you, too, but with a different *modus operandi*."

She had put the empty cognac bottle between her legs and was gently pulling it back and forth, up to her stomach and then down again, the brown glass sliding over her pink-white skin. The perfect murder. She'd pulled off the perfect murder, and it had been sitting inside her for all those years, and she finally had to tell somebody. It wasn't just her doing the talking, however. It was the champagne and the wine and cognac and those purple pills. But spaced out as she was, she knew there wasn't anything I could or would do about it. There was no tape recorder, no witness, my word against hers. And I knew right then that if I tried to tell anybody, if I ever crossed her in any way, I would die too. Because killing Guido hadn't meant a thing to her. She'd gotten the old man off her back, and she changed Tony into the boss. I shivered even though the heat was coming out of both the fireplace and my belly. She was a match for any of the Pardos, including Tony, and I wanted no part of her, including her body. The problem was how to get out of there without making her mad.

She didn't look so scary right then, lying there with her robe wide open—full frontal nudity, as the court order says when we close down some strip joint that's going beyond the licensing permit. One hell of a good-looking woman. And I had about as much desire for her as I would for my cousin Crispina, who has two moles on her face with bristly hairs sticking out of them. It was amazing, when you got right down to it. Despite her sweet look and softness, Constanza had no real idea of what love should be. Theresa was a degenerate. Angelina and Florence were gargoyles. The old lady was gaga. And Mrs. Pardo, who seemed so different from all of them in both her looks and manners made them all look like Sister Mary Ignatius, who was my teacher in the third grade. When you got right down to it, Renee and Claudine were the least whorey of the whole fucking bunch. I took a deep breath, and the pain in my chest was still there. No worse but still there. Mrs. Pardo's eyes were closed and she was snoring softly; little bubbles of spit pushed onto her lips and then pulled back again.

I became so dizzy that I would have fallen over if I hadn't grabbed the back of a chair. There was something wrong with me, something that wasn't just the booze and the rich food. I reached into my pocket and pulled out the little bottle of nitro, unscrewed the cap, and stuck one of the little white pills under my tongue. Nothing felt different. The doctor said it would help immediately if I had angina, but nothing felt different. The pain in the middle of the chest was still there. Time to get back to my room and, if it didn't go away, have someone call a doctor. Or an ambulance. That would be one way to get out of there. In an ambulance.

Mrs. Pardo was still lying there, and I figured she was good for at least the night. What the hell was in those purple pills?

I slipped into my jacket and walked across the room, but just as I was reaching for the bolt, there was a pounding on the door that sounded like a heavy-metal drummer warming up.

"Gretchen, you bitch," someone yelled from the other side, the pounding staying the same. "I know he's in there, bitch, and I'll kill the both of you. Let me in, you filthy cunt. I'm going to tell Tony everything, and then both of you will be dead. Dead!"

It was my late date for the evening, Constanza. I was amazed at how calm I felt standing there listening to her scream about what she was going to do to both of us and what Tony was going to do to us, and on and on until she must have run out of breath, and both the pounding and the yelling stopped. Maybe she'd gone away, and maybe she hadn't. She was a Pardo, wasn't she? Going out there then would have been a problem at the least and maybe death at the most. I walked over to one of the chairs and sank into it. Best to wait a little while before going out there. My head was so tired I could barely hold it up, and I could feel my eyes closing. Just rest for maybe twenty minutes and then take the chance.

But when I woke up, I knew it wasn't any twenty minutes. I looked at my watch. Twenty minutes past two. The gas jets were still roaring, but Mrs. Pardo hadn't moved an inch, the bottle still resting on her belly. I slid the bolt back as quietly as I could and stepped out into the hall. Nobody. Closing the door behind me, I moved out into the main hall and started down the wing my room was in. I could hear the grandfather clock ticking as I went by it, but there was no other sound. What could I tell Constanza in the morning? She'd probably checked my room. What could I tell her?

I was so busy trying to think of something that would hold water that I didn't see or hear them, but all at once two guys were holding my arms and another one was stepping in front of me. I tried to pull away, but these were real strong-arms. In my prime, I might have taken one of them, maybe even two, but not three and not right then.

The one in front of me pulled back his fist, and my stomach muscles tightened on their own. Just before it hit, I heard the guy holding my left arm say, "Just one. She said just one." And then the unspeakable pain went from my stomach to every part of my body, and my legs came off the floor, and when they let go, I dropped like a cannonball. I wasn't all the way out, but I couldn't move. I just lay there doubled up, my mouth open and screaming but no sound coming out. Faintly I heard the one who had spoken before say, "No kicks. She said just one, and you know how she is when you don't do it like she says."

I knew they were gone even though I couldn't hear their footsteps on the deep carpet. I was all alone with only the pain for company, and as soon as it eased off enough, I started throwing up, over and over until there wasn't even phlegm coming out. I don't know how long I lay there before the pain became a dull ache, but I finally was able to push myself to my knees and crawl. I moved only inches at a time, but I finally made it to my door. Those were heavy panels, and I had trouble pushing it open far enough for me to slide in. I leaned my weight against the door to make it close, and then I dropped to the floor. Maybe I fell asleep and maybe I passed out, but the clock radio said it was fifteen minutes past four when I came to.

I stood up and made my way to the bathroom, where I splashed water on my face until all the puke was gone. The pain in my gut was steady but bearable, and I sat down on the bed to peel my clothes off. When I bent over to slip off my shoes, I collapsed to the floor and lay there for a while until I felt strong enough to pull them off. The socks were just as tough.

Getting up and onto the bed was a lot harder than falling off it, but I finally made it and lay back, then slid my legs under the turned-back blanket and pulled it up over me. I turned my head to see if I could reach the bedside lamp, and there was my new box of mints on the other pillow. There was no way I was going to reach that lamp. My body was hurting too much for me to sleep anyway. Hurting. I took a deep breath, but there was no pain in my chest, just in the gut. Hurting. Where was my bedtime pill? On the bureau. No way. There was no way. What was I going to tell Constanza in the morning? If she was like she had been in the hall, there was nothing she would believe, and then where was I? All I could think of was Clark Gable. Frankly, my dear, I don't give a shit. So help me, I smiled before I went out again.

27

My throat was so dry that I couldn't swallow, and it felt like I was going to choke to death because the air in my nose wouldn't push through to wherever the hell it was supposed to go. My eyes had enough grit in them to pave a road, and all the bones in my body were grating on each other every time I tried to move.

Just as I was about to try to push the blanket as far off me as I could, the door slammed open and Constanza came through like she had rockets pushing out of her rear end. She was yelling something, but I couldn't make it out until she stuck her face right in front of mine and told me what a piece of shit I was, and she was going to see me flushed the hell out of there as soon as Tony came home.

I didn't say anything, because I not only felt too weak, but I also couldn't think of what to say. She was as mad as you can get when she came into the room, and she was getting madder by the second. She raised her hands above my head, and I tried to brace for wherever she was going to hit, but instead she reached down and yanked the blanket off me.

"Jesus, Mary, and Joseph," she said, lifting her hands to cradle her face. "What the hell happened to you?"

I looked down and smack in the middle of my stomach was a purple-black mark the size of an orange, and radiating out from it were purple streaks of different widths and lengths. It was like a whole kindergarten had used me for finger-painting practice. Constanza lowered her hands to about an inch from the bruises, but though she wanted to, she couldn't bring herself to touch the marks. You could sense that even breathing on them would make me hurt.

"What happened?"

Was she kidding me or what? She was the one who had told them to put me down. But she seemed so surprised, really surprised. *Was* she the one who had set me up? Who else could it have been? Had Tony's people been watching his wife's room? What happened? She wanted to know.

What happened, I wanted to know. My body was out of order, but the brain was working.

"I left Mrs. Pardo's office," I started, "and . . . and I was coming to your room when three guys jumped me in the hall and did this to me, and when I came to, I didn't know where I was, but I finally crawled back here and made it to the bed."

"Jumped you?" yelled Constanza. "Three guys? Who the hell were they?"

"I don't know. I never saw them before."

"Why would they do that?"

"That's what I'd like to know."

"You didn't recognize any of them?"

"No. They weren't any of the guys I've seen around the house or down at the barn."

"And they were roaming around our house in the middle of the night? And they did this to you and left you where?"

The barf. She had to have seen the barf in the hall. But if she had, she would have said something. I glanced over at the clock. Ten thirty-five. Had one of the servants already cleaned it up before she came here? Take a chance.

"It was somewhere around half past ten," I told her. "I left Mrs. Pardo's office and was on the way to your room when it happened." I couldn't repeat that often enough. "They must have dragged me someplace because I had trouble finding my way to my own room."

"I called you at eleven o'clock," she said, "and when you didn't answer, I came here. I looked in the office, and after a while I . . . I . . ."

She'd gone to Mrs. Pardo's room and pounded on the door. But she wasn't going to mention that. She wasn't going to say that she'd been screaming outside the door while I was lying somewhere out cold. She believed I was meeting Mrs. Pardo in the office and not the room. Might as well rub it in a little.

"Didn't you ask Mrs. Pardo what time I left the office?" I inquired, beginning to enjoy myself despite the pain.

You could almost read her face as she tried to work out an answer.

149

"No," she finally came up with. "She doesn't bother me, and I don't bother her."

She bothered her, all right. No matter what Constanza said, the young Mrs. Pardo bothered all of them. They'd never encountered her kind before, and I had to admit, neither had I. My family's reaction would be almost the same as that of the Pardos if I brought someone like Mrs. Pardo home with me. My family was nicer, and for the most part they weren't crooks, although I always worried that someday I might have to take my uncle Salvatore in. But their reaction would have been the same for the blond Amazon.

"I'm supposed to see her again this morning," I said, "but I'm not sure I'm up to it."

Constanza was all womanly concern. "What do you want me to do?" she asked.

"I think I'd like to soak in a tub," I told her.

She rushed off to get the bath ready, and I pulled the blanket back over my belly. Maybe it was just as well that those guys had clocked me. Who knew what the hell this crazy girl might have done? And if she didn't put the finger on me, who did? How many enemies did I have in this place? As many as there were people? Only some of them, including the three who had bagged me, couldn't be classified as people. If they had been told to, they would have killed me as easily as punched me, and still walked away without making any noise. Or taken my body someplace where even Brady couldn't find me.

And then it hit me as the memory flooded back. Mrs. Pardo—Gretchen—had murdered the old man, had snuffed Guido, and I was the only one who knew about it. Would she remember telling me, after all the stuff she'd put into her body? And if she did remember, would she have me microwaved or whatever to keep the secret safe? What would Tony do if he found out his wife had murdered his father so that he could take over the empire? Carlotta had made me go to the high school production of *Macbeth* that she had directed, and now I realized it wasn't as ridiculous as it had seemed at the time. Except that they didn't have microwaves in those days, so the wife had to use a dagger. Did Tony know his father was trying to bang his wife? And had she done it to get the old man off her back literally or to make herself queen? What would happen if the rest of the family found out about it? The old lady? Aldo? Cissy? How could anyone named Cissy be a Mafia killer? Or the sisters. Angelina? Florence? Theresa? Constanza?

"Your bath is ready," said the last named.

She helped me out of the bed and put her arm around my waist, and then gently lowered me down the three steps into the tub. There was some kind of sudsy bath oil in the water, and it felt good to slide my hands along the bottom of the tub and let the warmth sink in.

"How does it feel?" she asked.

"It feels good. It feels better," I told her.

"I'll rub you down with some of this," she said, holding up a bottle.

"I'm going to stay here for a while, Constanza," I said. "It's going to take time to get some of this ache out."

"That's all right," she said, sitting down on the small white stool next to the tub. "I have nothing else to do."

I lay there, feeling some of the hurt being sucked out by the warm water. This had gone on long enough.

"Do you have any idea at all who might be trying to kill your brother?" I asked out of the blue.

"No," she said.

"How do you feel about him?"

"He's my brother," she said.

"Do you like him?"

"I used to. He never hurt me like Aldo and Cissy did. They're pigs. They could die and go to hell, and it wouldn't bother me."

"How about your sisters? Did you ever wonder how their husbands died? Could Tony have had something to do with that?"

"They died when Babbo was still alive. Tony was in college."

"Do you think your father had something to do with them disappearing?"

That hit home. She was squeezing the oil so hard that her fingers were bone white against the red bottle.

"Babbo didn't like them, that was for sure. I was in the room when Tino told him about their whoring and the other things they were doing when they went to Las Vegas."

"Do you think Tino took care of them for your father?"

The squeezing continued. "I don't know. I don't know about things like that."

"How about your sisters? Did they know their husbands were doing all those things?"

"I told them," she said flatly.

"And what did they say?"

"They didn't believe me. They said I was jealous."

"What did they do when their husbands disappeared?"

"They carried on like it was the end of the world. Angelina cried for two days without stopping. You ought to see their rooms. They've made shrines out of their rooms, and they keep lighting candles in their husbands' memory and paying for special Masses and all kinds of other bullshit."

"Then they wouldn't hate your brother for that, and if Tony lets Aldo and Cissy do anything they want, then they wouldn't really care that he was running the business."

"If you're asking me if they have enough guts to kill Tony, the answer is no. Sure, they think they're the ones who should be the boss, especially Aldo, but they wouldn't be any good at it, and everybody knows that. What they're good at is hurting girls and maybe beating up on somebody if they have eight other guys with them, but that's about as tough as they get. Tony could eat them for breakfast, and he wouldn't even have to spit out the bones."

"What about your mother and Theresa?"

"My mother's got Alzheimer's. She's in and out of it from day to day. Sometimes you can talk to her like she's normal, but other times she doesn't know us from the man in the moon. Theresa's a cokehead. Half the time she's as bad off as my mother."

"Do you think it's somebody from the outside, then? Somebody from another organization?"

"I don't know anything about that," she said. "Are you almost ready to get out?"

"Yeah. You want to get me one of those robes?"

She didn't take her eyes off me while I was getting out of the tub and slipping into the robe, and I knew that if I wanted her, right then or later, it was as good as done. But there was something so lonely-looking about her, so unhappy, so vulnerable, that what I really wanted to do was give her a long hug, like I did with one of my girl cousins when she was having trouble, especially boyfriend trouble. Those princesses in England, whenever I saw their pictures, I felt like I wanted to give them the same kind of hug.

My bottles of pills were on the bureau in the bedroom, but I couldn't remember what I had or had not taken, so I swallowed one of each of them. I took a deep breath, but there wasn't any pain in the chest. Constanza came out of the bathroom behind me, still holding the bottle of oil, but I could tell that she didn't even realize she was carrying it. The state of mind she was in right then might make her easy pickings for more information.

"I'll tell you what I'd like to do," I told her. "Let's go for a walk and take a picnic lunch with us."

It was like I had given her the kind of Christmas present she had always wanted. Her face lit up.

"I've never done that," she said. "I've never gone on a picnic here. Come to think of it, I've never been on a picnic anywhere. I'll go tell Cook, and I'll meet you at noon by the swimming pool."

All my clothes had been washed or cleaned except what I'd been wearing the night before, and I stuck those in the hamper, hoping whoever had to take them out wouldn't puke from the stink. I decided the best thing would be to see Mrs. Pardo in the office and find out what she remembered about last night. Things were beginning to sort out a little in my mind. Where they sorted to, I didn't know yet, but it would come to me. I put on the shoulder holster, and my sports jacket over it. There was never going to be another time in this house when I wasn't wearing a gun. They could still catch me by surprise, like they had last night, but from now on I would be listening and watching and walking on eggs so that I would know if even one cracked. Though my gut still ached something fierce, I felt pretty good. I didn't know why I felt pretty good after all that had been done to me, but it was nice to know I could still feel that way.

28

She looked as if she had just come from a health spa. The eyes were clear, the skin had the right amount of pink, and you just knew her breath would smell like some kind of flower.

"Good morning, Vincent," she said as I came into the office, my own eyes red, my skin pasty, and my breath like that of my uncle Pietro, who lives on garlic, onions, rancid cheese, and baccalà. She waited until I had closed the door behind me before she said, "That was quite a church supper we had last night. How are you feeling?"

"I haven't tied one on like that since the stag we gave for a buddy of mine, Denny Raspuzzi," I told her as I walked over to the desk.

She was looking at me with a frown on her face. "You're walking strangely," she said. "As though your pants are too tight for you."

Tell her or not. Maybe stir things up a bit. Tell her.

"I got mugged on the way back to my room last night."

"Mugged?"

"Yeah. Three guys grabbed me, and one gave me a punch in the stomach that made me remember every meal I've eaten in the past twelve years."

"In the house? Where did it happen?"

"In the hall when I got to the wing I'm staying in."

"They walked up and grabbed you just like that, and then one of them punched you?"

"They came from somewhere behind me, and, yes, it happened just like that."

"Do you know who they are?"

"I'd never seen them before, but there are a lot of people here I haven't met yet."

"Did they say anything?"

"When the guy was about to punch me out, one of the two holding me said, 'Just one. She said just one.' Then, after I was down, the same guy said, 'No kicks. She said just one, and you know how she is when you don't do it like she says.' "

"That's all they said?"

"That's exactly what they said. Believe me, I was tuned to their station."

"*She,*" Mrs. Pardo said, more to herself than to me. "That narrows it down a bit. I doubt if one of the servant women wanted you beat up. Therefore it had to be Mommie Dearest or one of the four harpies. Have you had a special problem with any of them?"

"No." I would have bet on Constanza if she hadn't been so surprised at my welt, but I couldn't think of any reason why the old lady or the other sisters would want me clobbered, except for the pleasure of having it done. "Give him one for the Gipper," one of them might have remarked to one of the lackeys, just for the hell of it.

"That's strange. And you'd never seen them before?"

"Never."

"We could line up the whole crew and have you check them out."

"I don't think that would be a good idea."

"Why not?"

"If we do find out who they are, what do we do? You

know these people. They won't tell who gave the order. I don't think we should stir the pot any more right now. I've just got to keep digging until I find out who's behind all this."

She stuck the barrel tip of her pen into the dimple in her chin and thought about it for a moment. It was as if last night had never happened, as if she was a boss and I was an employee, and nothing had changed.

"I think you're right," she said. "We don't want to dig too deeply into last night. Tony has had men guarding our door at night, but I called them off because he was away. However, we can't be sure they weren't there, and if they report this to him, we've got to have a story that will stand up. What were you doing in my room last night?"

"We had to go there because you thought someone had bugged the office," I came up with. "What I had to tell you was pretty important, and then we discussed strategy."

"That's good," she said. "What did you have to report that was so important?"

I had to tell her what I had. It might not have been smart, but it was all I had. If Tony Pardo ever found out about what had happened in that room last night, I was dead. And if those were his men in the hall, I might be dead anyway. But if they were *his* men, who was the *she* that had given them the orders to pop me just one time?

"Both Aldo and Cissy have twenty-two-caliber rifles in their rooms, and both pieces have been fired recently. Mama Pardo has a bottle of strychnine among her medicines," I told her.

I had called her Mama Pardo just as I would have done with one of my grandmothers, but old lady Pardo had about as much in common with my grandmother as Madonna had with the church choir. What

157

I told her didn't sound like enough, so I took a shot in the dark.

"I have the feeling that somewhere on this property there's a guy who's good with explosives. Nobody will tell me anything, but maybe Tony knows something about that."

"How long were you in my room?" she asked, and I could tell by the look on her face that she didn't know. There were little wrinkles in her forehead. The cool lady was feeling a bit nervous inside.

"A long time," I told her. "I fell asleep in a chair after you fell asleep by the fire."

"Tony's not going to believe that," she said. "Nobody would believe that. But nothing happened. Nothing happened, did it?"

She was really worried now and showing it. After pulling out a drawer, she reached in and came up with a bottle of pills and spilled them into her hand. There were four different colors, including the purple kind, but she popped a green one this time.

"Nothing happened," I told her. "We both fell asleep because we had too much to drink."

"We were drugged," she said. "Somebody put something in the wine. We went to the room for a dinner meeting to discuss strategy, and somebody had doctored the wine."

"I don't think that story's going to hold up if somebody takes us to court," I told her. "They'll want to know why we just didn't meet in the hall or outdoors if we thought the office was bugged. And I'd leave the dinner part out, if we can get away with it. That makes it sound too social. What we've got to worry about right now is who were those guys, and why did they punch me in the belly? There are an awful lot of sticky questions here. Maybe we should just say that you were scared to be alone, and I was the only one who was not here when all the murder attempts were made, so you used me as a bodyguard. You were afraid to go to sleep, and I stayed until you calmed down."

"Do you think he'd believe that?" she asked, and there was fear on her face. She had probably seen things happen since she married Tony that had never occurred in Durham, New Hampshire.

"We can only hope for the best," I said, and I felt fear in my belly, too. But I was also getting a little pissed off at the same time. Heart attack or no heart attack, the next guy who tried to jump me was going to find that I was once one of the best, and whatever I still had was good enough to take care of the situation. Even as I was saying that to myself, I was wondering what would have happened if I'd tried to muscle away from those guys. Would my heart have quit from the strain? I felt old, older than my uncle Pietro even.

"What are your plans from here on in?" she asked.

"I'm going to keep nosing around," I told her, "and try to find out who specializes in explosives. Maybe Tino will be able to tell me. The problem is tying everything together. There's no pattern yet, no center to work from. All I need is one thing to grab on to, and then we might be able to find out what the hell is going down. This is all so different from when I was a cop and I could pull people in for questioning and get court orders for documents and request backup and have a whole department behind me. Here there's just me and people who couldn't care less about what I want or am doing."

I realized after I said it that I was practically begging her for help, but when I looked at her I saw that her eyes were narrowed and she was staring just to the right of my head. You could almost hear the wheels spinning. The lady was figuring out her own defense, and if it meant that she had to tell Tony I had forced myself into her room and tried to rape her, that was the way the ball was going to bounce. Mobsters' wives were supposed to cook and clean, take care of the kids and keep their mouths shut unless spoken to. It didn't seem to work that way with Tony and Gretchen because she did none of these things. He was practically treating her like a full partner, and she had to be pretty goddamned good at what she did in order for her to sit up there on the throne beside him instead of down by his feet.

But even though she was up there, they weren't equals because the Mafia was still a few generations away from women's rights. And even though he was a graduate of the Harvard Business School, he was still capable of actions that would make any of those S & L crooks look like one of the husband wimps on TV sitcoms. I realized right then that I had better have a good story of my own about what happened because Miss Gretchen would throw me to the wolves as quick as she could blink if it was a question of whose ass was on the line. Her eyes shifted so that she was looking directly into mine again.

"However," she said, as though she had just been talking to me, "I must tell you that Tony's getting impatient. He likes things to happen instantly, no matter how difficult the situation is for other people. I like you, Vincent. I would hate to have anything happen to you."

What she said made me feel funny in the knees. The first few days there had been like living in a hotel, but the punch-out last night should have reminded me of where I was and who I was dealing with. It was time to tell Brady and my brother Petey where I was. And let Pardo know they knew. Maybe it was time for me to tell the authorities what was going on here. But then I would be out on my ass, if not dead. And that would mean no more briefcases with a hundred grand inside. Four hundred thousand down and six hundred thousand to go. Enough for me to live on easy street the rest of my life. Independence. Call my own shots. Marry Betty Wade and maybe have some kids. It was worth the gamble, wasn't it? Yeah. It was worth the gamble.

29

The rest of the day moved quickly. My picnic with Constanza was not a total success. She let me know right away that I could enjoy more than the food and wine, if I wanted. Her blouse was so peek-a-boob that you could see all the way to Palermo if she bent over only an inch, and there wasn't any bra inside it. She'd laugh at things that weren't even funny, and then she'd grab hold and give me a kiss as if it all was happening in the excitement of the moment. All I would have had to do was hold my face still enough, and she would have had her tongue down my throat, but under the circumstances I wasn't having any of that. We had barely spread our blanket when I heard a stick break in the bushes somewhere near us, and I wondered if there were just the bees and the birds keeping us company.

But even if she knew that people were monitoring our actions, Constanza acted like we were all alone in the Garden of Eden and it was time to take the first screw the world had ever known. However, I wasn't buying the package, and after a while she gave it up and just sat there pulling at blades of grass, not saying anything, not looking anywhere special. It was my turn to act as social director.

"Constanza," I said, "what do you want to do with your life?"

"What do you mean?"

"Do you want a career? Do you want to get married? Have babies?"

A different look came over her face, softer, close to a smile. "I changed my mind. I want to go away from here," she said. "Get married. Have babies. Would you take me away from here? Would you marry me? Would you make babies with me?"

She wasn't making jokes. Her eyes were wet, and her lips were parted, and the blade of grass in her hand was shaking as though the wind were blowing.

"You barely know me," I told her. "Why do you say something like that?"

"I know you're not like all the others," she said, waving her hand to indicate the people in the house, in the barn, on the grounds. "I never get a chance to meet men like you. They're all like them," and she waved her hand again to take in everybody.

"What makes you think I'm so different?"

She thought about that.

"They have no heart," she said. "They do nothing from the heart."

I could feel my own eyes filling up as a wave of sadness went over me. They did nothing from the heart. I could do nothing with my heart. I reached out and took her in my arms, pressing my head against hers so that the wetness in our eyes could fuse together. My heart ached with sorrow, and I took a deep breath to check on whether there was more than sorrow involved. For the rest of whatever was left of my life I would never do anything without taking that deep breath to find out if I was having real or imagined pain, whether it was going to let me keep going or put me under.

"Constanza," I said, "what do you want?"

"Help me," she answered. "Help me."

We pulled our heads apart a little and looked into each other's eyes. Then we kissed, a long, slow, steady kiss that had nothing to do with the next step being me grabbing her boob or her cupping my crotch. I haven't had many kisses like that, sad to say, and right then I felt that if there was anything I might be able to do to give Constanza a happier life, I would go for it. She gently tugged her lips from mine and looked down at her watch.

"Jesus," she said, "I was supposed to go to the hairdresser first today, and now Theresa will take my turn. We've got to get back."

A Pardo was a Pardo was a Pardo. She started off, and I bent down to put things back in the basket. When she realized I wasn't following her, she turned around and looked at me.

"What are you doing?" she asked.

"Picking up the stuff."

"Come on," she said. "Someone will take care of that," and she was on her way again.

I looked down at the food spread over the blanket and then at her retreating back. No matter how much I might try to help her, Constanza was going to have trouble adjusting to the outside world.

That night at eight forty-five I went to the dining room, and everybody was there ahead of me. Everybody but Tony and Gretchen and the South Americans. Constanza and Theresa chatted with me about nothing at all, but the rest of them just chewed their food with occasional grunts from Aldo and Cissy. The old lady ate almost nothing, spending most of her time staring down at her plate.

When we were drinking our coffee, Theresa announced that a new movie had arrived that day and if anybody wanted to see it, they were going to run it now. Only the four sisters got up, and I stood with them. I don't know what entertainment Aldo and Cissy had in mind for the evening, but I would have turned it down even if they had invited me.

The screening room was like a real luxury theater with maybe thirty seats, and on one side there was a bar with all kinds of booze and a commercial popcorn maker and shelves of different kinds of candy as well as bowls of fruit. When I was a kid, I would always buy myself a Milky Way, a Snickers, a Baby Ruth, and a box of popcorn. First you get yourself so full of chocolate that you're just this side of puking, and then you munch the popcorn to take the sweet taste out of your mouth. All that same stuff was over against the wall, and it took willpower to stop me from trying to bring back my childhood.

The movie was *Terminator 3* with Arnold what's-his-name, and Constanza, who had plunked herself down next to me, kept grabbing my arm and screaming whenever anybody got wasted, which was about every two minutes. Theresa yelled a little bit, but the two older ones just sat, the only sound their chomping of candy and popcorn. At one point when the good guy and the great girl were having some R-rated sex, Constanza reached down and ran her hand up my thigh, which nailed me right to the seat. I made no move to push her hand away, and we sat like that for the last ten minutes of the movie, me getting harder and harder and about to burst.

But when the lights came on during the closing credits, she stood up, said good night, and left with Theresa. The two older ones were back at the candy stand when I walked out of the room, neither of them paying the slightest attention to me.

I passed a maid and two guards on the way to my room; she gave me the faintest of smiles before averting her eyes, and the guards walked past me like I wasn't there. I looked closely at their faces, but they weren't the ones who had gut-punched me. What if they were? What could I have done against the two of them? I would be lucky if they didn't do it to me again. I could feel my face getting red. Moderation, I told myself. Moderation.

It was five minutes past midnight when I got back to the room, but I wasn't the least bit sleepy. In fact, I was so keyed up that I could feel myself bouncing on my toes. In the old days I would have gone to one of the all-night bars where cops congregated after their shifts or on their nights off, and maybe come across a woman I knew or even somebody new. Safe sex. One thing about me now was that I was really into safe sex. What could be safer than none at all?

I was running my hand along the videos in the case when the phone rang. Deep in my gut I knew, and when I picked up, Constanza said: "Do you think you could get over here without being mugged?"

I thought about a lot of things in those few seconds, ranging from what I was doing there in the first place, to Tony Pardo, to Mrs. Pardo, the sisters, the brothers, and who was trying to kill who. But most of all I thought about Constanza running her hand up and down my leg during the movie, and I knew why I was restless and why I wouldn't be able to fall asleep.

"If I'm not there in five minutes, call the police," I told her, and hung up.

I brushed my teeth and ran my hand across the stubble on my face. Good enough. In maybe four minutes I was tapping on her door. She was still dressed in the blouse and jeans she had worn to dinner and the movies, but the look on her face was much different as she bolted the door behind us. Then without another word she pulled me over by the gas fireplace that was roaring away. In front of it there were maybe twenty of those big pillows in a heap, and I wondered if these people had a set plan about this kind of thing.

Without saying a word, Constanza started stripping me down—pulling, unbuttoning, yanking, pushing—until she had me bare-ass naked in about three minutes. Then she peeled off her own stuff in twenty seconds, and we were down on the floor with her trying to eat my face as I went into her. No condom. No nothing. I remembered Betty Wade's warning, but it was too late. And I couldn't have cared less.

30

One great thing about a gas fireplace is that you don't have to keep getting up to put more wood on it. So we just lay there curled up in the warmth, dozing a little bit, rubbing cool hands along warm skin every once in a while, being nice to each other. We hadn't exchanged one word since I had walked, or been pulled, through the door, and at least an hour had to have passed. I was wondering how Constanza might be in my outside world and what it might be like to have Tony Pardo as my brother-in-law. Would I be expected to live on the estate with everybody else, and then one day disappear like the other two sisters' husbands? Would I be given a piece of the action? Would I be allowed to work my way up in the organization or maybe take over one of the legitimate businesses? I was smiling to myself all the while I was thinking this. There was no way I would live among this lot or work the rackets for or with them. They had bought me for a million bucks, that I had to admit, but that was the one and only deal I would ever make with them. If Constanza was willing to come with me and live in my apartment—or probably something better, with the extra money I would have—that was one thing. But we would never come back to this place, even on the holidays.

A tapping on the door brought me to my feet so quick that I felt dizzy. Constanza had been licking the inside of my left ear, and when I jumped up, my shoulder hit her in the jaw, and I could hear the click as her teeth banged together.

"Jesus Christ," she yelled. "Are you trying to kill me?"

"There's somebody at the door," I told her. "Somebody just rapped on the door."

"Calm down," she said. "It's only Theresa."

"What does she want? Why is she banging on the door in the middle of the night?"

"She wants to come in. That's what she wants."

"What for? What the hell for?"

The look she gave me was close to pity. "What do you think what for? She wants to party with us."

"Party?"

"Yeah. Theresa's great. You'll like doing it with her."

"But what about you?"

"I'll be here. You'll like doing it with both of us."

"No way," I told her, looking around for my clothes. "No fucking way."

"Okay," she said, getting up and stretching. "Don't get your balls in an uproar."

"Tell her to go away."

"I will. I will. Just take it easy."

She went to the door, unslid the bolts, and opened it a crack. "He says no," she told her sister.

There was some whispering from the other side.

Constanza looked back at me slipping into my pants. "I don't think so," she said. "Take something to put you to sleep. You'll be all right."

There were some more words from the other side, and I could tell that Theresa was trying to force the door open, but Constanza was holding firm. She looked over at me again, and I shook my head no as I finished buttoning my shirt. Then she shoved the door firmly until it clicked, and slid home the bolts.

"What are you doing?" she asked, coming over to stand in front of me. She sure was a good-looking girl.

"I'm going back to my room," I said.

"Hey, the night's still young. We only did it once."

"Once was plenty, thank you." I was so mad that I could feel my heart racing. What the hell was I? A stud for these two maniacs? Moderation, I told myself. Moderation. Say something to keep it light. For me, not for her.

"Theresa's something when she gets going. You're really missing out on something special."

"Yes," I told her, "but would you respect me in the morning?"

I pulled back the bolts, closed the door behind me, and stood in the very dim light in the hall. No matter how hard I tried, how relaxed I attempted to be, I couldn't stop my heart from pounding, and I was scared to start walking in case the exertion would be too much. So I stood there and breathed, long and slow, letting the air come in and the air go out until I felt I was strong enough to walk. But I guess I was still disoriented, because I went down the wrong corridor, and all of a sudden I was mixed up as to where I was.

As I stood there trying to decide what I had done wrong, I heard a door open around the corner from me and people talking in low voices. I walked up to the corner and barely stuck my head around, just enough so that I could see with my right eye.

It was Mrs. Pardo standing in the doorway to her room, the light behind her as dim as that in the hall. At first I couldn't make out who the man was, but as he turned his head, I realized it was Barzatti. She was wearing one of the terry-cloth robes, and he had his left hand between her legs, and I could see it moving up and down. She didn't budge an inch, just stood there smiling and saying something so low I couldn't hear, and then she laughed out loud, pushed his hand away, and closed the door.

I pulled my head back and looked for a place to hide. There was one of those grandfather clocks right behind me, and I went to the other side of it and pushed against the wall as hard as I could. The rug soaked up the sound of his footsteps, so I held my breath until there was the beginning of pressure in my chest. Jesus! Was I going to have a heart attack right in front of him? Either way I was dead if he knew I saw him with Mrs. Pardo.

He walked right by me and down the hall, unable to tell me from the clock. He might have seen me, but he was so busy looking at his left hand that he didn't notice anything else. I couldn't see his face in the dark, but I knew he had to be smiling. And I knew exactly what kind of smile it had to be.

I breathed slow and easy, letting the air soak in, and the pressure went away. Then I counted to a thousand, and then another five hundred for luck, before starting out for my room. As soon as I hit the next corner, I knew where I was. Two guys were standing almost in front of my door, but they just looked at me like I was a leaf blowing by in the wind, and I went inside, slid the bolts home, and then leaned against the door, still concentrating on the slow and easy breathing.

It felt as though my legs wouldn't hold me, but I walked over to the bureau, shook out my nighttime pills, and washed them down with water. I took two Valium tablets as a chaser. Sometimes you get too tired to sleep. I've never been able to go to sleep without first brushing my teeth, no matter how drunk or tired I was, but I thought about it for almost a minute before I went into the bathroom and did what I had to. My body felt sticky from being with Constanza, but I was in no shape for a shower or bath. Theresa would have killed me off. I would never have gotten out of that room alive.

Which brought me back to Constanza. Jekyll and Hyde. It was like when I saw *The Godfather*. Halfway through the movie I suddenly realized I was rooting for one scummy side over the others when all of them should have gone straight to hell. The girl played games with herself. And with me. She had the Pardo spots on her, and she could never change them. How could I have been fooled so bad? All these people were scum even when they forgot they were for a while, or playacted at being real people.

Which brought me to Mrs. Pardo. Barzatti had to be

twenty-five years older than she was, and ugly to boot. Yet I knew what had happened in that room as well as I knew what would have happened to us if she hadn't passed out from the booze and drugs. What kind of game was she playing? How many guys had toasted their bare asses in front of that fireplace when Papa was away on business? It took guts for Barzatti to cheat on Tony Pardo. But I had been ready to take the chance, so why not him? Why not who else? It wasn't that the lady was a minister's daughter from Durham, New Hampshire, who had fallen in with evil companions. If anything, it was Barzatti and me who had better watch out. My only advantage was that I knew about Barzatti and he didn't know about me. Or did he? I had to figure out what she was up to.

But just as I was setting my mind to it, I felt the Valium kick in, and I let myself drift into Nice Land. That's what my aunt Cecilia used to call it when she would tell me a bedtime story when I was a little kid. Nice Land. Nice . . .

31

It took the noise of the helicopter to pull me out of wherever my dream was taking me, and I had to squint against the light that was slipping through the cracks between the window drapes to keep the sun from blinding me. Two Valiums were at least one too many, and maybe even two too many. That was one rut I didn't want to fall into. It still bothered me that I was taking all those drugs, and I didn't need another one to be addicted to. Drugs were drugs. I knew what I was thinking didn't make sense, but it bothered me that my life depended on drugs. My life had always depended on just me.

I didn't want to get up and try to find out who was out to ace Tony Pardo; I didn't want to take my pills; I didn't want to eat; I didn't want to look at Constanza or any of the other Pardos; I didn't want to shower, shave, or get dressed. I just wanted to hide. So I rolled over on my left side, pulled my knees up almost to my chest, and fell asleep again.

When I woke up, I was still in the same position, and I had to unbend slowly because my joints felt like they were locked in place with wire. The sun wasn't trying to poke its way in between the drapes anymore, and the clock showed it was twenty-five minutes past five. I'd been in bed over fifteen hours. I still didn't want to get out, but that was beginning to scare me a little, so I elbowed myself to the edge and stood up. Though I had braced myself to accept it, there was no dizziness. I figured I was four pills behind, so I gulped them down with water. A bath sounded great, but I was worried that I would get all logy again so I showered and then shaved.

While I was in the bathroom, someone had come in to make the bed and freshen up everything. The place was ghostly when it came to service. You almost never saw any of the help in the house, but things always got done when you weren't there. No one had bothered me all the time I was sleeping, but the twenty minutes I had spent in the bathroom was enough for them to slip in and take care of everything. And when I came back that evening, the bathroom would have been cleaned, my dirty clothes taken away, and the fresh-washed ones put in the drawers. It was as if they had you under constant surveillance. Maybe they did. Who knew what the hell was going down in this crazy place?

I was just about to start blow-drying my hair when the phone rang.

"Vinnie," said Tony Pardo, "where the hell have you been?"

"I was a little under the weather," I told him, "but I'm feeling all right now. How was your trip?"

"It was one of those turnaround things, so I'm a little tired, but it went well. I brought back a couple of friends that I'd like you to meet at dinner. Gretchen filled me in on what you found out, which I consider very interesting. We'll talk about it when we get a chance. You're doing a nice job."

He hung up without saying good-bye, but he had seemed friendly. I wondered how he'd react if I filled him in on Mrs. Pardo and his trusted capo Barzatti. Not so nice a job. And what about me? He wouldn't be overjoyed at my little adventure in his bedroom. Maybe it was time to get out of there. Forget the rest of the money. I'd given him enough stuff to follow through on his own. And if he said I hadn't done enough, I'd give him back all the money in my closet and just keep the two hundred thou. Or maybe just the money my brother Frankie was using. A million bucks had been ridiculous right from the start. If I saved his life, that would be worth a million bucks or all the money in the world, but I wasn't going to be able to find out much more than I already had. There was a bad feeling in the pit of my stomach.

I dialed my brother Petey's number. He could come and get me if they didn't want to give me a ride back to town. Why wouldn't they want to give me a ride back to town? Everything had been on the up-and-up so far. But it was time to tell somebody where I was, and Petey would give me the best advice.

The phone rang five times and then Doris answered. She said Petey wasn't home, but he'd been worried about me, and he'd be glad to hear that I was okay. The trouble was that he had gone out of town for a client and wouldn't be back until tomorrow. Could he call me when he got back? That was a good question. Suppose whoever answered told him something that didn't sound right, and I didn't even know about it? What was I going to tell my brother's wife? That I was at Tony Pardo's house and he was giving me a million bucks to find out who was trying to kill him and . . . No, I couldn't do that. Too complicated and it might scare the hell out of Petey. So I just told her that everything was fine, and I would call again the next day.

"He won't be back until late," said Doris.

"Then I'll call him the day after."

"You all right, Vinnie?" she asked, and I could tell from her voice that Petey had been going nuts wondering about me.

"I'm fine, Doris," I told her. "I'm having a great time, and I'm catching a lot of fish."

"Petey said you never went fishing."

"Well, I'm going to do a lot of it from now on," I told her. "It's great therapy."

"You take care, Vinnie," she said. "You know how Petey feels about you."

After I hung up, I sat down on the bed and thought about that. I got along great with all my brothers, but there was something special with Petey. It was the same way that I had suddenly felt about Betty Wade. Before her I had gotten along great with a lot of girls, but the thing with her was like with my brother

Petey—special. And then I thought about Constanza.
I had to have been out of my mind to think some of
the things I had been thinking before Theresa
knocked on the door. I would tell Tony after dinner.
I'd tell him I wasn't feeling that well, and I had to go
home to see my doctor. When I thought about that, I
realized it was true. I was feeling unsure, and I wanted
to see my doctor.

I watched *Die Hardest* while I was waiting to go to
supper. The video was longer than I thought, and I
didn't want to miss the ending, so everybody was
already in place by the time I arrived. There was the
whole family, including Gretchen, who was sitting at
the end of the table opposite her husband, as if she did
it every night, and Tino was there, and two new guys
who were sitting on either side of Tony.

"Ah," said Tony, "Vinnie. I was just going to call
down to see what was holding you up. These are my
friends Vito Bolognini and Giuseppe Santini from
Sicily. They are gracing my house for a few days while
they conduct some personal business."

The two men barely looked at me. Bolognini, who
was somewhere in his mid-fifties, gave a slight nod to
show he knew I was alive, but the other one, who was
maybe thirty, give or take a couple of years, only
shifted his eyes a fraction. I could almost smell the
stink coming off their double-breasted silk suits.
These were bad ones—old-country bad. These were
like that mother creature in the movie *Alien,* the one
who spawned the things that ate your guts out. Just
looking at these two made me feel funny in the knees.

There was no menu that night because this was a
banquet in honor of the two visitors, and there must
have been about eleven courses, a few of them, like the
squid cooked in its own ink, specialties of my aunts.

They were all delicious, and I ate more than I meant to or should have, but it was my first meal of the day and I was starved. The wines were special, too, and I drank my share. Wine was moving up on the list of the things I missed most, and I knew I might never get another crack at vintages like these, so I said what the hell and drank. After all, I was eating enough food to soak it up.

Tony did most of the talking during the meal, with some help from the missus, but the rest of the family said nothing. Constanza and I made eye contact once, but it was like I was a complete stranger to her and she had no intention of getting to know me. The older Italian talked a little to Tony in very broken English, and once in a while he would say something to the other one in a dialect I couldn't make out. I got the idea that he was a very big boss and this was his capo or maybe just a bodyguard. The guy didn't look like he was paying much attention, but I could tell he knew what was happening at every seat at the table.

We didn't finish eating until half past ten, and when Tony asked his guests if there was anything they would like to do, the older man said he was tired from the trip and was going to bed. Tony himself escorted them to their rooms, leaving the rest of us still sitting there. When they were out of sight, the others stood up and went their own ways, with Angelina pushing her mother's wheel chair. Nobody looked at anybody else, and then they were gone, leaving me standing there with just the waiters and the maids. There was still a half bottle of the last wine we had been drinking on the sideboard, so I picked it up and waved good night to everybody as I left the room. The two maids smiled at me, but the waiters just stood there with their hands behind their backs like they were in the army, for

Christ's sake. As soon as I was out of the room I could hear them jump into action, clearing things away and chattering like a bunch of birds.

I used the rest of the wine to wash down my two bedtime pills and then thought about watching another video, but suddenly I was very tired and decided to go to bed. I wondered if something was wrong that I was so tired all the time. The bathroom had been cleaned while I was at dinner, the drapes closed, the cover on the bed drawn back, and the box of mints put on the other pillow.

I switched off the light and lay back. For a second I thought I was going to be sick to my stomach, but it went away as quick as it had come, and I fell right asleep. The dream had to do with Mrs. Pardo and Constanza fighting over me, grabbing my shoulders and my arms, shoving, pulling, and I could hear them saying "Vinnie, Vinnie," but the voice was exactly the same no matter whose mouth it came out of.

"Vinnie," said the voice, "Vinnie. You've got to wake up, Vinnie."

The light was on when I opened my eyes, and there was Mrs. Pardo—or was it Constanza?—kneeling on the bed beside me. It wasn't either of them. Claudine. It was Claudine.

"Vinnie," she was saying over and over. "Vinnie, you've got to wake up."

She pushed on my stomach and I threw up. Just like that. She was lucky my face was turned in the other direction or else it would have splattered all over her instead of the box of mints and the pillow.

"What? What's the matter?" I asked her.

The smell from the puke was so bad that I closed my eyes for a moment, but she didn't seem to notice it.

"Vinnie," she said, "you've got to come help."

"What's the matter?" I asked again, moving toward her and away from the messy pillow. "What's the matter?"

"It's that guy," she said. "He's doing something bad to Renée."

"What guy?"

"The guy who came in with Tony today."

I remembered. I remembered the two of them. "Which one?" I asked her.

"The younger guy," she said. "I had the old guy, but he fell asleep right after, and as I was going by Renée's room I heard her yell out and then I heard her crying, and she was begging him to leave her alone, but then she screamed again. He's hurting her, Vinnie. He's hurting her bad."

"Okay," I told her. "Just let me get some clothes on."

"There's no time," she said, grabbing my arm and pulling me toward the door. All I was wearing was my Jockey shorts, and I would at least have stopped for pants if I'd had the strength, but I was still groggy from the wine and the pills, and I just let her yank me along.

Two of the hall guards were standing outside what I took to be Renée's room, and I could hear the sound of her crying right through the heavy wood door. The two guys were listening, but they weren't making a move. Claudine shoved her way past them, pulling me along with her, and I reached for the knob.

"I wouldn't do that if I was you, buddy," one of them said. I was so surprised that I stopped and looked at the guards for a moment.

"She's crying," I said.

"She's paid to cry," said the other one.

I twisted the knob and pushed the door open. Even as I was doing it, the two guards were moving backward down the hall as fast as they could, close to running. What the hell kind of guards were they?

The bedroom looked like one of those horror movies, with all the lights blazing and Renée tied face down on the bed, her arms and legs spread-eagled and tied to the posts. She didn't have a stitch on, and I could see cuts on her rear end that were faintly oozing blood onto the pale white skin. The Sicilian was standing on the other side of the bed, just wearing his black socks, and in his hand he held what looked like an ice pick but was some kind of knife. The tip was dark from Renée's blood, and he had an erection that was almost as long as the knife he was holding. His face was all twisted, and his eyes were crazy.

"Easy, pal," I said, spreading my hands apart to show I wasn't carrying. Christ, all I had on my body was my Jockey shorts, and the thing underneath that could no longer be classified as a dangerous weapon.

He started yelling at me in Italian, but I could only make out a couple of words because of the dialect. I did pick out that my grandmother fucked the carabinieri. That could have been true in her younger days, but it carried no weight now. Claudine was standing right next to me, afraid to make any further moves in Renée's direction, so I took a couple of steps forward on the side of the bed away from the guy, hoping I could at least get Renée's hands free. She had stopped crying and was looking up at me, and I could see where one side of her face was swollen from what had to be a pretty heavy hand. The son of a bitch.

He was still yelling at me as I kept moving toward the headboard, and finally he ran around the bed and came at me, swinging the knife back and forth in a long arc in front of his body. You could see the pleasure in his face at the thought of cutting me up bad. I never felt so calm in my life as I took one step back and punted him in the balls, my leg stopping just under the swing of the knife. He folded in slow motion because the pain had frozen his body into a leaning position, but then when the agony flooded through to his brain he went all the way over, bouncing his face into the soft rug.

Without looking at him again, I went to the head of the bed and tried to untie the rope around Renée's left wrist, but all her tugging had tightened the knot to where it couldn't be budged. It would have to be cut. I looked on the floor for the Sicilian's knife, but I couldn't find it, so I got down on my knees to see if it had gone under the bed. Nothing. I stood up again and looked around. It had to be somewhere. Under him? Using both hands, I pulled him up on his side and flipped him onto his back.

There it was. You could just see the handle. The blade had gone all the way into his belly. I put my hand on his throat and felt the faintest pulse. Knife wounds are funny. A guy can be stuck in twenty places all over his chest and stomach, and yet the surgeons can patch him together again almost as good as new. Then again, one stab in the wrong place, and he could be dead. This guy was going to need a hospital.

I ran over to the phone on the other side of the bed, but before I could pick it up I heard a real loud "Jesus Christ" from the doorway, and when I turned to look, the two guards had their faces poked in and were staring down at the victim. The victim. I was the guy who had turned the son of a bitch into a victim. I looked over at Renée, still tied to the bed but relaxed a little now that she knew she wasn't going to be sliced up anymore. I couldn't cut her loose without the knife, but it would be worse to pull the blade out of the guy than to leave it in. This was going to be a great one to explain when the cops came. I could see my picture splashed all over the papers: "Ex-Cop Held in Stabbing Incident at Crime Lord's Hideaway."

"Will nine-one-one get you an ambulance in this area?" I asked one of the guys in the doorway.

"Don't do a fucking thing," he yelled. "We'll take care of everything." He turned to the other guy and said, "Go get the boss."

"Jesus," I heard the other guy answer, "he's probably asleep."

"You'll be permanently asleep if you don't get him," said the first one.

There was no time to wait for Tony Pardo to come, so I picked up the receiver and dialed zero, knowing the operator could give me instructions.

"Put down the fucking phone," said the guy in the doorway, stepping into the room with a .38 in his hand. "Put it down, or I'll blow your fucking nuts off one at a time."

Sometimes even when you don't know a guy at all, you can tell when he's being sincere, and this was one of them. He wasn't threatening to kill me. He was just letting me know that if I didn't do what he said, I was going to be badly damaged. He knew it was possible his boss didn't want me dead, and he didn't want to get into trouble if that was true. But if he just tore me up a little, that could be forgiven. I put down the phone. Tony Pardo wouldn't want his honored guest to die on him in his home. He'd do something as soon as he got there. Meanwhile the guy would have to take his chances.

"Vinnie," said Renée, "could you get me loose?"

Claudine ran over to her and tried to work on the knots, but they'd pulled solid from her bucking against the pain. She had rope burns on both wrists and ankles, and her face had swollen even more. I was just about to ask the guy with the gun if I could go look in the bathroom for a razor blade when the older Sicilian came into the room wearing one of the terry-cloth robes. He took a quick look around, and you could tell that he had put all the twos and fours together and knew exactly what had happened.

"Who?" he asked, looking directly at me.

"Nobody," I told him.

"Wha'?"

"He did it himself. He fell on the knife."

Turning to the guard who was still standing in the doorway, he asked again, "Who?"

The guard pointed his gun at me.

"Him," he said. "They were fighting, so it had to be him."

The older Sicilian looked again at me and then reached out his hand to the guard. The guy didn't know what he wanted, but I knew right away. This was a man who made instant decisions about life and death, and he had decided I was going to die. With his eyes off me for the moment, the guard didn't see me coming, and I twisted the gun out of his hand before he knew what had happened.

I waved the gun twice in an arc to cover the room, so everybody there would know who had the power. The Sicilian opened his mouth to say something but then thought better of it. I could tell from his expression that he could face death as easily as he could deal it out. They don't make many guys like that anymore. Except for crazy people, he was the first one I had ever come across.

"Claudine," I said, "go in the bathroom and find a razor blade or a knife that will cut Renée free."

She hesitated a couple of seconds and then went into the other room. Nobody said or did anything until she came back with a safety razor blade. She stood there looking at me until I waved the gun in the direction of the bed, and then she went over and started to saw through the ropes holding Renée to the bed. When the last one was cut, Renée gave a little moan and then rolled over on her back, wincing as the cuts on her rear hit the wrinkled sheets.

I was trying to think out my next move when Tony Pardo came busting through the door followed by two guys carrying AK47s. Mrs. Pardo had said he always had two guys guarding the room when he was sleeping there, and he had brought them along.

"What the hell's going on here?" he yelled as he came into the room, his eyes moving from person to person until they finally stopped at the guy lying on the floor. "Jesus Christ," he moaned. "Is he dead?" He immediately looked at the older Sicilian standing there with a look on his face that made me even more nervous than I already was. I had thought Tony Pardo was right up among them when it came to the leaders of the families, but this guy made him wet his pants. Since there was a God, then maybe there was also a devil.

"He-a killed-a Giuseppe," said the older guy.

"The guy's not dead," I broke in. "He's still got a pulse. If we get him to a hospital, they can probably fix him up."

"We can't take anybody to a hospital, for Christ's sake," yelled Pardo. "What the hell are we going to tell them? What the hell are we going to tell the cops? Why the Christ did you do this?"

"I didn't do it," I said, trying to keep my voice level. "He was working Renée over with the knife, and I told him to stop, and he came at me, and I kicked him, and when he fell over, the knife went into him. He did it to himself."

I looked around the room, but nobody was nodding to back up my story. Claudine had moved as far away from me as possible as soon as Pardo came into the room, and Renée was sitting on the side of the bed with her head hanging down. They weren't going to back up my story. They didn't want any part of me. These were definitely not whores with hearts of gold.

"He-a killed-a my Giuseppe," the old man almost moaned.

The look that Pardo gave me was about as pure as hatred can get.

"Take the gun from him," he told one of the guys with the automatic weapons. His gun was pointing belly-even with me. If there had been only one guy, I might have chanced it because I knew there might not ever be another chance. But there were three of them, and they were spread fairly well apart. I leaned over and handed the gun to him.

"I'm-a gonna kill'm," the old man said, starting to walk over to the guy holding the pistol.

"Hold on just a minute, Don Vito, please," said Pardo. "This man is an ex-policeman. People may know he's here. He's got to die in a way that they don't tie in with us, or else we're in big trouble. Please, let me handle it."

"He's-a gotta die," the old guy said.

"He's going to die," said Pardo. "He's going to die bad. But you've got to permit me to handle it."

"I wanna see it," said the old guy.

"You'll see it," said Pardo, the way my sisters-in-law spoke to their kids when they got hurt. "You'll see it."

I was looking at Renée, hoping she would lift her head and tell them how it had all happened, but there was no way she was going to mix in. And it wouldn't do me any good to ask her, because she would be afraid to say a word. Her job was to spread her legs and keep her mouth shut except for extraneous activities. Her mistake had been to yell when things got rough. And my mistake was to try to help her. The two guards in the hall had the right idea when they stayed clear. They had warned me to walk away. And now they were going to take me away.

"Where do you want him, boss?" asked one of the guards.

Pardo thought for a minute. "Lock him in the room with the stuff," he decided.

They got behind me, and one shoved me with the muzzle of his gun. I started to move toward the door. No one had yet made a move to get down on the floor and find out if the guy was still alive. Even the old Sicilian had written him off as too much trouble, no matter what he was worth to him. Nice people.

Just as we came out the door, Mrs. Pardo came hurrying up, wearing one of those terry bathrobes. She looked at me, then past me, and went into the room without saying a word. Nice person.

The guards took me down the stairs to the cellar and along a corridor until they came to a guy sitting in a chair in front of a metal door. He had an AK47 resting on his lap. Pardo must have bought them in bulk quantity for the discount.

"What you got here?" he asked as we came up.

"The boss wants him on ice for a while," said one of the men.

"In there?" asked the guard, standing up and pointing his thumb behind him.

"That's what he said."

"It don't make sense, but he's the boss," said the guard.

He unlocked the door and waved me in ahead of him. The room was huge and looked like some factory storeroom. Piled one on top of the other on shelves were plastic bags containing kilo after kilo of cocaine. This had to be the warehouse for Drugs "R" Us. If the narcs ever made a raid on this place, the headlines in the papers would be talking about billions in street value.

"Here you are, buddy," said the guard. "There's an open bag right over there. If you want, you can be the happiest fuckup in the history of the world. But don't touch any of the others or you'll be the unhappiest *goombah* in the world. And I know how to make people so unhappy that they cry a lot before they die."

I didn't know whether this guy considered himself funny or just took pleasure in his work, so I kept my mouth shut.

He didn't say any more either before walking out and slamming the door behind him. I could hear the key turn in the lock. There were fluorescent lights in the ceiling, and plenty of those wheeled gurney things to move the bags in and out of the place. I sat down on one of them and tried to think. There was a faint pressure in the middle of my chest, but my nitro pills were on the bureau in my room, and I doubted the guy outside would be good enough to get them for me. I was going to die anyway, so why should they try to keep me going? There was no doubt about that in my mind—that I was going to die. The Sicilian wanted me dead, and Tony Pardo seemed only too anxious to please this guy. The question was why didn't he have it done right away to show the Sicilian guy his heart was in the right place? I shivered a little bit even though the room wasn't too cold. I guess it was as much from having only Jockey shorts on as it was from the temperature.

Renée hadn't said a word. Claudine hadn't said a word. One time I stopped a pimp from beating his whore to death, and when I turned my back, she tried to clock me with a pipe. I told everybody on the squad I'd learned my lesson and would never do anything like that again, but here I was sitting practically bare-ass in a cocaine warehouse, waiting to see how they were going to ace me.

A million bucks. I was here because I couldn't resist an offer of a million bucks. In some ways I was better off than most people. At least I knew what my price was for going against everything I had ever believed in. And if that was the case, a million wasn't bad. I knew lots of guys who would have done much more for much less.

I'd never even stuck my finger in any of the bags of cocaine we had confiscated, or even when we had training sessions. I thought maybe I should take the guy's advice and put myself in the kind of condition where I wouldn't care what the hell they did to me. I walked over to the open bag and spread the top. Then I lifted the whole bag, turned it over, and dumped the cocaine on the floor. Then I walked around to see what else was in the room, and I came across a faucet low down on the wall in the farthest corner. Probably to fill the pails to mop the place out once in a while. I turned the handle and it worked, the water gushing on the floor. I turned it off again, thought about it for a few seconds, and then spun the handle all the way open. What the hell.

I went back to the racks and started opening bags and dumping cocaine on the floor. The water was spilling out on the concrete and spreading quickly. It had already reached the first spot where I had unloaded and was soaking into it. There was a drain on my side of the room, so I put a bag of coke on top of it to keep the water from draining out. It made a nice plug. Then I stuffed bags against the bottom of the door so the water wouldn't leak out that way. Then I began untwining the tops of the bags and spilling the cocaine every which way on the floor. The water was coming on fast. I choked a little on the coke dust, but that only meant that, win or lose, I was going to be the happiest horse in the race.

The guy said he would make me unhappy if I did any damage. What he didn't know was that I had a bad heart, and there was a tightness in my chest right then. All they had to do was squeeze me two or three times and I would be gone. Out of it. No pain. No more worries. No nothing. I really felt good for the moment, though. Why wouldn't I? I had been a cop, a good cop, and I was doing God's work. I wished I had a knife to slit the bags because it took time to untwine the "twistem" things, but I made pretty good progress. A million bucks. I was getting paid a million bucks to work there. But that wasn't out of line, considering the cost of the merchandise.

32

If I lived long enough for anybody to ask me if I had much to do with cocaine in my career, from then on I would be able to say, "Hey, I've been up to my ass in it." The cocaine mash didn't come anywhere near that high, but I think under the circumstances I should be allowed a little leeway.

I don't know how much time passed, but I became so excited that I was working like one of those robots in the automobile factories that keep going as long as they're plugged in. I was plugged in all right. Untwist-

ing the top of each bag took a lot of time, but I quickly
discovered that if I jammed a bag on the sharp corner
of one of the gurneys, it would cut right through the
tough plastic and spill everything into the water. That
was the most expensive soup ever cooked up by
anybody. Coke dust started sticking to the hair on my
arms and legs and chest, so every once in a while I
would kneel down and scrub it off as best I could. I
was beginning to feel a little light-headed, but I didn't
know if that was from the coke, from my heart, or just
because I was having such a good time.

Sounds crazy, doesn't it? Under two death
sentences—one from them and one from me—not
knowing which was to be my last second, continually
bracing myself for the opening of the door, and yet I
was enjoying my work, which is something you can't
say for most Americans. Opening bags, however, was
not the same as saying "sesame" and having the door
open. The door! Why not use the door myself instead
of waiting for them? There were only a few more kilos
left, and I threw them quickly into the batter. Then I
took the bag off the drain so the stuff could empty into
the septic system. Then I took the bags away from the
bottom of the door so the water could start to seep
through the crack below the door. That should wake
the guy up when his feet got wet. I waited for what
seemed like forever, but nothing happened. So I
started banging on the door with my fists, yelling as
loud as I could.

It finally swung open, and there was the guard
standing back a little, the gun held loosely in his right
hand. He must have seen the puddle of water after I
had pounded, but he obviously hadn't expected a
stream of white froth to come roaring out at him, and
I stepped forward and belted him in the jaw as hard as
I could. He went down so quick that he barely went

backward, and I was worried that I had popped one of my knuckles.

Grabbing the gun, I dragged the guy away from where the water was flowing. I would have been able to hear footsteps on the tile floor, but there didn't seem to be anybody coming from either way. So I stripped him to his underwear and put on his shirt and pants. The fit on those wasn't bad, but I ran out of luck with the shoes because he had tiny feet. It was just as well to be able to move around without making any noise. There were two extra magazines in his jacket, so I stuck them in the back pants pocket. My watch was still on the bed table in my room, and the guy wasn't carrying one, so I had no idea how long I'd been there or what time it was. The one thing for sure was that it was time to get going, but to play it safe I dragged the guard into the cocaine room, rolled him on his back so his nose would be just above the sludge, and locked him in. Then I smashed the head of the key with the butt of the gun to jam it into the hole.

The last thing in the world I wanted was to have to use the gun, because the noise would bring the whole army down on me, but if I was going to go that way, other people were going to go with me. When I reached the first floor, I found it was still dark outside, but I wasn't sure which part of the house I was in. There were supposedly ten guys guarding the place, but some of them had to be asleep, and two were stationed outside Pardo's bedroom door. So there might be only two roaming the floors, but they would be quite enough if they caught me with my pants down. Or rather the pants of the guy I had taken them off of. I could feel the adrenaline shooting through me like in the old days, and it felt good. It might kill me, but for that moment it felt as good as hell. If only Brady had been there to back me up, we could have taken the whole shooting match—the guys from the house, the barn, wherever. But Brady wasn't there, and I was the one who was wherever.

The occasional lamps gave a dim light, and I went up the first flight of stairs I found. It brought me to Pardo's wing, and I decided to try for my own room on the chance that they figured they had me tight in the cellar and why bother with it. Just as I was about to go around the corner, I heard voices, so I backed up to the first door, opened it, slid in, closed it as quietly as I could, and held my breath. There was no sound. If there was another person in the room, he was holding his breath the same way I was. I couldn't hold it forever, so I started letting it out as slowly as I could, but nobody yelled or grabbed me. I heard voices going past the door, two men talking about a game between the Boston Red Sox and the Texas Rangers. A no-hitter. Someone had pitched a no-hitter. The voices got lower and lower and then disappeared.

I opened the door a crack, peeked out, and then pushed it open far enough to squeeze through. In twenty seconds I was in my room. The bed had been remade, and it looked so inviting with the corner turned down and a second box of chocolate mints on the other pillow that I stared at it for almost a minute before getting down to work. Who the hell came in after midnight to tidy up a place from which a person has just been rousted? You know the joke about the guy whose wife makes the bed if he gets up to go to the john in the night? I have a cousin whose wife is so driven that she makes the bed when they stay in a motel. He swears that if there was a vacuum cleaner handy, she would do the rug. Compulsive. Some of her relatives must have been on the staff at the Hotel Pardo.

Even though it was a crazy thing to do, I took a fast

shower and got into my own clothes. The Beretta was not where I had left it, so the room had really been cleaned. Since I would have to carry the AK in one hand, I had to make up my mind about luggage. There were my clothes and the brand-new electric razor. Not really essential. I finally tied the handles of the two briefcases together with a sock, and was ready to go. Go where? Time to think. Take time to think.

There was the gate. There were the guards. There were the guys roaming the grounds with the dogs. The best bet would be one of the paths into the woods that I had walked with Constanza, and hope to come out on a road where I could maybe hitch a ride into the nearest town. It would be easy to stop a car if you were waving an AK47 in its face. But then there would have to be some explanations. I wasn't going to kill any innocent passersby, and these people would tell the cops about the guy with the automatic weapon, and unless the cops were members of the National Rifle Association, they would take me in, and then the whole story would come out. If Pardo didn't get me first, that is. Then there wouldn't be any story at all. But if there was a story, it would be one I would have to live with for the rest of my life, and that wouldn't make me happy. What would my family think of me? And Brady? And all the other guys I had worked with? A no-win situation. When you got right down to it, the best thing would be to let them stash me alongside Angelina's and Florence's husbands. In a grave or in deep water? Take your choice.

No, goddammit. These bastards had been winning the war too long. The least I could do was give them a run for their money, a hundred thou of which I was then holding in my left hand. Putting out all the lights in the room, I slowly opened the door to the hall. Clear. Which way? The only one I knew was the way I had first come into the place—the front door. If I tried to find the back door, who knew what I could bump into in the way of guards or even servants?

It was so weird to be going down that marble staircase at something around four o'clock in the morning with the weapon half raised in my right arm and the two cases of money hanging from my left. It was like visiting a museum after hours.

The front door opened easily enough, and I quickly went out to the end of the brick terrace because the spotlights were shining all over the place. And there it was. Right there. At the bottom of the steps. The biggest, blackest Rolls-Royce I had ever seen. Right there. With nobody in it. If I could get that baby rolling down the driveway, it would go through that gate like coke up Theresa's nose.

I ran down the steps and around the back of the car to the driver's side. And there they were. I could see them through the window. The keys were right there on top of the dashboard. When there is more than one driver, you leave the keys for the next guy. Tony Pardo didn't have to worry about anyone stealing one of his cars. If by chance somebody made the mistake, the car would be delivered to one of his own chop shops within the hour. The fucking keys. Right there.

I set the case on the ground, lifted the latch with my left hand, and all hell broke loose. The noise was like a bunch of fire engines racing through the streets in the middle of the night. The howling was enough to wake the dead, and that was what I was about to be. Tony Pardo wasn't as trusting a soul as I had thought. It was okay to leave the keys on the dashboard, but then you set the theft alarm before walking away.

It so caught me by surprise that I stood rooted to the spot for a few seconds and then took off across the driveway to the grass. That was when my greed did me in. I suddenly remembered that I had left the case of money on the driveway, and by the time I turned around and ran back, the dogs had come from wherever the hell they had been roaming, and were going straight for my throat. Knowing that I would be either dead or horribly mangled if I missed, I took out both of them with two long bursts until the magazine went dry, and by the time I had pulled it out and was reaching for another from my back pocket, four guys were standing there with their weapons trained on me, screaming that I was to drop the gun or die. I dropped the gun. If I'd had some bullets in the weapon, I might have tried for it, at least to take some of them out with me. Because it didn't make any difference. They had called it exactly. First I was to drop the gun. Then, at their convenience, I was going to die.

33

In about five minutes there were maybe eighteen men standing around me in various stages of dress. Or undress. Was the glass half full or half empty? The outside guys had all their clothes on, but the ones from inside the house were wearing everything from pants to bathrobes to just their skivvies. The only thing they had in common was the guns they were carrying.

Pardo had on a deep maroon bathrobe, the kind that looks like it's made of velvet. He was the only exception to the rule as far as guns were concerned. Guys like him just need a finger to kill somebody. They point the finger and somebody else takes it from there.

My gun was still lying on the ground exactly where I had dropped it, because nobody had come near enough to pick it up. They knew something was wrong, but they couldn't tell what it was. As far as most of these guys knew, I was still the investigator who'd been hired by their boss to find out who was trying to kill him, and who supposedly was calling the shots. I cursed myself for being so stupid. Only the ones who had been with Tony in Renée's bedroom knew what had happened. I might have been able to bullshit myself off the grounds through the guys who still thought I was in charge. After all, Barzatti had told them that was the way it was, and they were somewhere else when the Sicilian tried to make a loin roast out of Renée's ass and dicked himself instead of her. My brains had been in my own ass ever since I had taken on this thing.

So now here I was standing in the middle of a horde of wiseguys who just needed to see a finger pointed at me to end it all. Once and for all. If I made a break toward any one of them, they would start shooting from reflex alone, and then all my problems would be over forever. But the thought of those bullets tearing into me was more than I could handle, so I just stood there. Is it that people hope for miracles even when they haven't a shot in hell of getting out of the mess? The people in the concentration camps during World War II. Some of them made it. The guys on death row. They hoped for their sentences to be commuted to life, probably to life without parole, but deep down inside they were always figuring that maybe a governor would come along who would take the chance, or maybe the parole board could be bullshitted into believing that Christ had been found and a new man born, or maybe the Supreme Court would come down with something new, or maybe they would escape and never be found. There was always the maybe. I don't know what the maybe was at the back of my mind, but it was enough to keep me from running toward death. It would have to come to me.

"What's he doing out here?" Pardo yelled from the porch.

Nobody answered.

"Didn't you put him in the cellar like I said?"

Nobody answered.

"Who's watching the room?" Pardo asked, his voice rising with his temper.

"I think Freddy was down there," somebody ventured.

"Then go find out what's going on," said Pardo. He pointed at me. "Bring him into the house, for Christ's sake. It's chilly out here."

Without waiting for anybody to come get me, I turned and started for the steps. Behind me came what had to be the inside people while the rest of them either faded into the dimness beyond the spotlights or gathered around the dogs scattered on the grass. Nobody seemed too put out about them. Those were my first kills in all my years of police work, and I was relieved to find that I didn't feel bad about it. It might not be the same with people, but it was nice to know that I could handle putting down anything that came at me with its fangs bared.

While we were gathering in the hall, some new additions to the group came down the stairs—Mrs. Pardo, the Sicilian, Aldo, Cissy, Constanza, Theresa, and Jefferson, who was the only one fully dressed. No other servants were in attendance, and I wondered if they were all upstairs busily making beds before people returned to their rooms. Who were the people who worked there? I hadn't heard one of them speak English, and I wondered if maybe they were smuggled in from Sicily so they could see no evil, hear no evil, and tell no evil. And I wondered how the guy who had stabbed himself was doing. Maybe better than me.

It was then that the pain hit right square in the middle of my chest. Not a strong one, not a big one, a little one. But right in the center, under the breastbone. The classic spot. On one of my stress tests the doctor had used an interesting expression. He said that there had been the beginning of angina, but that the constriction had stopped. "It didn't flower," he said. That word got me. *Flower.* I could just see all the arteries of my heart flowering into one giant bouquet that was going to put me under for good. So I stood there wondering if this tiny spot of pain, this tightness, was about to flower and put me beyond the range of even Tony Pardo. Did I want it to or not?

"I've got to reach in my pocket and take out a bottle of pills," I told Pardo.

"What for?"

"I'm having a chest pain, and I want to take a pill bottle out of my pocket to keep me from dying."

"Fuck you and your pain and your dying," he answered.

"Tony," said Constanza, and there was a real look of concern on her face, "let the man take his pill."

"He's going to die anyway," answered her brother, "so what difference does it make?"

"Tony," said Mrs. Pardo quietly, "let him have his pill."

"Okay," he yelled. "Okay. Take your fucking pill."

I reached in for the little bottle, but had trouble unscrewing the cap. I hadn't needed any since the one time I had experimented with it, so maybe it had rusted in a little. And my hands were shaking. I tried like hell to cover it up, but my hands were shaking. I rolled two of the little white pills into the palm of my hand and then slid them under my tongue. It was supposed to work almost instantly, but nothing happened. The pain was still there. The faces all around me seemed to be waiting for some kind of reaction, and I almost smiled to reassure them, but then I decided to hell with it. Let them wonder.

One of the guards came tearing into the room. "Boss," he said, "Freddy ain't there, and there's some kind of water all over the floor."

"Is he inside the room?" he asked. "Did you look for him?"

"We yelled all over the place, we checked his room, nobody seen him."

"Not his room, stupid. What was in *the* room?"

"We couldn't get into the room. Somebody smashed the key so it wouldn't work."

Pardo turned to me. "Where's Freddy?" he yelled. "How did you get out of the room, and where's Freddy?"

My elementary school days took over. I did what we used to do whenever the teacher picked us out from the crowd for possible punishment for an unsolved misdemeanor. I had nothing to lose.

"He went off with Aldo," I told him, "after Aldo let me out."

Everybody's face turned toward Aldo. He wasn't showing any expression because he did not yet understand what was going on.

"Aldo," screamed Tony, "why the hell did you let this guy out, and where is Freddy?"

"I never . . ." Aldo began, but then he didn't know what to say.

"Why did you do this?" yelled Tony, walking over to Aldo and grabbing him by the shoulders. "Why did you do such a thing?"

"I never let nobody out," said Aldo. "I don't know where Freddy is. I been sleeping."

"Aldo was carrying the twenty-two-caliber rifle," I said, "and he had it in Freddy's back when the door opened, and then he told me to get the hell out of there, and I left him there with Freddy when I came up here."

"He's full of shit," roared Aldo. "I never did none of that. I don't know where the hell Freddy is, and I ain't got no twenty-two rifle."

"You have too got a twenty-two rifle," Tony said, his voice back at a normal level now. "It was seen in your room."

"Somebody put it in my room," said Aldo, "and then it was gone. The same thing happened to Cissy. Ask Cissy."

All heads turned toward Cissy. He had to be the dumbest one in the family. You could see the wheels trying to turn in his head.

"He's crazy," he said, wanting no part of whatever was happening. "I ain't never had no twenty-two-caliber rifle in my room. That was the gun that shot at you, Tony. I ain't never had no gun like that."

Things had gone deathly quiet, and I could feel the spot in my chest growing to the size of a dime. Without asking anybody's permission, I reached in my pocket again, pulled out the bottle, and popped two more pills. Nothing.

"He's-a gotta die," the Sicilian yelled, pointing his finger straight at me. "He-a killed-a Giuseppe and he-a gotta die."

I knew it wasn't any use to start yelling that it really wasn't my fault, so I kept quiet. The guy had died, and his boss wouldn't be happy until I was dead too. The pain spot got a little bigger. The guy might be satisfied sooner than he thought.

"Give-a me a knife," the Sicilian said. "Give-a me a knife, and he die just like Giuseppe, only it take a long time longer."

"Don Vito," said Tony. "I told you this guy was a cop, and we couldn't just dump him without the police going all out. It's got to look natural. There can't be a mark on him."

"Then-a how you-a gonna do it? You-a gonna let the angels take care of it?"

A big smile lit up Pardo's face. He liked the idea of angels doing his dirty work. "Yeah," he said, "that's just how we're going to do it. Jackie, get me Burkhardt."

He turned and swept his glance over all the people on the stairs and in the hall.

"Get out of here," he told them. "Go back to your rooms. Except for you, Aldo. You and me got to have a talk. Why the hell did you let this guy out, and what did you do with Freddy?" He turned to his wife. "Gretchen. Bring me the other key to the strong room."

"Where is the key?"

"How the hell do I know?"

"You're the one who had it. You never let me have it. I don't know where it is."

"Look in the office. Look in our room. It's got to be somewhere."

"Is it by itself or with other keys?"

"It's by . . . It's with . . . Christ, just find it."

Both Mrs. Pardo and Constanza gave me looks before they left, but the rest of them started to move out. There was only me, Tony, Aldo, the Sicilian, and three of the guards.

A husky guy wearing coveralls came in through the front door. "You wanted me, Mr. Pardo?" he said.

"Yeah. Remember you told me how in Vietnam you would take a gook up for questioning in a helicopter, and if he didn't tell you what you wanted to know, you just kicked him out the door?"

A soft smile of remembrance went over the pilot's face. "Yeah," he said. "I remember."

"Well, I've got a guy here"—and he pointed at me—"who's fucked me over, and I want to find out a few things, but he's got a bad heart. I was wondering if you could take him up in the chopper, and if he didn't cooperate, you could hold him out by his heels until he talked."

"If he's got a bad heart, he could die."

"That would be all right, too, as long as there wasn't a mark on him."

"I could rig him in a sling," said the pilot, getting a little bit excited, "and we could lower him out when we got up a few thousand feet and swing him around a little. Then we could just haul him up again, and no outside damage done."

"Hey, come on," I said. "The joke's over. You've already got a lot of explaining to do to the police, and this kind of crazy stunt won't make it any easier."

"Georgie," said Tony, to one of the guards standing in the hall, "would you be able to plant Altobelli's body back in his apartment so that it looked like he went quietly in his sleep?"

"Hey," said the guy, "I could put him in Madonna's bedroom and even she wouldn't know how it happened."

"I wanna be there," said the Sicilian. "I wanna see him swinging in the air. I want to be there when he dies."

"Okay, Don Vito," said Tony, putting both his

palms in the air toward the old guy. "You'll be there. You'll be right with him."

"I wanna be able to tell Giuseppe's mama what-a we did," said the Sicilian. "I wanna her to know we did-a the right thing by her baby."

I wished Giuseppe's mother could have seen her baby standing over Renée's ass with the knife in his hand.

I had a sudden picture of my mother walking into the bedroom of my apartment and finding me there. She still called me her baby sometimes. And the pain in my chest reached the size of a quarter. But I wasn't going to die just like that. I wasn't going to give these bastards a free ride by not having to take me on a ride in order for me to die. I closed my eyes and put my mind to it, and I shrunk that pain back down to the size of a dime. I went so deep into myself that I almost forgot where I was until the hands grabbed me and started to drag me out the front door.

"They know where I am, Tony," I yelled at him. "My people know where I am."

"You made two calls," said Pardo, "one to your mother and one to your brother, and you didn't say squat about where you were. Get him the hell out of my sight."

Jesus! They even had the phone monitored. The pain in my chest went up to the size of a quarter again. "I made four calls," I screamed back. "Four calls. And there's a deadline on two of them."

"Wait," he ordered the guys holding me by the arms, "Bring him back."

I threw them off by flinging my arms out, and they were so surprised that they let go. Then I turned all by myself and walked back to be within spitting distance of Pardo.

"Who else did you call?" he asked.

"I called the right people," I told him. "You'll be hearing from them if they don't hear from me."

"You're bullshitting," he said. "We monitor everything."

"I used the phone on your desk," I told him, and I could tell from the look on his face that I had hit on the exception to the rule. He got very calm looking, very Harvard.

"Burkhardt," he called to the guy waiting just outside on the porch.

"Yes, sir?"

"See if you can find out if this piece of shit made any calls from my phone. And if he did, who he made them to. Can you do that for me?"

"Yes, sir."

"Then he's all yours. Report to me when you get back."

"What do I do with him after I find out?"

"Bring him back, too. We may have to change some plans."

Whatever the change was that he had in mind, I knew it wasn't going to make life any easier for me.

34

The dogs were gone except for the blood on the white stones, but the black Rolls was sitting in the same spot, and I was shoved into the back seat. The Sicilian was ushered into the other side a lot more gently, the pilot sat up front with the driver, and the other guy pulled out the jump seat so he could sit opposite me. I could already see the movie title: *Driving Mr. Altobelli.*

I couldn't understand at first why I wasn't taking all this more seriously. I was on my way to some kind of horrible death, and yet my heart wasn't pounding in my chest, and my breath was going out and coming back in quite easily. Maybe it was the spot of pain in the middle of the chest. I think that deep down since my heart attack I had figured myself to be a dead man already, so these guys were maybe just jumping the gun a little. All in all, life had been mostly a lot of laughs with my big brothers looking out for me when I was a kid, and then having Brady protecting me when I was a cop. Being a cop gives you a special feeling, and if you think it out, what it does is make you feel that you're above the law, that you're not just like anybody else. So the women I was drawn to were impressed by that, plus the fact that I carried a gun, that I could kill or be killed at any moment. It didn't matter that the only things I had ever killed were those two hounds from hell. As Carlotta had said to me, one of the many times I had not understood what she was talking about, "You're part of every woman's dream, Vincent. You're part of the myth." And then she tore the clothes off me and went at it.

So, according to the way I was putting it together, they were on their way to kill a man who was already dead. There had been a few times in the past months when I had forgotten for a short time about my heart condition, when I had laughed without thinking, but something always came along to stick it in my face again, whether it was a pain in the middle of my chest like the one I had now, or just the way somebody looked at me. As much as anything, I didn't want any more of those looks. Right then I didn't give a shit one way or another.

We were driving slowly over some kind of bumpy road, and after about five minutes we stopped and the driver turned the engine off. Just before the headlights went, I saw the concrete pad with the helicopter sitting on it, a big black one with two windows on either side. The guy in front of me jumped out and then pulled me after him. We were standing in the dark until the pilot flicked a switch somewhere, and red and green lights flared up from the ground around the pad. They weren't strong enough to read by, but they must have been visible for miles from the sky.

There was a shed near the pad, and the pilot came out of it dragging some kind of harness. He threw it to the guy standing next to me. "Strap him into this," he told him, "and then bring him over to the ship."

It was a bulky thing with wide leather belts, and it took him a few minutes to figure out how to get it on me, but finally I was lashed into it as tight as he could yank the bands. It looked like the kind of thing they used to pull people off the roofs of buildings or from burning ships. When he finally finished, I could barely move, but he dragged me over to the side of the ship and shoved me against the fuselage.

The pilot had taken one of the side panels off the chopper, and there was about a five-foot open space in the side of the body, which exposed one of the seats. He then grabbed the rope that held the harness, threaded it through a winch on the floor of the ship, and wound it until it pulled me toward him.

"Okay," he said, when we were almost touching, "we can make this easy or make it hard. The boss wants to know about the telephone calls you made."

"He'll find out about them soon enough if something happens to me," I told him.

"Okay," he said again, and you could hear the anticipation in his voice, "then I guess we go for a ride. You'll get another chance to talk when we get up there, but if the answers aren't right, you're gonna swing, baby, swing."

This was one of the guys who had never left Vietnam, and probably never would. Brady had been a Marine there, and once in a while we would pop a few beers with some of his buddies, and you could pick out the ones whose minds were still "in country," as they called it. There had never been anything as exciting in their lives, and there never would again, and they hung on to their memories in a way that was scary. You could tell that this guy was one of those in the way he looked at me. In his eyes, I had turned into a "gook," and whatever happened to me would not keep him awake nights.

"Let's get him up in there," he said, and he and the other guy grabbed my legs and heaved me onto the floor. They helped the Sicilian to step over me, then strapped him into the back seat on the other side.

"Joe," the pilot said to the guy who'd been driving the car, "we'll probably be up about a half hour, depending on how long he takes. You wait here."

It took him ten minutes to explain to the other one how to handle the winch, and about five minutes after that we were up in the air, the pilot sitting alone up front, the Sicilian in the rear seat, and the guard squatting on the floor beside me.

Somehow or other what was about to happen hadn't really registered in my mind when they were talking about it. But as the cold air hit my body in the weird darkness of the night with the giant fan vibrating above my head, it suddenly became too clear. If I didn't tell them what they wanted to know, they were going to lower me out of the ship into the nothingness until I had a heart attack. They were about to frighten me to death. You had to hand it to Pardo. The old-fashioned way would have been for me to disappear into the ocean with chains around my feet or be found in the trunk of a recent model Cadillac or become part of the foundation of a new building in a major city or maybe even just be buried in a shallow grave right on the estate. But this was modern technology. They were setting me up to die of natural causes. There might be some marks on my body, because the guy had pulled the strap awful tight, but the autopsy would show heart failure, plain and simple.

"Okay," the pilot yelled to the guy beside me, and before I could even think about it, I was over the edge of the doorway, all my weight hanging on the harness. They hadn't even tried to ask me about the phone calls again because it wouldn't have been any fun if I had decided to spill my guts.

"Let him down about ten feet," the pilot yelled, and I dropped quick as the guy flicked the switch. Too quick, maybe, because I stopped with a jolt something like fifteen feet under the ship, though it was hard to tell distance in the darkness. I looked down and could see lights in various places, including the ones at the Pardo place. I waited for my heart to stop, but it didn't. All of a sudden I started going around in circles as the copter banked this way and that, my body swinging out and back, out and back. My heart didn't stop. I could feel it going faster than usual, but the pain was gone. My body was cold from the air, but I could feel the sweat pouring out of my armpits. Hot and cold. And excited.

This wasn't that much different from the rides I had gone on at Disneyland and at all the carnivals that came to the city. I loved to go on those things, whether it was Space Mountain or the roller coaster or whatever, and my brothers once told me I should have become a test pilot after they chickened out on the Death Thrill ride at the last carnival we took their kids to before my heart attack. It may seem strange, but under different circumstances I would have called what they were doing to me fun.

They couldn't kill me with this kind of thing; I knew that. But as soon as they realized it, too, they would cut the rope and let the authorities identify the pieces of the body as best they could. I couldn't understand why Pardo had not had me killed on the spot. He was being Harvard Business School clever instead of wise-guy realistic. I wanted to beat him at his own game. I had to beat him.

So I let my body go slack. Dropped my head to the side and let the arms and legs hang loose. I was doing the dead man's float we had learned at the police academy, except that I was using air instead of water. They were still banking and swinging me around in circles, but then I felt the tug that meant they were pulling me up on the winch.

You can't make plans in situations like this, you just hope that it's your turn for the luck. Since I was playing the thing to the hilt, I even had my eyes closed, and it came as a surprise when I bumped into the fuselage. Hands reached down and tried to pull me up, but the combination of me and the harness was more than the guy could handle by himself. I heard him yelling something into the wind, but couldn't make out what he was saying until I felt another pair of hands grab hold of another section of the straps. There was one big heave, and I was on the floor of the ship. I opened my eyes a slit. It was pretty dark except for the lights on the instrument board and the sides of the copter.

The pilot turned back to get into his seat, and while he was doing it, I reached up for the legs of the other one and threw him out the door of the ship. Just like that. I hadn't thought about it. I just grabbed and threw. He might have yelled, but if he did, the wind tore the sound away and all you could hear was the chopping of the blades. The pilot had settled back into his seat and had no idea what had happened behind him, but when I looked over to where the Sicilian was sitting, I could tell he had seen everything. Why hadn't he yelled? Here I was trussed up on the floor like a chicken, and the guy didn't even make a move. I started grabbing at straps and buckles, hoping to loosen some of them enough to crawl out of the harness, and this was where the luck came in. One of the handles I pulled stripped the whole thing off me. It was some breakaway device they probably had for emergencies, and that was the one I had grabbed. I was free.

Rolling over onto my knees, I stood up and walked over to the Sicilian. He was still staring at me, his eyes like moons in the glow from the instrument lights, but I could see his hands holding on to the sides of the seat like death itself. The guy was terrified. I wondered if he had ever been in a helicopter before. I unbuckled his belt and pulled him to his feet. It was like carrying a load of putty in a paper bag that could break open any minute. I held him up with one hand and frisked him with the other. No gun, but a knife just like the one his buddy had used on Renée. I was barely able to hold him with the one hand and the knife with the other, so I was going to inch him back into the seat when the pilot banked the ship sharply, and we were thrown toward the door. The lady or the tiger? The Sicilian or the knife?

I let go of the man and dropped to my ass to keep from sliding out the door. He wasn't so lucky and plummeted out like a sack of potatoes as I let go of him. I would have gone right out with him if the pilot hadn't suddenly banked the other way, shoving me toward the opposite wall. He still hadn't looked back, and I could see he was concentrating on the cement pad straight ahead out the window. I stuck the tip of the knife into the side of his neck, which almost turned out to be a tragic mistake, because he froze and the helicopter started dancing in a crazy pattern.

"Fly, you son of a bitch," I screamed at him. "Fly this fucker."

He put his hands back on the controls, and we steadied. I felt under his leather jacket and came across the gun in his holster. I now had a gun in my right hand and a knife in my left.

"Bring her down easy," I yelled in his ear, "and you make one fucking sound and you're dead meat."

I know he was trying, but he was obviously upset, because we bounced hard four times before he turned off the engine and we stopped. The driver of the car had been smoking a cigarette while sitting on the fender, and he started walking over toward us. The knife went a little too deep into the throat of the pilot and he uttered a moan, but he stopped that in a hurry when I stuck it a little deeper.

"Hey," said the driver, "I thought you guys were going to stay up there forever."

I couldn't take any chances on missing, so I aimed for the center of his chest and pulled the trigger twice. Both bullets caught him and he went down. It could have been the bucking of the gun, or the pilot might have jumped when the shots went off in his ear, but there was this tremendous tug, and the knife was pulled out of my hand. I whipped around to put the gun to the pilot's head, but it was the last thing I needed to do, because whatever motion had been made had stuck the blade halfway through the side of his throat. Grabbing the handle, I pulled as hard as I could, and it came free, but his face fell forward onto the control board, and I could see the blood covering the instruments.

I jumped down to the ground and checked the guy I had shot. I had aimed for the middle of his chest, and both shots had gone into his left shoulder. Whenever we were out on the range, Brady would act like I couldn't hit the broad side of a barn. What a laugh he would have gotten out of this.

I threw the knife into the deep brush and pulled the guy's automatic from his holster. He was breathing nice and steady, but he was out cold. Shock. Those two bullets must have torn his shoulder to shreds, and when he came to, the pain would be something else. I hoisted myself back to the floor of the helicopter and checked the pilot. The blood had slowed to a trickle, but he was unconscious too. Eventually someone would get around to helping both of them, but right now it wasn't going to be me.

This time the car only purred when I started it up, and as I headed back up the narrow road with no lights on, using the feel of the ruts for guidance, I tried to figure the next move. Since the gates opened out, I was pretty sure this baby would ram its way through them, and I could drive like hell to the city without them catching me. If I went straight to the precinct and told the lieutenant the story, the guys would put a ring around me that not even Pardo could break.

But the closer I got to the house, the more I realized that running wouldn't do me any good. They couldn't guard me forever, and unless I took off for parts unknown, Pardo would get me some day. With the kind of lawyers he could afford, the case could go on for years and the charges could eventually be dropped. All they had to do was mop the floor in the coke storeroom, and all the evidence would be gone. One day a car would come out of nowhere, and they'd have to scrape me off a wall. Hit and run. Parties unknown. Case closed.

If I wanted to live, I would have to run, leave my family and way of life, and give up everybody I loved in order to protect them. And even at that Pardo could still kill off some of my family to teach me a lesson. Revenge was part of the code. The Sicilian couldn't go back to his country unless he could tell the younger guy's mama that his death had been avenged. No. No way. Not my family. Not my parents and grandparents and brothers and their families. Not them. Pardo wasn't going to be allowed to kill them. But in order for my family to live, Pardo had to die. If the head of the snake was cut off, the rest of it might wriggle away and leave me and mine alone. It wasn't even anything to think about twice. Pardo had to die.

35

I stopped the car when I saw the first glow from the spotlights around the house, but I kept sitting there after I turned off the engine. What was holding me was the realization that I was about to deliberately kill a man. He no longer would be the first because there were two dead men lying somewhere in the fields around the house, and I was the one responsible. There was no question about the one I threw out of the copter; the Sicilian I counted as a present from God. But those killings had been to preserve my life. If I were still a policeman, I would be getting a commendation for what I had done. But as a private citizen, I would be arrested for homicide and tried. I might get off on justifiable cause, but that would open the whole can of worms for the world to see, starting with Pardo coming to my apartment and offering me a million bucks. Who the hell would believe that? Even my own family would have trouble swallowing that big a dose.

So what was happening was a war, between me and them. They were out to kill me, and I had a right to protect myself by killing them if I had to. I knew I had to ace Tony, because with him it would be a matter of pride as well as business, and they might let it go without even thinking about it. The Sicilian visitors were obviously big men in the organization, and since they had died while under Tony's protection, he would have to offer up some kind of a lamb just in hopes of maybe getting off the hook. You can bet that the people he dealt with in the old country made him look like a Miss America contestant. They had traditions he never even dreamed of.

So what I had to do was get into the house, find Tony, and put him away, then get the hell out of there and hope for the best. It was an impossible setup no matter what happened, but this wasn't like the multiple choice tests that I used to mark for Carlotta. This time all the possible answers to the question—a, b, c, and d—were "kill Tony Pardo."

It was fifteen minutes past five in the morning, and the light would be breaking within the hour. The dark right then was my only safety, but I would have to go into the light to get to where Tony might be. He would almost definitely be in his room, and there were probably the usual two guards, but his biggest worry right then would be how to square things with the Sicilian when he came back from offing me. So he wouldn't be thinking much about the return of Vinnie Altobelli's body. Well, the body had returned on its own two feet, and it was carrying two guns.

Working my way through the shrubbery, I came to the side where the swimming pool was and zipped up the stairs to the terrace. The lights were fairly dim there because of the trees, and I found a pair of glass doors that slid open when I pushed. Barzatti had explained to me that so many people were moving in and out of the house at all hours that they'd turned off the security system that had cost nearly half a million bucks to install after one night in which the alarms had gone off twelve times.

There were no lights in the room I moved into, but

there was just enough coming in from the outside so that I didn't bump into any chairs or tables. The hall was empty when I worked up enough nerve to try it, but I wasn't sure which way to go until I came around a corner and found I was near the dining room. I suddenly realized I was carrying a gun in each hand, so I stuck the .38 into my pocket and went with just the Uzi. The wing with Tony's room was to the left, so I slipped down that corridor holding as close to the wall as possible, except for the chairs and tables and clocks and all the other shit that rich people decorate with. I might as well have gone straight down the middle.

One more corner and I had to figure what to do when I got to the room. The bolts would almost definitely be in place, so it wouldn't be a matter of shooting out the lock and crashing in. It would take a battering ram to knock down a door that big and thick. I suppose I could knock on the door and say "Flowers for Mr. Pardo." That was about as good a possibility as any of the others. No, the only chance would be to hide in a room nearby and get him when he came out in the morning. That wouldn't give me much chance to get out of there, but even if I didn't make it, at least my family would be safe. That's all I kept thinking about—my brothers and their wives and kids. I couldn't let anything happen to them.

There wasn't a room directly opposite Tony's, but there was one about ten feet down, with the door slightly ajar. I slipped inside and turned around to see how far I had to keep the door open to have a good sight with my gun. But just as I put my eye to the crack, the door slammed shut and the lights came on. There was Tino Barzatti with two of his boys, and they all had their weapons trained right on my belly.

Barzatti had a big smile on his face, but his being glad to see me had nothing to do with friendship. I handed the Uzi to the guy standing to my left, and he took the .38 out of my pocket on his own initiative. How stupid could I be? Guarding the boss didn't necessarily mean standing in the hall outside his door. It was smarter to be in a room with the door open a crack so you could surprise whoever was trying to surprise you.

"I heard the copter come back," said Barzatti, "but I didn't expect you to come with it. Where's Burkhardt and Don Vito?"

"They went to their rooms," I told him.

"What do you mean, they went to their rooms?"

"Tony changed his mind about the whole thing. He called it off."

Barzatti's face creased even more than its usual deep grooves, and his smile turned into a frown. "What the fuck's going on here?" he asked.

"I just follow orders, like you," I told him.

He turned to the two men in the room with us. "Take him down to the cellar," he ordered, "and beat the shit out of him until he's ready to talk straight. That's what should have been done in the first place instead of that crazy helicopter thing."

"We can do it right here," said the one who had taken my guns.

"No, I don't want any noise here right now. If he tries to yell or anything before you get him down there, knock him out. I'll be down in ten minutes to see if he's ready."

"Tino," I said, "I'll tell you what you want to know for free."

"So start in," he said, "and then we'll see."

"I don't think you want your friends to hear this."

The frown came back. "What are you talking about?" he wanted to know.

"Just give me a minute and you'll know."

There was something about me that made him uncertain.

"Go out in the hall," he told the other two. "We'll be right with you."

After the door had closed, he stuck his gun right above my groin and pushed hard. I went back a step, flat against the wall.

"Talk," he said, "and if you're bullshitting me, it's gonna hurt worse than if you weren't."

"Tony didn't hire me to find out who was trying to kill him," I said. "He wanted me to find out about you and his wife."

There was that moment when my nuts could have been blown through the wall as his whole body stiffened, but then he relaxed the pressure a bit. The idea had sunk in.

"I bugged the room," I told him. "I've got tapes. I've got pictures."

You could see his mind working back on what had taken place in that room between him and Mrs. Pardo. Whatever it was caused fear to move through the crags of his face.

"Tony knows about this?"

"I gave him a preliminary report but not the tapes and the pictures."

"Where are they?"

"In a safe place."

He moved the gun up a little and stuck it into my belly while his left hand came around my neck and he squeezed me against the wall. "You motherfucker," he said, "you better tell me where they are or you're going to die real slow."

"If I die," I said, "fast or slow, he gets the works within ten minutes. And after that, you're the one who's going to die real slow."

He thought it over.

"He looked at me funny," he said. "He was looking at me funny, and I couldn't tell why."

He pulled me away from the wall, and opened the door about ten inches. "Joe," he said, "you go down to the barn and get the rest of them up here. Tell them the time has come, and we're going to take over. Stay clear of Tony's guys until we're ready. Angelo, you come in here."

The guy who had taken my guns came into the room.

"We've got to put him on ice," Barzatti said to the guy, "until things are in place. Find something to tie him up with and put a bird in his mouth."

The guy wandered around the room until he came across some lines from the drapes, cut them off, tied my wrists behind my back so that I could feel the rope biting through the flesh, and then stuck his filthy handkerchief in my mouth and snugged that in with another piece of cord. I was having trouble breathing, but they couldn't have cared less. The bird in the mouth. It was an old Mafia custom to put a dead bird in the mouth of someone they thought had talked to the police—a canary. Tino wasn't a Harvard grad; the old ways were good enough for him.

"We going to keep him here?" Angelo asked.

"No," said Barzatti. "Take him down to the basement and leave him outside the strong room until I come down. We're going to have to protect the stuff that's in there once we get the fucking door open."

"This is going to be it, huh, Tino?" asked the guy.

"This is it, Angelo," said Barzatti. "Today we take over the business."

"You'll do what you promised?" Angelo asked, almost drooling.

"You're going to be a rich man, Angelo," said Barzatti. "You're going to wipe your ass with hundred dollar bills."

They dragged me into the hall, and we split at the corner, Tino going one way and me and Angelo heading for the elevator, where he shoved me so hard that my head hit the wall, and I rode to the basement sitting on the floor. He dragged me to my feet again and hauled me down the hall and over to the strong room door, where the floor was still covered with the pasty white water. I wondered if anybody had made the connection yet. Then my feet were tied together and a rope attached me to the handle of the door, pulling so tight that I was forced to stay up on my knees, facing out. If I moved even slightly, the pressure on my shoulders was unbearable.

"I'll be back for you," he promised, "and I pray to the saints that Tino lets me be the one to do it."

Angelo wasn't gone two minutes when another man came around the corner and straight for me. He was dressed in black pants and a tank top, and he was carrying the biggest butcher knife I had ever seen. This guy was so wired that he kept stumbling over his own feet, looking every which way as if something terrible was going to jump out at him from the wall. Tino had sent somebody else to do the job, and my body shook at the thought of what that knife could do to me before I reached the point where I didn't feel any more pain.

When he finally reached me, he stood there a moment looking down, his face all twisted up. There are some people who can fine-slice a living human being with pleasure, but their numbers, thank God, are few. This was one of the guys who didn't like what he was about to do.

My body tried to jump away from the knife as it came down toward me, and the effort almost ripped my shoulder sockets loose. I closed my eyes, and then I fell right on my face. I looked up to see that the rope holding me to the door had been cut, and now my wrists were being cut free, and then he did the legs. I lay there, unable to move because of having had my circulation cut off, but then I rolled over and got up on my knees again.

"Signore," said the man, *"grazie, signore."* He handed me the knife, then turned and ran out of there.

There was a look on his face that reminded me of something, and then it hit me all of a sudden. *Signore. Grazie, signore.* It was the waiter I'd caught screwing the maid when I blundered into that room. This guy wasn't one of the guns. He was just a waiter. What kind of guts did it take to do what he just did?

I headed down the corridor toward the stairs with the knife in my hand. It wasn't the equivalent of an AK47. But two guys had already been put out of business that night from a knife that had been in my hand. There might be another one. There just might be another one.

36

As I walked up the stairs again, the ridiculousness of the butcher knife sank in. It worked fine in a zombie movie because the bullets went right through the creep holding the blade, but in my case the slugs would stay put. The first thing would be to work my way up in the world and trade the knife for a gun.

When I reached the top, I stood there for a second trying to decide the best thing to do. Hell, I couldn't think of anything to do, let alone the best. But before I could make up my mind, around the corner came Renée and Claudine, both wearing the house terrycloth bathrobes. Before I had come here the only person I had ever seen wearing a bathrobe as a regular part of his wardrobe was my uncle Pietro, who never wore anything else. Even when he came to dinner in the month of August, he wore his bathrobe over his pants and shirt, and if it was February, he wore it under his overcoat. Nobody ever gave him a hard time about it because that was what he wanted, and he was too old to change his ways. But in this house the bathrobe was almost a uniform, and it looked as though the girls were going off to morning roll call.

They both opened their mouths to scream and I froze where I was, but then nothing came out of their mouths.

"Vinnie," whispered Renée as she came running toward me, "we thought you were dead."

"It wasn't because they didn't try," I told them as Claudine came up with us.

"The halls are full of guys," she said. "Two went by a minute ago."

"What do you need, Vinnie?" asked Renée. "Are you trying to get out of here?"

"Yeah," I answered, "that's the main plan. But first there's one thing I've gotta do."

"What do you need?" asked Claudine.

"I need a gun," I told her. "Automatic if possible, but any kind of a gun will do."

"You come with us," she said, "and we'll get you whatever you want."

"There's guys looking for me," I told them. "We could run into something bad."

"Vinnie," said Renée, "I owe my ass to you. Whatever you need we'll get."

I couldn't tell whether she was making a joke or being serious, but either way I needed her help and this was no time to ask dumb questions. Renée took my free hand, and they led me down the hall to what turned out to be Claudine's room. It looked like it had been designed by the people who do honeymoon suites in those Pennsylvania hotels that have heart-shaped bathtubs. Her colors were various shades of purple—the sheets, the drapes, the furniture, the rugs, and even the bidet I could see through the open bathroom door.

"What kind of weapon you want?" asked Claudine.

"Uzi? AK? Whatever you've got along those lines," I told her.

"I've got them all," she said, rummaging around in the back of her closet. She came out with an AK and some extra ammunition, and handed them over.

"Where did you get this stuff?" I asked her.

"The boys forget them when they leave," she said, "and then they're afraid to come back for them, and I ain't going to be carrying them through the house to their places, you can bet your sweet ass."

"What boys?"

"Well," she said, a little smile on her face, "sometimes when things get slow, I let one of the boys come up for a little fun. Your gun belonged to Mario, the guy that punched you in the stomach the other night."

"How did you know about that?"

"He told me, that's how."

"But they were looking for me. Why were they looking for me?"

"The three guys were having a party with Theresa when Constanza came banging on the door and screaming that you had dumped her and were in with Mrs. Pardo. So Theresa told them if they came across you, they were to give you one good one for her little sister."

It's amazing how complex questions sometimes have very simple answers.

"Thank you for helping me," I said, "and I hope your lives go well in the future. It might be best if you got out of here real soon, because some big things have gone down, and there could be serious trouble."

"We were just talking about that," said Renée. "One of the guys Mr. Pardo brought here is the president of a bank in New York, and he wants to set me up. Claudine's got enough stashed away so she doesn't have to work another day in her life."

"The only problem," said Claudine, "is that I like what I do."

She and Renée broke into the giggles, and then both of them grabbed me and started kissing me all over the face—lips, eyes, cheeks, everywhere.

"Hey," I said, "there's a time and place for everything, but I don't think this is the time or the place."

"We were just saying good-bye, silly," said Renée. "You're about the nicest guy that ever came here, and I'm only sorry we never made it together, because I'm positive you would have liked it."

"And as for me," said Claudine, "I would have blown you out of your fucking mind."

They started laughing so hard that they fell into each other's arms. Whores. Go figure.

"I have to find Tony Pardo," I said, "so when I leave here I—"

"He's in the office," said Claudine. "They're all in the office. You never saw such running around as was going on in the last fifteen minutes. Tony called everybody to the office. That's why we came out. To find out what was going on."

"Do you know what's going on?"

"We haven't the foggiest," said Claudine. "But you have to go to the office if you want to find Tony."

"That's what I want to do," I told them. "Find Tony."

As I closed the door to the room, Claudine said something, and they both started laughing like crazy again. I wished them long life to balance out what I was going to try to do to Tony Pardo, the biggest whore of them all.

37

For the first time since I had come to this house I knew exactly where I had to go to get where I wanted to be. The main office door was shut tight, so I went around the corner to the secretaries' office, which was also closed but opened right up when I twisted the handle. There was light showing from the connecting door to the main office, which was open maybe two inches. Several voices were going at once, but then Tony Pardo's voice howled above all the others and dead silence hit.

"Listen!" he was screaming. "This is not like anything that has happened before. Santini was Don Vito's nephew, his favorite nephew. He's not going to be satisfied with just Altobelli's head. Nothing will happen until he gets back to Sicily, but then there's going to be dues to pay, and I've got to hit the mattress until it's all sorted out. Gretchen has power of attorney, so she'll handle the business deals, and there's plenty of cash to take care of anything that comes up. There's also enough stuff in the strong room to get us all the money we need if we can ever find the fucking key. If not, Tino will have to blow the door. But I have to truck the stuff out of here tonight before the word gets out about what happened. Do you all understand me?"

Although the crack wasn't wide enough to see everything, it looked like the whole family except for mama was in the room, plus a guy standing with his back to me. He looked familiar, and when I thought about it, I realized that every time I had seen Tony Pardo in public, this guy had been close by. *The* bodyguard. Pardo wouldn't let the whole crew know his private business, so this had to be the one guy he felt he could trust as much as he would ever put his faith in anybody but himself.

"Where are you going to be," asked Angelina, "and how do you know they won't come after us when they can't find you?"

"They've got nothing to gain by doing anything to you until they find out what kind of deal they have to make with me," Tony told her. "I've got the stuff."

"But from what you're saying," said Florence, "you're the one who's got to make a deal with them."

"I agree," said Tony, "but we've got maybe half a billion dollars' worth of coke in the strong room, and they're not going to let this incident interfere with business. If the pipeline dried up now, the Colombians and Jamaicans would move in right away, and Don Vito doesn't want that to happen. I can straighten it out. I'm just going to need a few days to contact the right people and set up the meetings." He turned to his bodyguard. "Georgie, go see if Don Vito went back to his room," he ordered, and the guy, who was standing just inside the office door, turned and shoved it open, knocking me backward onto my ass. It was so unexpected that I threw my arms out trying to catch my balance, and the gun went flying from my hand into the dark.

"What the fuck?" yelled the guy, and the next thing I felt was the barrel of his gun stuck in my throat. The other gunman and Aldo ran over, grabbed the front of my shirt and hauled me into the office while I was still on my back. The man was stronger than he looked.

As soon as Tony realized it was me, he came tearing over, and when he reached me, I could see the red building up in his face. Without saying a word, he kicked me in the side, but he wasn't wearing any shoes so he was the one who yelled out in pain. Only a small satisfaction because he grabbed the gun out of his man's hands and pointed it right at my belly.

"What are you doing alive?" he wanted to know. "What are you doing alive?" He was so close to pumping the whole magazine into my belly that I didn't dare breathe, let alone answer. He must have stood there a whole minute with nobody even twitching, and just as suddenly he handed the gun back to its owner.

"Where's the don," he asked almost wearily, "and Burkhardt? Tell me what happened before I have your nuts cut off and stuffed in your mouth."

"You've got a problem," I told him, my mind working along the lines that had come to me the last time one of these guys had shoved a gun in my belly. "Barzatti's turned, and he and his men are coming for you. They killed the don and the pilot, but I got away."

Now, who would believe a story like that? He did. It took him a few seconds to sort out what he thought were the circumstances, but he bought the whole fish—hook, line, and what I hoped would be a sinker. But he wasn't dumb. The man was blind in some ways but not stupid.

"How do you know all this?" he asked, his voice so calm it was like he wanted the salt passed to him. "We didn't hear any shooting. How do you know all this?"

"They knifed them," I said. "I ran into the bushes and they couldn't find me in the dark, and then I watched. I was there. I saw it. I'm also a detective. That's why you hired me. And while I was digging away at your problem, I started coming across strange things, little ones that didn't add up until they ambushed us at the helicopter pad. Barzatti's an explosives man. Who do you think did the bombs in your desk and your car? He's tied in with someone in your family, and they're planning to take over any minute."

There's bad luck, such as squatting outside a door when a goon slams it open, and there's good luck, which works in your favor every once in a while. Just as I finished talking, unable to think up any more crap that might be crammed into the toilet bowl, there was yelling outside the house that came faintly through the boarded-up windows, and then there were two sharp bursts of gunfire.

"Jesus Christ," said Tony, "they're here. Aldo, you son-of-a-bitch, your friends are here. Georgie, go get the rest of the boys. Cut those mothers down when they try to come into the house."

Then he picked up a gun from his desk, turned around and pointed it at his brother Aldo's head. The two older sisters screamed as one, and ran over to shield Aldo's body with their own. Constanza and Theresa didn't even twitch, and I remembered what Constanza had said about her older brothers. Angelina turned and looked Tony in the eyes and the gun in the muzzle. There was no fear in that lady.

"Another one?" she screamed. "My Nino. Florence's Freddy. And Papa. You and she had them kill Papa. Now you want to kill Aldo. Kill me. Kill us all. Kill me first."

She put her hands up to her blouse and ripped it

open, her huge breasts straining into her brassiere. The gunfire increased from outside.

I stayed down on the floor, not wanting to attract any more attention than necessary, and I looked over at Mrs. Pardo, who was staring back at me like she was trying to get inside my skull to see what was going on there. Barzatti. Power of attorney. It clicked into place. She knew I knew. The look I tried to give back to her was a message that the secret was safe with me, that I would never talk, but I couldn't tell if she was getting it. I had nothing to gain by bringing her into it, and all I wanted was to save my own ass if that was at all possible, which did not seem the case at that moment.

The gunfire outside was spotty, but in less than a minute Barzatti burst through the door with a Beretta in his hand. So there we were like the border between two countries, guns pointing at guns, casualties unknown if the first shot was fired.

"Tino," yelled Pardo, "why are you doing this? You had everything you wanted. Why are you doing this?"

"I want it all, Tony," said Tino, his voice barely above normal speaking level. "Don Vito came over to see me, not you. They ain't been happy with you. He said I could have it all."

"No," said Tony. "There's got to be more to it than that. You're not smart enough to pull off a thing like this. Who is it, Tino? Who are you in with? It's Aldo, isn't it? Stay with me and we'll split it from here on in. Fifty-fifty."

"No, Tony," said Barzatti, "It's coming to me. I want it all."

The difference between Pardo and Barzatti was that Tony gave orders to kill but had probably never wasted anyone personally, while only Barzatti and

God knew how many he had personally sent to hell. It makes a difference as I found out when I thought I was shooting to kill at the helicopter pad. I was a good marksman, so when I pulled the trigger, something in my head shifted the target area to the shoulder instead of the chest. So Barzatti would have killed his boss while Pardo was still thinking about it.

Except that at the last moment Tony's bodyguard came back into the room behind Barzatti, and smashed him on the head with the barrel of his gun. The blood streamed from Barzatti's skull as he went down to his knees, still conscious but with no strength in his body, and the guard picked the Beretta up from the floor and stood there, waiting for further orders.

Tony walked over and shoved his gun into Barzatti's left ear, just under where the blood was pouring out, and I tensed for the blast of the shot. But there was Jekyll and Hyde, and there was Harvard and Mafia, and Pardo had a few things he wanted cleared up.

"Who?" he asked clearly. "Who's in this with you? You can live or you can die. All you have to do is tell me who."

Maybe if he hadn't been so groggy, Barzatti wouldn't have fallen for it, but he at once turned his head until he was staring straight at Mrs. Pardo, his look a mixture of pleading and hopelessness. I had already made the connection because of what I had seen outside the doorway of her bedroom, but Pardo made it on his own brains and instinct.

He turned slowly toward her, the pistol in his hand held loosely but pointed in her direction.

"You?" he said, "You! Mr. Minister's daughter from Durham, New Hampshire, you and Tino. He was old enough to be your father, for Christ's sake. His brains were in his dick. In his ass. But he never had enough in his head to run an organization. You and Tino. Who'd have thought it?"

"It's not true, Tony," she said. "You know it can't be true. Why would I want him when I have you? I have all I need or would ever want. You're my husband. You're . . ."

"Power of attorney," said Tony, and you could see his mind starting to put things together, all kinds of things. "I let you bullshit me into giving you power of attorney and all the rest of it. The companies. The controlling shares. Jesus, but I was stupid."

"It's not true, Tony," she said, her voice at a pitch I never would have expected from what I had learned of her. She knew she was about to die, and the ice queen was melting.

"Maybe it's not," he said, a little smile on his face. "Maybe it's not true. But even if it isn't, I'd never be able to trust you again. From now on I can only trust myself. Just me. Nobody else."

Just as he was bringing the gun up into position, I threw myself at him feet first and scissors-kicked him in the belly and back, knocking the gun out of his hand. He staggered back a few feet, but as I saw him reaching down for his gun, a shot rang out and the bullet hit him right in the throat. As I got to my feet, I saw Mrs. Pardo standing there with the gun in her hand, which had come from I don't know where, and I yelled as I saw the gunman turn his weapon toward her, but a blast shook the room as a shotgun went off, and the gunman's body went kicking through the air into a heap.

I turned toward the sound, and there was Jefferson, the butler, standing there with the gun pointing at me, and I knew that this time my luck had run out.

"No," commanded Mrs. Pardo, "let him be."

38

Even if the Beatles were all alive and still working together, their sound wouldn't have come close to the music of Mrs. Pardo's "let him be." Because that shotgun held five rounds in it, and I could tell from the look on his face that Jefferson had been ready to blow me into little pieces.

Another burst of automatic fire could be heard from somewhere on the grounds.

"We've got to get out of here," said Mrs. Pardo to Jefferson.

"What about him?"

She looked straight into my eyes, all cool again.

"Do you want to come with us, Vincent?" she asked. "Do you want to get out of here?"

I nodded at her, afraid that words might jar Jefferson's trigger finger.

"What about them?" he asked, and the shotgun swept the other side of the room where the rest of the Pardos were standing and Barzatti was still kneeling.

She walked over to Barzatti and looked down at him.

"You up for your end of the deal, Tino?"

Even though the blood was still running down his face, he pushed himself to his feet so that he was almost on an even level with her. Then he nodded slowly, but definitely.

"You can handle them all right?" she asked, waving her gun toward the six Pardos left in the room.

"They have nowhere else to go," he answered. "They belong to me now."

"And Sicily?" she asked "You can settle with them?"

"All they care about is the stuff in the cellar," he said.

"And him?" she said, pointing to her late husband. This was a woman beyond any coldness I had ever imagined. "Ice Lady" wasn't descriptive enough. She was made of the liquid hydrogen you dipped things in to make them freeze instantly.

"We'll take care of it. A car fire, maybe. They'll have trouble sifting the ashes."

I looked over at the Pardos, but their faces were set in stone. Barzatti and Gretchen could have been talking about a roast of beef. Constanza wouldn't meet my eyes.

"Okay," she said, "Then we're on our way. You keep your end of the bargain, and I'll keep mine. But if anything goes wrong, Tino, anything at all, to me or even to Vincent, the FBI gets the whole wad, and the people in Sicily get the leftovers."

Mrs. Pardo started out without another look at anybody, and when Jefferson waved the gun barrel in my direction, I took it that he wanted me ahead of him. We went down some back stairs, through some corridors, and then out a side door, where a jeep was sitting. The back of the jeep was packed solid with cases, so we stood there a moment until Mrs. Pardo said: "Vincent, you sit on the hood. I'll be going slow, so don't worry about falling off."

Which is how we traveled down some dark, bumpy road until we came to the helicopter pad. When we first started out, there would be little bursts of gunfire from somewhere around the house, but by the time we reached the pad everything had turned quiet. The pilot and the other guy were still lying in the bushes, where I had dragged them, but I could see that their eyes were open in the dim light. The pilot groaned when he saw me.

"It's okay," I told them. "We'll call and have somebody get you."

It was about time I called the police in on this, even if it was going to be an anonymous tip.

Jefferson took one look into the cockpit, and said, "This will present no difficulties once we get the blood cleaned off the instrument panel." He took out a handkerchief and started rubbing away.

"Help me load the cases into the ship, Vincent," said Mrs. Pardo.

"What good will that do?" I asked.

"So we can fly out of here," she said.

"But the pilot is in no condition to fly," I explained to her.

"My dad has many talents," she answered.

So there we were two minutes later, up in the air, Jefferson handling the controls, me in the seat in back of him, Mrs. Pardo in the one beside him. Jefferson! The butler did it. All those shots with the .22. The poison in the wine. He probably handled all of that. Jefferson! She hadn't said "Jefferson." She had said "dad." I closed my eyes and pictured their two faces together. Christ, that's where the resemblance was that had tickled something in me. I'd looked at enough mug shots in my time so that I should have picked that up somewhere along the way. But the butler!

We flew for something like forty-five minutes before setting down on a grass field somewhere. There had been only one light in the field below, but Jefferson had obviously been looking for it because we landed maybe five feet from it. There was a car, a small truck and five men waiting, and all of them pitched in to load the stuff that was in the back of the helicopter into the truck. Then two men got into the helicopter and flew it away. I was just standing there with the wind blowing dust in my face while nobody paid any attention at all until Mrs. Pardo walked over.

"This is where we part company, Vincent," she said. "Jack will take you home in the car, and the rest of us will be going off in the truck. It's unlikely that we'll ever cross paths again, so I want to thank you now for saving my life back there. I don't know exactly why you did it, but I'm grateful."

"Maybe because you were the lesser of two evils," I told her, an expression that Carlotta used to throw at me all the time.

She laughed.

"That may be truer than you know, Vincent," she said, "because I am going to devote my time to the legitimate businesses we built up. All the other stuff I bequeath to the people who will fill Tony's place."

"But it won't be that easy," I said. "You were there. I was there. We know what happened. How are you going to explain all those things?"

She laughed again.

"Vincent," she said, "I've been in Africa this whole past week on a photo safari. Inside of twenty-four hours I'll be in Zimbabwe, and it will take the authorities another three or four days before they will be able to reach me with the terrible news about my husband."

"But me? What about me?" I asked her. "I was there. I'm a cop. I can tell them everything that happened."

"You can tell them, Vincent, if you want, but who's

going to believe you? And if they do, how are they going to be able to prove it? Nobody who's left there is going to talk. You told your family you were fishing with a friend. I heard you say it on the phone tape. If you need to prove where you were, Jack's the friend who was your host. No, Vincent, I'm afraid you're stuck with this. I may be wrong and dad may have been right. Maybe we should have left you there. But you saved my life, and there's enough of my mother in me to honor that."

"You called Jefferson dad," I said. "You told me your father was a minister in New Hampshire."

"My father can be whatever we need," she said. "He has been a minister on occasion, a doctor, a lawyer, and even an engineer. But the important thing is that he is a full-time genius."

She took hold of my face in her two hands and kissed me a solid one on the lips. I was too stunned to relax, let alone enjoy it.

"Goodbye, Vincent," she said, and headed for the truck. I stood there, watching her. She started to go around the front of the vehicle, but then she stopped and looked back at me. She said something to the driver, and he yelled to the people in the back, and they hauled out a package and passed it to her. She then came back to where I was standing and handed me two of those attaché cases.

"Here, Vincent," she said. "These are my thanks to you. Tony never intended for you to keep the whole million. He didn't even intend for you to keep your life. Enjoy life, Vincent. That's what it's for."

Then she got into the truck and they drove off.

I was watching the lights disappear down the road when the other guy came over to me.

"You ready to move out?" he asked, taking the cases and putting them in the trunk of the car. "We better get going. It will take us nearly seven hours to get to your place."

He had it right almost to the minute, and it was afternoon before he drove up in front of my apartment building. We both got out and he pulled the cases from the trunk and delivered them to me. Then he dug into his wallet and slipped out a piece of paper.

"We've been fishing up at Lake Onota," he said, handing me a photograph that was all creased. "Here's a picture of the place and my phone number, in case anybody wants to take a look. It's nice there. You're welcome to visit any time. Good luck."

I had left all my stuff behind at Pardo's, but I had my car and apartment keys in my pocket, and when I opened the door, I stood there a minute and looked the place over. Everything was exactly the same. Everything. I went to the closet in my bedroom, and the original attaché case was still there behind the pile of shoes. I put the other two cases in with it, and closed the door. The money. I'd have to make some decisions about the money. And everything else.

But Mrs. Pardo was probably right. She was maybe the smartest person I had ever met. She'd had it all planned from the beginning, everything, probably including me, but I would never find out how or why. She was right then on her way to Africa, and would be properly horrified when they finally reached her with news about her husband's disappearance and probable death in the car accident. Unless there was a lucky break somewhere, and I doubted that there would be, no one would ever really figure that one out. I could tell them a lot about it, but I wouldn't be able to prove anything. And my family would be ruined for life. It would kill my mother and father, and sit on my brother's heads for the rest of their days.

But I was out of there. I was free. And safe. I was finally home safe.

The pain in my chest hit so hard that I yelled. The pressure was even worse than when I had chased the kid up the stairs, and I could feel the sweat breaking out all over me. I stumbled over to the phone and dialed 911, gave the dispatcher my name and address and told her I was having a heart attack. Handled it real calm. Then I went out cold.

39

The super had to let the paramedics in even though I had come to before they arrived. I was lying half on the couch and half on the floor when I opened my eyes, and I pushed myself up as best I could until I had support for my back and could prop my legs up on the coffee table. The pain had toned down to a light ache, but I felt too weak to stand up, so I yelled to them to get the super when they knocked on the door.

As soon as I told them the pain had been like my heart attack, they got an I.V. into me, radioed the hospital what they were bringing in, and had me in the ambulance before I could even protest that I felt much better. The stuff in the emergency room took about an hour, and then they had me up in CCU by the time Dr. McMurty had arrived.

He went through all the usual rigmarole, ordered some extra tests, studied the new cardiograms next to the old cardiograms they had dug up, and then looked down at the floor for a couple of minutes before coming over to me.

"What happened?" he asked.

I told him I had been away on a fishing trip and had just returned when the pain hit me.

"Did you do anything especially strenuous on the trip?"

I thought about that for a minute. Did I do anything especially strenuous?

"No," I said, "the biggest fish that was caught was me."

"You must have given yourself one hell of a fight, then," he said, and actually smiled. A joke. Dr. McMurty had made a joke. I smiled back at him.

"Your cardiogram is exactly the same as the last one taken at my office," he said, "so there hasn't been any new damage. I don't know what caused the pain. Have you been taking your medicines?"

"I forget once in a while," I admitted.

"You can't forget," he said. "Your life depends on remembering to take the pills."

"I'll remember," I told him, and I really meant it.

"I'm going to keep you up here overnight," he said, "and then put you down on a regular floor for a couple of days. Just as a precaution. When are you supposed to see me again?"

"I think it's next week."

"Okay, I'll see you here tomorrow."

"If I'm okay tomorrow, can I go home?"

"We'll talk about it."

Right after he left, the nurse came back. She was a nice-looking middle-aged lady who didn't seem too worried about my condition. You know, it's crazy, but when they told me in the emergency room that they were sending me up to CCU, my reaction was happy because I had the idea that Betty Wade would be waiting at the hospital for me. Crazy, huh?

The nurse had obviously been talking to me, but I hadn't been listening. She put a hand on my shoulder, a worried look on her face. "Are you all right?" she asked.

"Yeah, fine. I was just thinking about something."

"Your brother's outside. I'm going to let him in."

Petey was a mixture of happiness that I was alive and pissed-offness that I had gone away without telling anybody where I was.

"I was up at Lake Onota fishing," I told him.

"With who?"

"A guy named Jack Cassidy. I met him at a police convention once, and we've kept in touch."

"You never mentioned him before."

"Why should I?"

"I talked to the doctor," he said, "and you're going home to Mama's again when you get out. No arguments. Until you get your strength back. The doctor said he can't understand why this thing happened because everything looks fine. He may give you another stress test, but he didn't seem worried."

I told the nurse I didn't want a sleeping pill, so I kept waking up and dozing most of the night. CCU is quieter than a regular floor because the nurses are concentrating so hard on keeping everybody alive that they don't have time to yak, and I figured I could sleep without any help from one more pill than my usual number.

Sometime in the middle of the night I woke up because I heard a noise coming down the hall, and when I looked out I saw a gurney going by with somebody on it who had what looked like a dozen bottles draining stuff into him. And right behind it came that surgeon, Dr. Englund, and he was still wearing his long white coat, but I couldn't tell if there was any blood on it.

What got me was that when he came to the middle of my doorway, he stopped, turned, and looked in at me for what seemed like a whole minute. I doubt if he could see me in the shadow, but it was as if we were staring eye to eye. Then he turned back and walked on by.

"Not yet, you son of a bitch," I whispered after him. No more stress. Take my pills. Moderation. That was now my middle name.

So there I was two days later back at Mama's with everything that came with it, including uncles, aunts, and cousins who got on my nerves and platters of food that would have given the hospital dietitian a nervous breakdown. I ate every bit of it, even though I could see Dr. Englund's face staring up at me from the fork or spoon.

All my brothers came to see me, but nobody outside the family seemed to know about it so at least I was spared those embarassing visits. But on the fifth day an unmarked police car drove up while I was sitting on the porch rocking back and forth, and Brady unpeeled himself from the driver's seat.

"Jesus Christ," he said, heaving his huge bulk up the steps, "what the hell's going on with you now?"

"They don't know," I told him. "Some kind of fluke."

He started babbling about all kinds of things, some of them from out of nowhere, and I finally realized he wanted to tell me something but didn't know how to begin.

"Will you for Christ's sake spit out what's sitting in your mouth?" I told him.

"Today's my last day on the force," he said. "I've got the years, and I'm taking retirement."

"What the hell for?" I asked him. "You'll go nuts. You're too young to sit on your ass or take some kind of nerd job. I'd go back in a minute if I could. Why are you doing it?"

He chewed that over for a while and finally came out with, "I'm quitting because of you."

"Me? What the hell does it have to do with me?"

"It don't feel right anymore. They gave me a good boy for a partner. They gave me Jackson. You know him. He's good. But it's not the same like it was with you. My back's itchy all the time. It's not that I don't trust him. It's just that he's not you. I want to work with you again."

"Me again? You know they won't take me back."

"Not there. I want to open up an agency. I've got a lot of good years left in me, and I don't want to sit on my duff, and I think we could make a good living with a detective agency."

"But I can't do anything physical. What the hell good would I be?"

"You'd be the brains," he said. "I'd do the legwork, and you'd be the brains. And maybe after a while we could hire a few more pensioners and make some real money. We can't get by on just our pensions. Nobody can. You need this agency as much as I do."

"It's crazy."

He stood up, all six feet four of him, the giant hands curling and uncurling. "Think about it," he said. "I'll get back to you in a couple of days. I have to go now to the farewell party for me at the pub."

"I'll come with you," I told him, standing up.

He pushed me back down. "Like hell you will. Your brothers would kill me if I took you to a pub right now. Get your strength back, and then we'll do our pub-crawling. Think about it. It will take your mind off all the other shit. Think about it. You and me again. I'll call you in a couple of days."

"I'll be back at my own place by then," I told him.

After he zoomed off, I went into the house to tell my mother I was leaving the next day. The argument lasted fifteen minutes longer than I had feared.

40

Petey wanted to go upstairs with me, but I insisted he go back to work, that I was feeling fine, and he would only make me nervous if he kept fussing over me. The apartment looked the same as it had the week before, but this time I was different as I walked around it. Relaxed. I was taking my medicines right on the dot, and I felt good. The cases were still in the closet, and I lugged all three of them out, opened them on the bed, and looked at the neat stacks inside. I still hadn't thought through what I was going to do about the money. Declare it? Give it to charity? Keep it and stay quiet?

I had looked in the paper each day for something about Tony Pardo, and on the fourth day it was there. Two-column story on Page 1 with a headshot. Killed in a car crash. Burned beyond recognition. Identified by dental records. Police investigating. I wondered how long that file would be open. Barzatti had to have gone berserk when they opened the strongroom and found the slush. Maybe he was in too much trouble with the big boys to worry about what I had done. Or maybe he thought somebody else had done it. Or maybe I would be reading about him dying in a car crash in the near future. I wasn't sure I had heard the last of what had happened. It would always be hanging over my head, no matter how much time went by. In a way it was as if it couldn't have been real. I put it out of my mind like it was a nightmare in which you remembered a few things afterward, but everything else was cloudy. I wondered a little bit about the kind of deal Mrs. Pardo had made with Barzatti. Was he supposed to get all the rackets and she all of the legitimate businesses? She had to have planned the whole thing from the beginning. I was sure she had put the bug in Pardo's ear about hiring me. But why me? How had she even known about me? Had he mentioned to her that his aunt Clara was a cousin to an ex-cop's grandmother? She'd brought me, an outsider, in to stir things up, to get the pot boiling, to screw up Pardo's thinking. And then she'd killed him. Why hadn't she killed me? Because I had saved her life? I didn't want to think about it anymore. I never wanted to think about it again.

I sat down on the couch in front of the television and stared at the dark screen. There was nothing I wanted to watch, nothing I wanted to do. All that money sitting on the bed and nothing I wanted to do with it.

The red blinker on the answering machine caught my eye. I pushed the button to play back the messages. They were all the calls that had come in while I was away. Most of them were from Petey, my mother, and my brothers, but there were also four from Mimi Barnes, the last of which was a plea for me to call her, in what she thought was her sexy voice. There were two calls from Brady and some from other people, and then there was one that made me sit up straight, like I'd just been touched by lightning.

"Altobelli," the voice said, "this is Betty. Betty Wade. Your nurse. Betty Wade. I'm in terrible trouble, and I need help. He's trying to—"

That's all there was, and then the message ended. I reversed the machine and played it again, and it was cut off at the same point. I suddenly realized the tape had run out. There had been so many calls before hers that the tape had run out. Jesus Christ!

There was such fear in her voice that my hands trembled each time I played it. It was always the same, never changing.

I called the long-distance operator and asked her for the number of Betty Wade in Tucson, Arizona. No Betty Wade was listed there or in any of the surrounding communities. Then I called the operator again and asked for the numbers of all the hospitals in the Tucson area. She said there would be a separate charge for each one, which got no argument from me, and I finally had them.

At each hospital I was put on hold forever until I was finally transferred to the right place in Personnel, but each one told me there was no one by that name working at the hospital. I sat there a minute and then called each hospital back, and finally at one of them I reached somebody who dug a little deeper than the rest and came up with the fact that a nurse named Betty Wade had worked there for one month and then left without giving notice. Nothing more was known.

"Would you give me her home address, please?" I asked.

"I can't give out that information," said the voice.

"Look," I told him, "this is her brother. Our mother is dying, and I can't find Betty. You've got to help me."

There was a long pause, and then he said, "The only address we have is two-two-four Uxbridge Street in the town of Rancon."

I called information and asked for the number of a Betty Wade in Rancon, Arizona, but was told there was no listing.

"Could you tell me if there was a listing at one time?"

"I cannot give out that information, sir."

She couldn't and she wouldn't.

When I hung up the phone, I listened to the tape again. And twice more.

Then I called Brady at home. He sounded like I had just woken him up from a nap.

"What's doing?" he asked.

"I've got our first case," I told him.

"What?"

"Our first case. For our agency."

"You'll do it? You're going to do it?"

"Yes. And we start right now."

"What's the case? What do we do?"

"We have to track a missing person. We fly to Tucson on the first plane we can get."

"Tucson, for Christ's sake. Tucson, Arizona?"

"That's right. Pack a bag. I'll be over in a cab to get you."

"But what about money? Tucson, for Christ's sake. Did you get an advance?"

"A big one. All the money we'll need."

"Okay, I'll be ready. I've only been retired for two days, and I'm going nuts. You sure we've got enough money?"

"More than you've ever dreamed of. Get ready."

I went into the bedroom and packed a bag, including my gun. With my license they would let me take it on the plane. And Brady could show them his badge. They had never checked beyond that when I had gone to pick up prisoners. I looked down at the three cases of money on the bed and thought about how much to take and where I could stuff it. Then I closed all three cases and put two back in the closet. The third case would be my carry-on. I thought about my brother Petey, then decided to call him from Tucson, tell him I was there on vacation with Brady. He'd believe that. My doctor's appointment was the next day, but I called and postponed it for a week. Everything taken care of.

I picked up the two bags and placed them outside in the hall. As I turned to close the door, I thought that someone had called out to me, and I poked my head back in, but there was nothing. I suddenly realized the voice was in my ears, ringing out from my brain.

Nobody dies on me, Altobelli, the voice was saying. *Nobody.*

"And vice versa," I answered out loud. "And vice versa."